Charles A. Mann

Paper Money

The Root of Evil

Charles A. Mann

Paper Money
The Root of Evil

ISBN/EAN: 9783337529536

Printed in Europe, USA, Canada, Australia, Japan

Cover: Foto ©Andreas Hilbeck / pixelio.de

More available books at **www.hansebooks.com**

PAPER MONEY,

THE ROOT OF EVIL.

AN EXAMINATION OF THE CURRENCY OF THE UNITED
STATES, WITH PRACTICAL SUGGESTIONS FOR
RESTORING SPECIE PAYMENTS WITH-
OUT ROBBING DEBTORS.

BY

CHARLES A. MANN.

NEW YORK:
D. APPLETON & COMPANY,
549 & 551 BROADWAY.
1872.

PREFACE.

THIS book was written, but not published, in the winter of 1867–'68. It has now been rewritten and brought down to the present time as near as possible, and a chapter added on the tariff question.

The discussions of financial subjects seem to be confined of late almost wholly to that question, to the exclusion of that more important topic, the currency. The public mind is thus led on a false scent, and the cause of free-trade is likely to suffer in the long run by being forced into premature prominence. The object here proposed is in part to show the preliminary work to be done before revenue reform can be perfected. The refunding of the debt and the restoration of specie payments are of more importance than the adjustment of our revenue system, and ought to precede it. In fact, when those reforms are accomplished, "protection" will die of old age— a natural death. When the interest on the debt is reduced to four per cent., and the Government is administered with the economy that only specie can give, it will be possible to devise a system of taxation affording an ample revenue, and permitting at the same time as near an approach to free-trade as any this country has hitherto enjoyed.

The reason for the prominence given to the tariff question, to the exclusion of the more important currency question, seems to be the ignorance of the latter, so widely prevalent. Almost every standard treatise on political economy contains a full discussion of free-trade, and the principles that underlie it have been established in the domain of abstract truth beyond danger. But the conclusions of political economy on the subject of paper money are not yet settled. No treatise with which I am acquainted traces the phenomena it produces to their true causes. Even Mill has committed serious errors; and though he states, with reference to the law of the circulation of the precious metals, that few have had "an adequate conception of its scientific value," he must himself be numbered among the writers who have signally failed to apprehend its force. I am unable to perceive that our knowledge of currency has advanced much since Ricardo wrote; and, though I commenced with the intention only of proposing some practical measures looking toward the resumption of specie payments, I have found myself impelled

to begin with first principles, and to attempt the
elucidation of the whole subject of paper money.

In many quarters the idea seems to prevail that
either our country is excepted from the science of
political economy, or else that it has a special science
of political economy peculiar to itself. The idea is
as vain as to believe that, because the fauna of this
continent is peculiar, there is no place here for the
science of biology; or that, because the strata geolo-
gists have explored differ from and cannot be iden-
tified in time with those laid bare in other regions,
therefore we have a different science of geology. Undoubtedly the social phenomena developed in this
country differ from those witnessed among other
nations, because the conditions are unlike. The main
points in which we differ are in the character of the
people, leading to self-government, instead of a meddling government, and the cheapness and abundance
of fertile land, which enable us to endure the most
barbarous system of finance in Christendom, without
sinking the mass of the people in pauperism. We
are in a different stage of evolution from other nations; but similar causes produce here effects similar
to those produced elsewhere, and in studying those
causes, the conclusions of other nations, derived from
their own experience, can be made to us fruitful of
knowledge. The science of political economy has
been fully elaborated in Great Britain. To the

authors of that country must we turn for information on the subject; and, though their conclusions are not always applicable to the changed conditions of America, yet the general principles of the science can be derived from no other source. Political economy, as a science, has as yet been but feebly developed in the United States; partly because self-government and abundant land have saved us from those disastrous social phenomena which lead to the investigations of social science, and partly because we have never had any class that could spare time from money-grubbing to devote to study. Most of our books on the subject have been text-books containing no new investigations; and the chief attempt to pursue the subject originally—that of H. C. Carey—contains little that is reliable, being disfigured at every step by the vain endeavor to prove the absurd theory, that the way to diversify home industry is to put a duty on pig-iron. "Nothing can lie like figures, except facts," when manipulated to sustain a false theory.

In the following pages I have endeavored, starting with no pet theory of my own, to elucidate the one that seems most applicable to the currency of the United States. If that theory is correct, the facts will group themselves about it spontaneously; if false, I shall be satisfied if I have assisted others in searching for the truth. Facts and figures with reference to the financial condition of the country have been furnished in abundance by such productions as Welles's "Revenue Reports," Walker's "Science of Wealth," and Grosvenor's "Does Protection Protect?" There seems to be need of a generalization therefrom. To supply that need, an attempt is here made; and in those works, particularly the first, will be found, I confidently believe, facts sufficient to support every position taken in these pages.

The view of the functions of money here given is the exact opposite of that enounced by the Supreme Court of the United States in its latest decision on the legal-tender act. If any apology is needed for the publication of this volume, it is to be found in the series of decisions of which that is the culmination. When the judges of America are so deplorably ignorant that hardly a dozen among them know what a dollar is, any attempt, however feeble, to furnish an antidote to the black-letter political economy taught in our courts cannot be wholly wasted.

UTICA, *February*, 1872.

CONTENTS.

PAPER MONEY.

CHAPTER I.

OF THE PRECIOUS METALS AS A CIRCULATING MEDIUM, AND OF THE LAW OF THEIR CIRCULATION.

No branch of political economy presents more certain conclusions than that which treats of the functions of money. This certainty remains, however, only while the money treated of is that which is coined from the precious metals. Whenever paper money becomes the subject of consideration, certainty gives place to doubt and ignorance. There is no economical question, where so wide a difference of opinion exists, as in determining its true place.

In an investigation, therefore, of paper money, it is well to begin with that which is certain, and consider money which is coined before treating of that which is printed.

Money is defined to be the instrument which men use in exchanging the objects of desire, as the medium of exchange, and the standard by which values are measured in making exchanges.

Barter in kind is the first form of exchange; but
2

direct barter is possible only on a limited scale. The husbandman can take his wheat to the tailor, and obtain in return a coat, if the tailor desires the wheat, and they can agree upon the quantity to be given for a coat. The tailor can take the wheat to the cabinet-maker, and receive for it a chair, if the cabinet-maker is in want of wheat, and they can agree upon the quantity. The latter can exchange it again for some other article, whenever he can find a person possessing the article he desires, who is willing to give it for the wheat, and they can determine what amount of one article ought to be exchanged for a given amount of the other. But this process is slow and laborious. It is easier and simpler for the husbandman to barter his wheat for some article at once portable and divisible, desired alike by the tailor, and cabinet-maker, and the rest of mankind, and exchange that article for a coat, or a chair, or whatever else he desires, leaving the tailor and cabinet-maker to use it in the same manner to satisfy their desires. That the division of labor may be perfected, it is necessary that there should be some such common object which all the world is willing to receive in exchange for the objects of desire, and to use as a measure of their value. Such a medium is money. Without it the division of labor, and exchange on a large scale, are impossible.

But the use of money does not change the nature of a transaction. All exchange of the products of labor is essentially barter in kind. A common medium is used merely to facilitate the operation.

In considering this subject of exchange, the classification of values made by Adam Smith must always be kept in view. Every article has two values: intrinsic value, or value in use, and relative, or desirable value; which latter is expressed by the amount of other objects of desire men are willing to give in order to obtain it. This, for want of a better term, is called exchange-value or value in exchange.

When a common medium of exchange is used, the value in exchange of any given article is expressed by the amount of the circulating medium, or money, it will exchange for, which is called its price.

But value, evidently, cannot be measured by a mathematical abstraction of space or quantity. A dollar, like a bushel, is a unit of measure or calculation. It is also something more. A bushel of wheat, of oats, of rye, can be contained in the same measure, while a bushel of wheat may exchange for three bushels of oats, and two of rye, and each of these quantities may exchange for a dollar. The dollar, therefore, is the standard by which the relative or exchange-value of these articles is measured, and, as it will exchange for any one of these quantities, it possesses also value in exchange as much as the wheat, or oats, or rye. The measure dollar is a unit of calculation; yet a dollar is a thing as well as a name. There must be a substance or commodity possessing exchange-value, to which the name is given, and which then becomes money. The choice is not necessarily restricted to the precious metals. Whatever article or commodity is accepted by a community as the common standard of value and medium of exchange becomes money by virtue of such consent, whether it be the wampum, or cowry shells of savages, or the paper to which, in civilized communities, an imaginary or credit value is given. Money derives its force, as such, from common consent. The common consent of mankind, however, has fixed upon the precious metals to be used as the only money of universal circulation, owing to the fact that of all known commodities they are best adapted for the purpose. They are portable, durable, divisible, and always of the same quality. Above all, their value is more stable than that of any other article. On the importance of this quality it is needless to dilate. A fluctuating measure of value, like a fluctuating measure of quantity, or distance, fails in the most essential particular. The fundamental idea of measure is stability.

The stability of the value of the precious metals arises principally from the fact that, unlike paper, their quantity can never be artificially increased. They can only be produced by actual labor. A coined dollar, therefore, always represents a dollar's worth of labor. The amount of gold designated in the United States to be stamped as a dollar is 23.22 grains of pure gold, or 25.8 grains of gold, nine-tenths fine.

The precious metals, however, do not furnish an absolute standard by which values, at considerable intervals of time, can be compared. Corn and labor have been set up as such standards by different writers, but without success. There is no such unvarying standard, nor is there need of any. Its use would be fanciful. The value of money is sufficiently stable, if the variation extends only over long periods, so that current transactions can be closed before the change has accumulated enough to be felt. Although, therefore, gold and silver vary in value from age to age, and from one generation to another, this fact does not disqualify them for their office. The precious metals declined in value after the discovery of America, and again after the settlement of California and Australia, owing to the increased supply. But the decline being secular, current transactions were not appreciably affected thereby. Nor is there any danger to be apprehended from this source in the future. The decline, if any, will be gradual, and the only consequence will be, that each succeeding generation will transact its business at a higher scale of prices.

When gold and silver are accepted as the circulating medium, it becomes desirable to put them in the form best fitted for that use. For every dealer to keep a pair of scales, ready on each sale to weigh "the dust," and estimate its purity, is an inconvenience submitted to only in remote mining districts. It is much more convenient to have that part of these metals used as money divided into pieces of suitable size, and their weight and fineness guaranteed by a recognized authority. This is done by government, which coins them into pieces whose denominations are multiples or decimals of the unit of calculation used to compare values.

But to make gold and silver into coins is a matter of convenience merely. It does not affect their nature, or the laws which regulate their value.

It is the general practice of governments to receive all bullion that is offered at the mint, assay it, and coin it into money at the request of the holder, charging him only the bare cost of the operation. If we suppose this cost to be one-half of one per cent., then, if coin is worth more than bullion by at least that percentage, the holders of the bullion send it to the mint to be coined. If, on the other hand, coin is not worth more. than bullion by a fraction equal to the expense of coinage, it goes to the melting pot. The only difference in value between coin and bullion is the expense of coinage. When they vary in value more than this difference they are interchangeable. The laws, therefore, that regulate the value of bullion regulate the value of money in exchange.

But gold and silver, like other metals, are mined from the earth; and their permanent value throughout the world is determined by the same causes that determine the permanent value of other metals. It depends principally on the cost of production, and in the cost of production the main element is the quantity of labor. But the cost of production of the precious metals varies little, if any, from year to year. No new methods of mining nor new processes of reducing ores have yet been discovered which increase the amount produced for a given quantity of labor, except in such temporary instances as the placer mines of California and Australia.

There is a difference, however, between the precious metals and other products of labor in one respect. The demand for other articles is limited. Men are willing, ordinarily, to receive of them only enough for consumption. These products must seek a market. But the precious metals find a market wherever there is a civilized man. They exchange for every thing else, and hence are always in demand in the sense of always being desired. Consequently, gold and silver vary less than any other article from their natural value, or that which is proportioned to their cost of production. They are not subject to the fluctuations of other articles of commerce—bought and sold in open market. They are, therefore, more stable in value than any thing else.

But it must not be supposed that they are actually free from temporary fluctuations. They are subject, like other products of labor, to the law of supply and demand, though in a less degree, and in a different manner.

The fluctuations in value of all articles that are bought and sold are marked by variations in their price—that is, the amount of money for which they will exchange; and under the law of supply and demand, if the demand for any article remains the same, an increased supply thereof thrown on the market will cause its price to fall. But price cannot be predicated of money. Money exchanges for every thing that can be bought and sold, and not for any single article by which its exchange-value can be measured. If the amount of the goods that are bought and sold in a country, that is, the number of exchanges to be effected, remains the same, and the amount of money is increased, the increased amount of money will exchange for the same amount of goods as the smaller sum: the greater sum will have the same purchasing power as the smaller; but the prices of the goods, being measured by an increased amount of money, will be raised. Each particular sum, therefore, will have less purchasing power than before. Ten dollars after the increase will not buy as much as ten dollars would before. If, on the other hand, the sum of money is decreased, and still exchanges for the same amount of goods, the prices of the goods will be decreased, and each particular sum will buy more than before. An increased supply of money, there-fore, in a country, the uses for it being the same, increases the prices of the goods bought and sold, and a decrease of the amount of money lowers prices. It does not follow that the price of each article will be affected equally; but the average increase or decrease of prices will be proportioned to the increase or de-crease of money, the other causes which affect prices remaining the same. When, therefore, average or general prices are high, money will buy but little; when general prices are low, money will buy much. The purchasing power or value of money is inversely as general prices. That quality in money which cor-responds to price in other articles, is general purchas-ing power, and the value of money is subject to the law of supply and demand, like that of any other com-modity. The demand for money being considered a constant quantity, an increased supply lowers its value. The purchasing power of money then falls. There is an advance in general prices.

But it must not be supposed that there is any gain by such an advance. The country is not enriched by it. The values of different articles, relative to each other, are not necessarily changed. The change is in their value compared with money. They will bring in exchange more money, but not more of each other. There is, and from the nature of things there can be, no general advance of values.

But, while the temporary value of money, like that of every other product of labor, depends on the law of supply and demand, the supply of money, unlike that of other commodities, may be increased by another means than the actual introduction of more money. The money on hand may be made the instrument of effecting more exchanges than formerly. It may be made to do more work. Thus, if one dollar is used to make a single purchase, and is then hoarded by its last owner, while another dollar is used to make one purchase, and then another and another, until it has been so used by ten successive holders, the last dollar does ten times as much work as the first, and is equivalent in its effect on the supply of money to ten such hoarded dollars. The supply of money, therefore, may be increased by an increase of its rapidity of circulation, that is to say, of the amount of work which it does. But this increase of supply does not necessarily enhance prices. For an increase of the demand for money, that is, of the amount of the exchanges which the business of the country requires to be effected by it, may be met, not by an actual increase of the supply of money, but by an increase of the rapidity of circulation, or effective power of that on hand.

It follows further, that, although general prices are increased or decreased by an increase or decrease of the quantity of money in a country, the increase or decrease of prices is not necessarily in the same ratio as the increase or decrease of money. If the amount of the circulating medium is increased or diminished one-quarter or one-half, prices will rise or fall, but not necessarily one-quarter or one-half. The extent ot the rise or fall will depend on the rapidity with which the money circulates. While an increase is in progress, money will be likely to circulate rapidly, and prices may increase more than one-quarter, or one-half, and after the increase of money ceases, or a diminution commences, money will be withdrawn from circulation by hoarding, and prices will recede toward the point from which they started; so that there will be no time at which the increase of prices will be exactly as the increase of money. The effect of money on prices depends on two factors, the quantity of money, and the rapidity with which it circulates.

From this brief summary of the functions of the precious metals as a circulating medium, it is evident that all exchanges made through the medium of money are in reality barter. Instead of exchanging a bushel of wheat for two bushels of rye, we exchange it for a certain amount of the precious metals, and then exchange the latter for rye. But things that are equal to the same thing are equal to one another. Things that exchange for the same thing exchange for one another.

In the immediate distribution of the produce of labor the same holds true. A house is built. One man furnishes the lumber. Another paints it. Others give their time and labor toward its construction. Each, therefore, is entitled to an interest in the house when completed: the lumberman to a room according to the value of his lumber; the painter to another room for his paint; the carpenters each to a room for their services. But they are not all desirous of receiving rooms for their shares. Therefore they take money, and with it buy such habitations as suit them. But that, in effect, is the same as if they had bartered their labor and supplies for a dwelling.

These are the simplest cases; but commerce in all its ramifications is an extension of this fundamental idea. Money is merely a means of exchanging different articles for one another.

In the commerce between two nations this fact is even more evident. Thus, an American merchant sends wheat to England. An English merchant sends cotton goods to us. The American who sent the wheat, having sold it, has money to his credit in England against which he can draw a bill of exchange. The Englishman, having sold his cotton in America, and wishing to remit the money home, buys the bill of exchange, which represents funds in England, and receives there the money for which he sold his goods. The effect of the transaction is, that the wheat and the cloth have been bartered for one another. This is true of the whole commerce between the two countries. We are constantly sending cotton and bread-stuffs to England, and receiving manufactured articles in return. If, as is generally the case, we import more from England than we export to it, it will happen that there are not enough bills of exchange procurable in New York, at a rate less than the cost of shipping specie, to remit all the money that must be sent, and gold or bullion will be sent instead. The exports are bartered for the imports, and the difference only is paid in gold.

But men do not barter one article for another, unless each expects to make something by the trade. The prospect of profit is the impelling motive on both sides. The same is true of foreign trade. It is only barter, and it is entered into because both parties gain by it. It is mutually advantageous. It increases the producing powers of both countries.

But bullion is an article of merchandise, like any other product of labor, and it is therefore exchanged by one country for the goods or merchandise of another, as any other community, for the reason that it is for the mutual advantage of the countries to do so.

It has already been stated that the cost of production of the precious metals, being always nearly the same, their permanent value throughout the world varies little, if any, while their temporary value, at particular places, may fluctuate with variations in the supply and demand, and that the part of the precious metals which has been coined, cannot vary from the value of bullion above the expense of coinage. It follows that money may sometimes be of higher value in one country than in another. The country, then, in which it is higher, will wish to buy it as an article of trade from the country in which it is cheap, by exchanging something else for it; while the other country where it is cheap will be willing to part with it, and obtain in its place something more needed. But as, where money is high in value general prices are low, and where, on the other hand, money falls in value prices rise, it often happens that in one country prices are high because money is plenty and cheap, while in a neighboring country prices are low because money is scarce and dear, in which case the country last named would send a part of its goods to the former, and that country would pay for the goods with the article of which it had the most, and which it could part with at the lowest rate, namely, money, and not other goods. Thus, England sends woollens to France and receives silks in return. But suppose an addition suddenly made to the money in active circulation in England; the increased amount of money would have the same purchasing power as the smaller amount to which it had been added, and general prices would rise, including, probably, woollen goods. England could not then continue to exchange with France the same amount of woollens for the same amount of silks, as formerly; but the value of money having continued the same in that country, the same amount of money would buy the same amount of silks as before, and instead of sending woollens for the silks, England would send that which was cheapest, money. Silks and other goods would then pour in from France to realize the high prices, and, as the precious metals are the only money current among nations, the money sent to France in payment would be gold or bullion. A stream of gold would flow from the former country to the latter. But England has no mines of the precious metals. It would be compelled, therefore, to obtain from those countries which have mines a supply of gold and silver, by exchanging therefor such of its products as those countries were willing to receive. Thus, England exports to the United States manufactured articles, and receives in return breadstuffs and cotton. But, as it sends more goods to the United States than it receives from them, the difference is paid by the latter in gold or bullion. For bullion, being a product of our mines, is just as much an article of merchandise as our cotton or wheat, and we send it to England in exchange for manufactured articles, for the same reason that, in the case first supposed, England would send it to France in exchange for silks; it is the cheapest thing we have to send at that time. General prices may be higher in this country than in England, because we have proportionately more money in circulation, and money consequently has less purchasing power; and though the money used for our internal trade, and which has raised prices, may not be gold, the money of commerce that we send abroad is necessarily of that kind. Thus it would happen that a stream of gold would flow from this country to England, and thence to France.

This is but a single instance of the manner in which the precious metals flow from one country to another in the course of trade, owing to differences in the value of money. But it is enough to show that, between countries having intimate commercial relations, gold tends toward the one where it has most purchasing power; that is to say, where its value is highest, as measured by the quantity of goods it will exchange for. Such has usually been the state of prices and exchanges between England and the United States.

To examine fully the causes affecting the values of commodities themselves, apart from the causes pertaining to the value of money, which influence and determine the circulation of the precious metals from one country to another, would require an examination of the whole subject of international trade in all its complicated relations. This cannot be done at the present time. It is sufficient to remark, that the low prices of commodities—that is, the high value of money prevailing in the older countries—may be attributed to the tendency of profits to a minimum, in the absence of new fields of employment for accumulated capital, to the low wages resulting from the pressure of population upon the means of subsistence, and to the effective power of machinery, and the consequent diminished cost of labor. These causes tend to keep prices in general at a low range, even though bread-stuffs and raw materials are largely imported, and to attract the precious metals to those countries from the mining regions.

The last mentioned of these causes is the most potent. The saving of labor which the use of machinery affects, is the chief source of the accumulated wealth of the highly-civilized nations, and the means by which they attract to themselves the necessary supplies of the precious metals. A commodity which, produced by direct labor, would require the time of a workman for weeks, or months, can be produced by the aid of machinery in a few days. But to those who have no machinery such a commodity represents as much labor as it would cost them to produce it without machinery. Thus, a piece of cloth, which in England would require labor equivalent to that of one workman for two days, would require, if made in the mining states of South America, or in the wheat districts of Russia, the labor of one workman for a month, and the home-spun article produced would be a sorry substitute. The South American, and the Russian accordingly, are glad to unite their rude labor directly with the gifts of Nature, and to exchange the gold and wheat which result for the cloth of the Englishman, the product of skilled labor aided by machinery. Commodities, then, may be said to attract the precious metals according to the amount of labor they represent. Raw produce attracts them the least, manufactured articles the most.

There is still another cause influencing the circulation of the precious metals which deserves mention, as its influence is increasing rapidly with the progress of civilization, and is particularly potent in our own country at the present time. I refer to the movement of capital from one country to another for purposes of investment.

Foreign capital may be attracted to a country for security of the principal, or in order to realize higher rates of interest.

Thus, suppose an English capitalist, attracted by the high rates of interest paid in the United States for the use of capital, desires to take advantage of the fact by investing in American securities. He meets in London a railway projector from America, who sells him railway bonds. The American thereupon with the proceeds of his bonds buys railway iron of the English makers, and ships to New York the iron with which his road is constructed. Here is a transfer of capital without any transfer of money. But the railway constructor may prefer to buy his iron in Pennsylvania. He, therefore, if exchange, as is usually the case, is in favor of England, deposits the money realized from the sale of his bonds in London, and, with the proceeds of the sale of his bill on London, pays for his iron. In this case, again, the capital is transferred without any shipment of gold. But the bill on London, having been sold in New York, has been purchased by some one, who, without it, would have been compelled to have shipped specie to England to have met his payments there.

Thus it happens that a high rate of interest, confidence existing, tends to attract capital to the country which can afford to pay it, and either draws gold into the country, or keeps at home a portion of that already there, and this influence may act irrespective of the purchasing power of money, as marked by the scale of general prices in the respective countries from which the money is drawn, or to which it comes. But when capital is sent abroad for investment, it usually takes the form of a loan. A debt is then created which must sooner or later be liquidated, and the interest on which must be paid as it accrues. The effect, therefore, of the movements of capital seeking investment on the circulation of the precious metals is temporary, and as the rate of profits which can be derived from the differences of prices is greater than the interest paid for the use of capital, it follows that the controlling cause in determining the circulation of the precious metals remains the exchange-value of money. They seek the country where they buy the most. Gold flows from California, where interest is two per cent. per month, and commodities are correspondingly high, to Holland, where interest is two per cent. per annum, and commodities are low. The flow of the precious metals to India and the East proceeds from the same cause. Prices being exceedingly low, the purchasing power of money is very much greater in those countries than in the so-called civilized portions of the globe, and it is probable that for generations to come the Orient will furnish a vacuum for the reception of the surplus products of our mines.

The foregoing is but an imperfect sketch of the causes determining the movements of gold and silver through the commercial world. Enough has been said, however, to show that, like other articles of merchandise, these flow from country to country in accordance with the demands of trade, and the ability of each country to attract them, and to indicate the foundations on which rests the law of the circulation of the precious metals, first pointed out by Ricardo, viz.:

"Gold and silver having been chosen for the general medium of circulation, they are, by the competition of commerce, distributed in such proportions among the different countries of the world as to accommodate themselves to the natural traffic which would take place if no such metals existed, and the trade between countries were purely a trade of barter." *

This statement is not made with the usual felicity of that author. What would take place if no such metals existed may be known in some other planet, but can never be known in this. What is really meant is, that the use of coined money has no effect on the laws which determine the exchange-values of commodities, including therein the precious metals themselves, and consequently has no effect on the exchanges of commodities one for another.

The law of the circulation of the precious metals correctly stated would be as follows:

Gold and silver tend to circulate from country to country, in the course of commerce, as if all trade were barter, and as though they had never left the form of bullion. The precious metals, coined and uncoined, are shipped from one country to another for the same reason that other commodities are sent. All merchandise seeks the best market. Commodities for sale are sent to the places where they fetch the highest prices. But, while the precious metals furnish no exception to

---

* "Principles of Political Economy," chap. vii.

the rule, the fact is disguised, as price cannot be predicated of money. But, though they assume the form of money, they tend to flow none the less to the country where they find the best market; where they have the greatest value in exchange; where money has the most purchasing power; where, in short, the prices of commodities in general are the lowest. Gold, like water, seeks its level. Each country, other things being equal, has a share of the circulating medium of the world proportioned to its wealth and necessities. Prices in each country must bear their proper relation to prices in every other, and this relation is adjusted by the flow of the precious metals through the channels of commerce, and, as no other commodities possess the same quality of universal circulation, nothing else can ever be substituted for them as money. Paper, it is true, may be used as money within the jurisdiction of the government under whose authority it is issued, but it cannot become the money of commerce. Gold only is current between nations, and its most important function is to act as a regulator of international prices.

The amount of the precious metals which naturally flows to and is found in each country may be called its natural circulation; and it is as sure to come to any country that is well governed, and inhabited by an enterprising people, as the right amount of blood is sure to circulate through the veins of a healthy man.

From the consideration of this law of the circulation of the precious metals, the folly is made evident of some of the ideas commonly current in the United States on the subject of money. The fallacies of the exploded Mercantile Theory, prevalent in the beginning of the century, still linger among us. It is commonly thought that, so long as the money current is gold, or its equivalent, there cannot be too much of it; and it is gravely proposed to make our currency equivalent to gold, without any regard to its quantity, or to the fact that paper, convertible on demand, is equivalent to coin in its effect on prices and the international exchanges. On the other hand stand those who fear that gold cannot again be used as money, because so little of it is left in the country; forgetting that the amount of gold in a country is a thing with which legislators have nothing to do, and that commerce, unfettered by foolish legislation, will regulate the currency in accordance with natural laws.

But, unfortunately, it seldom happens that commerce is left free to follow its own laws. The natural circulation of the precious metals, consequently, which would exist in each country if commerce were free, seldom exists in fact. Men, who think they can improve upon natural laws, are apt to begin their experiments by tinkering with the currency; and the law of the circulation of the precious metals through the world, which is as fundamental in its place as the law of gravitation, is seldom recognized by legislators. How far and in what manner the introduction of paper money conflicts with that law, will be shown hereafter.

CHAPTER II.

THE DIFFERENT SORTS OF PAPER MONEY.

THE instrument with which the exchanges of commerce are effected 'is of minor importance compared with the exchanges themselves. It is not the machinery that we study, but the work it accomplishes. It is only when the machine is out of order that our attention is called from its work to itself, and we are compelled to learn the nature of its construction, and the remedy for its defects. Or, perchance, when new patents are offered for our use, we are impelled to investigate the principles on· which they are made, and test the merits they are said to possess.

The place money would naturally fill in the science of political economy is narrow. The part the precious metals perform as a circulating medium is easily understood. When, however, by the substitution of paper money for natural money, the machine has been thoroughly put out of order, a subject presents itself at once intricate and unsettled.

A preliminary step in the investigation of that subject is to examine the various sorts of paper money commonly used in civilized states, and determine the grounds of difference between them.

The first introduction of paper money arose from

the weight and bulk of gold and silver. For retail
traffic these qualities are not objectionable. Fifty
dollars in gold are a little heavier, but occupy no
more space, than the same amount in small bills. But
in the extensive operations of wholesale trade it
becomes a great labor to count over the coin, piece by
piece, for each transaction, particularly when it is
partially worn away, and consists of coins of many
denominations, issued from the mints of numerous
petty states; while to transport it from place to place
becomes another labor. Hence arose, at an early day,
the custom of depositing coin in a bank, which issued
its bills or certificates to represent it. Such was the
origin of the banks of Genoa, of Amsterdam, and of
Hamburg. Their bills or receipts circulated as money,
but were supposed to represent always coin actually
in their vaults, and were issued for convenience
merely. The working and effects of such a currency
differ in no manner from those of one composed of the
precious metals solely, and present no new principles
for examination.

The advantages of such a currency depend on the
manner of doing business in the country where it is
used. There was a time when its use was a necessity.
But it is not easy to see the advantage, in this age, of
issuing notes to circulate as money, if they represent
coin actually held to meet them, dollar for dollar, and
are issued only for the sake of convenience in counting and transportation. In former days the means of
communication were slow and difficult. Then each
load was hauled, at great expense, in lumbering
coaches, drawn by horses, over rough roads, exposed
to all the dangers which beset the king's highway in

a lawless age. Now it is taken to the office of an express company, and, for a small compensation, delivered in a few hours to any part of the country, without any appreciable risk to the owner. At that time confidence did not extend through society, and it was necessary to count out the money for each transaction. Now a check is given, and the matter is ended. Steam transportation, express companies, banks of deposit, clearing houses, and bills of exchange, have done away with all necessity for complaining of the weight and bulk of the precious metals, and demanding a paper substitute. All the stupendous operations of modern commerce could be conveniently transacted without a dollar's worth of bank-notes. For the exchange of values is made almost wholly by means of bank deposits, and the percentage of money retained in the bank vaults for the occasional payment of depositors, is as convenient in the shape of coin as in the shape of paper, and can be paid out by weight faster than notes by count. In modern times, it is only in retail trade that money circulates actively from hand to hand, and, as will be shown hereafter, the use of any other money than gold and silver in retail transactions ought to be prevented by law, on grounds of public policy. The age for using paper money for convenience' sake only has passed. And, in fact, that motive has but little to do with the issuing of modern bank-notes.

It was early discovered that the bills issued by a bank of good repute would be presented for redemption but slowly, and that the bank was under no necessity of retaining coin on hand to the full amount of its bills outstanding. Hence has arisen the second class of paper money, viz.: when the notes intended to circulate as money are convertible into coin on demand of the bearer, and have superseded a portion of the coin that would naturally circulate in the country, but do not exceed such natural circulation in amount.

Suppose the natural circulation of a country to be ninety millions of dollars, and that this amount of coin comes into possession of the banks, and they, thereupon, issue their circulating notes, payable to the bearer on demand, to represent it. If they retain the ninety millions of dollars in their vaults, and issue notes only to that amount, the circulation will be the same as before; but suppose they issue more notes than this sum representing the natural circulation of the country. The amount of money in circulation having been increased without any increase of the demand for it, the increased money will be of the same value, that is, will have the same purchasing power as the original money, and general prices will rise. But, in foreign countries, prices will have remained unaffected. Foreign goods will, thereupon, be imported to realize the high prices, and will be paid for with a part of the gold from the vaults of the banks. This process will continue until the surplus gold has left the country, and its circulation, consisting partly of gold and partly of bank-notes, has been reduced within its natural limits. If the amount of gold that remains is thirty millions, and bank-notes are issued to the extent of ninety millions, sixty millions of these will be in place of a corresponding sum of specie which has been exported, and the country will be the gainer by that sum. The gold has been exported, and in return foreign products have been received, and added to the wealth of the country; while its business continues to be transacted with money which has cost only the expense of the paper and printing. The principal gainers by the operation have been the banks. They have gained the use of sixty millions of dollars at a nominal expense; and the community at large has gained by the addition of that sum to the loanable capital of the country, which costs the borrowers the amount of interest they pay to the banks for its use, and which they are enabled to employ in productive enterprises.

We have not seen this process carried through in our day, because bank-notes have been issued from time immemorial, and we cannot go behind them. But their effect is precisely the same as in the case above supposed. A bank is started with thirty thousand dollars in gold, and issues ninety thousand dollars in notes which circulate as money. The gold it retains in its vaults. The notes which have cost only the expense of printing, it loans to its customers, and thus adds sixty thousand dollars to the loanable capital of the country, which is used to increase its production and wealth.

Bank-notes have all the characteristics of money, except that of value depending on cost of production. The question whether they are money, it is true, is one which has been much discussed, and many distinguished authorities have denied that they are, basing the assertion on the ground that they are not a legal tender, and do not finally close transactions. But the author,* on whose opinion this view chiefly

* Mill, "Principles," etc., Book III., chap. xii., sec. 7, and sec. 1.

3

rests, while asserting that, "it seems to be an essential part of the idea of money that it be legal tender," asserts also, in the same chapter, that "bills of exchange and cheques circulate as money, and perform all the functions of it." These two statements are totally inconsistent, and might be left to neutralize one another. The question, however, whether bank-notes are to be classed with the other instruments of credit, or with money, is not a mere question of nomenclature, but one of vital importance, well worthy of examination.

Money derives its force from common consent. Men, for the sake of convenience, and to render a division of labor possible, have been impelled to fix upon certain commodities to use as a circulating medium. The custom being a necessity has become universal. A legal tender law, therefore, merely gives sanction to a custom which existed before the law was passed, and which would continue in full force if the law were repealed. So strong, indeed, is the custom, that it sometimes overpowers the law, and makes that money which legally cannot be such. Thus, during the suspension of specie payments in England at the beginning of the century, bank bills were never a legal tender. The remedies of arrest for debt and distraint for rent were removed, in case a tender of Bank of England notes had been made; but it was decided in 1801 that every contract was legally payable in specie only. Yet the suspension continued twenty years thereafter, and the law was never enforced. Certainly, it cannot be denied that bank-notes were money during this period, for no other was used. Yet, according to law, they were no more money during the suspension than before or after it, and when finally, in 1834, Bank of England notes were made by law a legal tender, they acquired no new use in practice thereby. So during any ordinary suspension of payments by our banks, though specie is still the only legal medium, and though perhaps the banks have legally forfeited their chartered rights by refusing to pay specie, their notes nevertheless are the only money in circulation. Yet bank-notes when convertible into coin on demand are just as much money as when inconvertible. They are not only a medium of exchange, but a standard of value and a means of discharging indebtedness. Whether they have become so by custom or by the strict letter of the law is immaterial. Every man who makes a contract, whereby he is required to pay money, expects to pay it with bank-notes. They are, or are supposed to be of equal value with coin, and are referred to equally with coin as the standard by which the value of the property parted with or acquired is measured. No other form of credit is used as a standard of value. It matters little whether bank-notes are called "coined credit" or money. If men choose to coin credit instead of gold, and receive it in all their transactions in the place of gold, it becomes money as distinguished from other kinds of credit. If bank-notes were not used, gold and silver to the same amount (less the reserve) would necessarily circulate. They take the place of the precious metals, therefore, and perform all their functions, though, owing to their unstable value, in a defective manner. Of so little avail is the law making specie the only legal tender, that even the courts are compelled to evade it. In this country, no State has the power to make bank-notes a legal tender between individuals; and probably no such power has been conferred on the general government. But the courts have partially nullified this provision by holding that a tender of bank-notes is good, unless specifically objected to at the time of the tender, and statutory legal tender required instead. In England, also, country bank-notes are a good tender, unless objected to. This quality belongs to no other form of credit, nor to any article of merchandise. A tender of a bill of exchange, or of a note of one individual, or of a check on a bank, would be bad, whether objected to or not. So a tender of a barrel of flour, or of a bale of cloth, in the place of money, would be no avail, without any objection on the part of the creditor. Bank-notes before 1862 were the only thing in the United States, except gold and silver coin, which could be used in immediate payment of pecuniary obligations, and were commonly so used to the exclusion of the latter. So that, though our currency was nominally of gold, practically gold was used as a legal tender only in special cases. Bank-notes by force of custom had usurped its place, and all contracts were made with reference to the custom.

It may still be said that bank-notes do not finally close the transactions in which they are employed. The bank which issued the notes may become insolvent, and then the transaction would not be complete. The receiver of the broken bill would have recourse to the person from whom he received it; but this fact makes no essential difference. In the case of a counterfeit coin, the person paying it out is bound to make it good; but if out of one hundred dollars ten are found to be counterfeit, the remaining ninety do not cease to be money. So if, out one of hundred bank-notes, ten are the issue of insolvent banks, the remaining ninety still possess the characteristics of money. The courts of most of the States hold that the receiver of a bill of an insolvent bank must return it forthwith to the person from whom he received it, and that any delay in so doing discharges the latter. And the courts of some of the States have gone so far as to hold that bank-notes do close transactions in which they are employed; that giving them for a debt without objection is payment, and that the risk of the solvency of the bank is thrown on the receiver. Where it is held at the same time that a tender of bank-notes is good unless specifically objected to, it is difficult to perceive why they are not for all practical purposes as much money as if made by express enactment a legal tender, like Bank of England notes. It should be remembered, too, that in this country the ultimate payment of bank-notes has generally been assured by a pledge of bonds or other securities, in the hands of an officer of the State, under whose laws the banks have been incorporated; and though the security has sometimes proved fallacious, the practice has imparted confidence to the holders of bank-notes, and has helped to make them current as money.

But the opportunity for profit to the issuers of notes circulating as money is so great, that they are constantly tempted to issue them in excess of the amount naturally required by the trade of the country; and hence arises the third class of paper money, viz.:

When notes have been issued, nominally payable in coin on demand, and superseding a portion of the coin which would naturally circulate in the country, but exceeding in amount such natural specie circulation.

This species of paper money differs in some of its effects from the preceding, but in its nature is identical with it.

The paper money of a country may, at one time, just equal in volume the specie that it has displaced, and at another time exceed it. For one period it may be of the preceding class, and for another period belong to the class now under consideration, while the people using it would not be aware of the change; and, though having a dim consciousness of the fact that their currency was redundant and imperfect, would not perceive the amount of the excess, nor be able to detect the cause. Bank-notes would continue to be redeemed in coin on demand, when presented in small amounts; and as long as confidence continued, small amounts only would be presented for redemption. But whenever, from any cause, such as a demand for specie to ship abroad, or because distrust had entered the public mind, notes were presented for redemption in large amounts, the fact would become patent, that bank-notes had driven too much gold out of the country, and that they were in excess of the natural specie circulation. Thereupon, specie payments would be suspended, and the fourth class of paper money would be reached, viz.:

When the notes, circulating as money, are not convertible into coin on demand.

Such has been the circulating medium of this country, periodically, after every commercial crisis. But such circulation of inconvertible bank-notes has always been of temporary duration, and in violation of law.

It has been the result of a panic, and has belonged to a stage of transition from a period of speculative excitement, to one of ordinary quiet. Its characteristics are to be studied, with those of the other classes of bank-note circulation.

There is another species of paper money more properly belonging to this class. It is that which by law is made a legal tender for the payment of debts, and is not required to be redeemed in coin. Such is the present currency of the United States, which is paper money proper.

When a nation habitually uses as its circulating medium, bank-notes issued to an amount exceeding the natural circulation, so that the percentage of specie left in the country is small, it will find itself in the event of a great drain upon its resources to support an exhausting war, left without any money but paper. The gold and silver on hand will at best be insufficient for the occasion, and the financial distrust which accompanies civil commotion will cause that little to be hoarded. To borrow gold will then be difficult, while to borrow inconvertible bank-bills will be to pay the banks heavy interest for the use of printed slips of paper, which the Government can print as well as they. The opportunity of making a forced loan without interest will become a temptation too strong to be resisted, and the sinews of war will be obtained by issuing legal tender notes.

The principle upon which such notes are based, so far as they are based upon any principle but that of the thief, seems to be this : money, it is said, is a mere unit of calculation. "The dollar is wholly an arbitrary conventional standard." Value can be measured by an abstraction, just as distance or quantity. A yard measure is obtained by marking off a space called a yard upon a stick, which thereupon becomes a measure of length. So Government can stamp a piece of paper as a dollar, and it thereupon becomes a measure of value. This theory may not always be present to the minds of those who issue legal tender notes, but it always finds advocates among them, and is the theory upon which the issue of such money in preceding generations has been based. Its first conspicuous advocate was the celebrated John Law. "Money," said that writer, "is only the sign which represents riches in circulation. A crown is a note of which the impress of the prince is the signature;"* and he supposed that by increasing these signs which represented riches, he could increase equally the riches of a country. Failing to put his schemes in practice in his own land, he succeeded afterward (1716) in procuring their adoption in France; with what disastrous results, history has recorded.

Probably no civilized government could now be induced to countenance this theory of money except under the pressure of a supposed overpowering necessity. Paper money in these days is made a legal tender only as a revolutionary currency.

But the theory that the value of money rests in a name is one which cannot be carried out consistently in practice. The present value of money, like that of wheat or any other commodity, depends on the supply of it compared with the demand for it. Its

---

* "Money and Trade Considered, with a Proposal for Supplying the Nation with Money." Edinburgh, 1705.

ultimate value depends on the value of the thing used as money, and this value depends on the cost of production. But while in issuing a revolutionary currency the fact is usually overlooked that its immediate value will necessarily be determined by its quantity as compared with the amount of exchanges to be effected with it, the other fact is often recognized, that its ultimate value will depend on that of the thing to which the name of money is given. The attempt accordingly is made, to add to the value of legal tender notes, by giving them other qualities than that of circulating as money. Thus greenbacks are made receivable for taxes, and for government loans whenever contracted, and an ill-defined expectation is constantly kept alive that they will some day be redeemed in gold.

The assignats of the French Revolution belonged to this class of currency; and value was given, or attempted to be given, to them by making them convertible into the forfeited property of the church and nobility at fixed rates. The attempt to sustain their value failed, however, owing firstly to their excessive issue, and afterward to the fact, that as the title to the property depended on the permanent success of the Revolution, it was not then deemed secure.

It should be observed that an inconvertible currency is based on credit; but not in the same manner as bank-notes. The latter are debts of the banks issuing them, payable in coin on demand, and it is the credit of the bank that makes them current. Their value depends on the prospect of their being redeemed in coin on presentation. Bank-notes, therefore, are strictly a credit currency, and specie and bank-notes together constitute a mixed currency.

But the element of credit in government notes made a legal tender is extended several degrees further. Such notes are not payable in gold on demand, and may never be paid in gold at all. But they can be used as the equivalent of gold in the payment of taxes, and in subscribing to government loans, and it is only when thus transmuted into bonds that a fixed time for their payment is named.

It has been claimed by a late writer that legal tender notes " transfer debts but cannot pay them. The creditor may accept the promises of the government in place of that of an individual, but he receives no value." *

This statement is erroneous, in not recognizing the fact that such notes are as much money in the United States, as gold in other countries. The circumstance that they are ill-fitted for the office, and perform the functions of money imperfectly and unjustly, does not alter the case. The law has made them money, as far as the law can make money. They possess value in exchange. They measure the price of every thing that is bought and sold. They are the standard of value, and the medium of exchanges, and they discharge indebtedness, just as fully and completely as any other money, how cruel soever the wrongs they inflict in the operation.

But while paper promises are the instruments used in this country in buying and selling every thing that is bought and sold, they themselves are referred by

* A. Walker—" Wealth of Nations."

the rest of the world to the standard of gold. Where
our law cannot make them current as money, they are
bought and sold for money like other government securities. But because they are not money in other
countries we cannot conclude that they are not money
here. The law has given them with us every quality
of real money except the fundamental one of stability
in value, which law cannot give.

It is indeed supposable that a legal tender currency not convertible into gold, but consisting merely
of counters, stamped under government authority,
might exist and not vary much from gold. So long
as its quantity continued just equal to that of the
specie which would naturally circulate in the country, and confidence in its ultimate value remained
unimpaired, exchanges would continue to be effected
at about the usual range of prices. But to keep the
volume of a revolutionary currency within this limit
is always found impossible. The only restraint on its
issue is the will of the government issuing it. When,
therefore, more money becomes necessary, it is obtained by printing more paper. It is always pleas-
anter to borrow without limit, and without interest,
than to submit to the terms demanded in open market; and when confidence is shaken so that the latter
course is difficult, the former method, to a nation using
such money, becomes inevitable. It is safe therefore
to conclude, that until human nature changes, no government can issue inconvertible paper money without
eventually making it redundant and depreciated, and
that after the experiment has once been tried, most
men will be willing to restrain the government within

its proper sphere, and leave commerce free to use the currency of nature.

From this examination it appears that paper money may be classified according to its nearness to specie, and that when paper is used as money it constitutes a credit currency. The paper is taken on the credit of the issuers, and this credit differs from other forms of credit. It is "coined credit." It circulates from hand to hand as money. Price is calculated in it. Contracts are made with the expectation that it will be used in their fulfilment. By the force of custom, or of law, it possesses all the characteristics of the real money, whose place it has taken, except stability in value, and may properly be called paper money. Nor does the use of paper as money conflict with the statement that money is a commodity. When it is said that money is always a commodity, what is meant is, that the value of money in exchange is determined by the same laws as the values of other commodities. When gold and silver are the only money, this is sufficiently obvious. When paper is substituted, the rule still applies, though it is not so apparent. Ordinarily a note or bill is simply a means for postponing the time of payment. But when bank-bills are used, though nominally they are only used to postpone the time of payment, practically they are received as payment, and become money. Yet as redemption of them can always be demanded, they follow directly the value of coin. Bank-bills resemble wheat-certificates. The latter are issued by owners of elevators, and call, not for a specific parcel of wheat, but for a certain weight of that commodity of a certain quality. The former in like manner are certificates issued by bankers, calling for a certain weight of another commodity, the precious metals, of a certain quality. When a wheat-certificate is presented at the elevator, the wheat it calls for is weighed out of the bin containing the proper grade. When bank-notes are presented for redemption, the metal is counted out, having been previously weighed and assayed at the mint, though in some places, as in London, it is usual to pay out the coin by weight, and not by tale. The only difference between the two, is that bank-notes have the qualities of negotiable paper, and it is not necessary to keep in bank the commodity they represent to the full amount of the notes outstanding, though even this practice the warehousemen know how to imitate, when speculation runs high. The further difference, that wheat-certificates are bought and sold, and bank-notes are used to buy and sell, results from the difference in the commodities they represent. The precious metals being used as money are universally exchangeable; while wheat being used for one purpose only is exchanged for consumption. But as far as the laws of value are concerned, there is no difference between a wheat-certificate and a bank-note. Both represent given amounts of certain commodities produced by labor applied to the earth.

When inconvertible paper is made by law a legal tender, it becomes money legally as well as practically. But even in that case, though the time of payment is left indefinite, the expectation that such paper will finally be paid in coin is always kept alive, and though its present value does not follow coin, its ultimate value is determined by the likelihood of its redemption. In both cases the value of paper used as money is determined by the same laws as the values of other commodities. Its immediate value depends on the supply of it compared with the demand for it, and its ultimate value upon its conversion into coin, and through coin upon the cost of production.

CHAPTER III.

OF THE INSTRUMENTS OF CREDIT USED AS CURRENCY.

BESIDES bank-notes circulating as money, there are several other instruments of credit that act an important part in facilitating exchanges, and which, being current from hand to hand, bear a certain likeness to money, and perform some of its functions. These are promissory-notes (other than bank-bills), bills of exchange, and bank checks, or deposits.

1. That promissory notes act as currency, is often denied. It is said that, as they are not payable on demand, they can for the most part be converted into money before due only at a discount from their face value, and hence are merely an evidence of debt, like any security for the payment of money. This is true in many instances, but not always. Suppose that A, a country dealer in dry goods, purchases a bill of merchandise to the amount of $1,000 of B, a jobber in a neighboring city. A receives the usual time on his purchase, say ninety days, and is put down in the books of B as his debtor for the price of the goods, which debt he pays at the expiration of the time of credit. In this case the purchase on credit, so far as concerns the currency used to effect it, is the same as a purchase for cash. But suppose that, instead of

receiving a book credit, A gives his note for the amount, payable to the order of B. B can then use the note in several ways. He can take it to his bank, and have it discounted, and with the money thus real-ized buy other goods to replace his stock. In this case, the note has been used merely as an evidence of indebtedness, or security for the payment of money, though by its agency one purchase more has been made within the time of the credit than could have been done without it. But, instead of having the note discounted, B may endorse it over to C, a jobber at the commercial centre of the country, in payment for a bill of goods, and C may endorse it over to D, an importer, for merchandise purchased of him, and D receive payment of it when due. In this case there have been two new transactions, within the time of the credit, by means of the note, which in case of a simple book credit from B to A, either would not have been made, or could only have been made by the ac-tual use of money. The note, therefore, has been the instrument for making these exchanges, just as much as if it had been one thousand dollars, in bank bills pay-able on demand, and has been a part of the currency of the country for that purpose. The quality which causes a promissory note to differ from a simple credit, and gives it its efficacy as currency, is the quality of negotiability under the Law Merchant. Not only is the note transferable from person to person, but A, who made it, cannot set off against the bank which discounted it, or against any of the other holders for value, any claim he may have against B, but must pay it when it falls due, without question.

But B might have put the note to another use

still. He might have held it as a security until paid; in which case, the note would have been like any other money security, a mere evidence of indebtedness, and would have performed none of the functions of money.

So to the bank which discounted it, it would be a mere security bought for money, like a government bond. The use of promissory notes as currency in this country is comparatively limited. They are usually either held for investment, or discounted by the banks, or bought and sold like other money securities.

2. Bills of exchange are frequently current in the same manner as promissory notes, by virtue of their negotiability. In England, domestic bills of exchange are largely used in cases where, with us, notes have taken their place. They are often made between parties living in the same place, and are the evidence of indebtedness frequently given by traders, in the course of their dealings, and being endorsed from one person to another in the course of trade, act as a medium of exchange. The use of bills and notes of individuals as currency seems to be more extensive in that country than here. It is stated, that at one time bills of exchange composed almost the entire currency of Lancashire, for sums above five pounds.

In the United States, however, inland bills of exchange, and drafts, are generally used for the purpose for which they were originally introduced; for facilitating the exchanges between different places, without the expense and risk attending an actual transfer of money.

In making these exchanges they act the part of currency. For example: A, a merchant in New York, sells dry goods of the value of $1,000, to B, a merchant in Chicago. C, another merchant in Chicago, sells breadstuffs to the same amount to D, a merchant in New York. B, instead of remitting the money itself to A, buys of his neighbor C a bill of exchange drawn by him on his debtor D in New York, and remits it to his creditor A, who collects it of D, and thus both transactions are closed by the one payment made in New York, and without two transfers of money from one city to the other, passing one another on the journey.

It is true that this precise transaction does not always occur in the course of trade between the two cities. But it represents the manner in which exchanges are made. The merchants of Chicago are owing in the aggregate large sums to the merchants of New York, and the merchants of that city are owing large sums to those of Chicago. The bills of exchange drawn in New York on Chicago, and those drawn in Chicago on New York, or the promissory notes made payable in that city, or with exchange on it, are collected through the banks, either directly, or by being received on deposit, and the drafts of the bankers substituted. The banks settle the accounts between each other, and make an actual transfer of money only to adjust the balance of exchange. These bills and drafts perform one of the functions of money, that of being a medium of exchange. It is not simply that they are an obligation to pay money, transferable from one person to another, but it is the quality of being negotiable, so that no other claim can be set off against them in the hands of a *bona fide* holder, that causes them actually to represent money, and act the part of currency. Nor does it follow that they are always currency. That is only one of the uses to which they may be put, as is the case with promissory notes.

In foreign commerce, bills of exchange act a part even more important than in internal trade. The goods that are shipped from one country to another are represented by bills of exchange drawn against them, which bills are current from hand to hand; and the country that receives more goods from another than it sends, must pay the balance in coin or bullion. Of the exchanges between two nations, therefore, but a small part are made by an actual transfer of money. Bills of exchange transferable from person to person are the currency of commerce, and it is estimated that nine-tenths of the trade of the world is transacted by means of them. It has already been stated, that the trade between two nations is essentially barter. By the use of bills of exchange, the actual transfer of money may be wholly dispensed with, and then this fact becomes even more evident. The goods are bartered against one another, and the balances are settled by the shipment of bullion instead of coin. But though, in appearance, money is thus entirely superseded, it still continues to perform one of its original functions. It remains the standard by which the values of the different goods are measured, and by reference to which it is determined what quantity of one article shall be exchanged for a given quantity of another. The parts filled by bills of exchange, and money, respectively, are apparent. The latter is the standard by which the exchange-values of the different articles are determined, and the former are the media of exchanging or bartering them for one another.

3. Bank deposits, and checks drawn against them, fill a place in domestic trade as important as that of bills of exchange in commerce. They differ essentially in some of their characteristics from any other form of credit, and as their true place in facilitating exchanges has not always been recognized, they are worthy of careful consideration. The idea, that the chief use of banks is to issue notes to circulate as money, is so prevalent, that the other uses of those institutions, of far more importance in economizing capital, and in ministering to the public good, are usually forgotten.

Banks of deposit increase the amount of loanable capital in a country.

Where no banks exist, every trader must keep by him unemployed a certain sum in ready money for immediate use, or to answer occasional demands or contingent liabilities. A person doing a large business must necessarily have on hand at all times a considerable sum in cash, and those doing a small business must each have a proportionate sum. In addition to these, capitalists not in active business, and persons acting in a fiduciary capacity, such as guardians, trustees, and the like, have idle funds constantly on hand awaiting investment. The aggregate of all these sums in a country of extensive commerce is very great. If in that country banks of deposit are not used, these sums would be hoarded. When, on the other hand, the habit of using banks of deposit is universal, all these funds are brought from their hiding-places into active employment. The persons composing each of the above classes would retain the usual amount of cash on hand, when using a bank of deposit for its safe keeping; and the bank, knowing the average amount of such funds in its possession, could loan them out to borrowers, being careful not to exceed that average. The capital of the country would not be augmented by the operation, but it would be rendered more active, and this in its effect would be equivalent to the creation of new capital out of nothing. The capital loaned by a bank is commonly employed for the purpose of increasing the production of the country. By far the larger part of it is used in discounting the notes received by manufacturers and merchants in the course of trade, who are thus enabled to give credit to their customers without tying up their capital, and rendering it for the time being unavailable in their business. Banks of deposit, therefore, simply by bringing idle money into use, save millions every year.

But they also economize capital by increasing the rapidity of circulation of money in general.

Suppose that A, residing in a town where there is only one bank, makes a sale, for which he receives $1,000, and, while waiting to invest the money, or to use it in making a purchase, leaves it on deposit at the bank. Knowing that he is likely to leave it some little time, the bank loans it to B, one of its customers, who uses it in making a purchase of C. The latter receives B's check, which he deposits, and the bank, knowing that C will not be likely to call for the money immediately, loans it to D, who makes a purchase with it of E, when the same process is repeated, and possibly the $1,000 may thus be used ten times before A calls for it. The money during all these transfers reposes quietly in the vault of the bank. Each owner checks against it as he uses it, and the person to whom payment is made deposits the check, which is then credited to his account; and when A, the first depositor, finally draws it out, he also checks against it, which check, instead of being paid in cash, may be re-deposited, and the money still remain in the bank, transferred to a different account. The money, therefore, in the coffers of a bank, so far from being idle until drawn out, has the greatest effective power of any in the community; with this exception, however, that the portion of it held by the bank as a reserve to meet its circulating notes is itself idle, though each dollar of it has three or four paper representatives actively at work. But it will be observed that the bank incurs a new liability at each transfer, and at the same time receives a new obligation in return. Thus, in the case above supposed, it is bound to pay C and E, as well as A, $1,000 on demand. But it has only $1,000 in its possession, and the promises of B and D to pay $1,000. It has not money on hand to the full amount of the deposits it has credited on its books, but only a percentage thereof. But, as a deposit is a debt of the bank to the depositor payable on demand, all that is necessary on the part of the bank is to keep its funds in a condition where it can fulfil its part of the obligation. Where the habit of making exchanges of property by checking against money on deposit is general, the money itself, as has already been stated, is seldom actually called for. The checks given are deposited, and a credit written in the account of the depositor for the sum of money represented by the check. If there are several banks in the place, checks on each bank may be deposited in each of the others ; in which case the banks, at the close of business, exchange the checks they respectively hold against each other, and each one pays each other in money the balance, if any, over and above the amount of its checks it holds. In large cities, where clearing-houses are established, even this payment is made without the actual use of money. Checks on one common bank are substituted, or securities are deposited in a trust company, for which certificates are given, or money is loaned to the government, for which certificates are issued, and these are used to settle balances at the clearing-house. The banks, therefore, in order to fulfil their obligations to pay depositors on demand, are under no necessity of keeping money on hand to the full amount of the debits inscribed in their books. They know the proportion of their deposits, which, on the average, they will be called upon to pay in money, and they keep on hand in cash such a reserve only as will enable them to meet these demands. If men are willing to make their exchanges of property by means of the credits they have given the banks, without reference to the amount of cash in the vaults of those institutions, the exchanges are made just as effectively when a percentage only of the sums represented by the checks is cash on hand, as when the whole of it is cash. If the banks are able to answer all demands that are made upon them, no more can be required. When, therefore, a bank is started with a capital of one hundred thousand dollars in money, it can loan, by inscribing credits in its books to be checked against, not only that sum, but such an amount of deposits as one hundred thousand dollars in cash is found sufficient, on the average, to keep afloat. The reserve, which it is usually considered necessary to keep in actual money, within the limits of prudent banking, is one-third of the demand liabilities. Such a bank, therefore, could loan, by means of deposits, three hundred thousand dollars, thus actually adding to the money in the country, available to effect exchanges, two hundred thousand dollars. Hence is seen the important part acted by banks of deposit in a commercial country. By their agency one hundred thousand dollars in cash can be made the instrument of effecting as many exchanges as three hundred thousand dollars without them, and that, too, without the issue of a single dollar in the shape of bank-notes circulating as money. Thus, by increasing the amount of work done with a given sum of money, banks of deposit lessen the quantity of money needed to do the business of the country. It has already been stated that they likewise bring into use a large amount of money that would otherwise be hoarded. In this country, however, where capital is scarce in proportion to the uses for it, bank deposits consist largely of loans made by the bank, by crediting the account of its customers with certain sums, and taking obligations for the repayment thereof.

By the use of these economizing expedients, the wholesale business of the United States is effected by the actual handling of an amount of money comparatively small. When the parties reside in the same town, checks are given; when their places of business are in different cities, payments are made by means of banker's drafts, which are merely the checks of a bank in one city upon a bank in another city, and which are credited to the account of the depositor like any other check. In retail dealings and in payment of wages, money for the most part is actually used; while in the rural districts, where banks are far apart, more money is used in proportion to the business done than in the cities, and the amount of bank deposits is proportionately smaller. The purchase of farm products from first hands is generally made with money and not checks. Large shipments of currency from the commercial centres are accordingly made every year to move the crops; which currency finds its way back in payment for the goods purchased by the country merchants.

As we have always been accustomed in the United States to the use of banks of deposit, we are not conscious of the economy there is in using them. The saving they effect becomes apparent, however, when we contrast the amount of money that circulates in this country and Great Britain with that which circulates in France.

In making such a comparison, bank-notes will be included with coin in estimating the amount of money in circulation, as it has already been shown that they are properly classed as money. In like manner the bullion held as a part of the bank reserves is as much money as the coin held for the same purpose. Nor can the coin and bullion which are thus held by the banks as a reserve be deducted from the money in circulation. That portion of them which is held as a margin for deposits, so far from being idle, has the greatest effective power of any in use. The portion, however, which is held as a margin for the redemption of circulating notes acts only through its paper representatives. If no notes were issued the amount of

4

specie necessary to effect the exchanges would be equal to the sum of the specie and notes, less the amount of the reserves held to meet the notes. Yet in this country the two funds are mingled together, so that it is impossible to distinguish the coin which is held to meet deposits from that which is kept for the redemption of the notes. In the Bank of England, however, these funds are kept separate, as the issue department of that institution and the banking department are compelled to maintain independent reserves of specie. In the following figures, then, the specie which is used as a reserve for the redemption of notes is counted twice, once for itself and once for its paper representative; but as the specie reserves are larger in the English banks than in ours, the total deduction to be made on this account is greater for that country than for the United States.

At the beginning of the year 1860 the circulation of the banks of the United States amounted to two hundred and seven millions of dollars in notes. They also held specie to the amount of eighty-three and one half millions. In addition there was a considerable amount of specie in the hands of the people, of which various estimates have been made. But these estimates are necessarily based on imperfect data, and are exceedingly unreliable. There is no reason to believe that the total circulation of the United States in 1860, including both specie and bank-notes, was much above four hundred millions of dollars, leaving the Pacific States out of the calculation.

The total bank-note circulation of Great Britain ranges near two hundred millions of dollars, varying slightly in different years according to the state of business. There is relatively more specie in circulation in that country than there ever has been in the United States, owing to the limited use of bank-bills of small denominations. The total amount of specie, including bullion held as part of the bank reserves, is equal in our money to four hundred and fifty or five hundred millions of dollars, and the entire circulation of Great Britain in specie and bank-notes together is not far from six hundred and fifty to seven hundred millions of dollars. Ten years ago, by the same methods of computation the specie was fifty millions of dollars less. The amount of bank-notes, however, was a little greater then than now, which shows that there is a tendency in that country to diminish the paper money in circulation, while the number of exchanges to be effected is increasing.

The total circulation of France, including specie and bank-bills, was, previous to the Prussian war, a little less than one thousand millions of dollars. The amount tends to decrease as habits of hoarding are broken up, and the circulation is probably less now than ten years ago. The amount of bank-notes in 1868 was two hundred and fifty-six millions of dollars, which was an increase of a hundred millions in two years.

But, in comparing the amount of the circulating medium used in different countries, the most important consideration to be kept in view is the total sum of the exchanges effected in those countries. The population and the amount of the circulation *per capita* is of minor importance. Now, England is pre-eminently the trading country of the world. Its commerce and manufactures are greater than those of any other country. Its accumulations of personal property are enormous, and are constantly changing hands. Its accumulated or moneyed capital is greater than that of France or the United States, and is constantly seeking investments. A large portion of the international transfers of other countries also are effected by means of bills of exchange drawn on London, and that city is the clearing house for the commerce of the world. The amount of the exchanges effected every year in England, therefore, is many times greater than in either France or the United States. That country, also, is the receiving and distributing market for the precious metals produced in the mining regions, and a portion of its coin and bullion being merely *in transitu* is not properly a part of the circulating medium of the country. The effective power of money, therefore (including under that designation bank-bills as well as specie), as measured by the amount of exchanges it effects, is at least three times as great in Great Britain, and was twice as great in the United States as in France. This increase of efficiency comes principally from the use of banks of deposit. By their agency the work of eight hundred millions of dollars was done in the United States with four hundred millions of dollars, and by their use we saved the latter sum to be added to our productive capital, in addition to what was saved by the use of bank-notes in the place of real money. In France, on the other hand, owing to the revolutionary experiences of the nation, confidence does not permeate society, as in England and America. Credit and the transferable instruments of credit are not so extensively employed to economize the use of money.

Hoarding is a habit generally diffused, and banks of deposit do not act the important part assigned to them in our social economy, the amount of bank deposits in that country being only one-eighth as large as in the United States. France, therefore, requires at least twice as much money as we do to effect the same amount of exchanges; and, as the precious metals can only be obtained for value, that country is kept from accumulating wealth by having so much of its capital invested in them.

On the other hand, the inference may well be made, that, in Great Britain and the wealthier portions of the United States, capital would be economized sufficiently by the use of banks of deposit, and of the transferable instruments of credit, without any issue of bank-notes. By the use of the latter the economizing of specie is carried so far that it ends in insecurity, and the fluctuations that result produce a waste of both labor and capital.

The action of bank deposits as currency is very similar to that of bills of exchange, and the promissory notes of individuals. When checks are negotiated from person to person, by endorsement, they are identical as currency with those instruments. But when the checks are not negotiated, but simply deposited, the process is different. The credit is then transferred from one account to another on the books of the bank, and the bank becomes debtor to a new creditor. But while deposits are currency they are not money. They are used to exchange values, but not to measure them. The quantity of one article that ought to exchange for a given quantity of another is determined by reference to money, the universal standard, while the exchanges are effected by transferring a debit of a bank from one person to another.

What effect bank-notes, and the other transferable instruments of credit, have upon prices, is a question as little settled as any in political economy. At the same time, it is a question of vital importance; and on its determination must rest our conclusions as to the benefits derived from paper money.

Mill denies to them any direct effect upon prices. His opinion is expressed in the following terms: "But we have now found that there are other things, such as bank-notes, bills of exchange, and checks, which circulate as money, and perform all the functions of it; and the question arises, Do these various substitutes operate on prices in the same manner as money itself? Does an increase in the quantity of transferable paper tend to raise prices in the same manner and degree as an increase in the quantity of money? There has been no small amount of discussion on this point among writers on currency, without any result so conclusive as to have yet obtained general assent."

"I apprehend that bank-notes, bills, or checks, as such, do not act on prices at all. What does act on prices is credit, in whatever shape given, and whether it gives rise to any transferable instruments capable of passing into circulation or not."

If the conclusions heretofore reached are correct, this statement contains several errors. It has already been shown that neither bills of exchange, checks, nor deposits, perform all the functions of money. They are instruments used in making exchanges, but they are not the standards of value, by reference to which it is ascertained how much of one article ought to exchange for a given quantity of another.

There is a second error, however, of greater importance. It consists in supposing that it is credit which acts on prices. The real cause, of which credit is but an effect, is still more remote. Whatever affects values, affects prices; as price is only an expression of the value of one commodity in terms of another commodity—gold. But credit has no effect on values. It is brought into use when some cause that changes values, changes prices. Thus, in case of a short crop of wheat, the value of wheat is increased, and its price rises. A speculative demand ensues, and credit is resorted to. But it is not the use of credit that causes the rise of price. The scarcity of wheat enhances its value, while the value of gold remains stationary. The same gold, therefore, will buy less wheat, and the price of the latter rises independent of credit or currency. In like manner the transferable instruments of credit (other than bank-notes) are not the cause of the rise of prices, any more than credit itself. They are employed simply to economize the use of gold. They are capital-saving machines. Of the double functions of money they perform only part. They become the means or instrument of exchanging commodities for one another, but they are not used to compare values. They are not the standards to which prices are referred. The use of credit and its transferable instruments, therefore, has no effect on the values of commodities compared with each other. But it may be said that they might elevate all prices in the same proportion, thus leaving prices higher, but relative values the same. But here another limit is met. Gold is the regulator of international prices, and, under the law of its circulation, prices in different countries are too closely related to permit such an enhancement in any one country. It follows, then, that neither credit, nor the transferable instruments of credit, have any effect on prices. This conclusion, however, is to be received only with proper limitations. It is true that they have no such effect in the long run; but the course of prices, while they are in the process of adjustment to values, is fluctuating and irregular. Thus, if a scarcity of wheat increases its value, its price rises gradually, and with many fluctuations, until an equation of demand and supply is established. Over the final adjustment of its price to its value, neither credit, nor its transferable instruments, have any control; but over the intermediate fluctuations of price they may have a temporary influence. The same is true of other commodities. While the adjustment of prices to values is in process, the extent to which purchasers can use credit, and its transferable instruments, may have a certain influence over the fluctuations of prices, without changing this ultimate adjustment.

Allowance must be made, also, in estimating the relation of credit to prices, for defects in the machinery for effecting exchanges. The value-saving machines which credit supplies are not perfect. The most common defect in them is that of carrying the economy of gold so far as to produce a scarcity of that article, and a consequent rise in its value. A derangement of the whole machinery then results; for credit, like steam, misused produces explosions.

A third error of Mill is in failing to distinguish

between bank-notes and the other instruments of credit. The reasons for classifying bank-notes with money were given in the preceding chapter. If those conclusions are correct, bank-notes must have an effect on prices which the other credit documents do not. Money acts upon prices directly. In the words of the author before quoted, "that an increase of the quantity of money raises prices, and a diminution lowers them, is the most elementary proposition in the theory of currency." The scale of general prices is directly affected by the amount of money in circulation; and this is the only direct effect that money can have on prices. For while the scale of prices can vary with the quantity of money in circulation, the price of each article is influenced by a multitude of different causes, and it is only the average price of all which is influenced directly by the ratio that exists between the amount of money in circulation and the amount of exchanges it is required to effect. When the scale of general prices in any country in one year is compared with their state in a prior year, the difference is found to depend principally on the amount of money in circulation at the respective periods.

If bank-notes are money, they must be included with coin in obtaining the amount of money by which general prices are determined. It does not follow, however, that they have the effect of rendering prices higher than would be the case if gold only were used. That inconvertible bank-notes issued in excess of the natural circulation have this effect is undeniable. That they can sometimes have it, before the stage of inconvertibility is actually reached, cannot be demonstrated, but many facts can be adduced tend-

ing to prove it. These will be given in another
chapter.

Credit and its instruments, on the other hand, can
have no effect on general prices. In proportion as
they are available, they may make more or less effective on prices any cause that acts on values. But, as
before stated, it is not credit that is at work, but the
cause behind it. The change in prices is confined also
to some single commodity or class of commodities,
and the rise in the prices of these may not affect general prices. In the average that constitutes general
prices, not only the prices at which the commodities
sell enter, but also the quantities of them sold. If, for
instance, there is an actual scarcity-caused by poor
crops, bread-stuffs will rise in price, but general
prices may not be changed. The same amount of
money will effect the exchanges of a small crop at
high prices, as of a large crop at low prices.

Another difference between bank-notes and the instruments of credit proper is in the way they are used.
Bank-notes are paid out as money. Checks and notes
of hand are given, that the holder may collect money,
or transfer the right to collect it, and the money finally collected is usually bank-notes. When a purchaser
enters a shop, and pays for his purchase partly in
coin, and partly in bank-notes, it would be difficult to
say why one acts as money, and the other not. The
notes are not taken on the credit of the purchaser who
pays them out, but of the bank which issues them, and
are taken to be paid out again just like the coin;
while a check would be taken under the same circumstances on the credit of the purchaser, either as
maker or endorser, not to be paid out, but with the

expectation of collecting the money. It may be said, that checks could be used in this case precisely like bank-notes. The statement is true; but the fact remains nevertheless, that they are not commonly so used, and do not in practice perform the functions of money, like bank-notes. If the time ever arrives that bank checks are used as freely as bank-notes, they will become as much money as the latter.

Another difference is, that bank-notes displace specie dollar for dollar, or nearly so, less the reserve to meet them; while the other instruments of credit displace specie to an amount much smaller than their own sum. They economize the use of money by increasing its activity of circulation. They add to the effective power of the money on hand; while bank-notes drive coin away, and take its place. The limitation on the amount of the latter that can circulate is imposed by the law of the circulation of the precious metals, and until that limit is reached, they can be issued, while used in retail trade, and in payment of wages, without regard to the supply and demand of commodities. But credit and its instruments cannot increase, while the demand for commodities remains the same. They are the effect of such a demand, and not the cause of it.

The difference, then, between bank-notes and the transferable instruments of credit may be stated in a few words. An increase of bank-notes is an increase of money, and may affect general prices. It may raise prices without regard to the demand and supply of commodities. An increase of notes, bills of exchange, and loans by bank deposits, increases, not the quantity of money, but its activity of circulation, and it is only special prices, or those toward which speculation runs, that are enhanced, while it is the special demand resulting from a change in values, and not the credit given, which causes the enhancement. An increase of bank-notes is possible without any increase of the amount of exchanges to be effected. An increase of notes, bills of exchange, and loans by deposit, can only take place on account of an increased demand for money, that is, of the amount of exchanges to be effected. Bank-notes perform both of the functions of money. They are used to measure values, as well as to effect exchanges, though in measuring values they fill the place of gold partially and imperfectly; while the other instruments of credit perform only one of these functions, that of facilitating exchanges.

It follows, from this distinction, that, in statistics of the amount of a mixed currency, bank deposits should not be included with bank-notes and coin as part of the circulating medium. Their amount should be included with the prices of commodities as one of the things augmented by an increase of notes or coin. They should be regarded as an effect, and not the cause. This error, however, does not invalidate such statistics. For the money held as a reserve to meet deposits ought, in theory at least, always to increase in proportion with their amount. That such is not always the case in practice is, unfortunately, true. Bankers cannot always resist the importunities of borrowers, and frequently increase their deposit-loans beyond the sum which their reserve justifies. Such increase, however, is temporary, and brings its own punishment. It does not change the conclusion, that the amount of deposits is as directly affected by, and dependent on, the quantity of money in circulation, as are the prices of commodities.

From this examination of the nature of credit, and its transferable instruments, it is apparent that their use does not change the conclusion reached in the first chapter, that money is always a commodity, and trade is equivalent to barter. They have no effect upon the laws of value. They facilitate the exchanges of commodities, but do not change their relations to one another. They diminish the amount of capital necessary to keep in the form of coin, but do not fill the office of money, as the standard of values by reference to which commodities are exchanged.

Some obscurity has arisen in the science of political economy from not distinguishing between capital and money. Money, like any other tool, is a form of capital, but the accumulations of labor called capital may exist in almost as many forms as there are objects of human desire. But when capital is loaned it is usually computed in money. The name dollar, in expressing capital, is more nearly a mere unit of computation than at any other time. A loan of moneyed capital is usually made by means of some of the transferable instruments of credit, most frequently by a check on a bank, and it rarely happens that the money is actually counted out ; just as commodities are paid for by transferring a credit, without counting out any money. Yet, in both cases, the receiver is entitled to demand the dollars in actual specie ; and the fact that specie is rarely called for, does not make the transaction in the one case any less a payment of money, or in the other case any the less a loan of money. Capital, undoubtedly, is the thing loaned, but it is capital in the form of money. Popular usage, therefore, is correct in speaking of the loan market as the money market, and the interest paid for the use of capital as the interest of money. If credit did not exist, a loan of moneyed capital would always be made by actually counting out the coin. The name was given before credit existed—when a loan of money and the interest of money were paid in specie, and not by a symbolic transfer. A serious error, however, has proceeded from this source. Because the interest paid for the use of capital is said to mark the value of money, it is supposed that there is a direct connection between these two things. The rate of interest, however, depends on the supply of capital compared with the demand for it, and the worth of the security offered. The value of money depends on what it will exchange for; that is, on the prices of commodities in general. The connection between the two, therefore, is remote, and rates of interest constantly vary without any corresponding change in the prices of commodities, or the value of money as marked by its purchasing power. *

When, again, it is said that money is a mere ticket or order, so that the one who lends it only transfers the right to receive a certain portion of the produce of the country, the fact that money is itself a commodity is apt to be overlooked, and the dangerous inference drawn that, like any other ticket or order, it is a mere symbol, and may be printed without regard to the intrinsic value of the thing on which the impression is stamped. But money, in itself, is no more a ticket or

* Mill, Book III., chap. viii.

order than wheat or any other commodity. The only difference is, that money is universally exchangeable, while wheat and other commodities must usually be exchanged for money before they can be exchanged for one another. Money itself is as much capital as the wheat or other commodities, though it is also the instrument of transferring capital, and paper money, so long as it remains convertible into coin on demand, is equivalent to capital, and costs every holder of it, except the issuer, as much capital as if it were coin.

A certain amount of obscurity has resulted, also, from confounding the words money and currency, or using them as equivalent terms. Much of the discussion that has arisen in reference to the classification of bank-notes, and the transferable instruments of credit, has come from a difference in the use of these words. But money is both a medium of exchange and the standard of value; while, as the instruments of credit, except bank-notes, are used only to transfer money, or exchange property, without measuring values, they are not properly money. There is need, therefore, of a word of wider signification to include them, and, as they are current from hand to hand, they can justly be called currency. Bank-notes are both money and currency. Bank deposits and bills of exchange, and promissory notes when endorsed from person to person, are currency, though not money. In the nomenclature of business, currency has a more limited signification. It is used simply to designate paper money, meaning usually bank-notes. In political economy the word has also a still wider signification, being used to designate the kind or class of money in use, such as a mixed currency, an inconvertible currency, and the like. Much fruitless discussion would be saved if a sure definition of the word currency could be agreed upon. A prerequisite to such agreement, however, would be an agreement in opinion as to the functions performed by the various instruments of credit.

CHAPTER IV.

OF CONVERTIBLE BANK-NOTES IN EXCESS OF THE NATURAL CIRCULATION.

WHETHER bank-notes are classed with credit or with money in their effect on prices, is a question of no practical importance, unless it can be shown that, while retaining their convertibility into coin on demand, they can be issued in excess of the specie, which, without them, would naturally circulate in a country.

It is maintained by many writers, and those of the highest authority, that a paper currency cannot become redundant and excessive, so long as it remains convertible into coin on demand, both in fact and in public belief. It is asserted that the banks have no power of increasing their circulation, except as a consequence of, and in proportion to, an increase of the business to be done.

Thus, Adam Smith says: " The whole paper money of every kind which can easily circulate in any country, never can exceed the value of the gold and silver, of which it supplies the place, or which (the commerce being supposed the same) would circulate, if there was no paper money." *

* " Wealth of Nations," Book II., chap. ii.

Mill asserts that "the banks will not be able to maintain in circulation such a quantity of convertible paper as to sink its value below the metal which it represents." *

On the other hand is that school of "currency theorists" who attribute almost every rise or fall of prices to an enlargement or contraction of the issue of bank-notes, and who argue as if the banks could increase their issues at discretion, regardless of the wants of commerce or the specie circulation of the country.

Among American writers, Mr. Amasa Walker, in his recently published "Science of Wealth," has ascribed to the banks great power of expanding their issues, and thus engendering a rise in prices. While relying but little on abstract reasoning to sustain his positions, he has collected a mass of facts and statistics in reference to the action of the mixed currency of this country for the last generation, showing, without regard to theories, that our machinery for effecting exchanges has worked badly.

That the motive to expand their circulation to the utmost limit is always present to the issuers of bank-notes can hardly be denied. This sort of money costs only the expense of engraving and printing, and yields to those who lend it as high a rate of interest as real money. The more of it they can keep afloat, the greater their profits.

That the banks impelled by this motive can issue their notes in excess of the specie which has been superseded, and that such redundancy frequently ex-

* Mill, Book III., chap. xiii., sec. 1.

ists, while the notes are still nominally redeemable in coin on demand, and that consequently the classification of paper money made in the second chapter is correct, can be shown with reasonable certainty. The best proof of the allegation is found in the instances where such a state of affairs has existed.

One memorable example of such a currency is seen in that of Great Britain in the latter part of the last century.

It was in the year 1705 that the celebrated John Law published, in Scotland, his visionary schemes for vitalizing the industry and augmenting the wealth of the country. It was his belief that to whatever extent paper money was issued, it would still continue to quicken the industry of the nation, and fill the land with riches. Though his schemes were not adopted, yet his ideas made a profound impression in Great Britain, and contributed largely to that excessive use of paper money that afterward existed.*

The extent to which, under the influence of these ideas, the issues of paper had been pushed, is indicated by Adam Smith. While asserting that paper money, consisting of bank-notes issued by banks of undoubted credit, is in every respect equal in value to gold and silver money, and that its issue does not increase the quantity of the whole currency, he nevertheless admits that in his time (1775) the paper money issued by the different "banking companies of Scotland was fully equal, or, rather, was somewhat more than fully equal, to what the circulation of the country could easily absorb and employ."

It appears, by the following passage from "The

---

* "Wealth of Nations," Book II., chap. ii.

Wealth of Nations," that there was then a constant tendency for gold to rise to a small premium both in England and Scotland :

"By issuing too great a quantity of paper, 'of which the excess was continually returning, in order to be exchanged for gold and silver, the Bank of England was, for many years together, obliged to coin gold to the extent of between eight hundred thousand pounds and a million a year; or, at an average, about eight hundred and fifty thousand pounds. For this great coinage, the bank (in consequence of the worn and degraded state into which the gold coin had fallen a few years ago) was frequently obliged to purchase gold bullion at the high price of four pounds an ounce, which it soon after issued in coin at £3 17s. 10½d. an ounce, losing, in this manner, between two and a half and three per cent. upon the coinage of so very large a sum. Though the bank, therefore, paid no seigniorage, though the government was properly at the expense of the coinage, this liberality of the government did not prevent, altogether, the expense of the bank.

"The Scotch banks, in consequence of an excess of the same kind, were all obliged to employ, constantly, agents at London to collect money for them, at an expense which was seldom below one and a half or two per cent. This money was sent down by the wagon, and insured by the carriers, at an additional expense of three quarters per cent., or fifteen shillings on the hundred pounds. Those agents were not always able to replenish the coffers of their employers so fast as they were emptied." *

* "Wealth of Nations," Book II., chap. ii.

This statement shows conclusively that at that time the circulation of paper money was excessive, and that its value was somewhat depreciated as compared with the metal it represented. If it took four pounds in bank-notes to purchase one ounce of bullion, which was subsequently issued in coin at the mint price of £3 17s. 10½d. to the ounce, counting the expense of coinage at nothing, then the difference between those two sums expressed the depreciation of the bank-notes as compared with gold; that is, between two and a half and three per cent. This difference in value between the currency and bullion is ascribed to the worn state of the coin. But, as Ricardo has shown, it was really owing to the excessive issues of paper. If the bank had refrained from reissuing the notes presented for redemption, the value of the whole currency would have been raised.* In the case of the notes of the Scotch banks, as it cost from two and one quarter to two and three quarters per cent. to keep them convertible, that rate marks their excess as compared with coin, though the loss was borne by the banks, and not by the holders of the notes. The mistaken ideas then prevalent in reference to the nature of paper money were the main cause of these excessive issues; while the principal means by which the notes were kept afloat was the circulation of notes of small denominations. In Scotland, at first ten and five shilling notes were allowed. At the time when Adam Smith wrote, none for a less sum than twenty shillings were issued, and at the present time that is still the lowest denomination permitted. In England,

---

* "Ricardo's Political Economy," chap. xxvii.

the issue of notes under five pounds was prohibited in 1826. Before that time small notes were in circulation, though never to the same extent as in Scotland.

Such was the currency of Great Britain previous to the wars with Napoleon. The suspension of specie payments for twenty-four years that followed, was the inevitable result of such a system. The shock to credit, and the drain of gold for the payment of subsidies, and the support of armies in foreign lands, rendered it impossible to keep bank-notes, already redundant, at the par of specie. A large part of the debt of Great Britain, consequently, was contracted in irredeemable paper, and though the depreciation was never very great, yet the use of paper money must be assigned as one cause of that incubus which, however skilfully prevented from paralyzing industry, has continued to degrade the mass of the British people.

A second instance of a redundant bank-note currency nominally convertible into coin is found in that of the United States prior to the year 1862. The mania for paper money in the last century was no where more prevalent than in North America. Most of the colonies emitted bills of credit made by law a legal tender. The Continental money of the Revolution, therefore, was but an extension of the currency used before the war commenced. The loss and suffering which resulted from the excessive issues and final discredit of that currency disgusted the nation with paper money. A party favoring "hard money" arose, and for a time its principles prevailed. The attempt to establish a single controlling bank, after the pattern of the Bank of England, signally failed. But paper money was not so easily disposed of. Intrenched behind State laws, a multitude of petty banks succeeded in flooding the country with their circulating notes. There has never been any power of general authority to limit the amount of this currency. The poorer money always supersedes the better. Each person prefers to part with that of doubtful value, and retain that in which he has more confidence. Few States, consequently, were ever able to elevate the character of their own currency. If, for example, one State had prohibited its own banks from issuing small notes, it would only have made room for the paper of the banks of some neighboring State less mindful of the public welfare. The bank-note currency of the United States, accordingly, for the generation prior to 1862, though fluctuating constantly in value and amount, has much of the time been excessive and redundant. There are several facts which tend to strengthen this conclusion.

It is shown by the discount imposed upon the bills of the country banks in the city of New York. The banks of that city, impelled by the necessities of their situation, had early learned to rely for profit on their deposits, and were not inclined to occupy the equivocal position of "banks of circulation." Their notes, therefore, being based on more specie than those of the country banks, exceeded them in value. The bills of the latter, at the same time, were for the most part redeemable only at the place of issue, and those of some of the New-England banks at the city of Boston. It naturally followed, that the country bills were not receivable on deposit by the city banks at par as

current money, but were subject to a discount, rang.
ing from one-half of one per cent. to two or three per
cent., and higher, according to the State from which
they came, and the supposed responsibility of the
bank issuing them. This discount, so far as it exceeded the expense of sending the bills home for redemption, and bringing back specie in return, marked
their depreciation below the standard of the metal
they were supposed to represent.

The rates of exchange on New York paid in different parts of the country expressed the same thing.
The bank-notes of each State were current at par in
all home transactions; but, when a merchant wished
to remit funds to New York in payment for his purchases, he was obliged to buy bills of exchange at a
premium ranging from one-half of one per cent. to ten
per cent., and sometimes even higher. This premium,
so far as it exceeded the cost of transferring the money
itself, was a proof of the depreciation of the paper current when it was paid.

Another circumstance which cannot be accounted
for without referring it to the excessive use of paper
money, is the fact that the expenses of living were
greater in the United States, during this period, than
on the continent of Europe, where the money current
was specie. The economy of a residence in the
European cities long ago became apparent to those
living on fixed incomes, and the American colonies
long settled in many of those cities testify to the fact.
Nor did this greater purchasing power of a small
income depend merely upon a difference in the relative
standard of living. It is true that, on the Continent,
people are satisfied with a suite of rooms, or a single

story; while in America each family must have an independent "homestead." But, on the other hand, most articles of consumption, and all the luxuries of life, have always been very much cheaper there than with us. In most parts of France, Germany, and Italy, one dollar in gold would buy as much as two or three dollars in the United States. In many cities of those countries, two thousand dollars, when expended by a native, or one understanding the language and modes of dealing of the place, would maintain an establishment on the same scale of comfort and luxury as double that sum in most American cities of the same size. This state of affairs existed when the weight of taxation was greater there than here; and, though this difference in the expenses of living can be accounted for in part by reference to other causes than the currency, no explanation of the fact would be sufficient which did not assign to that cause a leading place.

There is still another fact, which proves the excess of our bank-note currency during the period under consideration.

More paper money has been used in the United States than in Great Britain, where the method of doing business is similar, and the use of the economizing expedients of credit is but little greater. The usual amount of the bank-note circulation of England, Scotland, and Ireland, together, is about two hundred million dollars. That of the United States reached its highest point in 1857, when the amount in circulation was $217,000,000. The amount of bank-notes issued *per capita* has been a little greater here than in that country. But a comparison of the currencies of two countries *per capita* of the population would lead

5

to very inaccurate results. The proper comparison to make is between the total amounts of the exchanges effected in the two countries, with a given amount of currency. But, as was shown in the preceding chapter, the sum total of the exchanges made each year in Great Britain is very much larger than in the United States. The work, therefore, annually done with a currency of which only $200,000,000 are bank-notes, is very considerably greater there than here. It is but natural to infer, then, that paper money has commonly circulated in this country to an amount exceeding our reasonable wants.

The weakness of the old bank-note currency is quite apparent when we consider the percentage of specie to their liabilities usually held by the banks. For this purpose the deposits are on the same footing as the notes. They are equally payable in coin on demand, and, though the claim is not often made in times of quiet, yet when confidence is disturbed, or a panic sets in, the calling up of deposits is the great source of danger. The following table * shows the percentage of specie to their circulation and deposits, held by the banks of each State at the end of the year 1859:

STATES.	Per cent.	STATES.	Per cent.	STATES.	Per cent.
Louisiana	88.6	Pennsylvania	21.8	Delaware	9.9
Missouri	87.	Iowa.............	20.	New Jersey......	8.9
Georgia..........	23.7	Virginia	16.7	Connecticut......	7.5
Kentucky..	23.4	New York........	15.6	Rhode Island....	6.3
Tennessee.......	23.	South Carolina...	15.5	New Hampshire.	5.7
North Carolina..	22.08	Ohio	15.2	Wisconsin.......	5.5
Indiana..........	22.3	Massachusetts...	15.1	Vermont.........	4.2
Alabama	22.2	Florida...........	10.5	Michigan........	4.
Maryland........	21.4	Maine	10.	Illinois	2.3

* Walker, p. 168.

In the year 1859 the percentage of specie was above the average, and exceeded that of any year since 1842. The limit of safe banking, it will be observed, was exceeded by the banks of every State but two; while in the State of New York the fact, not apparent from the foregoing table, should be remembered, that the clearing-house banks of the city of New York were much stronger in specie than the country banks. The hold which any bank-note currency has on specie is very weak where the banks issuing it have on hand in coin less than ten per cent. of their demand liabilities. The chief element of weakness, therefore, in the mixed currency of the United States, has come from the country banks of the New England and Middle States. Where every village must needs have a bank, without regard to the accumulated capital of the neighborhood, those institutions cannot thrive as banks of deposit. They are compelled, therefore, to become banks of circulation, and to live by preying upon the rest of the community. Adam Smith complained of the "beggarly bankers" common in his day and country. The clan long ago migrated to America, and has thriven apace.

The paper money of the United States, consequently, has seldom been truly convertible into coin on demand. Under ordinary circumstances, when every thing has gone smoothly, and bank-notes have not been presented in too large amounts, they have been redeemed according to their tenor. But the currency has never withstood successfully any unusual pressure, and it is estimated that specie payments have been suspended eight times in sixty-four years.*

* R. J. Walker.

Since the complete adoption of the State-bank system, there have been three general suspensions—those of 1837, and 1857, and the one now in progress. Besides these, there have been several bank contractions that have caused "hard times," and produced partial or local suspensions. Such a currency cannot be justly called convertible, and, although it is commonly stated that the currency of the United States before the war was on a specie basis, the statement is only partially true. It could have been justly said of that of some of the States, while in other parts of the Union bank-notes have frequently been at a discount as compared with exchange, and as a whole the banks have never been proof against the pressure of a financial crisis.

The means by which an excessive quantity of paper money has been kept in circulation, and the causes peculiar to the United States which have aided them, deserve attention.

One of these is the habit, universally diffused, of using paper money. We have been accustomed to it from childhood. The habit has been transmitted from former generations. Having been brought up to confide in banks, we have confidence in one simply because it assumes to be a bank. An American seldom presents a bank-note for redemption, except because his suspicions have been aroused, or because he needs coin for some particular purpose. Bitter experiences of uncurrent notes and unpaid deposits have not shaken the public confidence in the system. Where this habit of confidence has been so universal, it has required but little specie to float much paper.

Another cause is found in the speculative habits of our people. In a country where wealth is increasing at a rapid rate, where an enterprising population, constantly reinforced by immigration from abroad, is joining its labor to lavish gifts of nature with never-flagging industry, where the occupation of new and fertile lands is ever going on, and new fields for the employment of capital are constantly opening, rates of profit are high, and the opportunities for speculative investment are enormous. Habits of speculation consequently become a national characteristic; and prudence in the use of credit, particularly of credit in the available form of bank-notes, is less practised than among more conservative communities. At the same time fixed capital tends to increase more rapidly than circulating capital; and, as the speculative class must gain the use of the latter, they are ever pressing the banks to increase their loanable funds, by expanding their issues of circulating notes to the utmost limit.

The great extent of our country has also been a means by which bank-notes have been kept from coming home for redemption. The device of issuing notes in one city, redeemable only in a distant city, was long since discovered to be a very effective means of hindering them from being presented for payment, and of diminishing the margin of specie necessary to keep on hand. It is said* to have been employed first by a banker of Aberdeen, in Scotland, who made his notes redeemable in London, and circulated them at home. The practice was subsequently adopted by the Bank of Ireland, which caused its branches to issue bills payable only in Dublin. The country bank-

---

* Benton's "Thirty Years."

ers of England about the same time discovered the profit in the operation, and issued notes redeemable only in London. This practice was finally suppressed in Great Britain by the statute of 1826. In this country the Bank of the United States attempted, by the same trick, to evade the limitations of its charter, and issued its branch-bank currency, which consisted of drafts or orders for small sums on the parent bank at Philadelphia, and which were circulated as money by the branch banks issuing them. The latter, in order to give them currency, made it a practice to cash them voluntarily, though they were legally payable only in Philadelphia. A person having but one or two small bills would not be at the trouble of sending them on for redemption, and such notes would circulate for a considerable period among the people before becoming aggregated in a single hand in amounts large enough to justify the expense of sending them forward for collection. After the decease of the Bank of the United States, this device was never directly employed by the State banks. But, indirectly, the same thing has been accomplished with ready facility. For instance, the headquarters of a bank would be nominally established in a remote or inaccessible place, where the bills purported to be issued and to be payable, while the real place of business for every other purpose, and the place where the notes were actually put in circulation, would be some distant commercial city.

The same device was practised in another indirect manner. Loans were not unfrequently made with the express understanding and agreement that the notes should receive what was called a good circulation. This consisted in taking them to a distant place and paying them out for purchases in the rural districts, where envious brokers and rival bankers would no longer be able to hurry them back forthwith to their issuers. Many of the small banks, particularly of the Eastern and Middle States, lived wholly by their circulation, which was thus kept afloat in the Western States at high rates of interest. The scarcity of loanable capital in those States rendered it easy to circulate any thing that purported to be money.

But the most effective means yet devised of driving specie out of a country, and making paper redundant, is found in the issue of notes of small denominations.

A note for a small sum will pass with less objection, and circulate more rapidly, than one for a large sum. A dollar bill will be received without question, when one for a hundred dollars would be rejected, unless the responsibility of the issuers were known, and the certainty that it represented specie existed. Large notes circulate only in wholesale business. Their use is confined to transactions between the dealers themselves, or in adjusting balances between the banks. Small notes, on the other hand, are employed in retail trade; they are paid out for wages; they circulate among the people in the thousand petty transactions of daily life. It is impossible for every one to know the worth of each note; they are passed from one person to another on the implied understanding that the person giving them will take them back if bad; they circulate rapidly; they move from hand to hand so fast that there is no time to present them for redemption. It requires, therefore, a less percentage of specie to keep small notes afloat than large ones.

It also happens that where small notes circulate, specie always disappears. The reason of this disappearance is sometimes supposed to be that bank-notes are more convenient, and are generally preferred to coin. This view is far from the truth. The real cause of the displacement of specie is found in that most elementary principle, that the poorer currency always supersedes the more valuable. A person who has in his pocket both gold and doubtful bank-notes, naturally prefers to rid himself of the latter. As between the two, there is always some doubt attached to the bank-notes. In order to know their value, it is necessary to know the circumstances of those who issue them, while gold is value itself. Accordingly, where small notes are crowded into circulation, coin is hoarded by individuals, or collected into the bank vaults, and drops out of general circulation.

The profit made by banks of issue is realized largely from the small notes. The large ones being used only in large transactions are generally deposited forthwith, and thus come into the possession of a bank by which they are returned to the issuer for redemption, or to settle balances, having had but a limited circulation. In the redemption of large notes, therefore, each bank acts as a check upon every other. But small notes are carried in the pocket-books of individuals to meet daily expenditures, or are collected in the money-drawers of the shopkeepers; and when at last they are deposited in a bank, instead of being sent home for redemption, they are paid out to meet a particular demand for them, and to commence another round of circulation. Thus more small notes can be kept afloat than the commerce of the country really requires, and, as the banks are under the strongest temptation to press them into circulation, they soon exceed in amount the specie that would naturally circulate if no paper were issued.

Prices accordingly are enhanced. But this enhancement is not always shown by the. market reports and trade statistics. It is much more observable in retail dealings than in wholesale transactions. It is marked better by the expenses of living than by statistics of prices. The latter are derived from sales by the quantity in open market, where the causes that determine exchange-value are the cost of production, and the law of supply and demand, and where the currency ordinarily has but little effect on price, save as it can be made a means of speculation. Prices at retail, however, are determined by quite different causes. They depend largely on custom and combination. The retail dealers generally manage to adjust their prices to the amount of money in the hands of the community; and, when there is a multitude of small bills circulating, not only have they a pretext for asking more, but the capacity of the consumers to pay more is increased; while, as a certain degree of discredit attaches to such money, and to the one paying it out, it does not feel so valuable as the solid metal, it is parted with more easily, and for less value in return. When it is said that an increase of the quantity of money raises prices, and a diminution lowers them, the proposition is much truer of prices at retail than of prices at wholesale. The latter are determined by general laws, while the former are determined by what the

shopkeeper can extract from his customers. When by
the issue of such bills a higher scale of retail prices
has been established, it requires, of course, more
money to make purchases. Nor does a temporary
scarcity of small bills have any effect in inducing the
retailers to lower their prices. Accordingly, whenever such a scarcity arises, the complaint is made at
once that there is not enough currency, and the
banks are urged to increase their issues, and they,
taking advantage of the circumstance, press their
small notes into the channels of retail trade without
much regard to the amount of specie in their vaults.
So potent is the effect of small notes, that it may well
be concluded that convertible bank-notes cannot become redundant, when those for small sums are forbidden by law. It is the unanimous testimony of the
English bankers, who have been examined before successive Parliamentary Committees, since the suppression of small notes, that the banks have no power of
increasing their circulation so long as it remains convertible, unless there be an increased demand for currency, caused by an increase of the business to be
done. It is admitted, however, that after a speculative movement has set in, an over-issue of bank-notes,
even when subject to this restriction, may be made in
order to prolong the duration of the movement, and
delay the inevitable reaction.* There is this difference to be noted, however, between England and the
United States: that, in a small country, covered with
railways, bank-notes can be sent back to their issuers
for redemption more readily than in a land of great

---

* Mill, "Principles of Political Economy," Book III., chap. xxiv.

distances; while in an old country, where rates of interest are low, and the accumulations of moneyed capital are enormous, there is not the same opportunity to circulate paper money, as in a newly-settled country, where new enterprises are daily developing, and the demand for loanable capital largely exceeds the supply. Even though small notes had been suppressed in the United States, the country banks would have been tempted none the less to have circulated their bills in the remote States of the South and West, and they might still have found it possible to have issued them in excess of specie. It is certain, however, that such a restriction would have gone far toward elevating the value of the currency unaccompanied by any other repressive legislation.

Mill, while sustaining the position of those who deny the bank-notes any power of increasing prices so long as their convertibility is maintained, admits that the rule ceases to apply when small notes are issued.

"I cannot but think," he says, "that this employment of bank-notes (in retail trade) must have been powerfully operative on prices when notes of one and two pounds value were permitted by law." *

If he had witnessed the effect of one and two dollar notes on retail prices, he would have admitted the power of the banks to issue paper in excess of the natural circulation, and would probably have classed bank-notes with money, and not with credit in their effect on prices.

Another cause which has tended to make the issues of bank-notes in this country excessive is the

* "Principles," etc., Book III., chap. xxiv., sec. 2,

practice established in many States of requiring the banks to deposit with a public officer collateral securities for the redemption of their circulating notes. Such laws, just in proportion as they secure the ultimate value of bank-notes, diminish their present value. They give them a *quasi* government endorsement. They relieve the holders from the necessity of watching the coin reserves of the banks, and, by thus giving the notes a wider circulation, impede their return for redemption, and enable the issuers of them to keep a greater amount afloat with a limited reserve of specie. That bank-notes thus secured circulate on the credit of the securities as much as of the banks issuing them is shown by the fact, that at the outbreak of the Rebellion the Western bank currencies, founded on Southern State bonds, depreciated as those bonds declined in price, with occasional exceptions of solvent issuers, involving in ruin merchants who received such notes in the course of trade, and bankers who took them on deposit.

But while from these causes the mixed currency of the United States had reached previous to the war a stage of development similar to that of the currency of Great Britain at the end of the last century, and bank-notes were frequently issued in excess of the natural circulation, the periods during which such excess lasted were always limited. The ultimate regulator of the amount of bank-notes that can be kept convertible is the movement of the precious metals. When not redeemable in coin, there is no limit to the amount that can be circulated. The simple effect of issuing them is, that, as the money in circulation is increased, prices rise. But the limit to which prices in coin can rise is speedily reached. If commodities are high, coin is exported until prices decline. The precious metals seek the best market. They flow to the country where prices are low, and from the country where prices are high. So long, therefore, as bank-notes are convertible into coin, the banks have no power of issuing them so as to permanently elevate the prices of commodities. Yet this does not affect the conclusion that they have this power temporarily. When prices rise, the gold is exported gradually, and an inflation may continue for a considerable period before the natural check of an exportation of specie brings it to an end. It is natural, also, that the banks should exercise this power, where small notes are issued more frequently than when they are prohibited. For, in the latter case, the enhancement of prices begins in the wholesale markets, and is felt immediately on the international exchanges. But, because the effect of issuing notes of the large denominations is more limited and temporary, the conclusion does not follow that they differ in their nature from small notes. The difference is one of degree, and not of kind.

From these considerations, it seems reasonable to conclude, that paper money, while nominally convertible on demand, is sometimes issued in excess of the quantity of the precious metals that the laws of commerce would assign to the country in which it is issued, and that in few countries has such excessive use of paper money been more prevalent than in the United States.

CHAPTER V.

To many minds, every attempt to reduce to laws actions apparently so erratic, and closely allied to gambling, as the speculative operations of the stock-exchange and the markets, will seem fruitless. Yet the limits within which men are free to act are as narrow in speculation as in any other department of human effort. As the facts of political economy can be classified, and through them all the sequence of cause and effect can be observed, so in that minor branch of the science of exchanges which includes speculation, causation can be traced. Men act from motives, and in this case, as in every other, their actions can be followed back to their causes.

The motive in speculation is the love of gain, and its apparent object is to turn to advantage changes in the prices of things bought and sold. But as price is the value of any commodity stated in terms of another commodity, the value of which is taken to be constant, to know the probable changes of prices the causes that affect values must be understood. The one who perceives, or thinks he perceives, a cause likely to affect values, attempts to make money by his foresight.

He buys the commodity affected for a rise of price. He speculates, and the cause of his speculation is the change of values that acts on prices. Hence speculation may be defined as an effort of those making exchanges to profit by real or expected variations in the values of commodities or securities. When a merchant buys goods to distribute them to the consumers, he adds a new value to them. When he buys them because he thinks their price is going up, he founds his expectation on something affecting, or likely to affect, their values on which he speculates.

The changes in the values of commodities resulting from an increase or diminution of the cost of production are usually so slow in coming that they do not lead to speculation. It is the change of the immediate value of a commodity produced either by a diminished supply of it, or an increased demand for it, on which most speculations are based. In the markets for merchandise, it is commonly a short supply of any thing that changes its value relative to other commodities, and thus puts up its price. The harvests are bad. The stocks of bread-stuffs consequently are lessened. A war or political disturbance may hinder importations. Some important article of foreign production cannot therefore be obtained to the usual amount. As soon as it is seen that the supply of any necessary commodity is likely to be deficient, and that, as the demand for consumption will remain constant, the price must be enhanced, dealers in that commodity begin to lay in a stock in order to gain the increased price. The prospect of realizing an easy fortune by buying at one price to-day, and selling at a higher to-morrow, attracts numerous buyers from those engaged in other pursuits, and a speculation for a rise takes place. A similar effect may be produced by a new demand for any commodity, or class of commodities. It is witnessed when the breaking out of a European war creates a sudden demand for arms, saltpetre, or naval stores in our markets; and an example of the effect of a new demand concurring with an expectation of a reduced supply is furnished on such an occasion by the course of bread-stuffs.

But the speculative effect of an increased demand is more directly visible in the market for securities than in the markets for commodities. During any period of speculative quiescence, loanable capital accumulates. Rates of interest thereupon tend to decline, and the demand for securities increases. A speculation in the stock-market follows, during which the prosperity of the enterprises whose stocks are dealt in is frequently misrepresented or overlooked. Such accumulations of capital sometimes occur on a large scale. In countries which are in a rapidly progressive state of wealth, like Great Britain and the United States, the accumulations of new capital are enormous. The amount of it which is in a loanable form is subject to periodical enlargement. The ability of the banks to accommodate their customers is then enhanced. Rates of interest and of profit tend to decline. Outbursts of overtrading, and wild speculation result. During these, capital is destroyed, or changed from the circulating to the fixed form, and, after the inevitable commercial revulsion that follows, profits and interest again rise. These accumulations of capital cannot affect directly the values, or consequently the prices of commodities. But if they are contemporaneous, as is always the case, with changes in values arising from other causes, overtrading is greatly increased. At such times, also, too much capital may be drawn into banking, and excessive issues of notes may take place depressing their value as marked by a general rise of prices. It is, however, the quotations for securities that such accumulations of capital affect the most conspicuously. They are powerful on the stock-exchange, where values can be made to order, and room is left for the imagination to play with them its most fantastic tricks. They are absorbed also in purchases of real estate, where the rise of twenty years can be discounted in a single season. The most prominent instances of these speculative outbursts are those which occurred in this country in 1837, and again in 1857. . In the latter case, accumulated capital acting through the banks produced such an over-issue of bank-notes, and so great a rise of prices, that Prof. Bowen, writing before the culmination of the movement, ascribed the rise to a marked decline in the value of the precious metals, an explanation which overlooks the main cause at work. Such a general rise of prices has been seen in this country since then, caused by a decline of the value of the money by which prices are measured, and the depreciation of greenbacks has been accompanied with the excessive speculation such a change of values would naturally cause.

If these conclusions are correct, but little place is left for those " currency theorists," who ascribe almost every rise or fall of prices to an enlargement or contraction of the issues of bank-notes. An over-issue of the latter cannot be the proximate cause of speculation, and the prevention of such issues cannot do away with it. Speculation is a necessity which cannot be escaped, until supply and demand never vary, and capital ceases to accumulate. In its right place it is a benefit. It opens a proper outlet for human activity. It is the excess of it that is an evil.

Intemperance in speculation is stimulated by nothing so much as by an excessive use of credit, and particularly of bank-notes. While the allegation that bank-notes create speculation cannot be sustained, the fact that they foster its excesses cannot be disproved. The effects of the different instruments of credit in stimulating speculation will be best seen by observing them separately, and it will be found that in proportion as credit supersedes specie, and drives it away, speculation thrives, and the worse become the effects of the subsequent reaction.

The manner in which credit is employed in purchasing commodities has been touched upon in a former chapter. Its most simple form is that of a book credit. In most branches of trade, by the custom of merchants, a buyer is allowed a specified term of credit on his purchases. At the end of the term only is his account presented, and payment asked. Or, if a note is given, it is only when it falls due that the maker must be prepared with the funds to meet it. Any dealer, therefore, can make large speculative purchases within the term of credit customary in his business, without laying out a dollar in money. But the credit of most merchants is limited. If, then, to his own responsibility a buyer can add that of another person, the confidence of the seller is increased. Two names are better than one; accordingly, a speculator, by transferring any notes or acceptances he may have, is enabled largely to increase his purchases. Negotiable paper, whether given in the course of business, or made for accommodation merely, is an instrument largely employed in speculative transactions. But, even when the buyer actually pays for his commodities at the time of the purchase, the element of credit may enter into the transaction, and form its basis. The money used may be obtained on credit—and it is in this manner that the majority of speculative transactions are carried on. The banks furnish the money to conduct them. This they do, either by discounting commercial or accommodation paper on the security of the names thereon, or by directly loaning the money to be used in making the purchases, and taking a pledge or hypothecation of the commodities bought, or their paper representative, as security for the loan. At the stock-exchange the custom of call loans has long existed. One who purchases securities on speculation, either buys an option, by which he is entitled to call for the delivery of the securities purchased at any time within a fixed period, or else he pays for them at the time of the purchase, and they are regularly delivered to him. The money for this payment is furnished by the banks or money-lenders, to be repaid on call, and as collateral security, the certificates of stock, or the bonds purchased, are pledged. The whole transaction is consummated by a broker, who borrows the necessary money, and keeps the loan good, if possible, and who receives from his customer a certain percentage of the purchase-price, which is held by him as a margin to cover any fluctuations in the market-price, and save him harmless. This custom of the stock-exchange has extended to most speculative transactions, and the operations of the corn-exchange are conducted in a similar manner. The transactions there, also, may be conducted through the agency of a broker or commission merchant, who receives a margin for his own protection, and the purchases are made either on time options or for cash. In the latter case the money is usually furnished by the banks, though not necessarily on call. When the fever of speculation runs high, there is hardly any of the leading articles of commerce that cannot be bought or sold on a margin, or time option. But as speculative transactions are altogether at wholesale, the money is paid, not by actually counting it out, but by transferring a credit on the books of a bank. It is by means of their deposit-loans that the banks furnish the money "to carry" the securities, bread-stuffs, provisions, and other commodities held on speculation. When the speculative spirit is strong, and buyers are anxious to increase their stocks, the pressure brought to bear upon the banks for increased discounts is very hard to withstand, and increased accommodations are generally granted. But a bank does not ordinarily expand its loans by crediting deposits in its books without having some increase of the percentage of cash on hand to correspond. This increase cannot be had by obtaining more of the precious metals. Gold will not come at the bid of speculators. The desired money is gained, therefore, by adding to the issue of circulating notes. It is true that deposits are legally payable in specie on demand, just as much as the notes circulating as money. But this legal liability is effectually escaped in practice. It is usual

for the banks to receive the accounts of their depositors with the understanding that payments are to be
made in current funds—that is, bank-notes. It is frequently expressed in checks that they are to be payable in current funds. Though the legal validity of
such agreements has been questioned, practically the
banks retain the power of paying deposits in whatever funds are current. It is obviously just that a
depositor should be paid in the same money he deposited. To give bank-notes and demand gold seems
inequitable. Public opinion, therefore, does not require of the banks the same punctuality in paying
deposits in coin, as in redeeming their circulating
notes in coin. Nor usually are the same penalties
imposed by law for such non-payment in the former
case as in the latter. Besides this, is the further consideration that every depositor desires to retain the favor
of the bank, that he may obtain loans when desired.
This feeling is carried so far that money is left on deposit
at one time expressly in order that the depositor may
become entitled, according to the custom of bankers,
to receive a corresponding favor at some future time.
Thus the practice of "compulsory deposits" has
arisen, and many business men are compelled to keep
"good accounts" that the bank may gain more interest, and grant them more extensive loans at times of
urgent necessity.

Under these circumstances it is evident that, ordinarily, the percentage of cash retained by the banks
to meet deposits may be in bank-notes, just as safely
as in coin. When, therefore, speculation runs high,
and the pressure for greater discounts weighs heavily
on the banks, they expand their loans by inscribing

new deposits on their books, and increase their circulating notes to correspond with the increase of deposits. As the notes are issued to meet an increased demand, caused by the increase of the business to be done, they are not likely to be returned for immediate redemption. It is in this way that the percentage of specie to their demand liabilities has at times dwindled down to so narrow a margin. If no circulating notes had ever been issued, the banks would have had much less power of increasing their deposit-loans, particularly if the percentage of specie necessary to have on hand had been fixed by law. By the aid of bank-notes, therefore, speculative purchases have often carried prices to a higher point than would have been possible without them.

It is further to be remarked, that while the banks of this country have had the power, from causes mentioned in the preceding chapter, of issuing their circulating notes beyond the natural specie circulation, it is particularly in times of speculation that this expansion has taken place. When banks can have no money but coin in their vaults, there is a fixed limit to their power of assisting speculators, by inscribing deposits in their favor. In that case, speculative purchases would be restricted, for the most part, either to the term of credit customary among merchants, or to time options. Overtrading by dealers in merchandise would still be likely to happen; but as the usual term of credit of any particular trade would be given only to merchants actually engaged in business, the facilities for "outside operators" and the general public would be materially lessened, while the merchants making the speculative purchases would be compelled frequently to find a market within the time of the credit, and would not be able to carry the commodities for an indefinite period on borrowed capital. The effect of speculation on prices, consequently, would be diminished. For it is the real purchases that determine prices, and not those on time options.* The latter are gambling transactions, or bets on prices, and have little influence on the general markets, as they are usually closed by paying the difference between the agreed price and the market-price, at the time of the settlement.

If no circulating notes were issued, or the amount were diminished, it would also result that the percentage of specie to their demand liabilities held by the banks would be much greater. The precious metals, which, superseded by paper, had gone to other lands, would then return, and would become the basis of bank deposits. That the deposits would at times be expanded beyond just limits, is probable. But, as the amount of money required to transact the business of the country would remain the same, the percentage of cash necessary to keep on hand to meet deposits would not be diminished, and would consist of coin only.

It is evident, then, that credit in some of its forms is the means always used to produce a speculative enhancement of prices, and that the efficacy of the several forms of credit, when used in enhancing prices, is in the order in which they have been named. Book credits have the least effect. Negotiable paper ranks next higher, and bank deposits are above either;

---

* Except in case of "a corner."

while as bank-notes, besides the quality of being current as money, possess the additional power of increasing the capacity of the banks to make loans by inscribing deposits, they have the greatest efficacy of all.

To defend bank-notes, as has been done by Mill,* following Tooke and Fullarton, on the ground that without them credit, and particularly bank deposits, would still be used by speculators as a means of enhancing prices, is to take an imperfect view of the subject. The assertion that credit and its transferable instruments can be abused, does not disprove the other assertion, that the abuse can be carried further when they are based on bank-notes than when they are based on coin. Nor does denying to the banks "any power of increasing their circulation, except as a consequence of, and in proportion to, an increase of the business to be done," settle the question. For the increase of business may be purely speculative, and the demand for accommodation may proceed from visionary operators who need restraint instead of encouragement. To assert that banks never make excessive issues of their notes, is to assert that bankers are always prudent. The proper conclusion for those writers to have made would have been that, if bank-notes need regulating by law, so also do bank deposits.

But it is in the panic which follows over-speculation that the bad effects of excessive issues of bank-notes become clearly visible. A speculative enhancement of prices almost always ends in a financial revul-

* Mill, "Principles," etc., Book III., chap. xii., sec. 6; and *Id.* chap. xxiii., sec. 4.

sion. In no country are these disasters so common or so destructive as in England and the United States. The credit system adds immensely to the capital that can be employed in production, and is one great source of the material prosperity of the Anglo-Saxon people. But it has also its dangers. It sometimes collapses, wrecking fortunes, causing widespread misery, bringing to a stand-still many productive enterprises, and blighting the whole business community. If its disadvantages could be removed, without at the same time diminishing its benefits, credit would become worthy of the praises of its advocates. This can be done, in part at least, by resting it on a broader foundation of gold.

Paper money is the principal source from which flow the evils of the credit system. While there is doubt as to the influence exercised by bank-notes in creating speculation, there is none as to their effect in aggravating panics. In them is found the most active agent in causing that total collapse of credit which is called a financial revulsion. Under a system of mixed currency, credit is an inverted pyramid resting on a narrow point of specie. Bank-notes are based on a percentage of coin, deposits on a percentage of bank-notes, while bills of exchange, promissory notes, and book credits, are paid principally by checks against deposits. In Great Britain, according to high authority * the pyramid of transferable credit is composed " of gold, three per cent. ; of bank-notes, eight per cent. ; of checks, thirty-six per cent. ; of bills of exchange, fifty-three per cent." In America,

* Robert Slater.

6

its composition is not materially different, promissory notes being included in the class of bills of exchange.

. When a part of the coin is withdrawn from a country whose exchanges are effected under such a system, the foundation of the edifice of credit is weakened. If the withdrawal goes too far, the whole fabric falls, and the whole machinery for making exchanges ceases to work. Suppose a foreign demand for gold causes its continued export; the amount of specie held by the banks is thereby diminished. This compels them to withdraw from circulation a part of their circulating notes; this, again, causes a contraction of loans and deposits. There is less currency left then to meet the bills and promissory notes of individuals, and to pay for goods bought on simple credits. Each form of credit is necessarily contracted, but the more specie the currency contains at the outset, the less will be the extent of the contraction.

Take, for example, a case that has not unfrequently occurred in this country. A bank, having thirty thousand dollars in gold, uses that sum as a margin on which to base one hundred thousand dollars of circulating notes. The one hundred thousand dollars of notes are used as a margin for three hundred thousand dollars of deposits. To meet its total liabilities, payable on demand in coin, it would have then only thirty thousand dollars in coin; that is, seven and one-half per cent. If from any cause a demand for specie is made upon such a bank, it is compelled forthwith to contract all its liabilities. This demand, when made, will be by means of the circulating notes, which will be presented for redemption. The specie in its vaults will forthwith begin to diminish, and in place of that withdrawn will remain its own notes. These can no longer be used as a margin for deposits, unless the bank suspends specie payments altogether. In the struggle to avert that catastrophe, with its accompanying penalties of bankruptcy and loss of chartered rights, the loans by way of deposit will be greatly curtailed. The depositors, engaged, perhaps, in a similar struggle to maintain their own credit, or losing confidence in the bank, will then demand payment of the obligations to them ; and as the seven and one-half per cent. of specie will be speedily exhausted, a suspension of specie payments will be necessary, no matter how great the assets of the bank over its liabilities may be. If, instead of thirty thousand dollars in specie, it had held one hundred thousand dollars, though the loss of ten thousand dollars of the specie would have necessitated a curtailment of the demand liabilities, yet the contraction plainly would have been much smaller, and might have caused but little inconvenience. That which happens to one bank may happen to all. When the total percentage of specie to their demand liabilities, held by all the banks together, has sunk to a small fraction, a foreign demand for specie, causing the withdrawal for exportation of a portion of that in the bank vaults, compels an immediate contraction of the demand liabilities of all of them. A number of the banks may have kept the necessary reserve, but this fact will not save them. Even those which are strongest have only gold enough to meet a quarter or a third of their notes and deposits. Ordinarily it is the weak banks which are in the power of the strong ones; but as soon as the former have suspended specie payments, and still continue their business, this condition is reversed. Whenever any checks or drafts on the banks which have not suspended come into the possession of those which have, the latter immediately present them for payment in order to strengthen their own position. In a panic, therefore, the banks all go together, just as much as when banking was monopolized by a single corporation with numerous branches. Thus, one bank in the city of New York may boast that it has never suspended payment of its circulating notes. By retaining enough specie to meet the notes dollar for dollar, this was not difficult to do. The same bank, however, has been compelled to suspend payment of its deposits in specie whenever its fellow-banks could no longer resist the pressure. When, therefore, a financial crisis compels a general contraction, the extent of it will be increased if the gross amount of specie to their demand liabilities, held by all the banks of the country together, has been reduced to a small percentage. At the same time, after a reaction in prices has begun, the desire of each person to realize the funds necessary to meet his engagements, and the shock communicated to the nerves of the public, cause the contraction to be carried much further than in the ratio of the gold to these demand liabilities. A complete collapse of the whole fabric of credit then ensues. Distrust succeeds confidence, and stagnation follows. Capital diminishes its aid to productive enterprises, and is hoarded on call-loans at nominal interest, but on unquestionable security. This state of affairs may continue for months or years before confidence is fully restored, and capital again seeks employment in speculative enterprises.

Now, a speculative enhancement of prices in any country necessarily causes an unusual exportation of specie. If the enhancement is in the price of bread-stuffs, for instance, the people who have been in the habit of drawing their supplies from that country seek a cheaper market. If the enhancement is in the prices of foreign products, they are immediately imported to realize the rise, and gold is sent back to pay for them. In accordance with the law of the circulation of the precious metals, gold flows from a country where prices are high, to the countries where prices are low. Every general speculation, therefore, causes a foreign demand for specie, and, when a mixed currency is used, has, as its logical termination, a commercial crisis and a suspension of specie payments. It is the struggle of the banks to avoid suspending payment of their circulating notes that causes a large portion of the suffering which ensues. Stringent penalties for such a suspension are usually provided by law. The banks, to save themselves harmless, sacrifice their customers, and the latter, in desperation, withdraw their deposits, demanding gold therefor, and driving the banks into the pit so much dreaded. The suspension of specie payments is generally looked upon as a calamity to be averted at any expense. Such, however, it is not. The evil lies in the expansion of the demand liabilities of the banks which precedes. The suspension is an effort of nature to throw off the disease. It diminishes the export of specie from the country. Foreign goods, after it happens, are sold for suspended paper at lower prices than when bank-notes were convertible, and, if gold is remitted in payment, it must be bought at a premium. The profit on foreign importations, therefore, is diminished both by the fall in prices of commodities and the rise in the price of gold. Importations accordingly fall off until commerce is restored to its natural condition.

The immediate cause of the great financial revulsions with which this country has been smitten, has been the loss of gold by the banks. It is possible to suppose, however, that a panic might happen before a dollar in specie had been withdrawn from their vaults. When speculation has caused a general rise in prices, a point will finally be reached where the number of persons selling to realize profits will exceed those buying for a further rise. As soon as the sellers are more numerous than the buyers, prices begin to fall; confidence is broken; the panic becomes contagious; a rush to realize takes place; and, as the specie on which the whole edifice of credit has been built is the only money perfectly free from doubt, every one will desire to possess it, and will make any sacrifice to obtain it. The cause of the panic will be the general desire to realize on a falling market, and might occur if there were no paper money in use. Under a mixed currency, however, the banks commence with the fall in prices to contract their liabilities in order to strengthen their own position, and this contraction operates to increase the panic. The effort to obtain gold is not the only thing that aggravates the disaster; for in every general speculation large amounts of capital are destroyed, or, being tied up in an inconvertible form, are wholly withdrawn from the loan market.

The extent of the contraction, however, which the banks will be compelled to make, will depend mainly in this case, as in that of the exportation of specie, upon the percentage of reserve they hold to their demand liabilities; that is to say, upon the extent to which the expansion has been pushed.

But, while a mixed currency has a decided effect in increasing speculation and aggravating panics, it may have a similar though less apparent disturbing effect on prices when the markets are in an ordinary state of quiet, and speculation is confined within narrow limits. As the notes of the banks constitute the currency which is the medium of exchange for the greater part of the commodities of the country, if this currency varies in amount without a similar variation in the amount of exchanges to be effected, an element of doubt and uncertainty is introduced into all business transactions. Such a variation in the circulating medium would affect the prices at which commodities would be exchanged, and another cause would be added to those which nature prescribes, necessary to be taken into account in conjecturing the probable price of commodities at any future time. If the amount of bank-notes is diminished while the business to be done remains the same, prices will fall. The same amount of business cannot be effected immediately with a less amount of money, except by exchanging commodities at a lower range of prices. But we have seen that even metallic money is not perfectly free from variation. The exchange-value of the precious metals is subject to slight temporary variations, caused by a diminution of the supply. Now a mixed currency intensifies any such variation in the value of the precious metals. The withdrawal of gold causes a contraction of the circulating notes, and this again causes a contraction of the deposits; the variation in the value of gold is multiplied; and this may take place at any time, independent of speculation or the state of the markets. The outbreak of war, a political disturbance, or a financial revulsion in a neighboring country, may cause a demand on us for gold to ship thither, and we máy suffer from overtrading in which we have had no part.

These vibrations of a mixed currency depend on the percentage of specie it includes. The longer the pendulum, the greater the arc through which it swings. The more credit the currency contains, the greater its contractions and expansions. Where none but metallic money is current, the contraction is not double; though credit may be contracted, the amount of money still remains the same. In that case, also, the gold for exportation is drawn in part from private hoards, and not from the coffers of the banks; or, if it comes from the banks, the consequent rise in the rates of interest draws in a fresh supply from the hands of the people, and thus diminishes the stringency. The more metallic money there is in circulation, the greater is the reserve to meet a foreign demand, and the broader the foundation of credit. In that case a collapse of credit would not destroy a part of the circulating medium, and there would still remain enough money to transact the business of the country without waiting to attract back the value-money, which, superseded by paper, had been driven to foreign lands, or without resting in a state of stagnation, until the renewal of confidence had restored credit-money to its usual proportions.

The subject of the relations of bank-notes to credit and its transferable instruments, and the several relations of each to prices, has been much obscured by the discussions of the English economists. On one side are the advocates of the "currency principle," who attribute every change of prices to an increase or diminution of bank-notes; and who infer that, by a law regulating their issue, speculation can be held in check, and panics can be prevented. On the other hand, their opponents, in contending against the interference of the law, have taught that there is no difference between bank-notes and the other forms of credit, and have concluded that banks are unable ever to make over-issues of convertible notes. Yet the truth remains, that bankers are gifted with no more foresight and prudence than the rest of humanity. They sometimes become infected with the sanguine hopes of their speculative customers, and end by finding their liabilities dangerously expanded. Credit economizes capital, just as steam saves labor. But as a boiler which can safely run with a pressure of seventy-five pounds becomes dangerous when the pressure is trebled, so a bank, which is strong with a specie reserve of thirty per cent., is weak when only ten per cent. is left.

The conclusion, however, that the reserve should be regulated by law is wide of the mark. Men cannot be made prudent by law any more than they can be made honest by law. All that the law ought to do, is, to punish wrong-doers—those who are dishonest, and steal, by imprisonment—bankers who are imprudent, and suspend, by bankruptcy.

CHAPTER VI.

THE EFFECT OF A MIXED CURRENCY ON THE DISTRIBUTION OF WEALTH.

THE produce of human labor and saving is divided primarily into three shares, and under the name of wages, rent, and profits, is distributed among the laborers, landlords, and capitalists, who are entitled to it. This distribution is made by a process of exchange. The wages of the laborer, the rent of the land-owner, and the profits and interest of the capitalist, are measured out to each by the same means by which the exchange of commodities is effected. Money is used as the medium, and as the common measure of values, in making the division. The distribution of wealth, therefore, cannot be just, unless the measure by which it is made be true. If the yardstick varied from thirty inches in one week to forty inches the next, while prices remained the same, injustice would enter into every transaction in which it was used. If every dealer kept by him two yardsticks, one forty inches long to measure off the purchases of the rich, and another but thirty inches long to measure off those of the poor, not only would cruel wrong be done, but the face of society would be changed. It is the strongest objection to paper money that it frequently acts with precisely this inequality. It becomes an instrument by which, in the distribution of wealth, the capitalist obtains a greater proportionate share than the laborer. It is one of the causes owing to which those who work for wages own in the end the smallest portion of the products of labor.

As society is at present constituted, the reward of the laborer is not a proportionate share of the profits of the enterprise in which he assists, but consists of the market value of his services paid to him in money by the capitalist who employs him. The market value of these services, or the rate of wages, depends mainly on the ratio between the demand and the supply of labor. That portion of the capital of a country which is laid out, or intended to be laid out, in hiring laborers, is sometimes called the wages fund. It is on this fund that the demand for labor depends. The supply, on the other hand, consists of that portion of the population who offer their services for hire, in which class are included, as well those who work for wages, as those whose compensation is called a salary. It is the competition of the laborers among one another to meet the demand, which is said to regulate the rates of wages. But the wages fund is not a fixed quantity. It can be increased by adding to it a portion of the profits of the capitalist, if the latter can be induced to make the transfer. The laborers, feeling this fact, without understanding it, have begun in latter times to substitute combination for competition, and by strikes, labor unions, or simple moral pressure, to induce the capitalist to subtract from his profits to add to the wages fund.

The first peculiarity of a mixed currency, to be

noticed in tracing its effect on the distribution of wealth, is the fact that, while certain classes gain immensely by the issue of circulating notes, the one which works for wages does not share in the gain. No part of the profit derived from issuing them is allotted directly to the laborer. It is by the common consent of all the members of society that paper is permitted to have the force of money. The laborer, as well as the capitalist, receives bank-notes as the equivalent of gold, and consents to their use as money. It is not just, therefore, that the former class should monopolize all the profit derived from this substitution of credit for value, and as there is no practicable means, except the imperfect one of taxation, by which all the members of society can share in the gain, this inequality is a valid objection against bank-notes.

But a mixed currency is made to injure the laboring class more directly by its use in fostering speculation. It was shown in the preceding chapter that whatever opinion is held, as to whether the issue of bank-notes is ever the proximate cause of a speculative enhancement of prices, it must be admitted that they are often made the instrument of enhancing prices beyond what would be possible if specie only were used, and that they always intensify the ruin of a panic. Now, those who suffer most from a speculative rise in prices, and the subsequent depression in business, are those who work for wages. A speculative demand for some one or several of the leading articles of commerce, may carry prices to a point unreasonably high, and if, as is usually the case, the commodity which is the subject of speculation is a necessary article of consumption, the cost of living may be greatly enhanced. The rates of wages, however, may remain wholly stationary, while their purchasing power is thus diminished. For the number of laborers still continues the same, and there is no increase of the demand for labor. It is true, wages may advance somewhat, for the laborer must have what are termed necessary wages. He must be enabled to obtain the things absolutely necessary for his own support, and for the maintenance of his family, in the manner customary in his rank in life. If flour or provisions are enhanced in price for a considerable length of time, wages will be likely to advance enough to enable the laborer to maintain his family after his customary manner. But this advance in wages will not be immediate, and, if the speculation is not long protracted, none may take place ; nor when it does come are wages likely to rise in the same proportion as other things. For " no one speculates in wages." * There is no way of buying them for a rise. They are forced up by the demands of the laborers, who, spurred on by the pressure of necessity, are impelled to act in combination, while the advance is resisted by the capitalist as far as possible ; for it must be paid out of his profits. Hence, it is sometimes maintained that some necessary article of consumption is a more just instrument for the payment of wages than money. The experiment of paying them on the basis of a barrel of flour for a week's work of a common laborer has been tried, and, it is stated, has been found satisfactory. Certainly the money wages are a most deceptive measure of the real wages, or the share of the prod-

---

* A. Walker, "Science of Wealth."

ucts of labor which the laborer receives for his services.

But the laboring class suffers, also, from the depression which always results from a financial revulsion. At such a time the wages fund is diminished. Capitalists hesitate to engage in new enterprises. Confidence is impaired, and capital is hoarded. It can no longer be borrowed on the usual terms, and the amount of it available for the purchase of labor is therefore diminished, while the number of the laborers remains constant. A portion of them, accordingly, are left idle, and, as they must live, a sharp competition for employment begins, against which combinations are powerless. The rates of wages are then lowered, perhaps even more than the prices of commodities have fallen. Hence, in times of speculation, wages go up the last and the least of any thing, and fall the soonest and the lowest.

But it is when a mixed currency is composed in part of small bills, issued as largely as the circulation of the country can absorb, that the result to the class living on wages is the most unequal and unjust. This injustice arises from the effect of small bills in enhancing retail prices. The extent of the enhancement will appear from an examination of the nature and characteristics of retail trade, a subject to which attention has already been directed.

The causes that determine prices at wholesale and prices at retail are very different. In wholesale transactions, commodities are bought in open market, by those whose business it is to know the lowest price at which they can be had, and are sold by those studious to obtain the highest price current. Competition is the ruling influence, and the laws which determine the point above which the buyers do not rise, and below which the sellers do not go, can be ascertained. The permanent price of any article in open market is determined by the cost of production, and the temporary fluctuations depend upon variations in the supply and demand for consumption. It is of prices which can be referred to fixed laws that political economy treats, and to analyze and investigate those laws in one of its most important functions. But prices at retail are little treated of in that science. They are not determined by any established rules. The motives by which retail buyers are influenced are quite different from those which determine wholesale purchasers. The former do not always seek the lowest prices. They buy perhaps for the sake of display, often from a passing whim, and seldom after a careful study of the market; while the poor, or those who buy on credit, are often coerced into paying extortionate rates. Retail prices, accordingly, do not follow with regularity the variations of the general markets. It is true, that a continued change in the wholesale rates will finally affect the prices in the shops. But the effect is neither immediate nor uniform. A decline at wholesale is stubbornly resisted by the retail dealers, and those who yield do so irregularly, according to the times of replenishing their stocks. On the other hand, a rise in the wholesale markets becomes a ready pretext for marking up all goods on hand.

Competition has but little power among retail dealers. It removes striking disparities in the same neighborhood, but it does not prevent two prices for the same article at the same time. There are other influences more powerful in determining retail prices. Of these, combination is one of the most important. Instead of competing with one another, the dealers of any town are quite likely to confederate together, either tacitly or expressly, to keep up prices to what they call living rates. Only goods enough to satisfy the wants of the community can be sold in any event. The profits, therefore, can be more readily increased by raising prices than by enlarging sales. If the number of dealers is augmented, the number to share the profits becomes greater, and, instead of lowering prices, this may become a reason for putting them up. Hence it follows that the accession of a new dealer to those of any town seldom has any permanent effect in bringing down prices. His expenses are as great as those of his neighbors, and he is under the same necessity as they of realizing the usual profit. He may begin by underselling the rest in order to draw off their customers, but he soon finds that he can gain more by joining the confederation than by opposing it. The manner in which the retail dealers of a town can organize to keep up prices and prevent competition is shown by the following notice, which lately appeared in a Western newspaper:

"ORGANIZING.—The dry-goods merchants of this city held a meeting yesterday morning, at the Chamber of Commerce rooms, for the purpose of perfecting an organization, having for its object the establishment of a uniform scale of prices for dry goods, below which none are to sell. In the evening, another meeting was held, at which a constitution was under consideration."

Custom is another potent regulator of prices in

retail trade. When the price of an article has become established in any community, people continue to pay it merely from habit. The sellers have become accustomed to exacting, and the buyers to paying it, and they continue to do so, without much regard to the percentage of profit realized by the former, or to the variations in distant markets. If one dealer breaks through the custom, and endeavors to establish lower prices, he makes himself obnoxious to the rest, and is perhaps coerced into harmony with his fellow-tradesmen, either directly or by a sort of moral pressure. Another powerful cause in increasing retail prices, is the practice of selling on credit. When that practice exists, it becomes necessary to dealers to make profits enough to cover losses by bad debts, and the honest are thus made to pay for the purchases of the dishonest.

For these reasons, it happens that prices of the same articles are often quite different in neighboring towns, without any apparent cause. Different classes of people also become accustomed to different prices, and in the same town are found shops in one street where certain articles are sold at one price to a certain set of customers, and shops in another street where precisely the same articles are sold at quite different prices to another set of customers. It frequently happens, also, that in the same shop sales of any article are made at different prices, according to the persons who make the purchases. In this respect the custom that prevails in England and the United States is very different from that of the countries of continental Europe. In the latter each dealer attempts to adjust his price to his customer. He always has several prices for any article, and does not begin by asking that at which he expects to sell, nor does the buyer expect to pay the price first announced. A process of beating down commences, and the price finally paid depends very much on the sharpness or knowledge of the buyer. A native learns the lowest rates of the dealers in his own town, and is seldom imposed upon at home. The dealer however expects to obtain a higher price from one who can afford to pay it, and will not abate so much for the rich as for the poor. Prices are adjusted somewhat to the purses of the buyers. Take for example a town in South Germany. There lower prices are demanded of a resident than of a stranger. A North German pays more than a South German; an Englishman than a Frenchman; and an American obtains less for his money than either. It is mean, according to his notion, to beat down the price; while the European, accustomed to the practice, expects it. It is noticeable that the French word "marchander" does not carry with it the opprobrium of our higgle, or jew down the price. Our shops, for the most part, are on the plan of "prix fixes," and if lower prices are desired they must be sought in some other shop or in some less fashionable quarter. The continental system admits of competition between dealers, which ours does not.

It is worthy of notice in this connection, that in England the principle of coöperation has been applied for the most part to coöperative stores; while in France, and the adjoining countries, coöperation is practiced more frequently in the form of associated labor, and in the still more desirable form of a direct admission of the workman by the capitalists to a participation in the profits of the enterprise. This difference in the application of coöperation seems to result directly from the difference in the manner of conducting retail business.

A partial remedy for the evil of our system has arisen in some of the large cities, where a tendency to assimilate retail business to wholesale has developed itself. Certain large houses possessed of sufficient capital have drawn to themselves the retail trade, by underselling the dealers of smaller means, relying for profit on the magnitude of their sales rather than on high prices.

But, in considering the remedies for the evil, the effect of the currency should not be overlooked. It necessarily follows from the peculiarities of retail trade, that. bank-bills of the smaller denominations have a direct influence in enhancing retail prices. As has already been mentioned, such bills, circulating rapidly from hand to hand, are not often presented for redemption, and by issuing them the banks are enabled to make their circulation excessive. The community, therefore, has more money to expend, and is prepared to submit to higher prices. In the case supposed by Mill, that if, to every pound, shilling, or penny, in the possession of any one, another pound, shilling, or penny, were suddenly added, there would be an increased demand, and consequently higher prices for things of all sorts, it is evident that the increased prices would be at retail; for the demand would come from those buying for immediate consumption. Small bills have precisely the effect of such an increase of money. They cause more money to circulate in the channels of retail trade, and the retail dealers adjust their prices to the amount of money in the hands of the people for expenditure. When money is abundant, they expect and obtain a higher rate of profit than when it is scarce. When coin only is used, the amount in circulation cannot be artificially increased ; but, when notes of the smaller denominations are crowded into circulation, a pretext and an opportunity are necessarily given to the retailers for obtaining extortionate rates. An increase of small bills would not affect prices at wholesale to the same extent. The cost of production would still remain the controlling influence, leaving the surplus currency to be absorbed by a higher scale of prices at retail. The fluctuations in prices likewise, which result from the use of a currency weak in gold, render it necessary for tradesmen to have a larger margin of profit, in order to protect themselves against a fall in the wholesale markets. When the custom of high rates of profit for retailers has thus become established, competition has but little power in destroying its effect.

From this custom the community suffers, though the individual dealers are not all enriched. Whether the general percentage of profit is twenty-five per cent., or two hundred per cent., the total yearly profit of any retailer will depend on the amount of his sales, and, if a business is overdone, the share of profits, even at the highest rate, falling to each of those engaged in it may be small. But, as the public must buy all articles of consumption at these advanced rates, the expenses of living are largely increased, and this increase is felt most by those of small means. One who is living within his means has a surplus capital with which to buy his supplies. He can lay in a stock at wholesale prices in anticipation of his wants, while one who is living from hand to mouth must buy in small quantities at the highest retail rates. Often the prices of the necessaries of life, paid at the corner grocery in a side-street, are higher than those paid in the most extravagant establishment of a fashionable quarter, and always higher in proportion to the means of the purchasers. The effect of the high rates of living proceeding from this cause, is precisely like that proceeding from taxation in proportion to consumption, sometimes called indirect taxation. The amount consumed by any family does not necessarily depend on its wealth. Whether a man's fortune is ten thousand dollars, or one hundred thousand dollars, the appetites of those for whom he must provide remain the same. The price of flour, or of any other article of necessary consumption, therefore, is of much greater importance to the poor man than to the rich man. The latter, when prices have risen, finds a little less surplus added to his wealth at the end of the year. The former finds that he has saved nothing from his scanty earnings, or that the frugal savings of former years have vanished. It follows, that the higher range of retail prices, that results from the issue of small bills, affects most disastrously those who have no other means of support than their daily labor. Wages are not increased by small bills. The rate of wages depends on the demand for labor, and the supply of laborers; and, as both of these quantities are unaffected, the result of the increase of retail prices is to compel those who work for wages to be content with a lower standard of living. It may be said that the laboring class has been better off in this country, which has always been flooded with paper money, than in those European countries where specie has been used. The statement is true. But would not the laboring class have been even better off here, if paper had never circulated as money? When population has not yet begun to press on the means of subsistence, and-material wealth is increasing at a rapid rate, wages are higher, pay them in what currency you will, than in those overpeopled countries where the struggle for existence makes wages low. But with the occupation of all the new land east of the Mississippi, this country is entering upon another stage of growth. The time is approaching when the question, With what money wages shall be paid? will become worth considering.

The agriculturist, likewise, derives but little benefit from bank-notes, while he frequently suffers great injustice from their use. The demand for the products of agriculture, which are consumed as food, varies but little, the population remaining the same. The first thing that every man must have is the food necessary to sustain life, and when his appetite is satisfied he wants no more. The principal cause, therefore, upon which the variations in the prices of those products depend, is a change in the supply. The market rates for such articles are affected immediately by a good or a bad harvest. The causes which determine the prices of the things the agriculturist sells are very different, therefore, from the causes on which depend the prices of the things he buys; while the latter prices depend greatly on the amount of bank-notes in circulation, the former may not be much affected thereby. Agricultural products, it is true, are a frequent subject of speculation, and bank-notes are the most potent instrument of speculators; but, of the profit derived from a speculative enhancement of prices, a small part only falls to the share of the producer. The rise is very apt to come after he has disposed of his crop, and in any event he must sell, not simply at the lowest wholesale price then current, but at a price even lower; while in a country like the United States, where a surplus of agricultural products is produced, the price of the whole crop depends on the price which can be realized for the surplus. When, as is usually the case, we are exporting bread-stuffs, it is the Liverpool market which governs our own. But specie is the only money current between nations. The sales of the products of our agriculture, therefore, are made on a gold basis, though our farmers may never handle any money but paper. But while they sell on the basis of specie, and at wholesale, they buy for paper, and at retail. The effect of small bills on retail prices is quite as great in the country as in the cities. Competition has no power as a regulator of prices in the village and cross-roads stores. When the custom of high profits for retailers is established, it becomes prevalent throughout the land. Even when no money is used, but the farmers barter their products for merchandise, they are credited in account with the lowest wholesale prices, and are charged the highest retail rates.

The effect, then, of a mixed currency on agriculture is, that while the producers are sometimes benefited by a speculative rise in prices, they are constantly compelled to pay for their implements, groceries, clothing, and articles of luxury, the highest retail prices that result from the issue of bank-notes, and that they lose more than they gain by the operation.

The agricultural class in this country has been uniformly prosperous, notwithstanding paper money. But when taxes are low, and land is cheap and easily acquired, no defect in the currency can prevent that class from prospering. At the same time this prosperity does not excuse the injustice inflicted by the currency, nor is it safe to believe that the future will necessarily resemble the past.

The share of wealth which is distributed to the capitalist in the form of interest is increased by the used of a mixed currency. This results, in part, from the aid it gives to speculation. A period of speculation is usually preceded by an accumulation of capital, caused either by a natural increase of wealth, or consequent upon a state of depression and hoarding. At such times rates of interest are low. But when a speculation, fostered by bank expansion, is fairly under way, those who take part in it are willing to pay more for the use of money than when the markets are in a quiescent state. Prices are advancing, and the amount paid in interest seems small, even at the highest rate, compared with the expected profit. In the speculation, for instance, which culminated in the United States in 1857, there was a general advance in the rates of interest. But the advance was particularly observable at the West, where the common rates were two, three, and five per cent. per month. All real property was rising rapidly. The Eastern banks were sending on their notes to give them "a good circulation." Capital was attracted by the prospect of great gains; and as long as the fever lasted, and buyers could be found, no rate of interest seemed too high.

But it is usually at a later stage in a speculation that interest advances to the highest point. In the endeavor to avert a decline, the demand for capital increases, and an additional rate is paid for its use. When, however, the struggle to maintain prices has failed, and panic rages, the necessities of those who have obligations falling due compel them to pay the most extreme rates for the use of capital. The usury laws in this country have generally prevented the banks from making loans above the legal rate. But the "street rates," which have ruled at such times in New York, have been as high as three per cent. per month, and in other parts of the country even higher.

It is not, however, solely by the demand for moneyed capital that the rate of interest is governed. The nature of the security, or the risk of the return of the principal, is an element of the calculation. But it is the tendency of a mixed currency to increase the uncertainties of business. To the natural causes likely to affect prices must be added bank contraction and expansion. Under such a system the solvency of mercantile houses is more apt to be doubted, and those whose solvency is in doubt must pay, in addition to the current rate of interest, a premium sufficient to cover the supposed risk. The quantity of commercial paper that is rated as second-class is increased, and it often happens that, when rates of interest are nominally low, they are in reality exceedingly high to those who are in the greatest need. If specie only had been current in this country, the rates of interest would certainly have been more regular,

7

and probably, on the average, lower than under the system of bank money.

The effect of a mixed currency in increasing the share of wealth which is distributed to the capitalist in the form of profits, remains for consideration.

All the profit which is derived directly from the displacement of value money, by the various instruments of credit used as currency, goes to the capitalist. By their use his profits are increased enormously. But, by the substitution of credit for money, the standard of customary profit is raised in a manner which, without benefiting the capitalists as a class, greatly injures the rest of the community. Capital invested in any productive enterprise is exposed to risk. The danger is covered, however, by the expectation of profit. The greater the risk, the greater the profit that ought fairly to be obtained. When, to the ordinary risks, that arising from the uncertainties of the currency is added, the margin for profit must be raised. The manufacturer and the merchant must add to the prices of their commodities an insurance against this risk. If they only add enough to fairly insure against it they gain nothing on the average; while the consumers, who pay the insurance in the increased prices of what they purchase, are the sufferers. The rates of profit on capital in this country have always been higher than in older countries. Of this fact the uncertainty of the currency has been one of the secondary causes.

The insecurity resulting from the nature of the currency has also a more direct effect on the distribution of wealth. Frequent fluctuations in prices render a greater amount of capital necessary for the safe transaction of business, and give the strong a great advantage over the weak. A fall in prices, that would ruin a house of small means, would not only fail to seriously impair the capital of another of great wealth, but the latter, being enabled to purchase largely at low prices, would be enriched by the event which destroyed its neighbor. Credit, in some form, is an element of almost every business transaction. But when a decline commences, or confidence is weakened, the credit of a firm of slender capital fails at precisely the time when it is needed, while the credit of one possessed of accumulated capital may continue readily available. Hence the process constantly going on, of the weak disappearing and the strong becoming stronger. Hence the tendency of capital to become aggregated in the hands of a few.

So far as this concentration of capital results from the excess of credit in the currency it is unjust. If a merchant buys goods on time, and before his note becomes due a bank contraction depresses prices so low that he cannot realize enough to pay his note, he has suffered unjustly. His property has been transferred to another without his consent or fault. These involuntary transfers of property are constantly occurring under a mixed currency. An unnecessary element of hazard enters into all business transactions.

This incites, also, to speculation and gambling. The greater the fluctuations in prices, the greater the opportunity of those who are watching the markets in order to buy at a low price and sell at a high one. Speculation is not as unmitigated an evil as is sometimes supposed. The speculator has a necessary place in the economy of society. If he deals in merchandisc, he collects a supply of any article in anticipation of a dearth, and, by meeting the ensuing demand, diminishes the enhancement of prices. On the other hand, by buying after a decline he brings the decline to an end. It is his office to equalize prices, and prevent the extremes which without him would exist. Speculation, therefore, when based on variations in the supply and demand of commodities, is a necessity and a benefit. But, when stimulated by defects in the machinery for effecting exchanges, it becomes an evil. It is a means of diminishing production, and causing an unequal distribution of wealth. It causes capital to concentrate in fewer hands. The loss of that sunk in foolish undertakings is the least calamity attending a speculative outburst. It is the transfer of property from those of small means to those of greater wealth, which is the most deplorable circumstance occurring at such times. It is then that those possessed at once of capital and sagacity can hardly fail to swell their fortunes. The fluctuations which are the ruin of the weak holders, are the opportunity of the strong. Credit, then, more than ever, strengthens those who are least in need of its aid. So far as paper money increases speculation, and causes it to extend beyond its legitimate sphere, it has a direct tendency to cause the concentration of property among a few owners.

The effect of a mixed currency, then, on the distribution of wealth is, in brief, as follows: It lessens the share of the laborer by diminishing the purchasing power of wages; it injures the agriculturist by causing him to receive a smaller quantity of the commodities he needs for consumption, in exchange for what he produces; it increases the rates of interest and profits received by the capitalist, and has, at the same time, a strong tendency to aggregate capital in the hands of a few, while it is the capitalist who receives the direct gain from the substitution of his own credit for money. The same is true of the whole credit system. It is the capitalist who gains all the direct benefit from the use of the economizing expedients of credit in the place of value-money. To these causes, in part, may be attributed those striking inequalities in the distribution of wealth which have accompanied the great material progress of the age. Credit is to the capitalist what primogeniture is to the land-owner. In a country whose government purports to be founded on equality, the concentration of property in the hands of capitalists, which results from an excessive substitution of credit for money, ought to become as odious as the aggregation of landed estates in a few families by means of unjust laws of inheritance. If a just distribution of wealth is sought, the first thing to be done is to limit the element of credit in the currency.

There is another effect of the bank currency of the United States, relating more properly to the production than to the distribution of wealth, which deserves notice.

It has frequently had a tendency to give the foreign manufacturer an advantage over the home manufacturer in our own markets, and to destroy the protective effect of our tariffs. The importers of foreign merchandise have been enabled to sell their goods at paper prices, and remit the proceeds in gold without paying any premium for the latter. High prices in paper are as profitable for the importer as any other, when the paper is convertible into specie on demand.

The expenses of production, also, as measured in money, have been increased by the currency. When the purchasing power of money declines, the nominal or money cost of manufacturing increases. Wages rise enough to support the laborer in his customary mode, for he must obtain at least necessary wages, while all other expenses increase as money sinks in purchasing power. The enhancement is, in fact, only nominal. The cost, measured by the number of days' labor it takes to produce a given article, may remain the same. But as the money still retains its convertibility, the increased price of the manufactured article, which results from the decrease in the purchasing power of money, inures to the benefit of the foreign manufacturer. He converts the paper he receives for his goods into gold, and transports the latter to a country where it retains its natural purchasing power; and, accordingly, he can afford to undersell our manufacturers, who have conducted all their operations on the basis of paper prices.

A fluctuating currency also renders necessary a higher standard of profits as well in manufactures as in commerce. But of the manufacturers competing in the same market, the one can sell the cheapest who is contented with the lowest profit, supposing the cost of production to be the same. Foreign competition has often kept capital from investment in manufacturing enterprises in this country, not because our manufacturers could not manufacture as cheaply as their competitors, but because capital avoids those enterprises in which it cannot realize the customary profit. So far, therefore, as the insecurity of the currency has increased the standard of profit demanded by capital in this country, the currency has operated to retard the development of manufactures.

The statistics of our trade show that the imports have not diminished with an increase of the tariff; while they have, with persistent regularity, followed every increase in the amount of the circulating medium.*

When our manufacturers properly appreciate the law of the circulation of the precious metals; when they have learned that gold seeks the country where prices are lowest; that it flows to the market where it exchanges for the greatest amount of commodities, and commodities seek the country where they exchange for the greatest amount of gold, they will strive to foster manufactures by diminishing the cost of production as measured in coin; in other words, by ceasing to impose duties on raw materials, and by restraining the issues of bank-notes within natural limits.

* Walker, "Science of Wealth," p. 194.

CHAPTER VII.

To one who admits that the non-interference theory of government is correct, and asserts that in a democracy the chief danger to be feared is that individual liberty may be crushed by the majority that claims. to personify public opinion; that, therefore, no jealousy of the extension of the powers of government can be too great, no opposition to those restless reformers who seek to remedy sentimental wrongs by forcible legislation, instead of by convincing the public reason, can be sufficient, the preliminary question comes up, whether the regulation of the currency is beyond the proper sphere of government.

The question is particularly worthy of consideration at the present time. Nothing is the country more in need of than to learn the proper functions of government. The Puritan spirit of meddling, which in the preceding century found expression in "Blue Laws," is still actively at work among us; and those tainted with it are ever appealing to the law to aid them in carrying out their visionary reforms. Yet it was the triumph of the opposite principle in our politics which made our country great and our institutions a model. "That government is best which governs least," was the rule in our legislation until the supposed necessities of war reversed it. The attempted substitution of force for reason, as the motive power in government, is the most dangerous heritage the war has left us. Government meddling is the fruitful source of all our present wrongs. Yet it is not simply decentralization, or the restriction of the Federal Government within its proper sphere, that is needed; but rather to limit the functions of all our governments, municipal and State, as well as Federal. The complaint is made against our system of democratic equality, that it tends to keep the most intelligent and capable portion of our citizens in private life. The rewards of private enterprise are greater than any offered by official position, save when the latter is used as a means of jobbery and corruption. To a man of self-respect and capacity, commerce and the professions open a more inviting field than politics. Nor is the trouble wholly with this class. Where universal suffrage prevails, the office-holder will in the long run represent the average of his constituency ; and, when the legislator must reside within a narrow district, the choice of the electors is limited. The complaint, therefore, that the better class of citizens do not take an interest in politics is not likely to decrease. Occasional uprisings, compelled by unendurable outrages, may periodically bring to punishment the most flagrant wrong-doers among our rulers, but the tendency will always be to revert to the former state; and, for many years to come, " rings," corporations, caucus wire-pullers, and ward politicians, are likely to control our politics and name our legislators. The creatures, we may well believe, will not

forget their creators. The remedy for present evils
is to return to our primitive theory of a limited government; to restrict legislation to the establishment
of security and the administration of justice, and to
leave to an intelligent and enterprising people full
scope for the development of their energies, unfettered by crude legislation.

One method of limiting the powers of government
provided under our system, is through written constitutions. But these are of little avail unless the habit
of respecting them is thoroughly fixed. Unfortunately, the fact that slavery had intrenched itself
behind constitutional limitations, had long diminished
this habit of respect, and the inheritors of Federalism,
restive under limited powers, made this fact and the
necessities of war the pretexts for numerous usurpa-
tions. Written constitutions, accordingly, have been
brought into disrepute, and the efficiency of such limitations materially diminished. There is one limitation
left, however, which can be made effective—a restriction on the power of Legislatures to incur debts. Capitalists have learned to shun securities over which
hangs the question of a want of constitutional power,
and this restriction carries with it respect. But to
limit the power of a government to incur debts, is to
limit its power to impose taxes, and it is through the
latter power that many of the evils of government
come. If municipal corporations in the State of New
York had been restrained from incurring any debt for
any purpose whatsoever, the "Tammany frauds" would
never have been perpetrated, and a load of railway
indebtedness, improvidently incurred, would not now
be impending over our towns and cities. If such a

limitation could have been retained in the Southern States, they would have been saved from becoming fields of plunder for wandering demagogues. There is no necessity for a State, or municipal government, which is never brought into contact with foreign governments, and can never be at war, to ever incur any funded debt for any purpose whatsoever. Such restrictions have been enforced in many of the Western States with the greatest success. In Iowa and Minnesota the State governments are hardly felt by the people, and, though the Legislatures must occasionally meet to record the decrees of the great railway corporations, being prohibited from going in debt, they can do but little harm.

The limitations of government power in other matters are to be gained, for the most part, by enlightened discussion, and by appealing to the public reason. The necessity of restricting the power of government to meddle with the currency is to be taught in this way, and in no direction is the desirableness of such a restriction more evident. The instrument of exchange is the tool of commerce, and to permit government to tinker it is unendurable. Free banking ought to accompany free government.

It is maintained by some writers, that banking can be made as free as commerce, and that the law ought not to meddle with those who issue notes to circulate as money, any more than with those engaged in any mercantile pursuit, leaving the public to protect itself against bad money by discriminating in favor of the notes of responsible issuers. The system of banking, which, it is claimed, has proved the greatest practical success, is one of perfect freedom. "Though by law there has never been any restriction against any one issuing notes in Scotland, yet in practice it has ever been impossible for any unsound or unsafe paper to obtain currency." *

A mixed currency is self-regulating, and most of its evil effects result from attempts to regulate it by law. Such has been the case in the United States. The principal cause of the excessive use of bank-notes in this country. is the practice, which has long prevailed, of requiring banks to deposit securities with some public officer, as a pledge for the ultimate redemption of their circulation. Bills have circulated, not on the credit of the issuers, but on the credit derived from the provisions of the State law under which they were issued. They have circulated ordinarily without question, within their own State, and frequently far beyond it. If, however, no special security had been provided by law for the protection of the bill-holders, the bills would have circulated only where the responsibility of the issuers was known. Their circulation would have been, as it ought to be, local and limited, leaving coin the "uniform national currency."

The theory on which these laws requiring special security for bill-holders is based, is defective. The authors of them seem to have supposed that the first requisite of a sound currency is security for its ultimate redemption. They have accordingly permitted holders of public stocks and mortgages of real estate to turn them into money, by taking them as a pledge for the redemption of circulating notes, looking more

---

* Jas. Wilson, "Capital, Currency, and Banking." Herbert Spencer, "Social Statics" (Appletons), p. 435.

to the ultimate than to the immediate value of the currency. The latter value, however, is the one of chief importance, and it is determined almost wholly by the quantity of the money in circulation. Where the redemption of the paper medium in coin on demand is made doubtful by an excess of quantity, the currency is fatally defective, no matter how great the security for its ultimate redemption may be. And on the other hand, where the paper medium is certain to be redeemed in coin on demand, no other security is required.

If ever the laws requiring the deposit of securities for the redemption of bank-notes are done away with, it is possible that not a little suffering may be endured. It will be but temporary, however, and the lesson will be worth its cost. When the public has no security whatsoever against the notes of irresponsible issuers, it will soon learn by bitter experience to exercise a sufficient discrimination, and the people of the United States will be found equal to the successful management of their own money matters,* without the paternal care of the government.

While it is admitted, then, that the power to issue paper to circulate as money ought to be left free to all, in the same manner as the power to issue any other business paper, and that the proper remedy for its excessive use is to instruct the public mind and diffuse a correct knowledge of the evils of paper money, it is still claimed that there are remedies for these evils in the nature of police regulations, which the law

---

* Mill maintains that "some kind of special security in favor of the holders of notes should be exacted."—"Principles," etc., Book III., chap. xxiv., sec. 6.

ought to apply. The suppression of bank-notes of the smaller denominations is a matter of such vital importance that it will not do to wait until the people become so wise as to refuse to receive them.

Small notes are used in retail trade, and in payment of wages. They circulate among those who are least able to ascertain the responsibility of the issuers, while large notes are used in wholesale transactions, or in settlement at bank. Those who use them are certain to learn their value, not only on account of the greater sums at stake, but because they have ready facilities for making the necessary inquiries. The danger of loss by the public comes principally from the notes of the small denominations. The necessity of suppressing them was plainly pointed out by Adam Smith, and it is not creditable to American statesmanship that his suggestion, made upwards of ninety years ago, has not yet been adopted.

"Paper money," says that sagacious writer, "may be so regulated as either to conform itself very much to the circulation between the different dealers, or to extend itself likewise to a great part of that between the dealers and consumers. Where no bank-notes are circulated under ten pounds value, as in London, paper money confines itself very much to the circulation between the dealers."

It was repeatedly proposed, during the struggle against the Bank of the United States, to place upon all notes, circulating as money of a less denomination than fifty dollars, a stamp-duty heavy enough to diminish their use. If such a restriction had prevailed, the evils which the country so long endured from the excessive use of paper money, would have been materially lessened. The element of credit in the currency would have been diminished. By such a limitation probably one-third more specie would have been retained in circulation. The whole credit system would have been built on a broader foundation. Paper money could not then have been used to render the currency redundant, except in times of excited speculation, and, in case of the withdrawal of specie, the effect would have been less serious. Part of it would have come from private hoards, and not all of it from the vaults of the banks. The chief benefit, however, would have resulted from the restriction of paper money to the circulation between the dealers. It would have continued in use in all wholesale transactions, but, at retail, specie only would have circulated. Wages would have been paid in gold, and their purchasing power would have been increased. Paper would have been left to the rich. Gold would have rejoiced the poor.

Instead of suppressing small notes, the opposite policy has been pushed to its utmost limits. Whenever money has ceased to be plenty in retail trade, complaint has forthwith arisen of the scarcity of small bills. Instead of compelling the retail dealers to adjust their prices to the amount of money in circulation, and, by lowering them, to render less money necessary for effecting the usual exchanges, the demand for small bills has met with immediate response, and, by their aid the retailers have been enabled to maintain prices at the customary rates. If ever such bills are suppressed in this country it will cause bitter complaints of the scarcity of money, and some lapse of time must pass before the standard of retail profits can be reduced to the level of specie.

The easiest way of limiting the issue of small notes is by a graduated stamp-duty. The use of the taxing power for accomplishing incidental ends, it is true, has been brought into deserved disrepute by the exactions of the protectionists ; but the taxation of bank-notes is so just in itself, that it deserves to stand independent of the incidental benefit of limiting the use of paper money. As a medium of exchange a bank-note has all the efficiency of real money, and its cost is nominal. - If bank-notes were not used, specie which could be obtained only by giving for it an equivalent in value, would be necessary. The community which uses bank-notes as money saves capital equal to them in amount, less the expense of engraving, and the coin held as a reserve for their redemption. All the direct gain goes to the bankers who issue them. The public is benefited only by the increase of loanable capital. But it is only by the sufferance of the public that private notes can circulate as money. The forbearance is great which suffers men to charge interest for lending their debts. It is but right, therefore, that the public should share directly in the profit of the transaction. No juster tax can be devised than a stamp-duty on paper issued to circulate as money, and no more appropriate time can be found for imposing it than when all other negotiable paper is subject to such a tax. Business notes circulate only once. Bank-notes are issued over and over again, and the smaller the denominations the greater their circulation. They ought to be subject, therefore, to a heavier duty than ordinary negotiable paper, and the duty ought to be increased as the denominations decline.

There is a second restriction on the issue of bank-notes, which should be enforced by law, however free banking is made.   It is contained in a proposition set forth by President Van Buren in 1837.   That officer recommended, in his first message to the twenty-fifth Congress, the enactment of " a uniform law concerning bankruptcies of corporations and other bankers." *
Such a provision would be eminently proper in the ordinary administration of justice, independent of its effect in restraining over-issues of paper money, and ought to meet the approval of those who would set the narrowest limits to the powers of government.   Banks act in a fiduciary capacity both to their bill-holders and depositors.   Such debts need and deserve the watchful guardianship of the law.   In case of the insolvency of a bank, its creditors ought to share its assets without preference to any.   No favored officers or directors should be permitted to seize upon its property to the exclusion of too confiding customers.

* Even Herbert Spencer, while advocating the restriction of the powers of government within the narrowest sphere, admits this much:

" The State's duty in the case of the currency, as in other cases, is sternly to threaten the penalty of bankruptcy on all who make engagements they cannot meet; and sternly to inflict the penalty when called on by those aggrieved."—" Essays, Moral, Political," etc., p. 328. Appletons, 1868.

" That the State should compel every one who has given promises to pay, be he merchant, private banker, or share-holder in a joint-stock bank, duly to discharge the responsibilities he has incurred, is very true.   To do this, however, is merely to maintain men's rights—to administer justice; and therefore comes within the State's normal function.   But to do more than this—to restrain issues, or forbid notes below a certain denomination, is no less injurious than inequitable."—" Social Statics," p. 434. Appletons, 1869.

Any depositor or bill-holder, whose debt has not been paid in specie on demand, no matter how small the sum, ought to be permitted to throw the bank into the hands of a receiver, to the end that equal justice be meted out to all. If the merchant who permits his paper to remain under protest a limited time can be thrown into involuntary bankruptcy, much more ought the bank which fails to pay the least of its liabilities in gold on demand to be subjected to that process.

The increased stability, however, which such an enactment would give to the currency, would be its most important result. In this way could a restraint be put upon the tendency to expand deposits beyond the limits of judicious banking, and even those bankers who issued no circulating notes would be taught the lesson of prudence.

When corporations are created by law with the exclusive privilege of issuing circulating notes, the preceding restrictions can be enforced with peculiar propriety. Corporations, the creatures of law, ought certainly to be subject to the authority that gives them existence. Special privileges ought to be granted to them only, subject to such limitations as will prevent abuse. The issuing of notes to circulate as money is not a necessary part of the business of banking. Whenever it is found that the harm resulting from the issue of such notes exceeds the good, the power of limiting them ought to be exercised.

But when banking is not left free, and government intrudes beyond its proper sphere, it is found that other regulations become necessary. One violation of a sound rule leads inevitably to another. When security for the bill-holders is enforced by a public pledge of collaterals, the bills obtain an increase of circulation by virtue of the safety which the law assures. But it is not the ultimate value of the notes that the law ought to guard most carefully. Their immediate value is of more importance, and this can only be secured by compelling the banks to keep themselves constantly in a condition to redeem their notes in coin on demand. They cannot, however, keep themselves in this condition, unless they are equally well prepared to cash their deposits in coin on demand. The great danger in banking under a mixed currency comes from the constant tendency of bank managers to retain only enough specie to make a reserve for the redemption of their circulating notes, and to use their own notes, or those of other banks, as a reserve for the payment of deposits. From this practice it results that the percentage of specie to their demand liabilities is so often reduced to a minimum, and that, when an extraordinary demand for specie arises, they cannot meet it. They are then compelled to suspend, and by all going together they escape harm. The constitutional provisions and stringent penalties against the suspension of specie payments, which have always existed in this country, have not been sufficient to prevent the recurrence of that disaster at the usual intervals. When all are guilty, none are prosecuted. The public has then a greater interest in preserving the banks, than in punishing the violation of law. The penalties accordingly have been evaded, or the law suffered to remain a dead letter. Though a stringent bankrupt act stood *in terrorem* over the banks, it is doubtful whether it would always be sufficient to induce them to restrain their demand liabilities within prudent limits, so long as they are organized as corporations under laws which, by guaranteeing the ultimate redemption of the circulating notes, relieve the holders of them from all necessity of immediate watchfulness.

A third regulation, therefore, is necessary for such corporations. They ought to be compelled by law to keep a certain percentage of their demand liabilities in specie. Such a law was enacted in Massachusetts in 1858. By its provisions the banks of that State were required to keep on hand specie to the amount of at least fifteen per cent. of their notes and deposits. A similar provision has also been introduced into the present national banking law, substituting for specie lawful money.

By diminishing the reserve of specie, the banks gain largely in interest. But, as the public good requires stability, they ought to be compelled to secure it, even at the sacrifice of a portion of their gains. It is not the suspension of specie payments which is an evil, but the expansion which precedes it. The remedy, therefore, ought to be aimed at the disease, and not at its effect.

But such a restriction could never be enforced with unyielding severity. Occasions would occur when it would probably be found advisable to remove the limit.

It was maintained by Lord Overstone that the value of paper money ought to follow the fluctuations in the value of the precious metals. This is the view on which the English bank act is framed. The Bank of England is required, not only to redeem its notes in coin on demand, but also to give them in exchange for bullion whenever bullion is brought for the purpose. If, therefore, gold flows into the country, it is presented to be exchanged for notes, and the circulation is increased. If, on the other hand, there is a drain of specie for export, notes are presented for redemption, and the circulation is diminished. The contraction is double, including discounts and deposits as well as notes, and a general contraction of credit ensues. Thus the effect of the natural variations in the supply of the precious metals is increased. Commerce, accordingly, oscillates like a pendulum. Gold accumulates, and notes are issued. The bank has no power to prevent their issue if the public is in a speculative mood. Interest consequently falls, and capital becomes easily accessible. Then gold begins to be exported. The circulation and deposits are contracted, interest rises, credit in all its forms is restricted, and commerce trembles. The opinion that the paper currency ought necessarily to fluctuate with the metallic basis is founded on a misapprehension. The precious metals are selected by common consent to be used as money, not because their value never fluctuates, but because it fluctuates less than that of any other commodity. If their value were perfectly stable, they would be still better fitted for the office. Instead, therefore, of using bank-notes to increase the fluctuations in the value of money, we ought to use them for the opposite purpose. They can be made at times to give stability to the currency when it is most needed. They can be employed to fill the place of gold temporarily withdrawn, and to thus equalize the inevitable fluctuations in the supply of the precious metals. It is often preferable, therefore, to increase instead of diminish the issues of bank-notes in the midst of a commercial panic, and to support credit and restore confidence when the machinery for effecting exchanges has been brought to a stand-still. If ever our banks are compelled by law to keep a certain percentage of specie to their demand liabilities, it will be found necessary to suspend the rule in case of a commercial revulsion. This, however, will be a gain over the former practice of suspending specie payments altogether on such occasions. The present National Bank Act contains a provision for lifting the restriction in such a case. The banks are required to keep on hand a certain percentage of "lawful money," but in case of a deficiency are allowed thirty days of grace in which to make it good.

Against all propositions for limiting the amount of bank-notes, it is constantly objected that, if such a limitation were enforced, there would not be money enough to transact the business of the country. To this objection there is a sufficient answer: The amount of money necessary to effect a given amount of exchanges is wholly a question of prices. The higher the prices at which the articles are exchanged, the greater is the amount of money required, and the lower the prices, the less the amount needed; while, in accordance with the law of the circulation of the precious metals, gold will always flow in where a vacancy occurs. Prices, in any one country, must always bear a fixed relation to prices in every other country with which it has commercial intercourse. If bank-notes had at any time been wholly or partially driven out of circulation in this country, prices would have fallen until enough specie had come in to have filled their place.

Another objection constantly made is, that the limitation of bank-notes would diminish the amount of capital, and retard the accumulation of wealth. Specie can be obtained only for value. If bank-notes were cut off, the coin to fill their place would flow in only in return for an equivalent amount of the products of labor. But this loss, it should be remembered, would fall on the issuers of the circulating notes. Those who receive paper money in the course of business part with value for it, the same as if it were specie.

It is to be remarked, also, that to suppress small notes would not diminish the amount of capital by the full amount of their diminution. The issues of paper act as an increase of capital only so long as they fill the place of the specie which would naturally circulate. As soon as the paper becomes excessive, so as to enhance prices, it adds nothing to the circulating capital. Its purchasing power sinks, and a greater nominal sum is required to effect a given amount of exchanges. When it is asserted, that more money is needed to transact the business of the country, what is really meant is, that there is a deficiency of capital. The borrowing portion of the community is always in search of loanable capital, and always persuades itself that " an increase of the currency " would furnish the object sought. The absorption of the excess of the circulating medium in inflated prices is overlooked.

But even if a restriction on the issue of bank-notes would diminish the amount of loanable capital in this country, such a regulation has always been sorely needed. The rapid accumulation of wealth is less important than its just distribution. The methods of compensating the laboring classes, and of distributing commodities to the consumers, have long presented the weakest points in our social economy. The preliminary remedy for these evils—one which ought long since to have been enforced—is to compel the nse of specie in payment of wages and in retail trade. The diminution of the speculative feeling and element in business, and the greater stability in commerce which would follow from a proper restriction of banknotes, have likewise long been of far greater importance than any increase of the facilities for accumulating wealth. Capital invested in trade has been in greater need of reasonable security than of an opportunity for extraordinary profit.

These facts were well understood by those statesmen who opposed the Bank of the United States. The memorable struggle against that institution had a double object in view. It was waged principally to destroy an overgrown corporation, which would have become an oppressive monopoly in business, and a controlling power in politics. But the ultimate end sought was to limit or prevent the use of paper money. The first object happily was attained. The second unfortunately miscarried. Benton has stated, with true Bentonian afflatus, the intention to destroy paper money, and the cause of the failure.

"I am one of those," he has said,* "who promised gold, not paper. I promised the currency of the Constitution, not the currency of corporations. I did not join in putting down the Bank of the United States to put up a wilderness of local banks. I did not join in

* "Thirty Years' View," vol. ii., p. 10.

putting down the paper currency of a national bank, to put up a national paper currency of a thousand local banks. I did not strike Cæsar to make Antony master of Rome."

The defeat of the Democratic party, which was a consequence of the commercial revulsion of 1837, caused the abandonment of the war on paper money, and the subsequent sinking of all financial questions in the slavery agitation prevented its renewal.

But while bank-notes have thus had full sweep in this country, and have been used to excess, it must be admitted that the evil has not been without mitigation. By the profit derived from issuing them capital has been attracted into the business of banking, and the country has gained thereby. Where banks of discount and deposit exist, the use of capital is economized. Hoarding is brought to an end. Money is made to circulate more rapidly; and its effective power is increased. The amount of wealth necessary for each individual to keep invested in the fixed form of specie is very materially diminished. So necessary is it to the material development of a country, that banks of discount and deposit should become numerous, that it is desirable to give to bankers the right to issue their own notes to circulate as money, in order to attract as much capital as possible into the business of banking. The deposits are the chief source of profit in banking. But, in a country where moneyed capital has not accumulated, the deposits are necessarily limited. Circulating notes can then properly be used to fill their place as a source of gain to the bankers.

The progressive state of wealth in this country

8

which has resulted from the opening of new lands has kept the standard of customary profit in business, and the rates of interest for the use of capital at a high point. The demand for loanable capital has constantly been in excess of the supply. It is probable that the issue of paper money has filled this demand more completely than would have been possible, if specie only had been in circulation, and has attracted capital into the business of banking, which would otherwise have sought a different mode of investment. This process, however, has often worked unequally, and has given certain States an advantage over others; thus the West has constantly sent its breadstuffs and provisions to the East, and received in return the notes of Eastern banks, parting with value for such notes to the same extent as if they were gold. Such use of paper money has failed to allure capital into the business of banking at the localities where it was most needed.

But, while bank-notes in this country have had their advantages, there has never been a time when they have not intruded beyond their proper sphere, and when the regulation of the currency would not have been a blessing to the people. The subject is the more worthy of attention, because now the country has accumulated sufficient capital to be able to dispense with the excessive use of bank-notes, and because, moreover, it is possible that out of the present financial chaos may be evolved an opportunity to enforce a proper regulation of the currency.

CHAPTER VIII.

"THE THEORY OF GREENBACKS."

THE issue of government paper to circulate as money followed naturally from the situation in which this country found itself at the breaking out of the rebellion. The weakness of the mixed currency then in use rendered a suspension of specie payments inevitable. To borrow the bills of suspended banks, or to issue circulating treasury notes, became, thereupon, the only alternative. During the War of 1812, the former course was pursued, and the government sold its bonds at twenty per cent. discount, taking for them inconvertible bank paper at par. But in 1862 the borrowing was on a scale so enormous that an excessive issue of inconvertible paper was probable in any event, and it seemed better for the government to make a loan without interest, than to leave the profit of issuing irredeemable notes to the banks. War, it is true, can be carried on without borrowing. The necessary supplies can be obtained by taxation, or by living on the enemy. But to fit a nation to rely solely on taxation, two things are requisite: a sound currency at the outset, and a readiness on the part of the people to submit to the accompanying hardships. At the beginning of the rebellion, the United States possessed neither. That our bank-note currency was fatally defective, we can now realize. That the people were not prepared to make the sacrifices, which a reliance on taxation as the principal means of obtaining supplies would have called for, is probable. At all events the politicians in power feared to impose taxes, lest by burdening the voters they might imperil the success of their party. Taxation severe enough to cause the present generation to bear the whole cost of a war waged in part for the benefit of future generations, always finds bitter opponents; and, as the policy which guided the dominant party in the suppression of the rebellion was distasteful to a minority of the people, it became doubly important to the leaders of that party to use every expedient to allay opposition. Any present financial depression might have endangered their ascendency. Paper money, therefore, was to them a political necessity. The loan without interest, and the illusive prosperity, which resulted from ascending prices, they found a strong assistance at the polls.

The most important attempt at direct taxation failed, owing mainly to this political timidity. The draft was in the nature of a tax by lot. The endeavor to enforce it caused the New-York riots. Those disturbances happily were suppressed. But the principle, for which the rioters contended, unfortunately prevailed. Thereafter the draft was used chiefly as an appliance for stimulating enlistments, and, by the extravagant bounty system, the burden of recruiting the army was thrown directly upon the property of the country, lessening, thereby, its capacity to bear taxation for other purposes.

But however much the issuing of treasury notes, as a forced loan, can be palliated by the plea of necessity, the excessive issues and extreme depreciation of them which followed can be met by no such apology. The political expediency, which was one motive for their issue, was a principal cause of their depreciation. In making things pleasant to carry elections, the ruling majority refrained too long from severe taxation. The ignorance and moral weakness of the politicians, who were our law-makers, held them back from imposing the proper burdens on the people, and it was not until the people, more enlightened than their rulers, clamored to be taxed, that the money to conduct the war began to be raised in the only manner according with far-sighted prudence. Meanwhile the sinews of war had been provided by issuing greenbacks fast enough "to float" the loans placed on the market. The first internal revenue law went into operation October 1st, 1862, on which day gold sold at $123\frac{3}{4}$, and the premium had reached 70 per cent. before the effect of the law in producing revenue was fully felt.

Paper money, so far from being a source of strength in war, is the parent of all weakness. Excessive issues are accompanied by certain depreciation, and, if carried too far, end in a total collapse. In the latter case the war must cease or be carried on by taxation, and by drafting soldiers without pay. Common prudence, therefore, requires that paper money should be issued only as a last resort; that it should be preceded by taxation as severe as the nation can endure; and that taxation should accompany it at every step. It is to the pursuit of the opposite course in 1862, that the magnitude of the national debt, and the present depreciation of our currency, may be largely attributed. A partial excuse for the adoption of that policy is the total ignorance of the nature and the dangers of paper money, which then prevailed among those in authority; and also a failure to appreciate the magnitude of the contest upon which the nation had then entered. As it was, paper money wellnigh proved our ruin. It is possible that if the war had been continued another year, or had resulted in a protracted guerilla warfare, a collapse of the currency would have changed its results. Fortunately it was in the nature of things that the rebel finances should collapse first.

Before examining, by the light of political economy, the effects of the present legal-tender currency of the United States, it is desirable to understand thoroughly upon what theory of the functions of money that system is based.

It has already been stated, that an exchange of any article of merchandise for a given amount of the precious metals is as essentially an act of barter, as to exchange two articles of merchandise, the one for the other. Gold possesses value in exchange like any other metal, or any product of labor; and, when merchandise is sold for a certain amount of gold, value is exchanged for value. Coining the gold into money does not, in the least, affect the nature of the transaction. Value is still used to measure value. Coinage is a matter of convenience only. It is the means of assaying the bullion, and dividing it into pieces of equal weight. Coins are always mere "denominations of weight," like bushels. But in measuring value, as in measuring space, units of measure are necessary. It is only thus that different quantities or sizes can be compared with one another, and arranged in an ascending scale. As a portion of space first designated arbitrarily or by accident is called a foot, so an amount of the precious metals, fixed arbitrarily, is called a dollar. In the United States it is $25\frac{8}{10}$ grains of gold nine-tenths fine. Thus, by having a unit of calculation to which a name is given, the values of different quantities can be readily compared, and accounts can be kept. In addition to assaying the metal, and dividing it into pieces of equal size, coinage fixes the name of the unit of calculation, and provides a money of account. There is no necessity of making coin a legal tender by express enactment. If men agree to pay dollars, in the absence of any law, they would mean a certain amount of gold duly stamped, and the courts would be bound to enforce contracts according to the intentions of the parties, without any legal-tender act. It is so necessary, however, to have names for the measures of value, in order to compare values, that it is probable a unit of calculation would be fixed upon and a name given to it, even though it represented no value, and were a mere abstraction.

"It is said there are African tribes, in which this somewhat artificial contrivance actually prevails. They calculate the value of things in a sort of money of account called 'macutes.' They say one thing is worth ten macutes, another fifteen, another twenty. There is no real thing called a macute. It is a conventional unit for the more convenient comparison of things with one another." *

Inconvertible paper, when made a legal tender, resembles this contrivance. The most important function of money is then left out of view. A dollar is considered a mere unit of calculation, or money of account, and the fact that value only can measure value is ignored as much as possible. The name is substituted for the thing itself. The value of the thing called a dollar is wholly disregarded. A worthless bit of paper is stamped as a dollar, and is thus supposed to be made one. This theory, it is true, is not strictly adhered to in practice. Value has been imparted to greenbacks in an irregular way by making them receivable for taxes, and convertible into government bonds, as the equivalent of real dollars. But the idea which controlled their issue was, that the principal function of money is to be a mere unit of calculation, and that the quality of value in the thing to which the name of money was given could be disregarded. As a measure of length is obtained by marking off an arbitrary space and calling it a foot,

---

* Mill, Book III., chap. vii., sec. 1, quoting Montesquieu.

The following is the passage from that author ("Esprit des Lois," Livre XXII., chap. viii.):

"Les noirs de la côte d'Afrique ont un signe des valeurs sans monnaie; c'est un signe purement idéal foudé sur le degré d'estime qu'ils mettent dans leur esprit à chaque marchandise, à proportion du besoin qu'ils en ont. Une certaine denrée ou marchandise vaut trois macutes; une autre, six macutes; une autre, dix macutes: c'est comme s'ils disaient simplement trois, six, dix. Le prix se forme par la comparaison qu'ils font de toutes les marchandises entre elles: pour lors, il n'y a point de monnaie particulière, mais chaque portion de marchandise est monnaie de l'autre."

or a yard, so it was thought a measure of value could be obtained by taking a bit of paper, or any thing that government might choose to designate, and naming it a dollar. Whatever the law made current as a dollar, it was believed would be equal to a real dollar. Multitudes of people were unable to perceive why there should be any difference between a paper dollar and a gold dollar, and it was stoutly insisted, notwithstanding the premium on gold, that the currency was not depreciated, while the belief was universal (and still obtains) that a return to specie payments would be a speedy and simple matter.

That notions so crude should prevail in this country, and that a theory, resembling so closely that in accordance with which Law attempted to coin all the wealth of France into money, should be reproduced in this age, may seem strange. That such is the case, however, can be shown, not merely from newspaper reflections of the current opinions of the day, but from the laws of Congress, and the decisions of the Courts.

A correct conclusion on this point is desirable, not merely as a matter of historical research, but because, in settling the debts contracted in greenbacks, a disposition is now manifested to disregard the theory upon which greenbacks are founded. While in the beginning it was claimed that a dollar is whatever the law makes a dollar, now it is attempted to transmute paper into gold by insisting that a dollar is $25\frac{8}{10}$ grains of gold of nine-tenths fineness.

1. That the foregoing is a correct statement of "the theory of greenbacks," appears from the act of Congress authorizing their issue. A greenback purports on its face to be a promise of the United States

to pay to the bearer a dollar. It also purports on its back to be, and by law is, made a legal tender to pay all debts, public and private, within the United States. Each greenback, therefore, is a legal tender to pay every other, and the United States are under no legal obligation whatsoever to redeem these promises to pay a dollar by the payment of a coined dollar. The dollar that is intended is the dollar of account. This one incidental quality of the dollar is selected out as its sole function, and the essential quality of value is disregarded. The theory of money prevalent before the science of political economy had been developed, is revived; American dollars are made to resemble African macutes. The effect of the legal-tender act upon the treasury notes issued under it has been stated by a distinguished jurist in these words:

" By the arrangements of the legal-tender act, the notes are not payable in coin, for the quality which makes them receivable for all public and private debts authorizes the government to redeem them in other notes of the same kind, so that they are to constitute a medium of payment and exchange, which is to be quite distinct from gold and silver money, and not convertible into it." *

A greenback, therefore, whatever it may be as a government security, is, in its character of money, nothing but a stamped counter.

2. An apt illustration of " the theory of greenbacks " is found in the decisions of the Courts invalidating specific contracts to pay in coin. While the law making coin a legal tender remains unrepealed,

* Metropolitan Bank *vs.* Van Dyck, 27 New York Rep., p. 583, Denio, J.

such decisions can be arrived at only by disregarding
the quality of value in money. If it be true that a
dollar is only a unit of calculation, and not a fixed
amount of the precious metals, only a name, and not
a thing, then a contract to pay a dollar is satisfied by
paying whatever the law makes a dollar of account.
If the exchange-value of money is not recognized by
law, there is no legal difference between a treasury
note and coin. A debtor can then agree to pay coin,
and the law will none the less uphold him in paying
legal-tender notes. For the latter " are lawful money,
and have a legal value equal to that of coin in the
cancellation of debts." *

If, on the other hand, the teachings of political
economy and of common sense had been heeded, such
a conclusion could never have been reached. Value
is the essential quality of money, and every thing else
is incidental. When, therefore, the Government makes
two different things of unequal value a legal tender,
individuals ought to be left free to select whichever
class of legal tender they can agree upon, † and their
contracts ought then to be executed according to their
tenor. Courts of justice are instituted to enforce contracts as made, and not to make new ones. When
two things of unequal value are a legal tender, debtors, if left free to choose, pay their debts in that which
is the less valuable. It accordingly happened that
the law declaring coin a legal tender, though still
remaining on the statute books of the United States,
was, for a time, practically repealed by judicial legislation.

* Rodes *vs.* Bronson, 34 N. Y., 649.
† See Carpentier *vs.* Atherton, 25 California Rep., 575.

3. That in issuing greenbacks the name dollar was mistaken for the thing itself, appears plainly from the reasoning pursued by various judges in attempting to sustain the constitutionality of the legal-tender act. By one, this assertion is made: "If Congress can coin any metallic substance, under the power to coin money, and stamp it with an arbitrary value, as it is conceded it may, then it follows that it can make such stamped metal a legal tender at any designated value." * This jurist construes the constitutional power of Congress " to regulate the value of money," to mean a power to debase the coin after the manner of Henry VIII. He evidently mistakes the name dollar for the thing itself. He thinks that to stamp a piece of metal as a dollar gives it an arbitrary value as one, ignoring the fact that the value of a dollar is measured by what it will buy. Such a logician ought to believe that an act of Congress declaring two pecks to be a bushel would change the value of wheat.

Another judge says: " Gold and silver coin and money, are not necessarily convertible terms. The latter word is used in various senses, and has various shades of meaning, according to its employment or connection. It is generally the representative of values, and the instrument of exchanges. But it is no part of a contract of debt made at one time, for the repayment of money at another, that this representative or instrument should possess the same exchangeable value, or the same purchasing power at the time of payment, as at the time of incurring the debt. All that the debtor contracts to do, is to return to his

* Metropolitan Bank *vs.* Van Dyck, 27 N, Y. Rep., 430, Davies, J.

creditor in dollars and cents as much as he received, and the advance and repayment are alike to be made in that which by competent and valid authority is made the medium of account and payment."[*]

This jurist has evidently failed to learn that the fundamental quality of money is stability in value; that money which does not possess that quality is the most effective instrument of robbery ever devised.

But here are the words of another, whose studies plainly had never been extended beyond his law-books, and who had failed there to learn justice:

" The legal-tender act does not deprive any person of property, for it makes the notes issued under it as valuable as gold coin in the hands of every person receiving them for all commercial purposes. I of course lay out of view the difference created by brokers and speculators between the value of gold coin and such notes, as having no legitimate bearing on the question. That difference cannot be regarded, because it is not recognized by law, and all agreements to pay any such difference are utterly void."[†]

According to this luminary, the law looks upon money simply as an idea. The worth of a dollar is wholly in its name; whatever the law makes a dollar is a dollar, at least in Court. The theory propounded to account for the difference in value between greenbacks and gold coin seems very absurd at this day, but in 1863 it was generally entertained. Indeed, there is a still greater degree of absurdity in the following statement:

" A treasury note of the denomination of ten dol-

<hr>

[*] Id., p. 487, Emott, J   [†] Id., p. 472, Balcom, J

lars is legally as valuable for the purposes of money
as a coined eagle. The value of each is fixed at ten
dollars money of account. If a gold eagle be worth
more in the market than a ten-dollar legal-tender note,
it is because it is wanted to pay duties and settle
balances abroad. The market value of gold is therefore regulated by the demand and supply. This demand for gold may be for legitimate purposes, as
suggested, and it may be for speculative or illegiti-
mate purposes; and, unfortunately, at the present
time, most of the difference in value of gold coin and
legal-tender notes is the result of a species of gambling
in the metallic medium of circulation as private or
public stocks are gambled with. It cannot be said
that a measure of value thus affected by extraneous
causes, fluctuating in its character, which may be more
to-day and less to-morrow, can be any just criterion
of what a creditor loses or gains." *

To argue that a metallic medium of circulation
becomes fluctuating in its character, when superseded
by paper, and that the rise and fall in the premium on
gold measure fluctuations in the value of gold, instead
of greenbacks, denotes ignorance of the kind that can
never be enlightened. Gross, however, as are the errors contained in these opinions, they correctly represent the ideas prevalent at the time they were made,†
and are in strict conformity with "the theory of greenbacks."

This was the view of the functions of money entertained by the legislators who passed the legal-tender
act, as shown by their subsequent attempt to keep

* Id., p. 482, Wright, J.   † September, 1863.

down the premium on gold by act of Congress. The law, they reasoned, had made a bit of paper a dollar. The law recognized no difference in value between such a dollar and any other dollar. Therefore there was no such difference. The apparent difference "had no legitimate bearing on the question," being " created by brokers and speculators." By suppressing speculation, then, the premium would be kept down. The attempt accordingly was made. Speculation in gold was forbidden. The whole supply of that commodity was driven out of the market, while the demand for it remained constant, and the premium advanced sixty per cent. in a few days.

This " theory of greenbacks " differs in no respect from that in accordance with which the despotic princes of former ages debased their coinage and robbed their creditors. The theory upon which that proceeding was founded is distinctly stated by Montesquieu. " Money," says that writer, "is both a thing and a name. Civilized nations which use ideal coins only, do it because they have converted their real into ideal coins. At first their real money is a piece of metal of a certain weight and fineness. But soon bad faith or poverty causes a portion of the metal to be deducted from each piece to which the same name is left. For example, from a piece of the weight of a pound of silver, the half of the silver is deducted, and it is still called a pound. Thus the pound is an imaginary pound, and it may happen that no coin will be made worth exactly a pound. So that the pound will be purely an ideal piece of money. The denominations of as many pounds as are wished may be given to each coin, and the variations may be continual.

For it is as easy to give another name to a thing, as it
is difficult to change the thing itself. In order to remove the cause of the abuse, there ought to be a law
in every nation which desires to foster commerce, that
only real coins should be used, and that no expedient
should be resorted to for making money an idea only.
Nothing ought to be so free from variation as that
which is the common measure of every thing."

The expedient of paper money had not then superseded the more patent trick of debasing the coinage.
But, notwithstanding the difference in form, the two
are in fact identical. Both consist in diminishing the
value of the thing used as money, while leaving the
name unimpaired. The judges, accordingly, who have
sustained the power of Congress to issue legal-tender
notes, have been driven by inexorable logic to maintain the position that Congress has despotic power to
debase the coinage, and to make the debased coin
tenderable in payment of debts contracted in coin of
full weight.* In fact, the decisions made in the time

---

* The power of Congress to debase the coinage so as to affect
past debts was assumed in the case of Rodes *vs.* Bronson, before
cited, in these words :

"If by the legal-tender act the value of the creditor's claim has
been reduced, the same effect might have been caused, and to the
same extent, without the agency of the paper money, by simply debasing the gold and silver coin of the country to a sufficient degree—
a measure unquestionably within the power of Congress. A tender
in such debased coin would have been a literal compliance with the
contract."

The judges who made this decision displayed a perverse moral
obliquity, which the progress of knowledge has rendered rare in this
age, but which it is natural to expect in those who derive their
political economy from the Year Books.

In the opinion of the Court, in the case before referred to, of the of Edward VI. and Elizabeth, affirming the validity of the payment in debased coin of a debt contracted in good coin, were quoted, to show that the law recognizes in money only the name and not the substance. Such, undoubtedly, was the common law of England

Metropolitan Bank *vs.* Van Dyck, 27 N. Y., p. 455, the ancient authorities sustaining this power to debase the coinage were collected. The following is a synopsis of them:

After the debasement of money in 5 Ed. VI., debt was brought against a lessee for arrear of rent. The lease was dated Nov. 21st, in the thirty-first year of Henry VIII. At the time the rent fell due, the shillings, which, at the time the action was brought, were decried to 6*d.*, were current at 12*d.* The defendant pleaded tender of the rent, when it was due, " *in peciis monetæ anglicæ vocat* shillings, and said that every shilling at the time of the tender was payable for 12*d.*" The plea was held good. Barrington *vs.* Potter, Dyer, 81 b, fol. 67.

" In Pong *vs.* De Lindsay, and others (1 Dyer, 82 a), in debt on bond for payment of £24 sterling, plea of tender; that, at the time of the payment of said sum of money, certain money was current in England, in the place of sterlings, called pollards, viz., two pollards for one sterling; and that, at the day aforesaid, the defendant tendered a moiety of said debt in pollards. The tender was held good, and the note of the case is, that if, at the time appointed for payment, a base money is current in lieu of sterling, tender at the time and place of that base money is good, and the creditor can recover no other."

A similar case is cited from the Year Books, 11 Henry VII., 56.

A precedent for subduing a rebellion by tampering with the standard of value, and making law by proclamation, is also quoted, showing that there is nothing new under the sun:

" Queen Elizabeth, in order to pay the royal army which was maintained in Ireland for several years to suppress the rebellion of Tyrone, caused a great quantity of mixed money, with the usual stamps of the arms of the Crown and inscription of her royal style, to be coined in the tower of London, and transmitted that money to that kingdom, with a proclamation dated May 24, in the forty-third

should accompany it at every step. It is to the
uit of the opposite course in 1862, that the magni-
of the national debt, and the present depreciation
ur currency, may be largely attributed. A partial
se for the adoption of that policy is the total
rance of the nature and the dangers of paper
ey, which then prevailed among those in author-
and also a failure to appreciate the magnitude
he contest upon which the nation had then en-
d. As it was, paper money wellnigh proved our
. It is possible that if the war had been con-
ed another year, or had resulted in a protracted
rilla warfare, a collapse of the currency would
e changed its results. Fortunately it was in the
re of things that the rebel finances should col-
e first.

Before examining, by the light of political econ-
, the effects of the present legal-tender currency
he United States, it is desirable to understand
oughly upon what theory of the functions of
ey that system is based.

It has already been stated, that an exchange of any
le of merchandise for a given amount of the pre-
s metals is as essentially an act of barter, as to
ange two articles of merchandise, the one for the
r. Gold possesses value in exchange like any
r metal, or any product of labor; and, when mer-
dise is sold for a certain amount of gold, value is
anged for value. Coining the gold into money
not, in the least, affect the nature of the transac-
Value is still used to measure value. Coinage
matter of convenience only. It is the means of
ing the bullion, and dividing it into pieces of

shall be deprived of his property without due process of law, seems to be no greater protection against legalized robbery under the despotism of the majority than under that of the Tudors.

justly attacked by distinguished French economists ; and even the legists who support it are compelled to admit its injustice, and justify it only on the ground that each coin should be taken " at the value which has been imposed upon it by the prince," and that the creditor should receive it at that value "in order not to put himself in opposition to the laws of his country."

The blemish of the civil law is its servile yielding to despotic authority. Under a free government this defect ought not to be selected for imitation. Yet those who sustain the legal-tender act are driven, as a last resort, to invoke the " war power " in its favor ; that being the name which, in this land of freedom, for the sake of euphony is given to despotism.

CHAPTER IX.

An increase of paper money has the same effect on prices as any other increase of the circulating medium. The amount of exchanges to be effected remaining the same, an additional amount of money can be used only by advancing the scale of prices, and diminishing the purchasing power of any given sum. If the increase is of convertible paper, the enhancement of prices causes a part of the gold to flow off into other countries, and this produces a contraction of the paper and a decline of prices; while an increase of inconvertible paper, after it has filled the natural circulation, has the same effect in enhancing prices, without the check afforded by the exportation of gold. Prices then continue to advance as the paper is increased. Coin may still retain all its legal force as money, but it soon ceases to be current as such. The poorer currency supersedes the better, and the precious metals become articles of merchandise which rise in price as measured by paper. Coin is demonetized, and becomes the same thing as bullion. But, as all commercial communication with the rest of the world must be made by means of gold, it becomes an article of active traffic, whose price is subject to constant fluctuations. It is commonly believed that the price of gold, or the premium at which it sells in the paper money, is a just and accurate measure of the depreciation of the latter. The purchasing power of greenbacks is commonly said to increase or diminish with the variations of the premium on gold. When gold has fallen, it is constantly asserted that the purchasing power of the currency has been increased proportionately, and numerical calculations are made to show the precise amount of the appreciation.

This view has been expressed by Mill in these words: "But there is a clear and unequivocal indication by which to judge whether the currency is depreciated, and to what extent. That indication is the price of the precious metals. When holders of paper cannot demand coin to be converted into bullion, and when there is none left in circulation, bullion rises and falls in price like other things; and if it is above the mint price, if an ounce of gold, which would be coined into the equivalent of £3 17s. 10½d., is sold for £4 or £5 in paper, the value of the currency has sunk just that much below what the value of a metallic currency would be." *

That the premium on gold proves the fact that the currency is depreciated is undoubtedly true. That it can be relied on as a correct measure of the value of the depreciated currency is denied. A right understanding of this question is of the first importance, as many of the practical conclusions in reference to such a currency will be found to depend upon reaching a correct theory of the premium on gold.

* Book III., chap. xiii., sec. 2.

It appears from several considerations that the exchange-value or purchasing power of our present paper money is not now, and never has been, accurately measured by the price of gold. A diminution or increase of the value of money is measured, not by a rise or fall of the price of any one commodity, but by a rise or fall of the prices of all commodities, that is, of general prices; and, as gold has become an article of merchandise, it is one of the articles whose price enters into that average which constitutes general prices. But the price of no single article specially marks this average. Some articles range in price above the average, others range below it. The price of every article bought and sold in open market is affected by other causes than the currency. The price of each is subject to special causes peculiar to itself, or to the class to which it belongs. The precious metals are no exception to this rule. Indeed, the causes which determine their price, in paper, are more peculiar than the causes affecting the price, in paper, of any other article of merchandise.

One special cause, which, since the issue of inconvertible treasury notes, has at times had a potent effect on the paper price of gold is government meddling. The power of the government has been constantly exercised in vain attempts to regulate the premium on gold, interfering with the traffic in that article only, and leaving the prices of other commodities to be determined by the laws of trade. Thus, at one time, it was forbidden to speculate in gold. All transactions in that article were confined, by law, to actual deliveries over the counters of the brokers. The effect of this prohibition was to drive the supply of the precious metals out of the market, leaving the demand for them unimpaired. Gold accordingly rose rapidly in price, and, a few days after the passage of "the Stevens' Gold Bill," any one inquiring through Wall Street found a difference of from fifteen to twenty dollars on a hundred, between the prices for gold demanded by separate retail brokers. The premium on gold, certainly, at that time was not an accurate measure of the value or purchasing power of the currency.

At a later stage the policy has been pursued of accumulating enormous hoards of the precious metals in the vaults of the treasury, in order to depress the premium by holding those sums *in terrorem* over the market, and by disposing of a portion of them whenever the premium tends to rise. These efforts have been partially successful, and the price of gold has been frequently depressed so low as to make it the cheapest commodity in the country.

But the causes which have affected most directly the premium on gold have frequently been moral rather than commercial. An act of Congress has established certain government securities, called treasury notes, as the standard of value in all commercial transactions within the United States. But the value of these notes as securities, though not their purchasing power as money, has always been measured by gold, the true standard of value. The premium on gold, therefore, has frequently represented quite as much the credit of the government, as the exchange value or purchasing power of the lawful money. It has varied with the changing moods of the public mind. It has represented the hopes and fears of the people. Victories have strengthened the national credit, and the premium has fallen. Defeats have weakened confidence, and caused it to rise. While the inflation was in progress, the price of gold rose more rapidly than that of the great mass of commodities of domestic origin. The result of the war was still doubtful. No definite limitation of the amount of treasury notes was visible. All the doubts and fears natural to such a crisis found expression in the premium on gold. Other commodities, in like manner, rose in price; not because gold had risen, but because the supply of money had become excessive. Only imported articles and certain articles of export followed gold closely. The prices of the rest were slower in rising, and were less rapid in their fluctuations.

After the close of the war a reverse process took place. The issuing of treasury notes ceased. Their value as government securities was assured by success. Confidence in their ultimate redemption was created. The idea has been persistently pressed upon the public mind, that to raise them to par by resuming specie payments is a simple, easy thing, likely to take place at some day in the immediate future; and this belief alone has been sufficient to depress the premium.

But, while gold thus fluctuated with the state of the national credit, it is noticeable that the prices of commodities participated but partially and slowly in these fluctuations. The moral cause affects general prices less directly. It operates by increasing or diminishing the rapidity of the circulation of money.

But the credit of the government is now marked by the prices of its bonds which are securities only, rather than by its treasury notes, which are both securities and money. During the war the gold quotations of bonds were of minor importance. Our government securities had not then been exported in large amounts, and their price in gold abroad did not affect their price in paper at home. The premium on gold then fluctuated wildly without materially affecting the current quotations of bonds at our stock exchange. The gold prices of bonds then varied with the premium on gold. It was the price of treasury notes which marked the state of the government credit. But, since a moiety of the public debt has been transferred to foreign owners, it is the European price of bonds which denotes the government credit, and which steadies the premium on gold. It cannot advance without a decline in the gold quotations of bonds abroad, or a rise in their currency quotations at home. It cannot vary so as to leave a margin of profit on the shipment of bonds from one country to the other beyond the ordinary rate of profit of bankers. From this it has resulted, that the controlling influence since 1869 in determining the premium on gold has been the European prices of bonds. These have advanced to within a fraction of par, and being steady at that price the premium on gold represents the difference in value in our markets between the two kinds of securities, bonds yielding six per cent. in gold, and treasury notes yielding no interest, but in anticipation soon to be redeemed at par. But so long as the premium on gold depends on the quotations for bonds, it is determined by the state of the loan markets, and has little or no connection with the value of treasury notes as money. So little connection is there between the depreciation of the cur-

9

rency as marked by its loss of purchasing power, and the premium on gold, that it is probable the latter would fall to a nominal figure if the option retained by government of redeeming the bonds at their face did not prevent them from rising materially above par in the foreign markets, and that this decline in gold would take place without a similar decline in the prices of commodities in general, and irrespective of . them.

The only visible relation between general prices and the premium on gold is through the foreign exchanges. When the price of gold declines more than the prices of commodities, there is an increased profit to the importer of foreign merchandise, and a reduced profit to the home producer of merchandise for export. Imports are then stimulated and exports depressed. An adverse balance of trade is created to be liquidated with specie. Exchange on London advances. The shipments of gold increase accordingly, and the diminution of the supply of that article tends to enhance its price in paper.

If this were the whole case, a depression of the price of gold below the general level could not be long maintained. The resulting scarcity of it would cause its price to advance. But there are other influences at work. While the supply of gold in this country has been lessened, so also has the demand for it. There is but little use for gold as money except to pay duties, and the amount needed for that purpose is not great, as the same gold is paid in and out of the sub-treasury over and over again. The immense production of the precious metals in our mining States, therefore, finds no employment at home. It goes through our ports on its way to a market, leaving enough only for our limited wants, but tending to depress the paper price of the whole stock. If we had no mines, gold might become so scarce that an advance in the premium would be necessary to attract a supply from abroad.

The movements of capital for investment must also be taken into consideration. Attracted by high rates of interest, foreign investors have bought largely of our government and railway securities (which process is still going on), creating in the transfer of capital a balance in our favor, greater at times than the adverse balance in the merchandise account. But, even without any actual shipment of bonds, the portion of them on our markets is equivalent to a supply of gold. So long as the European quotations of our securities remain constant, the gold premium cannot rise without carrying bonds with it, or leaving an excessive profit in shipping them. Their effect on the gold market, therefore, is equivalent to an equal amount of gold. But the amount of our government securities is a known quantity, and the interest on the portion held abroad must be paid with specie, or by continued shipments of bonds. Here, then, lurks the possible cause of a future rise in the gold premium. When the supply of bonds in our markets is materially lessened, and the interest on them and on our railway indebtedness is called for by the foreign holders in cash, instead of credit, and the balance of trade on the merchandise account still goes against us, a scarcity of gold and of bonds may put up the currency prices of both. When in 1866, and again in 1870 on the breaking out of the Franco-Prussian war, a panic in London depressed securities, and compelled large shipments of specie from this country, gold rose independent of our home markets. In the case above referred to, the rise would take place from purely domestic causes, independent of the foreign markets. If it ever comes, it will probably be attributed to "a corner," as is usually the case when a scarcity of any article that is speculated in causes its price to rise. Such an advance would take place also, like the present depression, independent of the purchasing power of our paper money, except so far as the prices of commodities affect the course of foreign trade.

The premium on gold, therefore, is depressed or enhanced without any close dependence on the quantity of paper money in circulation, but as general prices tend to increase above a specie level, in a ratio with the increase of the currency above its natural metallic proportions, they cannot be permanently depressed without a decrease of the currency. The surplus money must be absorbed in price.

This is particularly true of prices at retail. When the purchasing power of money is measured, as it ought to be, by retail instead of by wholesale prices, the premium on gold is found a still more unreliable test of the depreciation of the currency. The quotations of gold, which govern its price throughout the land, are wholly derived from transactions at wholesale in one market. There is no separate retail price of gold which does not daily or hourly follow the regular quotation within a fraction. But retail prices of commodities are made in every shop throughout the land, without regard to the price of gold, and the nature of an inconvertible currency is such, that the percentage by which retail prices are advanced over wholesale is greater under it, than when the circulating medium is purely metallic. Retailers, then, require a greater rate of profit to cover the increased risks and expenses of doing business, while they do not lower their prices to correspond with a decline of gold. Having established the custom of high prices, they maintain them to the last. It is in the prices of the things we buy to supply our daily wants, that the surplus currency is absorbed.

But while the prices of the great mass of commodities of domestic production do not vary with the premium on gold, the prices of those articles of export and import whose values are determined in foreign markets necessarily follow its fluctuations. But this is at wholesale only. At retail, their prices follow gold at a most respectful distance. General prices throughout the whole land cannot vibrate with the varying transactions of the gold room. An increase or diminution of the currency raises or lowers them. But a real or expected change in the volume of the circulation that would effect the gold market immediately, might not be felt for weeks or months in the general markets, and in the retail markets later still.

One singular result has followed, perplexing, sometimes, to foreigners. The gold prices of commodities, obtained by converting paper into gold at the current premium, have fluctuated widely, while their currency quotations have remained nearly stationary. When the gold premium fluctuates rapidly, the gold prices of commodities vary more than their paper prices. The price of treasury notes as government securities, vibrates, while their value as money is but little affected. Those using paper money only, thus acquire the mental habit of looking upon it as the standard, and gold as fluctuating.

It is alleged, indeed, that the fluctuations in the premium on gold have been caused in part by changes in the value of gold itself. If temporary changes are referred to, arising from fluctuations of supply and demand, such changes are no greater under an inconvertible currency than under one of normal value, and have already been discussed in considering the effect of the exportation of specie. If a permanent decline in the value of gold is referred to, such decline evidently would have an effect only in depressing the premium, and not in causing it to fluctuate.

The alleged decline in the value of money, however, ascribed to the enormous production of the precious metals of late years, is not proved. The excessive use of paper in nearly every great nation of Christendom except Great Britain, namely, the United States, Brazil, France, Italy, Austria, and Russia, to which may be added Turkey, is sufficient to depress the value of money, gold included, without imagining an over-production of the latter. If all these nations should resume the use of specie, in the depression of prices that would necessarily ensue, it would probably be noted that the value of the precious metals had undergone no decline in the last decade.

This general use of paper money may have had some effect in depressing the premium on gold in our markets, by lowering its value in all markets. The three causes already stated, are sufficient, however, to account for the paper price of gold without any thing so far-fetched. Government meddling, the enhancement in the price of government securities following the restoration of its credit, and their exportation in the place of specie to make good the adverse trade balance, have acted together to depress the premium on gold, and have kept it since the close of the war below the level of general prices, rendering it a more inaccurate measure of the depreciation of the currency than the price of almost any other commodity.

The statistics are uniform in support of this conclusion. Thus, the Secretary of the Treasury stated in his report of Dec., 1865, that "rents and the prices of most articles for which there has been a demand, have been, with slight fluctuations, constantly advancing from the commencement of the war, and are higher now, with gold at 47 per cent. premium, than they were when it was at 185."

A comparison of the prices of commodities at the beginning of the year 1868, made in *Hunt's Merchants' Magazine* for January of that year, and also for May of the same year, shows an average advance of about seventy-five per cent., while the premium on gold was only at about forty per cent.

A similar comparison in Commissioner Welles's report for 1868, gives a similar result. In 1870, Amasa Walker and Prof. Bowen record the same state of prices, and, indeed, it is within the observation of all that the expenses of living have declined much more slowly than the price of gold, and have never fluctuated with it. Retail prices, particularly in the city of New York, are as high as when gold was "in the nineties."

The true measure of the depreciation of the currency at any particular time is its loss of purchasing power, not when laid out for any single commodity, like the precious metals, but the loss which results from the rise in the prices of all things that are bought and sold. The increase of general prices above the range which would prevail if specie only were current, is the true measure of the depreciation of paper money. Its depreciation, therefore, can never be determined with accuracy. To strike a general average of prices, excluding all causes affecting them but the excessive issues of paper money, would be wellnigh impossible. "General prices" cannot be used as a mathematical quantity. Yet nothing is more certain than that when the money in circulation is increased, without any increase of the exchanges to be effected with it, the general or average prices of the whole stock of commodities tends to rise in a ratio with the increase.

But the amount of the exchanges to be effected is itself a variable quantity. A small crop does not make as great an amount of exchanges, and require the use of as many dollars as a large crop. Its price accordingly ranges higher. When, during the war, a portion of the labor of the country was withdrawn in the army, the supplies of agricultural and manufactured products were curtailed. We had as a natural consequence "war prices." After peace was established, labor returned to its usual employments, and supplies of all commodities increased. The South also, reopened to commerce, required a supply of the circulating medium. The amount of exchanges to be effected with our paper money increased vastly, while by its partial contraction the supply was diminished. Accordingly, there was a general decline of prices.

In all these changes gold was one of the commodities whose price varied. Like other commodities its price was affected by causes peculiar to itself, and by the general cause affecting all prices, namely, variations in the supply of the circulating medium compared with the amount of the exchanges to be effected with it. Neither gold nor any other commodity can be selected as a measure of the effect of this general cause. The premium on gold, however, stands out in the boldest relief, and will probably continue to be used, though incorrectly, as a measure of the depreciation of the currency.

Some of the errors which have arisen from misunderstanding the nature of the premium on gold deserve notice.

It is in accordance with the theory that it is the sole and precise test of the depreciation of the currency, that such persistent efforts have been made by those in authority to keep down the price of gold. The belief prevails at the Treasury Department, that the lower the premium, the nearer the approach to specie payments. The opinion is erroneous. The premium on gold might stand at five per cent., and specie payments still remain as difficult and as remote as when the premium was at one hundred. The purchasing power of an inconvertible currency is the test of its nearness to coin, and when the premium on gold is reduced without a corresponding increase in the purchasing power of paper, no approach is made to a resumption of specie payments. Any forced depression of the price of gold, unless it is accompanied with a decline of general prices, is an evil. It drives specie out of the country, thus rendering specie payments more remote, and at the same time operates unjustly to a portion of the community. The home prices of those articles of export which are regulated by the foreign markets, decline with the premium on gold. To force down the premium, therefore, by governmental interference below the level of general prices, is to deprive the producers of those commodities of their just reward. They are obliged to pay an increased price for every thing they buy, and ought to obtain a corresponding increase of price for what they sell. Those who have been the most directly injured by the undue depression of the premium on gold, are the producers of petroleum, cotton, bread-stuffs, and the like, and the manufacturers of such articles as are subject to foreign competition.

The premium on gold is a natural result of the redundancy of the currency. It is an effort of nature to heal that wound. So far from being an evil, it is a benefit and a necessity. It ought to be left, therefore, to be regulated wholly by the laws of trade. It is as unjustifiable for the government to meddle with the price of gold as with the price of wheat or any other commodity. It is as great an outrage for the Secretary of the Treasury "to bear" the gold market, as it would be for him "to bull" it. Nothing would be lost by letting it alone.

Nor would speculators be enabled, by such a policy, to do any serious injury. It has long been popular to abuse speculators in gold, and to ascribe to them immense power over its price. There is but little ground for the opinion. The great mass of their transactions are mere bets, settled by paying differences, with but little effect on prices; while those who attempt to control the supply of gold, do not buy it in order to put up the price, but because they think it is going up. They buy in anticipation of a rise, that they may sell at a profit. On the other hand, when they anticipate a decline, they sell that which they have, or that which they borrow, in order to buy it in again at a lower figure. They are human, however, and fallible. Errors of judgment may mislead them. They sometimes stay temporarily the natural course of the market, and are crushed by it. But they always have as much power, and exercise as much influence, in putting the price down as in putting it up. They equalize prices as much in the gold market as in any other.

There is one speculator in gold, however, deserving of all the reproaches heaped on that class. That speculator is the United States. All the power of the government has been used, at times, to speculate in gold. By accumulating immense hoards of coin, throwing it on the market in large sums, and hoarding the notes received for it, the Treasury Department has frequently succeeded in depressing the price of gold, and in wrongfully benefiting one portion of the community at the expense of another.

It follows, further, from the fact that the premium on gold is not a correct measure of the purchasing power of the current money, that there is no method of obtaining accurate statistics of the prices in gold of commodities which have been bought and sold for paper only. To turn paper prices into gold, at the current rate of premium, does not furnish an accurate test of what gold prices would have been if treasury notes had never been issued. Comparisons of prices prevalent during the greenback era, with those prevalent before it, or which would have prevailed if the currency had remained metallic, when the comparison is made by reducing the paper prices to gold, taking the current or average premium as the measure of depreciation, give results which are approximations only. They are as near the truth, perhaps, as the case will permit, but are unreliable for many purposes. For instance, if the delusive paper standard were withdrawn from circulation, and a law were passed for the settlement of all contracts made in paper, according to the value of the money in whioh the debt was contracted, it would be preferable to arrive at that value, not by taking the premium on gold at that time as the measure, but by establishing certain rates of depreciation for given periods, to be fixed after a careful investigation, and averaging of general prices during those periods.

Another of the errors which has resulted from misunderstanding the premium on gold is the supposed necessity of making treasury notes a legal tender in order to prevent them from declining in value. The legal-tender act, however, has had no effect whatsoever in preventing gold from selling at a premium, or in saving treasury notes from depreciation. Gold, with all commodities, has risen in price, because more money has been put into circulation than there is any need of. The supply exceeds the demand, and the exchange-value of money has sunk. If, instead of paper, the surplus money forced into circulation had been wholly of gold, its value would have declined in the same manner. It was mentioned in the first chapter that the law of supply and demand applies to the precious metals equally with other commodities, and that an over-supply causes their value to fall, while coining them into money does not change that result. It changes only the manner in which the fall in value shows itself, causing it to be marked, not by a rise in the price of money (for money has no price), but by a decline of its purchasing power. Under the law of the circulation of the precious metals, it is impossible for the supply of metallic money to be permanently excessive. By causing prices to rise, it causes its own export. If, however, a nation could be completely shut off from all intercourse with the rest of the world, like Japan previous to the late treaties, and extensive mines of the precious metals were then suddenly opened, the increased supply of metallic money would cause its value to decline in a conspicuous manner, as measured by its purchasing power. The United States have been placed in a similar position since 1862. The supply of the circulating medium has been greatly increased without any corresponding increase of the amount of work to be effected with it, or any foreign outlet for it. Its value has consequently fallen, and if all the lands and property of the country had been specifically pledged for the final redemption of greenbacks, they would have depreciated none the less, and gold would have gone to a premium. The excessive supply of paper money has caused its purchasing power to sink, without regard to its value as an obligation of government. When, therefore, treasury notes had once got into circulation as money, the quality of being a legal tender between individuals made them circulate only more rapidly and surely; and had no effect whatsoever on their value, except to aid in depreciating it. Without a sufficient restrictiou of their quantity, they were consigned to certain depreciation, whether a legal tender or not.

But it is said, that without this quality they would have obtained no circulation as money; that they would have remained simply government securities bought and sold in open market. No conjecture, however, is hazarded as to the nature of the currency, for which they would have been bought and sold. It is not probable that they would have been quoted at a discount in the inconvertible notes of equal denominations issued by private corporations, which had already failed to meet their obligations. But even if they had been quoted at a discount, instead of gold at a premium, they could have been sold for the current money, and would probably always have gained greater purchasing power in that way than they obtained by preserving the illusion of quoting them at par. The case, so pathetically imagined, of a soldier receiving the notes of his government, and sending them home to his starving wife and children, who could buy no bread with them, is an absurdity on its face. Those who invent such suppositions have but little knowledge of economical laws. Money is made current, not by law, but by common consent. When the Rebellion broke out, specie dropped out of circulation. The whole business of the conntry was transacted with "current funds" before treasury notes were issued; and the latter, when of small denominations, payable to bearer, would have passed current as money, without being a legal tender, quite as readily as the bills of suspended banks; while contracts payable in current funds or treasury notes could have been enforced by the courts, according to their terms, with much less violence to logic and justice than was used in sustaining the legal-tender act. It was the convenient form in which treasury notes were issued, that made them current as money, and not the quality of being legal tender. Those who believe that without this quality they would not have circulated equally well with the bills of suspended banks, have but little faith in the power of patriotism. When the Bank of England suspended payments in 1797, meetings of business men were held throughout the country, who pledged themselves to use paper as the equivalent of coin, and for twenty-four years thereafter paper was current as money, without any act making it a legal tender. The same thing happened in the Southern States, during the Rebellion. Confederate treasury notes were never a legal tender; yet they passed current as money, and depreciated in a ratio with the increase of their quantity and the disasters of the Rebellion. The currencies of the two combatants went through almost precisely the same phases, differing in degree, though the one that depreciated the most and finally went out was not by law a legal tender.

There are those who claim, nevertheless, that there was a disaffected minority at the North who, without the legal-tender act, would have exercised some malign influence in preventing treasury notes from circulating, and in causing them to depreciate. The Secretary of the Treasury, who expressed this fear, and the faction who shared it, ascribed the effects of their own ignorant violations of the laws of currency to the machinations of speculators and political adversaries, like the savages, who, not knowing the source in Nature from which the thunder and lightning proceed, impute those phenomena to the power of some malignant demon whom they ignorantly worship. But even these partisans admit that a great majority of the Northern people sustained the war with the most ardent patriotism. To have objected to receiving treasury notes when inconvertible bank-notes were the only alternative, would never have occurred to them. The money paid out by government in purchases of supplies and in wages to soldiers would, by the vast majority of the people, have been received without hesitation or question. But, when money is once in circulation, no hostile minority can impede its circulation. The poorer currency supersedes the better. Every man keeps the better and parts with the poorer. If a currency circulates at all, the poorer it is, the more rapidly it circulates. All that the disaffected minority could have done them, would have been to have made greenbacks circulate more rapidly, exactly what the legislators attempted to do, who passed the legal-tender act.

But, if there had been any danger of this kind, the proper remedy would have been to have taxed bank-notes out of existence, leaving treasury notes to have filled the whole circulation. This was the proper course under any view. Whatever opinion may be held of the necessity of the legal-tender act, it cannot be shown that there was ever any necessity of issuing inconvertible paper in excess of the mixed currency prevalent before the war. The circulating medium of the Northern States, including bank-notes and specie, was, at that time, not far from $350,000,000. If all bank-notes had been summarily suppressed as soon as they ceased to be convertible into specie on demand,

and treasury notes had been issued, so as only just to have filled the natural circulation of the country, gold would never have risen above a moderate premium, and the expenses of the war would have been diminished by many millions, even though bonds had been sold at a discount. To that financiering which encouraged the issue of bank-notes convertible only into inconvertible paper, can be traced at least one-quarter of our present national debt.

The practical effects of the legal-tender act were two. By a most immoral and illogical decision of the courts, it was held to apply to debts contracted before its passage. A portion of the property of creditors was thus transferred to their debtors. The latter, to realize the gift, immediately commenced paying debts contracted in gold, with the depreciated paper. In this way, large sums of money which had been loaned on mortgage security were thrown on the market for reinvestment, amounting, probably, throughout the country, to three or four hundred millions of dollars. But as, under the legal-tender act, a loan on mortgage is merely an investment in government securities, investors preferred the higher form of security, bonds bearing gold interest, rather than treasury notes, yielding, when loaned on mortgage under the usury laws, a less rate. By thus sanctioning an act of barefaced robbery, the negotiation of government loans was facilitated.

The other practical effect of the legal-tender act is its effect on the construction of contracts made under it; a question likely to become of great importance before treasury notes are finally withdrawn from circulation, which will be fully considered in a future chapter.

If no legal-tender law is necessary to make inconvertible paper current as money, much less is one needed to give coin force as money. Such laws are useless. They only stand as a temptation to ignorant legislators to raise loans in any sudden crisis by a legalized fraud; in a barbarous age, by debasing the coin; in one more civilized, by depreciating paper. A legal-tender act is simply a trick of legislation by which money is made an instrument of robbery. When we have had a sufficiently painful experience of this fact, and it is fully understood that all trade is essentially barter, and money always a commodity, government will finally be restrained within its proper sphere. No legal-tender act will be passed, but in its place a simple definition of the word dollar, and its subdivisions, will be substituted. As sixty pounds of wheat, fifty-six pounds of maize, and thirty-two pounds of oats, make a bushel, so 23.22 grains of pure gold will be defined to be a dollar, and contracts will then be enforced according to their terms.

CHAPTER X.

THE EFFECTS OF AN INCONVERTIBLE CURRENCY ON THE PRODUCTION AND DISTRIBUTION OF WEALTH.

THAT the issue of inconvertible paper has a mysterious and potent effect in stimulating the production of wealth, and making every one rich, is one of those pleasing fallacies, which, though often refuted, both by unanswerable logic, and by cruel experience, finds new adherents in each generation. The present advocates of paper money, however, are not so confident as were the followers of Law and Hume, in the last century, and it is now pretty generally understood that prosperity, based on paper, is like the exhilaration produced by alcohol; the discomforts which follow the debauch exceed its pleasures.

That this is the correct view is plainly apparent. Wealth results from the union of capital and labor. The issue of inconvertible paper adds neither to the amount of capital in the country, nor to the efficiency of labor, and hinders, rather than aids, the union of the two. The only direct gain from the issue of treasury notes was the loan to the government without interest, and the consequent lessening of taxation. But, as the money received by government was sunk in war, nothing was added to the production of the country. Yet, while the emission was progressing, the general feeling prevailed that our national prosperity was at its highest pitch. To most minds, increase of price is as satisfactory as increase of wealth. In computing riches, dollars of account roll up the same as real dollars, and so long as the increase continues, the illusion is not discovered. A merchant, holding a stock of goods, had no more property when prices had trebled, than at the outset. Though the footings of his inventory were larger, he could not exchange his goods for any greater quantity of other goods than before. Many individuals, it is true, were made rich by the rise in prices, but that was because the gain in price was unequally distributed, and not because any addition had been made to the aggregate wealth of the country.

That production in some branches of industry is temporarily stimulated by the emission of inconvertible paper, is probable. The speculative class of the community is rapidly enriched by the operation, and its extravagance keeps pace with its riches. A demand for goods from those whose wealth is thus increased, springs up. But, on the other hand, the economies forced upon others by the gradual loss of purchasing power of their wages or incomes cuts off a large demand from that source, so that, on the whole, the increased demand is confined to articles of luxury. This increased demand for such goods is supplied by an increased production of them, which continues, however, only while the inflation is in progress, and when prices have culminated, production, so far from being further stimulated, is checked.

But, admitting that greenbacks stimulated the

production of certain articles of luxury, the fact still remains that, so far from causing any general increase of production, they had the effect of diminishing it. Capital was not attracted by them into productive enterprises, nor did they open to labor any new fields of productive employment. On the contrary, the best energies of the nation were turned from production to speculation. When prices of all commodities were rapidly rising, profits were made more easily by buying commodities to sell again, than by engaging in their production; while, as the advance in prices was spasmodic, and subject to sudden reactions, and as those buying on speculation could sell more readily than those keeping on hand stocks sufficient to meet the demands of their customers, gambling transactions were really less hazardous than legitimate business. At the same time, the frequent spectacle of fortunes rapidly acquired, almost without effort, fired the imaginations of the people, and the desire of sudden wealth became universal. Multitudes were enticed into living by their wits instead of by labor, and the drones in the hive daily diminished the substance of the workers. The number of middle-men and distributors was greatly increased. The fluctuations of prices and the discredit of the currency enhanced the risks of trade. Dealers, consequently, were forced to charge prices high enough to insure themselves against these additional risks. At the same time, from the nature of retail trade, they were enabled to fix for themselves the rate of this insurance, and to make it a source of profit. Though individuals were frequently unfortunate, the aggregate of profits received by the distributors as a class was largely enhanced, and both capital and labor were thus unnaturally attracted from other more productive employments; hence the increase in the number of distributors and middle-men; hence the tendency of population, so constantly witnessed, to flow from the country to the cities.

Nor should the effect of speculation, in causing the waste and destruction of capital, be left out of view. Capital invested in an enterprise which finally miscarries is destroyed, except that the portion of it expended for worthless lands or mines is transferred from one person to another without consideration. All of it, however, laid out for machinery or labor, without any productive result, is wholly lost. The amount of capital destroyed in this manner during the late war was immense. The amount for Boston alone is placed at $50,000,000, though the data for the estimate are not given. The Eastern capital sunk in unproductive mines of gold and silver, principally in Colorado and Nevada, would have wellnigh built a thousand miles of railroad. That sunk in oil-wells even more. There is hardly a strong-box in the country that does not hold, or has not held, worthless certificates of stock in some high-titled petroleum or mining company. Some of this loss would have occurred if gold had been the only money, but the wild excess of speculation may justly be attributed to inconvertible paper.

Though a great increase of banking capital followed the issue of greenbacks, the fact has added but little to the production of the country. Not only has banking capital been largely absorbed by government loans, but it has been used also to foster all manner of speculations, instead of legitimate enterprises. Gambling transactions on the stock and corn exchanges have been in better favor with the banks than the longer operations of commerce and manufactures.

But, while greenbacks have caused a great waste of capital swallowed up in profitless speculations, they have also retarded the progress of our national wealth by producing wasteful consumption. Habits of extravagance are inseparable from periods of speculation. Riotous living then takes the place of economy. Money easily won is recklessly spent. The percentage of capital saved for investment in productive enterprises is diminished, and unproductive consumption is vastly augmented. Nor is there any moral good from such expenditures in elevating the tastes or the intellects of the people. The ill-gotten gains of "shoddy" are laid out to tickle a vanity for foolish display. A passion for horse-flesh has accompanied the paper fortunes of the day. Fast driving seems to be the only culture known to those who have drawn prizes in the lottery of speculation.

But since the emission of treasury notes has ceased, and the question of resuming specie payments has been agitated, the currency has been passing through a different phase. Its effects, however, have continued equally disastrous. Probably no policy more fatal to production than the attempt arbitrarily to increase the value of depreciated money has ever been devised. When by a forcible withdrawal of treasury notes the prices of all commodities are steadily forced downward, and the speedy elevation of the currency to an equality with gold can be confidently relied on, every wise capitalist will withdraw his funds from investments likely to miscarry on a falling market, and seek instead inconvertible paper, soon to be transmuted into gold by the modern alchemy of contraction. Few investments could be found more secure and profitable than to buy treasury notes at seventy cents on the dollar, realize from them during a few months or years the ordinary rate of interest, and then sell them at par. Whatever doubt there may be, whether contracting the currency can produce specie payments, there is no doubt but that it drives capital out of productive industries into call loans and government securities. Treasury notes, as money, can only advance in value by a decline in the prices of the commodities exchanged for them. To buy commodities, or to invest capital in producing them, must then result in a loss of the rise in the value of the notes. The contraction of the currency, therefore, is a device to compel the hoarding of capital. It makes it for the interest of capitalists to shun productive enterprises, and keep their funds in the shape of money, or obligations to pay money. So long as that policy was pursued, stagnation was steadily creeping over the land. The changes in the employment of capital, and the natural reaction from war prices, which followed the termination of hostilities, would have disturbed the commerce and industry of the country in any event. When to these disturbing causes a steady withdrawal of the circulating medium was added, it is not surprising that in 1867 manufactures wellnigh came to a stand-still, and a general depression came over the business of the country.

Since the power to contract the currency has been repealed, industry and commerce have taken a fresh start. The people have adjusted their affairs to the actual condition of things, and production moves steadily on. Our material development, however, is still retarded by the use of an inconvertible currency. The evils that accompanied its emission continue, though in a less degree. The insurance against the uncertainties of the currency, which is added to the price of every thing that is bought and sold, though greatly lessened, still operates to increase the cost and diminish the amount of production. Speculation, though less potent than at an earlier period, still withdraws both capital and labor from productive enterprises. The lack of close economy, which is inseparable from paper money, still diminishes the annual savings of the nation; while the cry of a return to specie payments periodically produces a semi-stagnation, and business halts until it is seen what Congress is likely to do with the currency. But the native resources of the United States are so great, that no financial blunders can do more than retard the progress of our wealth. Vast tracts of fertile lands are still waiting for cultivators. In the Northwest, farms, within easy reach of railways and of markets, can be bought so low that one good crop at high prices will return the purchase-money; while, nearer the frontiers, "homesteads," with soil as deep and rich as ever gladdened the husbandman, can be had by simple occupation. Thither the hardy peasants of Northern Europe are irresistibly drawn. A few years of sturdy labor render them as rich in broad acres, and in flocks and herds, as the petty barons of their native valleys. States possessing these advantages not only increase in population and wealth with astonishing rapidity, but enrich also the older States by furnishing for their productions constantly - expanding markets. Notwithstanding, therefore, the depressing effects of pa-

10

per money and improvident taxation, this country is progressing in wealth at a rate more rapid than that prevailing in most others, though at a very much less rapid rate than before the suspension of specie payments.

The statistics establishing these conclusions have been collected by Mr. Welles, Special Commissioner of Revenue, in his several reports, and the rare talent for sifting facts which he has displayed, and the intellectual honesty with which he has sought truth for its own sake, render those reports invaluable to the student of political economy. His facts show beyond controversy that the production of wealth has been materially retarded, and he makes the striking inference, "that a cessation of progress in the United States, in view of the rapid developments of former years, cannot be regarded as other than retrogression."

Grosvenor, also, in his late work on protection,* has shown, by a comparison of statistics, that the increase of wealth during the decade just closed, after making due allowance for the disturbing element of the war, has been not over one-third as great as during the preceding decade. Some of this loss is properly attributable to the tariff. That the greater portion of it results from the currency, will appear in future chapters.

The evil effects of an inconvertible currency are visible less in retarding the accumulation of wealth, than in causing an unequal and unjust distribution of it. The insidious effect of greenbacks in adding to the wealth of a few, and degrading the mass of the

* "Does Protection Protect?" chap. vii.

people, ought, in a Republic, to cause their immediate withdrawal. After an unequal distribution of property has taken place, it is difficult to make a redistribution of it without an agrarian invasion of vested rights. But to change the laws, which are in process of producing this unequal and unjust distribution, is a legitimate remedy. To make gold the only money which the poor man will ever see or handle, is a reform next in order after the destruction of slavery.

An inconvertible currency has all the effects of a mixed currency in producing an unequal distribution of wealth, but developed in a far higher degree. It has also certain other effects peculiar to itself.

That greenbacks operated as a tax on each successive holder of them, so long as the decline in their value was progressing, is a fact which has now been thoroughly learned. Each man who passed them on to his neighbor can perceive that he was taxed to the amount of their depreciation while in his hands, as directly as if the government had taken a portion of his income. But it does not yet seem to be understood that, when the process is reversed, and the value of greenbacks is steadily augmenting, a tax is equally imposed, not upon the holders of them, but upon those who have debts to pay with them. A man who contracts a debt payable at a future day, and finds when the day of payment has arrived that the purchasing power of the money he must use has been enhanced in the mean time, is taxed to the amount of the enhancement. He must part with a greater quantity of commodities or property in order to realize the means of payment. All fluctuations in the purchasing power of greenbacks, therefore, operate as a tax upon some portion of the community. When they are depreciating, creditors are taxed. When they are appreciating, debtors are taxed. But such taxation is a very different thing from that levied for the support of government. It is confiscation. It is simply a means of transferring property from one person to another without the owner's consent. These vast transfers of property, made without any merit of the gainer, or any fault of the loser, are inseparable from a fluctuating currency, and render it a most unjust instrument for the distribution of wealth. When greenbacks were issued, contracts made in gold became payable in paper; debtors thus obtained a transfer of the property of their creditors. But when greenbacks were enhanced, creditors in their turn obtained an opportunity to repeat the operation. Thus an inconvertible currency becomes at every fluctuation an instrument of robbery. But its effects on the distribution of wealth will become more plainly visible when the shares distributed under its operation to the several producers of wealth are examined.

That convertible paper, when used in the payment of wages, becomes an instrument for depriving the laborer of a part of his just reward, has been shown in a former chapter. Inconvertible paper, however, is a far more potent instrument for producing the same injustice. Those who work for wages suffer the most severely from its use. As the emission of inconvertible paper progresses, all prices advance, and the rates of wages are enhanced with other things. But, unfortunately for the laborer, it is a rule almost without exception that the prices of all the necessaries of life rise more than wages.

By the issue of greenbacks an artificial stimulus was given at once to the prices of all commodities, and speculation forthwith ran riot. The markets were filled with buyers, who, confident of a further advance, were eagerly bidding up prices. The commodities which then became the subjects of the most active speculation were those composing the food we eat and the clothes we wear. Speculation caused by the issue of inconvertible paper affects most the prices of the necessaries of life. But for wages there can be no speculative demand. The employers of labor, so far from speculating in labor, oppose every advance to the extent of their ability; for any increase of wages is liable to diminish their profits.

Greenbacks made no addition to the capital which sought investment in the hiring of labor. The wages fund of the country gained nothing by their issue. Wages were advanced because the laborers must have their necessary wages. They must earn enough to buy the things without which life cannot be supported; and they will not descend to a standard of living below that to which they have been accustomed, without a struggle. They obtain, therefore, a nominal advance of wages; but not sufficient to make up for the loss of purchasing power which money undergoes.

The withdrawal of laborers in the army caused a scarcity of labor while the war was in progress, and concealed for a time this effect of the currency. With the disbandment of the armies, however, and the return of industry to its accustomed channels, the wrongs which the use of inconvertible paper in the payment of wages inflicts upon the laborers have been fully developed.

The Special Commissioner of Revenue, in his Report of 1866, after a careful investigation of the relative effect of the currency on the prices of commodities and the rates of wages, states his conclusions as follows:

"The general result of an examination and comparison of all the statistics gathered leads, therefore, to the opinion that the average increase in the prices of labor since 1860 has been about sixty per cent., and of commodities, as already stated, about ninety per cent."

In the Western States the condition of the laborers has been more favorable than in the Atlantic States. The prices of food have been lower, because food is there the chief product; while in a new and expanding country the demand for labor constantly exceeds the supply, and enables the laborer to sell his services on better terms. The above citation, however, fairly represents the relative advance of prices and wages in the greater portion of the country; but it fails at the same time to tell the whole story. It does not specify whether the prices of commodities from which the averages were made were prices at wholesale or at retail. The former are the only ones of which accurate statistics can be obtained, and from them numerical comparisons can be most readily drawn. But when the effect of inconvertible paper in enhancing retail prices is investigated, it becomes evident that the loss of purchasing power wages undergo is greater than that shown by comparisons with wholesale prices; for the issue of such money enhances prices at retail in a greater ratio than at wholesale. Greenbacks caused prices to advance because, though there was no more value to lay out in exchange for commodities, there were more dollars to expand for that purpose; and, as this paper money wholly superseded the metallic money, none other could be used in retail dealings. The retailers were entitled, on account of this increase of the money in circulation, to receive more for every thing they sold. But, from the manner in which retail trade is conducted in this country, they were enabled to take advantage of the occasion to increase their prices far beyond any thing they were reasonably entitled to. The retailers of the United States, never much restricted by competition, have, by the aid of greenbacks, formed themselves in many localities into "rings" for plundering the community.

Several causes, resulting directly from the nature of inconvertible paper money, have tended to enhance prices at retail more than at wholesale.

1. While the emission of greenbacks was in progress, there was no perceptible limit of the extent to which they would depreciate. It was possible that they might follow the path marked out in history for inconvertible paper, and become as worthless as assignats or Continental money. A doubt hung over them. There was danger in holding them. Every one, therefore, who was compelled to receive them in exchange for merchandise, endeavored to add to the price of the article sold an amount sufficient to insure himself against the risk of their further depreciation while in his hands. At the same time the value of the currency was constantly fluctuating. Prices of all commodities varied, not only according to the state of the markets, but with the variations in the value of

the circulating medium. These fluctuations were frequent and extreme. A dealer laying in a stock of goods, sufficient to last during the season, ran a risk of loss from a decline in their price before he could dispose of them to his customers. He endeavored, therefore, so far as he could, to add to his prices a sum sufficient to insure himself against the risks of these fluctuations. A higher rate of retail profits had become necessary. But the retail dealers, by tacit consent among themselves, made of this necessary insurance an additional source of profit. They fixed its amount themselves; and as, from the nature of things, there was no manner of fixing the amount with accuracy or certainty, they were always sure to stretch it to the utmost limit. The public was at their mercy. The wholesale dealers in like manner added the same insurance to their prices, but, being subject to the competition of open market, they were unable to make of it so great a source of profit.

2. That prices at retail go up much more easily than they come down, is a matter of common observation. An advance in the wholesale markets is a valid reason for increasing retail prices. The retail dealers, accordingly, mark up their goods to correspond with every upward surge of wholesale prices. The standard by which they are guided in determining the rates at which to sell, is the highest fluctuation of the season in the general markets, and not the average for that time, or what their goods cost them. But when high prices have thus become established, and people have become accustomed to paying them, the custom is continued after the reason for it no longer exists.

3. This practice of insuring against the uncertain-

ty of the currency, and the fluctuations in values, becomes prevalent in all commercial transactions. Every one must do it in self-defence. Hence, all the expenses, both of doing business and of living, are greatly increased. This circumstance, again, is made an additional pretext for enhancing retail prices, and the inability of the people to endure any further exactions becomes the only restraint upon retail dealers.

At the same time, that portion of the community that finds itself suddenly enriched by the transfers of property, which the fluctuations of values cause, gives itself over to all manner of extravagance. Goods are purchased simply on account of their dearness. The higher the retailers can put their prices, the better for such customers. But, in enhancing prices for this class, they enhance them also for the rest of the community, and the extravagant practices of a few thus become an injury to many.

4. There is still another quality of our greenback currency which assists this process of retail extortion. All coin, but debased copper or nickel, being driven out of circulation, paper takes its place in the smallest transaction. Small bills and fractional currency are issued to satisfy every demand for them, and become the most effective instrument in enhancing prices. If they were scarce, and difficult to obtain, it would become necessary to lower prices somewhat, in order to adjust them to the amount of money circulating through the hands of the people. But, so far from contracting that portion of the currency which most needs it, small bills and fractional currency are crowded into circulation, and retailers are enabled to put up prices until such excess of currency is absorbed. Ev-

ery clamor for small bills is immediately satisfied, as though such money were peculiarly the people's money, instead of an instrument for their oppression. Thus all the evil effects of issuing small bills under a mixed currency are aggravated tenfold when the currency becomes inconvertible.

It does not follow that all retail dealers get rich under such a system. Where prices fluctuate extremely, the risks of trade are greatly increased. The apparent high rate of profit also causes business to be overdone, and, though the gross amount of profit received by the retail dealers of the country has been greatly increased, the number among whom it must be divided has been correspondingly augmented. The net profits of each dealer, therefore, depend principally upon the two circumstances, whether his business is overdone in his own locality, and whether he is fortunate in making his purchases after a downward fluctuation in the markets.

But, while the profits of the retailers as a class have been vastly enhanced, the purchasing power of wages has been correspondingly diminished. When, therefore, the Commissioner of Revenue states that in 1866 wages had advanced sixty per cent. and commodities ninety per cent., he fails to show the real loss to the laboring class. It is probable that at that time commodities had advanced, at retail, over one hundred per cent., and that the purchasing power of wages in many parts of the country had fallen nearly one-half. Since that time, prices have been reduced somewhat, but the condition of those who work for wages has not been restored to what it was before the war. Speculation no longer exercises its former power. But it is observable that prices at retail have fallen in a less degree than at wholesale. The public has become accustomed to high prices, and the custom is still continued in force. Competition has less power than ever. The number of distributors remains excessive, while their expenses have been but little diminished. They attempt to live, therefore, by obtaining inordinate profits for what they succeed in selling. It is probable that nothing will reduce retail prices to their proper level but the use of coin as the sole medium of retail trade.

But, while the expenses of living are thus kept up at nearly war rates, wages have declined considerably. The disbanding of our armies increased the supply of labor; while the disturbance of business, and diminution of production, which necessarily resulted from the decline in the prices of commodities, lessened the demand for labor. At the same time, the policy of contracting the currency was long steadily pursued, the greatest sufferers from which have been the laboring classes. Contraction causes capital to be hoarded; to seek any investment, rather than productive enterprises. It brings production to a stand-still, and deprives the laborers of employment. One of the standing arguments in its favor is the ultimate benefit to those who work for wages. But if they starve before specie payments are reached, the remedy must be pronounced more fatal than the disease. It is better for employed workmen to be partially robbed by paper money than to be left idle by a general stagnation of business.

The foregoing conclusions can be supported by an ample supply of well-established facts.

The condition of wages and retail prices in Massachusetts in April, 1867, is stated by Amasa Walker in these words:

"By careful investigations made in this Commonwealth, it is quite satisfactorily ascertained, that the average advance of labor in all departments, male and female, in shops and factories, on farms and in families, is near fifty per cent. since 1860. If so, the laborer gains fifty per cent. in wages; but he must spend his wages for commodities, and these at the most moderate calculation have been raised in price at least one hundred per cent. above the natural average."

In the Revenue Commissioner's Report of December, 1868, the following statement is made:

"The result of long and careful investigations in respect to the retail prices of the leading articles of domestic consumption by operatives in the manufacturing towns of New England, the Middle and some of the Western States, have afforded data for accurately estimating the increase in the prices of such articles in 1867 as compared with 1860–'61. They establish the following conclusions:

"That the average increase in the price of groceries and provisions in 1867, as compared with 1860–'61, was 88 per cent.; or, calculated on the basis of the quantity consumed on an average by a number of workmen, a little in excess of 86 per cent.; of domestic dry goods, including clothing, 86½ per cent.; of fuel, 57 per cent.; of house-rent, 65 per cent.

"The average of these results, proportioned to the ascertained varying ratio of expenditure under the several heads, show that for the year 1867, and for the first half of the year 1868, the average increase of all the elements which constitute the food, clothing, and shelter of a family, has been about 78 per cent., as compared with the standard prices of 1860–'61.

"The result, in general, of this large increase in the prices of commodities of domestic consumption to the laboring man becomes evident, by comparing such increase with the increase in the rates of wages during the period under comparison—which rates, for the year 1867, as compared with 1860–'61, were as follows: For unskilled mechanical labor, 50 per cent.; for skilled mechanical labor, 60 per cent.

"The fact, therefore, is established by incontrovertible evidence, that the condition of working men and women in a majority of the manufacturing towns of the United States is not as good at the present time as it was previous to the war, notwithstanding that their wages are greater, measured in gold, in 1867–'68 than they were in 1860–'61."

In a speech made at Chicago, May 5, 1871, Mr. Welles shows that no improvement of condition has taken place since 1868, as tested by the consumption of certain leading articles—the best test of the general prosperity of the mass of the people that can be given, in the absence of such detailed investigations as those contained in his revenue reports. He says:

"I want to tell you, gentlemen, here to-night, and the directors of our financial affairs, that there was less coffee and sugar consumed last year *per capita* in this country than there was ten years ago. I want to tell you that we are consuming a proportionally smaller number of boots and shoes, hats and cloth, to-day, than we were in 1860; and that we consume less of cotton cloth, measured by the pound, in 1870, with 39,000,000 of people, than we did in 1860, with 30,000,000 of people."

Part of these effects must be ascribed to taxation and the tariff, and, though the effects of that cause and of the currency cannot be separately stated in figures, yet, from the *a priori* considerations above given, it is safe to conclude that the latter cause is by far the more powerful.

While those who work for wages suffer the most severely from the use of an inconvertible currency, the effect on the profits of those engaged in agriculture is scarcely less disastrous. In a country which raises a surplus of agricultural products, the price of the whole crop depends upon what can be got for the surplus. When there is more of an article produced than can be consumed at home, its price may decline indefinitely, unless the superabundance can be exported. Thus, in Illinois and Iowa, Indian corn has frequently been used for fuel. But, when a part of any crop is exported, the price of the whole is regulated by the foreign markets, as there can be but one price, after allowing for the expenses of transportation. There are times, it is true, when our markets control the foreign markets. We represent supply, and England represents demand. By controlling the supply, therefore, we can sometimes force up prices. This power is one, however, that we never have when most needed—when our crops are largest. The prices of most of our agricultural products, therefore, must depend in part on the price of gold. The quotations in the European markets rule, and the premium on gold is added in arriving at the paper prices in our markets. Hence, when the gold-premium is depressed below the level of general prices, the farmers suffer. They sell their products on the basis of gold, and buy the greater portion of the merchandise they need for consumption at inflated paper prices. When gold has advanced forty per cent. and commodities sixty per cent., or gold ten per cent. and commodities twenty-five per cent., they lose the difference. But this is not their only loss. Agricultural products are sold at wholesale prices, while the goods the farmers buy are at retail prices. Hence, when the products they sell have advanced only forty per cent., the goods they buy are really enhanced seventy-five per cent., and when gold is at ten the difference is yet wider.

The full effect of paper money on the agricultural class is only just felt. Successive short crops had so diminished the supply of breadstuffs throughout the civilized world, during the two years 1866–'67 and 1867–'68, that famine prices ruled, disguising the effects of our inconvertible currency, while owing to the short supply in our own markets, the prices of many agricultural products were independent of the foreign markets, and of the premium on gold. Speculation, accordingly, aided by its most convenient instruments, inconvertible paper, and banks freed from the restraint of paying specie, had full swing. But, since 1868, this has been changed by the return of our soldiers to farming pursuits, and by favorable harvests, and the evil effect of the currency has begun to weigh heavily on the agricultural class. As there is a surplus of their products for export, the premium on gold has become a controlling influence in determining prices, and as it ranges constantly below the average of general prices, agricultural products have become relatively very cheap. Thus, in many of the interior towns of the Northwest, spring-wheat of the second quality, of which the bulk of the crop consists, touched sixty-five cents in 1868, and in 1869 thirty-five cents a bushel in current money. At this rate a bushel of wheat has less power in exchange—will obtain for its producer less of other commodities, than ever before in the history of the country. During 1870 and 1871, wheat ruled higher, owing to the European war; but, on the other hand, Indian corn and hog products have ruled unprecedentedly low. At twenty cents a bushel for corn, and three cents a pound live weight for swine to the producers on their farms, these commodities have less purchasing power than at any former period in this generation. Now, our farmers, in their turn, are having a taste of the inequality and injustice of the greenback currency. After the poor harvests, it was made the instrument of enhancing the prices of the necessaries of life to the already overburdened laborers of the East. Now that the crops are superabundant, it is made the instrument of robbing the producers of a part of their just reward.

The increased use of machinery in agricultural operations and consequent decline of the cost of production have offset in part the evil effects of the currency. But that fact does not palliate the wrong. The currency deprives the agricultural class of the increased welfare the use of machinery would naturally bring.

The capitalist fares better than the laborer or the agriculturist, when inconvertible paper is used as the instrument for the distribution of wealth. The apparent gain to the owners of property from the issue of such money, it is true, is all in price. Production is in reality diminished, and there is less wealth to distribute. But, though capitalists do not gain so much as they would if gold were the only money, they receive a greater relative share of the wealth that is produced than before. Although a fluctuating currency causes many involuntary transfers of property, yet, as a rule, capital can protect itself. Money, always a power, is more powerful than ever when its value changes daily.

The manner in which an inconvertible currency increases the profits of capital employed in distribution, and particularly in retail trade, needs no further elucidation. The fact, however, deserves consideration, that the shares of wealth received by the several owners of capital under the operation of inconvertible paper are widely different. While the process of depreciating the currency is going on, capital which is tied up in trust funds, or which consists of debts payable at a future day, is steadily diminished. The property of every creditor is then, in part, transferred to his debtor, without his consent. Widows and orphans, and those living on fixed incomes, are then robbed under authority of law. But, on the other hand, active capital, skilfully handled, can have no better opportunity of increasing itself than is then afforded to it. An increase of prices, undoubtedly, is not an increase of values. A person holding the same property at the end of the inflation as at the beginning, would be no richer. But property does not remain constantly in the same hands. When prices begin to rise, people begin to buy in order to realize the increase. If, however, they use their own money they gain nothing, unless prices recede after they have sold. But, if they use borrowed money, they can sell at the advanced prices, repay the loan, and gain the difference. Commodities are thus bought on a margin, and by a rise the margin may be doubled. The apparent gain is nothing more than a depreciation of the currency. The money borrowed is repaid with money of less purchasing power. The property of the creditor is transferred to his debtor. Thus, many banks and money-lenders, insurance and trust companies, though having nominally the same capital to-day which they had in 1862, have really lost a part of it, unless they have gained enough by increased rates of interest to form a reserve.

But prices do not advance steadily as the emission of paper proceeds. The advance is always irregular and spasmodic. Reactions and fluctuations accompany it at every step. It is not every one, therefore, attempting to gain by the rise in prices, who succeeds. Only a few draw prizes. All business becomes gambling, and the most audacious are frequently the most successful. Success, however, is not wholly a matter of luck. In a market subject to frequent and violent fluctuations, those possessed of large capital have the most decided advantage over their less fortunate neighbors. A decline that ruins one operating on a narrow margin enables another having a large capital to buy at the reduced prices, and sell at the next advance. The risk of such fluctuations renders a large capital necessary to transact business with success. Credit also comes in to add to the inequality. The greater the risks of commerce, the more difficult does it become for those whose credit is not established to obtain the requisite advances ; while those whose credit is of high standing are enabled to profit by every fluctuation. Hence, under an inconvertible currency, capital tends more and more to become aggregated. It concentrates itself in the hands of a few extremely rich men. The effects of a mixed currency in producing such a concentration of riches (pointed out in a former chapter), are insignificant compared with this power of greenbacks. It is at the stock-exchange that this tendency is most plainly visible. A few great operators have swallowed up successive shoals of small ones, until many of the railway corporations of the country have become the property of a few men who have thus been rendered more powerful than the hereditary nobles of other lands.

The same tendency has been equally manifested in other departments of business. At the commercial centres the strong houses have constantly become stronger, while the weak ones have been swallowed up by the former, or have perished and disappeared. The tendency in commerce has been steadily toward the aggregation of a few immense fortunes, whose possessors can crush out their weaker competitors at a blow.

This tendency is inseparable from paper money, with its risks and fluctuations. These necessarily produce an unequal distribution of wealth, and thus divide society into separate classes.

But this inequality is not the worst result of such a currency. Those who gain the most wealth from its use are those who render no equivalent services in return. The speculators are the ones who are enriched; those who use their capital and credit as instruments for gambling, and not as a means for adding to the production of the country. Under such a system, they receive the largest share of the products of labor who assist the least in creating those products.

Not only do the speculators thrive on the natural fluctuations of prices inseparable from a fluctuating standard of values, but they are enabled also to create fictitious fluctuations, and thus to prey upon the rest of the community. As the amount of legal-tender paper money in the country is a known quantity, and cannot be increased by importations from neighboring countries, they can, sometimes, by withdrawing from circulation a few millions of greenbacks, at those seasons of the year when money is in active demand, produce an artificial stringency in the loan market, and a consequent decline in the prices of securities, to their own profit, and to the derangement of the commerce of the country to its remotest extremities.

When the effects of contraction, and a general decline of prices, are compared with inflation, and a general advance of prices, the same results are observed. It is still the speculators who gain the most. Capital which is used as an instrument for gambling has greater advantages over capital employed in legitimate commerce, on a falling, than on a rising market. The merchant who buys goods, when contraction is steadily forcing prices downward, is sure to lose before his stock is disposed of in the regular course of trade; while the speculator who stakes his capital on a bet that prices will be lower at some future day, stands a chance of gaining. The latter has the further advantage of always being able to wait until the bottom is reached, and of then buying for a reaction. Speculators can take advantage of a falling, as well as of a rising market. They thrive on fluctuations. Paper money nourishes them as much by contractions as by expansions. If, therefore, the policy of contraction is ever established in the United States, it will be for the interest of every merchant to close out his stock of goods, and, keeping his capital in cash or on call, enter the markets only as a speculator. If his business is conducted in part on borrowed capital, he can escape bankruptcy in no other way. If, on the other hand, his capital is all his own, he can, by simply waiting, add to it not merely the premium on gold, but the amount of the appreciation of the value of money.

But, while speculators will gain, and legitimate business will be destroyed, by the adoption of such a policy, it should be remembered that those who were shrewd enough to enrich themselves by speculation during the inflation, are the ones who will be most likely to display similar sagacity during the contraction. Not only will their paper fortunes be increased thirty or forty per cent. without any further effort on their part, but they will have another opportunity for successful speculation. The injustice of transferring the largest share of the products of labor to those who render to society no equivalent services in return, would thus be doubled. The crime of inflation would be logically consummated by the crime of contraction. If such a course is pursued, it will be found that ten years of paper money are equal to a century of the law of primogeniture in producing an unequal distribution of wealth.

Already the cry against a privileged class is beginning to be heard. It is called the bond-holding aristocracy. To exempt a particular species of property from taxation is undoubtedly to give to the holders of such property a special privilege. The exemption of United States bonds from state taxation, however, has comparatively little influence in producing the unequal and unjust distribution of wealth now going on. The most active agent at work is paper money.

Not only is the tendency of capital to concentrate increased by the fluctuations of prices, but an inconvertible currency has, like convertible bank-notes, but in a higher degree, the same effect on the condition of the mass of the people as indirect taxation. When taxes are imposed directly on property, the rich and poor contribute respectively according to their means. When taxes are imposed indirectly upon consumption, all are taxed according to what they consume. The poor man is then taxed on his whole income, or the greater part of it; while the rich man escapes taxation on the surplus which he adds each year to his principal. A diminution of the purchasing power of wages, it is evident, has the same effect on the laborer, whether it is caused by a tax on consumption, or by an imperfect instrument of distribution. It makes no difference to him whether the price of an article is increased by a duty on the raw material of which it is made, or by an insurance imposed by the middle-man in order to protect himself against the fluctuations of the currency. In either case he can afford to buy less of it than before.

But, contemporaneously with greenbacks, a system of indirect taxation has been put in operation, which, by diffusing taxes over an immense number of articles, instead of concentrating them on a few, has been rendered needlessly oppressive. It is not strange, therefore, that with two such systems of indirect taxation in operation at the same time, the mass of consumers should begin to feel that the holders of property are having an unjust advantage in the accumulation of wealth.

The remedy for the first of these evils is a speedy return to specie payments. The remedy for the second is not so much to make United States bonds subject to state taxation, as to reform the system of Federal taxation, and concentrate taxes on a few leading articles. A system of direct taxation is impossible. The provision of the Constitution which provides " That no capitation, or other direct tax, shall be laid, unless in proportion to the census or enumeration hereinbefore directed to be taken," precludes the Federal government from direct taxation. Population is not a test of the wealth of a country. The newer States possess much less accumulated capital in proportion to the number of their inhabitants than the older States, and any attempt to apportion to each its share of Federal taxes in accordance with the census must fail. The only direct tax possible is that on incomes, which, though a direct tax in political economy, is not in Court.

As Federal taxation then will necessarily be proportioned to consumption, instead of to wealth, it becomes doubly important to diminish its effects by lessening its amount. A situation has been reached where strict economy, in administering the government, has become the necessary means for alleviating the condition of the people. But, until specie payments are enforced, economy can only be talked of,

without being practised. Greenbacks and economy
cannot coexist. The product of the printing-press is
always parted with more easily than the product of
labor; and, when the currency is of fluctuating and
uncertain value, a close calculation of expenditures is
difficult. Nothing will bring the expenses of government within the limits of strict economy so surely as
to dispel the illusions of paper money, and reinstate
that which can be obtained only in return for an
equivalent in value.

De Tocqueville has predicted * that if ever a permanent inequality of conditions and aristocracy again
penetrate into the world, the channel by which they
will enter is manufactures. The tendency which
exists in a country, where manufacturing is the
chief industry, for society to become divided into
separate classes, consisting of a few employers and
many employed, between whom there is seldom any
sympathy, and often ill-concealed hostility, is undoubted. But when to this tendency, unmitigated
by any application of the principle of coöperation, is
added that of a financial system equally powerful in
producing the same result, society divides itself into
separate classes with great rapidity. The units of
which the favored class is composed, it is true, are constantly shifting, but to the mass of the people who
never enter that class this circumstance is of no benefit; while, as it prevents any concentration of hereditary culture, the community experiences all the evils
of an aristocracy without any of its corresponding
advantages. Universal suffrage then ceases to be

* "Democracy in America," Part II., Book II., chap. xx.

the means of producing equality, and becomes a blind for concealing a fraud. The principle upon which our government purports to be founded is equality. A Republic which is to exist permanently as a Republic, cannot well be founded on any other. A financial system, therefore, whose most direct effect is to produce inequality of conditions must be reformed, or it will change our institutions.

The tyranny of capital over labor at the South has been destroyed by our armies. But against this gain must be set off the unjust advantage which capital at the North has obtained over labor. Already, in the older States, the inequalities of European society are in process of being reproduced. While on the other side of the Atlantic the march is toward equality, on this side we are marching away from it. In these Northern States alone has the course of modern civilization been turned backward. A necessary preliminary to restoring its progress is a speedy return to specie payments.

11

CHAPTER XI.

THE EFFECTS OF AN INCONVERTIBLE CURRENCY ON FOREIGN TRADE, AND THE INTERNATIONAL EXCHANGES.

IT has been maintained by some writers, that the emission of inconvertible paper does not affect the foreign trade of the country in which such a circulating medium is used.

The opinion, and the reason for it, have been stated by Mill in these words:

" When the paper begins to exceed in quantity the metallic currency which it superseded, prices of course rise; things which were worth £5 in metallic money become worth £6 in inconvertible paper, or more, as the case may be. But this rise of price will not, as in the cases before examined, stimulate import and discourage export. The imports and exports are determined by the metallic prices of things, and not by the paper prices; and it is only when the paper is exchangeable at pleasure for the metals, that paper prices and metallic prices must correspond.

" Let us suppose that England is the country which has the depreciated paper. Suppose that some English production could be bought, while the currency was still metallic, for £5, and sold in France for £5

10*s.*, the difference covering the expense and risk, and affording a profit to the merchant. On account of the depreciation, this commodity will now cost in England £6, and cannot be sold in France for more than £5 10*s.*, and yet it will be exported as before. Why? Because the £5 10*s.* which the exporter can get for it in France is not depreciated paper, but gold or silver; and since in England bullion has risen in the same proportion with other things, if the merchant brings the gold or silver to England, he can sell his £5 10*s.* for £6 12*s.*, and obtain, as before, 10 per cent. for profit and expenses.

"It thus appears, that a depreciation of the currency does not affect the foreign trade of the country; this is carried on precisely as if the currency maintained its value." *

The conclusion follows logically from the premise which is assumed. If the premium on gold were a correct measure of the depreciation of the currency, and rose "in the same proportion with other things," foreign trade would be carried on in the manner described. While paper would be used for internal commerce, coin would continue to be the only money used in transactions with other nations. The premium on gold would be added to the quotations for bills of exchange, and the increased prices at which the importers would sell their goods would be exactly equalled by the increased cost of bills of exchange; or if the practice prevailed of dealing in exchange for coin only, as has happened in this country, the importer would pay for the coin with which to buy his

* "Principles," etc., Book III., chap. xxii., sec. 3.

exchange, a premium exactly equal to the increased price at which he had disposed of his goods, and the trade balances would be unaffected by the substitution of paper for gold.

But the experience of the United States since 1862 proves that the premise assumed by Mill is an error. Since the issue of greenbacks, gold has never risen nor fallen "in the same proportion with other things." The premium on it has never at any time been a correct measure of the depreciation of the currency, as marked by the prices of commodities in general. The reasons for this conclusion have been given in the chapter devoted to the subject. It remains to show the effect of the differences between the price of gold and general prices, upon foreign trade and the international exchanges.

When the premium on gold has risen more rapidly and higher than the prices of commodities, importations of foreign merchandise are diminished. In that case the importer sells his goods at increased prices in paper; but, as he is compelled to buy the gold to remit for them at very much higher rates, his profits are wholly cut off in making the remittance. On the other hand, one exporting goods for which he has paid in paper, and selling them for gold, is enabled to dispose of the gold at home for a large profit in paper; or a foreigner bringing gold thither to buy goods sells it for paper, and with the latter buys a larger amount of commodities than before. When, therefore, the premium on gold has risen above the average of general prices, the country where the inconvertible paper is used becomes a good country in which to buy. Its importations are then lessened, and if it has a surplus of products for export, its exportations are increased. But, when the premium on gold has fallen below the average of general prices, the process is reversed. One importing merchandise into such a country sells it for high prices in paper, and, buying the gold for remittance at a much lower rate, finds a broad margin for profit. In such case, the country using the inconvertible paper becomes a good country in which to sell. Foreigners forthwith take advantage of the market opened to them, and ship their products thither in increased quantities, while the products which are shipped thence for sale abroad are diminished.

It has become customary to attribute the present derangement of manufactures in this country to the depressing effects of internal taxation, and an oppressive tariff, overlooking the more serious evil of paper money. Such money, by increasing the cost of production, becomes a burden on all manufactures; but, in treating of the effect of the currency on the international exchanges, it is its influence on the production of those articles that come into competition with foreign-made goods which calls for particular attention. This competition may take place either in the home markets, or in foreign markets. Our manufacturers may be undersold, either in attempting to supply their own countrymen, or in supplying the wants of distant lands. When the field of competition is a foreign market, the disadvantages imposed upon them by the currency become very obvious.

When a fluctuating and uncertain medium of exchange is used, every dealer, as before stated, is compelled to add to the prices of the commodities he sells, a sum sufficient to insure himself against the risks of loss. The manufacturer, accordingly, pays this increase of price for every article he uses in his business, and the cost of production for him is increased. A general enhancement of wages also takes place. The laborer must receive a greater nominal sum, that he may live as well as before. This general advance of nominal wages will be another item to be added to the cost of production. But a manufacturer who works with a fluctuating currency, is compelled, also, to add to the prices of his products a sum sufficient to protect himself from loss by sudden depreciation. In addition to his ordinary profit, he must obtain an extraordinary profit as an insurance against the fluctuations of prices, or, when shipping his products abroad, against the fluctuations of the premium on gold. His standard of profits, therefore, is raised, as well as the cost of production. But, when manufacturers are engaged in underselling one another in foreign markets, the smallness of the profit they can respectively afford to accept, determines which must withdraw. A minute variation in the margin for profits will frequently drive one of the competitors out of the market. Our manufacturers, consequently, whose necessary standard of profits, and cost of production, have been raised by a fluctuating currency, are disqualified from competing in foreign markets on equal terms with those who have never been compelled to include in their calculation of profit an allowance for an uncertain medium of exchange.

But while a fluctuating currency, by thus increasing the cost of production, and raising the standard of necessary profits, diminishes the capacity of our manufacturers to enter the foreign markets, the excessive depression of the premium on gold since 1865 has been a still greater disadvantage to them in competing with their foreign rivals. Their whole business is conducted on a basis of inconvertible paper, by which general prices, including, of course, wages and materials, have been largely enhanced. But the goods they export they sell for gold, and the gold they convert into greenbacks, at the current rate of premium. If, however, the price of gold has only advanced forty per cent., while the average prices of commodities have advanced sixty or seventy per cent., or if gold has advanced ten per cent., and commodities twenty-five or thirty per cent., American-made goods, with the exception of those in the manufacture of which we have peculiar advantages, can only be sold in foreign markets at a loss. In that case, the price of the finished product, as reduced to paper, has not advanced with the cost of production. The statistics of our trade, particularly as collected by Mr. Welles in his several reports, show that our exports of manufactured articles have fallen off, in a marked manner, since the decline of the gold premium in 1865; and whatever opinion may be held as to the connection of cause and effect between these two facts, it cannot be denied that the United States do not succeed in competing, in the markets of the world, with the products of skilled labor.

The causes which have driven our manufacturers out of the foreign markets have, at the same time, endangered their possession of the home markets. Foreign producers, having no such disadvantages to contend with, are enabled to manufacture more cheaply than American producers, and thus undersell them at their own doors. The main thing in favor of the foreign manufacturers is the low premium on gold. The difference between the price of gold and the increase of the cost of production in this country is to them a source of profit, and constantly enables them to sell their goods at a less price in greenbacks than the American manufacturers can afford to take. Not all this increase of the cost of production is due to the currency. A portion of it comes from oppressive taxation. The heavy duties on imports, it is true, have always been intended to protect home manufactures. How far this intention has been successful, it is not necessary to consider here. Our protective tariffs evidently have wholly failed to protect our producers against the disadvantages of the currency. To have that effect, the tariff must be high enough to make up for the low premium on gold, as well as the heavy taxation, and such a tariff would tend strongly to defeat itself. Another way of protecting our manufactures would be to concentrate all indirect taxes on a few articles, and then, if possible, to raise the premium on gold above the level of general prices, and keep it there. The discussion of such a policy, however, may well be postponed until it has been finally determined to retain greenbacks as a permanent, instead of a temporary, currency. It is sufficient to observe that a rise of the gold premium would carry with it the prices of all raw materials which are imported, but would have much less effect on wages, and on most home products; while it would cause the prices of articles which are kept down by foreign competition to advance by the full percentage of the rise, and, as no increase of general prices could be caused by it, part of the currency now used in speculative operations would be withdrawn, and a stringency in the loan market would ensue. Such a policy might enable our manufacturers again to enter successfully the foreign markets with their products; while a protective tariff, so far from having such an effect, ignores the fact that there can be a foreign market for our manufactured products.

The effect of the currency on our commerce has been even more disastrous than on manufactures. The decline of over fifty per cent. in the tonnage of American sailing-vessels registered for foreign commerce, it is true, is not due altogether to this cause. Steam-vessels have largely superseded sailing-vessels in foreign commerce. But the causes which prevent us from building ships of wood equally prevent us from building them of iron. Nor can it be said that, in a natural state of prices, American builders of iron vessels cannot equal their British competitors; for, in 1859, ocean steamships of iron were built in Boston harbor, away from the centre of our iron industry, as cheap as they could be built on the Clyde in 1871.*

It is usual to attribute the stagnation in this branch of industry to the tariff on raw materials. The tariff, undoubtedly, is more severely felt in ship-building than in any other employment. But, after estimating at the highest this disadvantage, the currency is still found to inflict severer injuries. Ship-building is the branch of manufactures most sensitive to the adverse influences of inconvertible paper. Our ships are brought into immediate competition, at the commer-

* D. A. Welles.

cial centres of the world, with ships built on a gold basis; and our ship-builders, working on the basis of paper, do not find the increased cost of production it causes equalled by the premium they receive on the gold for which their vessels sell, or which is taken as freight money. The reform of the tariff, therefore, important as it is, unaccompanied by a reform of the currency, would do but little toward restoring prosperity to our ship-yards.

But it is not simply by transferring the American carrying-trade to foreign bottoms that the currency has injured our commerce. It has materially diminished the amount of commodities we are able to export. Our manufacturers find themselves handicapped when they attempt to furnish goods for foreign countries, and the greater portion of the articles left for exportation consists of the raw materials of agriculture. Our importations of coffee, tea, spices, and other commodities we cannot produce at home, are paid for with bills on London, which we buy with our agricultural products, gold, and bonds, and the markets for manufactured articles, throughout the world, are thus left open to the English without our competition. We very nearly fill, in general commerce, the same place as our semi-civilized neighbors of South America—as exporters of the products of unskilled labor. The great bulk of our exports consists of five articles of raw produce, cotton, petroleum, bread-stuffs, tobacco, and provisions, including, in the latter, "hog products," and cheese. By a barbarous tariff, and worse currency, the most inventive and skilful people that exists is shut out from competing successfully with its manufactures in the markets of the world.

If the commerce of the United States is ever to expand to the proportions Nature has marked out for it, the products of the loom and the forge must become articles of export. Commerce and manufactures must expand together. Our manufacturers, no longer pent up within the narrow limits of their own land, must seek the markets of the world, and, in so doing, furnish our merchants with cargoes for their ships. English commerce is founded on English manufactures. American commerce will one day build on a similar foundation. But it will not be until after specie has once more become the current money of the land.

The following table of our exports of manufactured articles at gold values, with fractions of millions omitted, shows but little progress since 1854, and a material decline if measured *per capita* of population:

Year.	Value.	Year.	Value.
1854	$36,000,000	1863	$37,000,000
1855	35,000,000	1864	24,000,000
1856	36,000,000	1865	23,000,000
1857	36,000,000	1866	29,000,000
1858	35,000,000	1867	35,000,000
1859	39,000,000	1868	37,000,000
1860	48,000,000	1870	33,000,000
1861	43,000,000	1871	43,000,000
1862	32,000,000		

The apparent increase in the last year is wholly due to shipments of arms and ammunition, a large part of which came from the government arsenals.

The following table shows the imports of dry goods at gold values, and, with the preceding, demonstrates the effects of our present system on the productions of skilled labor, and on the diversification of . home industry:

Year.	Invoiced Value.	Year.	Invoiced Value.
1854	$80,000,000	1863	$67,000,000
1855	64,000,000	1864	71,000,000
1856	93,000,000	1865	94,000,000
1857	90,000,000	1866	126,000,000
1858	60,000,000	1867	86,000,000
1859	113,000,000	1868	80,000,000
1860	103,000,000	1869	94,000,000
1861	43,000,000	1870	108,000,000
1862	50,000,000	1871	132,000,000

The lowest amount, it will be observed, is that for 1861, when the stagnation that preceded actual hostilities had diminished our capacity for consumption. From that time till 1864 the premium on gold, being in advance of general prices, acted as a most effectual protective tariff. In July of that year gold touched 285$\frac{1}{2}$, the highest quotation given. It ranged generally above 200 for the remainder of 1864, and, the first two months of 1865, declining steadily through March and April of the latter year, until in May it had fallen below 130. The effect of this sudden decline of the premium on gold is marked most visibly by the importations for the year 1866, the great increase having commenced in August of the preceding year. Since that time gold has constantly declined faster than other commodities, stimulating importations on a large scale, so that the value of foreign dry goods brought into the country was more than three times greater at the end of the decade than at its beginning.

That the theory is correct which ascribes the derangement of our foreign trade chiefly to the circumstance that the gold premium does not equal the depreciation of the currency, as measured by the advance of prices, can be shown by several facts collected by Mr. Welles. In his report of December, 1868, an apt illustration of the effect of our inconvertible currency on foreign trade is given.

"The statement," he says, "is furnished to the Commissioner by a manufacturer of furniture in one of the Middle States, who previous to the war had built up an extensive export business to the West Indies, Central and South America, of a variety of 'cane-seated' and 'cane-backed' furniture suited to warm latitudes.

"Thus, on the 1st of March, 1861, gold and currency being at par, $1,000 in gold possessed a purchasing power sufficient to obtain for the South American importer 111⅓ dozen of what are termed in the trade, 'ordinary square-post cane-seated chairs.' About the 1st of January, 1862, gold began to command a premium, and advanced during the next three years with great rapidity. This movement, however, was not participated in at first, to any considerable extent, by either labor or commodities, and, in consequence, the purchasing power of gold greatly increased; so much so, that on the 1st of July, 1864, the $1,000 gold which in 1861 bought 111⅓ dozen chairs, then bought 143 dozen. Under these circumstances, as was to be expected, trade increased, as the foreign purchaser found the American market by far the best for his interest; but from July, 1864, a movement commenced in an exactly opposite direction, gold receding, and labor and commodities advancing in very unequal ratios. Thus, in January, 1865, the $1,000 gold, which four years previous had a purchasing power of 111⅓ dozen chairs, and on the 1st of July, 1864, of 143 dozen, then commanded but 126⅔ dozen; in February, 1866, a still smaller number, viz., 91½ dozen, and ultimately attained its minimum in January, 1867, when the purchasing power of the sum named was only 89⅝ dozen. From this point the purchasing power has gradually increased, and for the past year, 1868, has remained at the rate of about 10⁹ dozen, or nine dozen less than could be bought with the same money in 1861.

"The result has been that the foreign purchaser now goes to France or Germany, while the products of American industry, in the form of furniture, being no longer available to exchange for sugars, spices, or dyewoods, gold has necessarily been substituted."

As gold could only be used to purchase the chairs by being first turned into greenbacks, it is evident that the principal cause in determining these variations of its purchasing power has been the amount of the premium. The lower the premium on gold, the less is the purchasing power of gold in our markets. Thus, on July 1st, 1864, gold was quoted at 250. In January, 1865, it fell below 220. In February, 1866, it ranged a little below 140, and in January, 1867, just below 135. During the last year mentioned, 1868, it averaged about 140.

In the same report he makes the following statement, showing that a similar state of affairs existed in other trades:

"There is hardly a single domestic article or product, agricultural or manufactured, in behalf of which the claim, either directly or indirectly, has not been made within the last two years, that the same could be produced to greater advantage or profit in some other country than the United States; increased protection even being demanded for oil paintings, rough building stone, Indian corn, firewood, Bibles, and ice —the latter to the extent of fifteen per cent. gold; and this claim the Commissioner is obliged to admit is to a very great extent in exact accordance with the truth."

In his report for December, 1869, he shows that he has learned that the trouble with our foreign trade is the fact that prices are too high in this country as measured by gold. He says:

"Gold would still remain what it is now, the cheapest commodity in the country, and for that reason, as now, would continue to be taken by foreign countries in preference to our other domestic products. That this now is the case, proves that gold is relatively the cheapest commodity we have to export. That gold also is relatively cheaper than the products of our domestic manufactures, can also be shown by a more specific illustration. Thus, in 1860, $1,000 in gold would purchase for export 111 dozen cane-seat chairs. The same amount of gold will purchase at the present time the same number in almost any part of Europe; but in the United States it will now purchase but 102 dozen, thus proving that, as measured by this commodity, gold is cheaper with us than it was in 1860, and cheaper also with us than it is in other countries. It is therefore sent to the points where it is most highly esteemed, and where it can be used to the greatest advantage; and the chairs, in common with the cotton cloth, furniture, tools and implements, nails, hardware, hats, wagons, etc., of domestic manufacture, are allowed to remain at home and depress the market with an excess of competition."

In his speech made at Chicago in May, 1871, he ascribes the perturbations in our exports and imports to the true cause. He says:

" And there was another incident connected with this period, which, I think, is especially worthy of notice, and that is, that the export of many of our domestic products was stimulated during the year 1864 and a part of 1865, to a very great degree, by the increase of the premium upon gold, which, often rising from 50 to 100 or 150 per cent. above the advance which had been experienced in labor and wages, increased, as it were, the purchasing power of the foreign consumer, or decreased the relative cost in our own markets of such articles of domestic product as were available for exportation and sale in foreign markets. For example, the export of bacon rose in the year 1864, as compared with 1860, from 4 to 10 millions; of tobacco, from 15 to 40; of cheese, from $2\frac{1}{2}$ to 12; of butter, from $1\frac{1}{2}$ to 7; while of many other articles, the increase of our exports was from 50 to 100, and sometimes 300 per cent. And the lesson, I think, which we can draw from this fact is, that the reduction of the premium upon gold without, at the same time, measures being taken to reduce also the cost of the production of articles of labor, brings no benefit whatever to the country; a lesson which, being not comprehended, or certainly not regarded by those who have the control of financial affairs at Washington, has, I think, cost the country, in the past year alone, certainly not less than one hundred millions of dollars."

If by reducing the cost of production he means revising the tariff and taxation, his remedy will not reach the root of the evil. It is good as far as it goes; but to diminish taxation will not increase the purchasing power of gold in our markets. It will not affect general prices. After its establishment gold will buy more of some articles, and less of others than before, but its general purchasing power will not be altered. While, therefore, some manufactured articles could be afforded cheaper, we would not be enabled, thereby, to regain our lost commerce.

His other remedy, contraction, would tend for a time, at least, to depress the premium on gold faster than the prices of commodities, and would still further lessen the purchasing power of gold in our markets. It would aggravate the evil rather than cure it, until universal bankruptcy had reduced prices to a specie level.

There is one practical result of the effect of our inconvertible currency on the international exchanges that deserves particular attention, on account of its bearing on the practicability of resuming specie payments.

While the emission of greenbacks was in progress, distrust prevailed. No limit to their depreciation was visible. Prices were steadily rising, and a want of confidence in the paper money spread throughout the land. A tendency to hoard gold was thus created, and, as importations were lessened at the same time, it is probable that until 1864–'5, notwithstanding the fact that gold had taken the place of cotton as an article of export, our due share of the precious metals remained in the country, stored away, in part at least, in private hoards. Since 1865, however, a different process has been going on. The price of gold has constantly ranged below the average of general prices, rendering it the cheapest article of export. At the same time the importations have been on a large scale, and the balance of trade to be paid in gold has been against this country. United States bonds, it is true, have in part taken the place of specie for shipment abroad. But it is probable, nevertheless, that the amount of the precious metals left in the country has fallen to a lower point than for many years.

It is from the hoards of coin in private hands that, under ordinary circumstances, any sudden demand for it is filled. If these private hoards have been thoroughly depleted in the United States, the resumption of specie payments will be found a task, the real difficulty of which has been as yet but faintly realized. That a comparatively small amount of specie is held by the banks, appears from their statements. The amount in the vaults of the Sub-treasury is known. But there are no facts on which to base an estimate of that stored away in secret hiding-places, ready to be called forth whenever real money again becomes current. Any estimates deduced from the statistics of the exportation of gold are unreliable. It can be shown, however, that the causes most likely to diminish the amount of coin held by individuals have long been and are still actively at work.

The idea has been persistently impressed upon the public mind that, the war having been brought to a successful termination, greenbacks would speedily be raised to the level of gold. The process of contracting the currency was long persisted in, and it has been made to appear for the interest of every man to sell his gold in order to realize the premium before it disappears. In the mean time there has been no use for gold. The courts for a long time refused to uphold contracts payable in coin; and, except in Wall Street, there has been no means of making it pay interest, and even there it has generally been necessary to pay for having it " carried." It has become, in short, the most unprofitable property in the country. When, therefore, a person has once sold his gold there is no motive for him to replace it. He can only obtain it by buying it of a broker. But one not a speculator, who has sold his gold in order to realize the premium, is not apt to buy it back again. There is no means by which the hoards of the precious metals in private hands, once broken in upon, can be readily replenished. The greater portion of the gold now in private hands, therefore, has been held since the suspension of specie payments. The amount held by the banks at the statement of June, 1871, was $19,924,955 against $83,594,537 in 1860. The same motives which induced the banks to turn their specie into greenbacks have acted with equal force on individuals, and it is probable that the amount left in private hands at the present time, as compared with 1860, has been diminished in a similar proportion.

There are other circumstances which strengthen this inference. It is known that a portion of the silver coin, which formerly circulated in this country, has found its way to Canada. The discount on American silver in that country marks its excessive supply. It is evident that the small change, which formerly circulated here through the channels of retail trade, has been sent thither to be made useful. The late excessive accumulations of gold coin and bullion in

the Bank of England and the Bank of France may
be attributed in part to the same cause. The disuse
of the precious metals in this country has driven our
share of them to countries where they can fill their
proper office, and the stock in European countries,
accordingly, has become over-abundant. It is safe to
conclude that a large portion of our share of the
precious metals is held in foreign lands.

In *Hunt's Merchants' Magazine* for January, 1869,
the stock of coin and bullion then "in the States where
resumption is to take effect " is computed at $150,000,-
000; which accords with the above *a priori* conclusions. It appears, further, that this stock was diminishing at about the rate of $20,000,000 a year, though
exports of government and railway bonds are delaying
the drain of specie.

So long as paper remains our only circulating
medium, it is better for us to exchange gold for
commodities which can be used, rather than to let it
lie idle. But, before specie payments can be fully
resumed, some way must be discovered for regaining
our share of the stock of precious metals. The policy
pursued at the Treasury Department for the last few
years is the least likely to produce that result of any
that can be devised. Gold will not remain in a
country where, commercially, it is the cheapest article
bought and sold for paper. It flows from the country
where prices are high to the countries where prices
are low. The law of the circulation of the precious
metals acts with greater force when the currency is
inconvertible than when it is purely metallic. Gold
prices, then, are regulated by the premium on gold, and,
when that is depressed below the general average, gold

prices are high. Gold, accordingly, is exported, and commodities imported, with the double effect of rendering specie payments more difficult, and of embarrassing manufactures and paralyzing commerce. The full force of this law has not yet been felt, as it has been neutralized in part by the flow of capital to this country for investment iu railway securities and government bonds. But that a day of reckoning must come at last would seem to be in the ordinary course of human events.

A singular effect of our present currency is seen in the relation of the manufacturers of the Pacific States to those of the rest of the country. The difference in the money used in the different portions of the Union is equivalent to a protective tariff in favor of the manufacturers of the States where coin is the only money current. The cost of production has been increased in the Eastern States by the use of greenbacks; while in California, where specie is the only standard, it has remained unaffected by the currency, and has tended to diminish, on account of the accumulation of capital and partial decline of the rates of interest. At the same time, the premium on the gold, for which the Eastern manufacturers sell their products in the California markets, falls considerably short of the increased cost of production to them, caused by our inconvertible currency. The discrimination in favor of the manufacturers of the Pacific States, however, is not so great as that in favor of the European manufacturers; for the former are harassed by the same system of taxation as the rest of their countrymen. The advantage of using a stable currency nevertheless operates strongly in their favor, and has already stimulated manufactures to some extent, narrowing thereby the markets for the products of the Eastern States. The greatest material benefit conferred by the Federal Union is free trade over a whole continent. That benefit has been partially weakened by the use of different currencies, whereby the trade with the Pacific States has been assimilated to foreign trade.

Instead of attempting to force an inconvertible currency upon a people who have had sufficient sagacity to decline it, the East will act the part of wisdom when it follows the example of those States in escaping the effect of the legal-tender act.

CHAPTER XII.

THE RELATIVE EFFECTS OF THE TARIFF AND THE
CURRENCY ON PRICES.

In the numerous discussions of financial questions
evoked by the wrongs which a barbarous system is
inflicting on the country, it is usually taken for granted that the prevailing enhancement of prices is due as
much to excessive taxation as to a redundant currency. It is claimed that the amount of the depreciation which our paper money has undergone in excess
of the percentage represented by the premium on gold,
must be ascribed to the accumulation and duplica-
tion of taxes. Prices of commodities, in general, it is
inferred, have been enhanced by the increased cost of
production which results from increased taxation.
This view is erroneous. Taxes, no matter how imposed, cannot add one iota to general, or average
prices. Taxation changes the natural relations of
prices to one another. It causes a redistribution of
prices, but it cannot increase them in the aggregate.
This follows from the theory of money heretofore ex-
plained, and from the incidence of taxes, or the manner in which they are distributed.

A given amount of money can only effect a given
amount of exchanges. A general rise of prices in-

creases the amount of exchanges, and requires a corresponding increase of money. If certain commodities, being taxed, rise in price without any diminution of the quantity on sale, more money must be obtained to exchange them in the ordinary course of trade. This money is set free for the purpose by a decline in the prices of other commodities. The rise of those taxed is offset by a decline of those not taxed, and the average of prices is unchanged. If a tax is imposed on profits, or, what is equivalent, on raw materials, prices of the manufactured products rise, that the manufacturer may gain the customary rate of profit of his business. The enhancement of prices naturally attracts merchandise from abroad, which must be paid for with specie. If the currency is convertible, the shipment of specie causes a contraction of its amount, and a decline of prices, in which the commodities affected by the tax participate but partially. If the currency is inconvertible, the effect is the same, but differently reached. The exportation of specie, in such case, affects prices only through the medium of the premium on gold. If the taxes are imposed while the issue of the paper is in progress they are immediately added into the prices of commodities, and, in the final adjustment of prices to the amount of the circulating medium, the articles affected by the tax are enhanced in price so as to leave the average rate of profit to the producers of them. The increased currency must be absorbed in price. If no taxes were imposed, it would still be so disposed of; but a different class of commodities would be affected by it. In either case general, or average prices would be the same. Taxation simply causes a different distribution of them.

The same conclusion is reached when the incidence of taxation is considered.

The whole produce of human labor is allotted to those who are entitled to it in the form of either rent, wages, or profits.   Out of these three all taxes must be paid.   If every man could add his share of taxes into his rent, wages, or profits, no one would be taxed. But to suppose that taxes increase general prices is to suppose that every man does add his taxes into his source of income.   If a system of taxation could be devised, by which every one would pay his just proportion according to his means, taxes would have no effect whatsoever on prices.   It is the attempt of each member of the community to shift the share of the public burdens, allotted to him under an imperfect system, to the shoulders of his neighbors, that causes taxation to disturb prices.

The redistribution of prices which results from indirect taxation is aggravated, and still further complicated, when the currency is inflated simultaneously with the imposition of taxes.   To estimate the effect of this disturbing element it is necessary to trace the manner in which taxes are diffused.

It was pointed out by Ricardo that, if a tax in proportion to profits is laid on all trades, the prices of commodities will rise in different proportions, according to the amount of fixed and circulating capital used in their production.   Their values, relative to one another, will be changed in proportion as the capital employed is expended in wages, or in wages and machinery combined.   When the capital is laid out in paying wages only, the price of the finished product must equal the money so expended, with the usual profit

12

added. If the capital employed is $10,000, and is all laid out in wages, and the profit is twenty per cent., the price of the finished product will be $12,000. When the capital is expended, partly in wages and partly in machinery, the price of the finished product will be equal to the amount of the wages, and the amount necessary to pay for the use of machinery, including wear and tear, with the usual profit on capital added. If, in this case, the capital and rate of profit are the same, the wages paid are $5,000, the cost of machinery $5,000, and $500 will cover the wear and tear of the latter, the finished product must sell for $7,500. The profit left in each case is, by the supposition, $2,000. But, if a tax on it of ten per cent. be laid, the price of the finished product will rise in the first case to $12,200, and in the other to $7,700. The percentage of advance is different in the two cases. The values of the two commodities relative to one another have changed.

But a duty on imports, whenever it is imposed on the material used in the manufacture of any article, increases the cost of production. It operates, therefore, as a tax on profits; and, if all duties were equal and in exact proportion to the values of commodities, they would have the same effect on relative values as an equal tax on profits in the cases above supposed. But duties are not levied equally or in proportion to values. Those levied on the raw materials of one trade are higher than those levied on the raw materials of another. An article, moreover, that in one stage is a finished product, is, with reference to some other branch of industry, a raw material. The effect, therefore, of a tariff diffused over a great number of articles is to redistribute their prices in a most complicated manner, and to change completely their values relative to one another. In a natural state of values three pairs of shoes may exchange for five hats; but, after prices are disturbed by indiscriminate duties, the different quantities of those commodities which will exchange for each other will be materially changed without regard to natural values.

But here again the currency comes in to increase the perturbation. The excessive issue of paper money causes all prices to advance. If no taxation were in force, all prices would tend to rise in the same proportion, and relative values would not be changed. But when prices are deranged by taxation, the rise proceeding from the inflation is unequally distributed. If commodities taxed rise in the same proportion as those not taxed, the part of the price which represents the tax rises also. There is, then, greater profit in producing an article that is taxed, than one that is not taxed, and capital would thus be attracted from one employment to another, until prices and. profits were equalized. But all commodities are not taxed equally, which has the same effect as if one were taxed and another not. The rise of prices, caused by the increase of money in circulation, tends, therefore, to distribute itself in some sort of proportion to the effects of taxation on prices, that profits may be equalized; while the effect of the currency and the tariff combined is to cause a new and irregular distribution of prices, and this cause acts independently of any thing affecting the values of commodities themselves.

This disturbance of relative values changes the employments of capital, and renders the industry of the country less effective. In the long run, it must materially diminish the production of wealth.

But to compare the effects of the tariff and currency on manufactures, and to determine which is the more pregnant with evil, it is requisite to trace still further the effect of duties on prices.

A duty on a commodity that is imported is a tax. It increases the cost of the article on which it is imposed, but not necessarily by the whole amount of the duty. Foreign manufacturers, producing for this market, must keep it, or diminish their business; and, to keep it, they are frequently obliged to share in the duty. They must sell their products in this market at a price, with the duty added, that will not materially diminish consumption. Yet the cases when this happens with manufactured articles are few and temporary. When the foreign producer, to meet a market, must accept a profit less than the usual rate in his country, he will abandon that market. Duties, therefore, not high enough to be prohibitive, increase, in the long run, the price of the article on which they are imposed by the amount of the duty, or near it.

When the article is produced in part at home, and the deficiency is made up from abroad, the price of the whole supply is increased by the amount of the duty, as there cannot be two prices for the same commodity. But the increase of price does not stop with the article on which the duty is imposed. Every one is trying to shift his share of indirect taxes to his neighbor. The merchant, of course, adds the duty in the price of his merchandise, and charges a profit on it. The manufacturer pays the duty in the prices of his raw materials, and charges it in the price of his finished product with a profit. Raw materials, in our tariff, are not put on the free list. They are selected as special subjects of taxation. Iron, wool, hides, leather, lumber, coal, chemicals, dye-stuffs, and the like, are all subject to duty. But a tax on a raw material is a tax on every thing produced from it, and an article which in one stage is a finished product, is the raw material for another, and that the raw material of something else. Duties, consequently, are diffused in the prices of all articles of consumption, and go into the cost of production and of living. The manufacturer pays his share of them in the increased prices of the things he and his family consume. He may pay also another share. Taxes, as we have seen, cannot affect general prices. They must come out of profits. But, when duties are so numerous and widely distributed, they lower the general rate of profit on capital. Of this loss also the manufacturer must stand his share.

But the workman also finds the duties included in the prices of the things he consumes. A duty on raw materials operates as a tax on wages. To obtain the same reward for his labor, therefore, he must receive a greater nominal sum. His wages rise, as estimated in dollars, that they may retain their former purchasing power. A general advance, not of real, but of nominal wages, takes place. This expense comes out of the manufacturer's profits. It does not follow, however, that the workman can compel such a rise of wages as will wholly indemnify him for the taxation. He cannot escape his share of taxes on consumption. He is fortunate, indeed, if he does not pay a greater share of them, in proportion to his means, than any other member of society.

But while the cost of production to our home producer is thus wantonly raised by duties on raw materials, his foreign competitor labors under no such disadvantage. When, therefore, the two meet in the markets of the world, our manufacturer finds himself undersold, and is obliged to withdraw. A tariff, which by taxing every thing seeks to protect every thing, ignores the fact that there can be such a thing as a foreign market for our wares. It imprisons our manufacturers within the home market, without any power of expansion. It destroys our foreign trade.

At the same time, it fails to give our producers the expected monopoly of their own market. The increased cost of production, which the tariff causes, is offset by a duty on the finished product. But this duty, in many instances, and particularly in the case of the finer products of skilled labor, barely equals this increased cost of production. The British manufacturer, accordingly, hampered with no such burden, can pay the duty, and still undersell our manufacturers in our own markets.

The effect, then, of indiscriminate duties imposed on the whole list of imports is to shut our goods out of the foreign markets, and to give them no better hold, on the average, on the home market; to which must be added the fact that increased prices diminish consumption.

There can be no such thing as a tariff generally protective. The idea that, by imposing duties on every thing imported, home industry will be fostered, is utterly fallacious. History records no more stupid hallucination.

The test of a duty is, how far is its subject a raw

material? Does the duty affect the prices of any other articles than of the one upon which it is imposed? Is it confined to the price of that commodity, or is it distributed in other prices?

The best duties are those on wines, liquors, and certain articles of luxury, which affect only the prices of the articles upon which they are originally placed. The next best are those on tea, coffee, sugar, and the like, which affect other prices, if at all, only to an infinitesimal extent, through the efforts of those who are taxed in the consumption of them to shift the burden. The most objectionable of all duties is that on iron. A tax on iron is a tax on the tools of the mechanic and the implements of the farmer. It is a tax on the machinery of every manufacturer, and, worst of all, it is a tax on locomotion and transportation. Iron is the great raw material. The air we breathe and the water we drink are as fit subjects for taxation as the iron that vivifies all industry. Nothing protects home manufactures so effectively as cheap iron.

The direct loss from the duty on pig-iron far outmeasures the gain. If the home supply is not sufficient, the price will rise until the deficiency can be supplied from abroad, and the duty will be added to the price of the whole. If, however, the duty is so high as to be prohibitive, the price will be enhanced, but not necessarily, by the full amount of the duty. The furnaces are differently situated with reference to advantages for cheap production. Some can produce much more cheaply than others; and, if no iron is imported, then the price will rise until enough furnaces have been built to supply the demand. Those most favorably situated will realize extraordinary profits. Those least favorably situated will realize only the ordinary rate of profit on capital. The value of the whole supply of pig-iron will be determined, in that case, by the cost of production at the furnaces least favorably situated, and the price will be enhanced, but not by the full amount of the duty. The greater part of this enhancement will be total loss. Those furnaces which, by reason of their natural advantages, make profits above the usual rate will gain this excess. Those which make only the usual rate will enrich the country no more than if the capital had been employed in any other kind of production. If by the effect of the duty the price of all the pig-iron made in one year is enhanced fifteen millions of dollars, a part, say five millions, goes to the favorably-situated furnaces as extra profit, and the remaining ten millions are as completely lost to the country as if they had been sunk in the sea. Worse than this. The enhancement of iron increases the cost of production of every thing made of or with it, and is distributed in the prices of other commodities until it is doubled or quadrupled. Part of this loss is equivalent, practically, so far as the American people are concerned, to a bounty paid annually by them to the consumers of British exports, to enable the British manufacturers to undersell us. We formerly had a large export trade in steam-engines, machinery, agricultural implements, and the like. But since a tariff has been devised, which is equivalent to paying a bounty to those who purchase these articles of the English makers, we have naturally lost a part of this trade.

If the duty on pig-iron were repealed, its price

probably would not decline by the whole amount of the duty. The consumption would be stimulated, and the price would advance in foreign markets. But this great advantage would result: the prices of pig-iron in this country and in England would be equalized. The prices in Liverpool and New York would differ only by the cost of transfer from one city to the other. Our manufacturers would be placed on an equality with their British rivals, and we would cease to pay a bounty to their customers. All this is true of wool and of many other articles. By a repeal of the duties, our manufacturers would get their raw materials as cheap as their competitors, and would find cheapened production much more protective than a duty on the finished product.

The present tariff violates the theory of protection as much as that of free trade. The arguments in favor of a protective tariff, usually urged, are two: the desirableness of diversifying home industry, and the advantage of turning the balance of trade in our favor. The tariff now in force, so far from accomplishing these results, has the opposite effect.

The object of diversifying employments is to produce social and intellectual progress. Civilization cannot expand if all men are engaged in rude labor. It is sought, therefore, to diversify industry by encouraging skilled labor, and putting a premium on intelligence. Our present tariff, however, does the reverse of this. It encourages labor in its rudest form at the expense of skilled labor. Raw materials are taxed, and the production of the finer and more costly articles of manufacture languishes. Crude labor finds employment in making pig-iron, in growing wool, and in boiling salt. While skilled artisans find no increase in the manufacture of machinery and of textile fabrics; and ship-building has almost ceased.

The effect of the tariff on our foreign exchanges is equally violative of the protective theory. If it be admitted that it is desirable to turn the balance of trade in our favor by legislative enactments, an idea now happily exploded, it is evident that a tariff which, by taxing all raw materials, increases the cost of production, can have only the opposite effect. The protectionists of the last century were wiser than their ignorant imitators of the present day. The advocates of the Mercantile System, while favoring protective duties, admitted that there were exceptions required by the system itself.

"The materials and instruments of production were the subject of a contrary policy, directed, however, to the same end; they were freely imported, and not permitted to be exported, in order that manufacturers, being more cheaply supplied with the requisites of manufacture, might be able to sell cheaper, and therefore to export more largely." *

The protective effect of a tariff cannot be measured by the average rate of duties imposed. As the cost of production is increased by it, those articles the duty on which is below the average rate are not protected, those on which it is at the average may be protected somewhat, while it is only those commodities, such as carpets and blankets, the duties on which are so high as to be nearly prohibitive, that are fully protected.

The idea of making a tariff generally protective seems to have resulted from our democratic equality.

---

* Mill; Book V., chap. x., sec. 1.

A duty was supposed to be a blessing of itself, which every producer was entitled to. Duties were bestowed accordingly on all, and the present practical *reductio ad absurdum* of the protective system is the result. A protective tariff cannot be made to respect equal rights. Its essence is monopoly.

To the question "Does protection protect?"* it can be answered, therefore, that our present tariff, so far from protecting the aggregate industry of the country, has the opposite effect, but that a protective tariff can be devised. One, for instance, which would put all raw materials on the free-list, and impose duties on the finished products of the finer kinds of manufactures, silks, fine cottons, broadcloth, and the like, would give the favored producers of those articles an advantage over their foreign competitors. Such is the tariff Prof. Bowen,† representing the Massachusetts school, advocates. When the claims of the active protectionists are narrowed to that point, it will be time enough to discuss them.

From this investigation, it is plain that our present tariff well deserves all the reprobation heaped upon it. It ought to meet with as much opposition from a consistent protectionist as from the most ultra free-trader. It is unfortunate, however, that all the light of discussion has thus far been concentrated upon it, leaving in the background that greater source of evil, the currency.

Bad as is the effect of the tariff on our commerce and manufactures, that of the currency is worse. Paper money with its fluctuations, and its power over

---

* Grosvenor, "Does Protection Protect?"   Appletons, 1871.

† Bowen, "American Political Economy."   Scribner, 1870.

retail prices, increases the cost of production far more than any tariff. It has also a peculiar effect still more disastrous. It causes an enhancement of general prices, leaving the price of gold below the general average. The increased cost of production and the increase of paper prices are not measured by the gold-premium. In most instances, the tariff duty and the gold-premium added together, fail to measure them. Gold, consequently, after being converted into paper, will exchange for less of manufactured articles in our markets than in others, that is, manufactured articles will exchange for more gold here than else-where. Foreign producers, accordingly, are making the exchange as fast as we can consume their commodities. We are importing finished products, and confine our exports to raw produce. Our commerce is all one-sided, and our manufactures have lost all power of expansion.

To revise the tariff will not remedy the evil. It will leave our producers laboring under all the disadvantages the currency inflicts upon them. It will not restore the cost of production to a normal state, nor increase the purchasing power of gold in our markets. Indeed, our home producers might claim that the defects of the currency impose upon them a burden from which their foreign rivals are free, and that they are entitled to a duty to offset this disadvantage. Even the gatherers of ice might claim with reason that the expenses of their business have been increased thirty per cent. by the use of paper money, and that, as the premium on gold only makes good ten per cent. of this difference, they are entitled to a duty of five to ten per cent., sufficient, when added to the cost of transportation, to prevent their Canadian neighbors from underselling them. The same claim might be made with equal reason by any of our producers who are subject to foreign competition. The tariff troubles them the least. Paper money is the root of the evil.

The true way to protect and diversify our home industry is to cheapen the cost of production, as measured in coin; to increase the value of gold in exchange; to let prices seek their natural relations, so that our merchandise will be cheaper than gold, and not gold cheaper than our merchandise. If we desire to foster our commerce and manufactures we must make it an object to foreigners to exchange their commodities for our commodities, and not their commodities for our gold and bonds. We must learn the lesson our British cousins know so well, how to undersell at gold prices.

There are two things needed to cheapen the cost of production in this country, as measured in gold. The first and most important is to make gold, or its equivalent, our only money; to restore specie payments in fact as well as in name, and then to restrain the issues of bank-notes within natural limits.

The second and less important is to confine the tariff to a few leading articles, and leave all raw materials on the free list.

But the first remedy should precede the other. To enlarge the free list to its proper proportions while paper money is giving to foreign manufacturers an advantage of twenty to thirty per cent. over home manufacturers would bring free trade into disrepute. On the other hand, when both of these measures are adopted, the surpassing natural resources of our country, and the greater efficiency of our more intelligent labor, will enable us to so completely undersell all competitors, not only in our own markets, but in the markets of the world, that a protective tariff will never again be mentioned save in derision.

The law of the circulation of the precious metals is at the bottom of the tariff, as well as of the currency question. When we have learned to obey it, we shall gain the leadership of the commerce and manufactures of the world, and make England as much a commercial appendage of the United States as Canada now is.

When the effect of the tariff is contrasted with that of paper money in diminishing the profits of those engaged in agriculture, the latter is still found to be the greater source of evil. In this country the agriculturist is unable to escape his taxes by adding them to the prices of his products, whether the taxes are imposed directly on his land, or indirectly in the prices of what he consumes. There are conditions under which he can do so. Thus, in a country where agricultural products are neither exported nor imported, the value of such products will be regulated by the cost of producing them on the least favorable lands, in accordance with Ricardo's theory of rent. In that case, all taxes, being additions to the cost of production, are charged in the prices of the produce. But in the United States a surplus of agricultural products has always been raised, and is likely to be for many generations to come. But when the price of a whole crop must come down to that of the exported surplus, the producers evidently cannot add their taxes to the prices of their produce. In addition to this, the opening of new lands, which follows the extension of railways at the West, is equivalent, so far as the Eastern farmers are concerned, to the importation of supplies from a country where the cost of production is less, and deprives them of the power to enhance prices in their own markets. It is only when supplying the local market of some great city that they can increase the prices of those articles which are too bulky for distant transportation. Our farming class consequently has the least power of shifting the burden of taxation of any portion of the community, and the tariff, so far as it is a tax on consumption, bears more heavily on that class than on any other.*

It has also a direct effect of its own in depressing the prices of agricultural products. This follows from the nature of money. As the amount of exchanges which can be effected with a given amount of money is limited, taxation cannot affect general prices. It causes a redistribution of prices enhancing certain commodities, and depressing others. Under a tariff on raw materials, the commodities enhanced are manufactured articles into which raw materials enter, and

* The statement contained in the report made in 1871 by the New York commissioners on local taxation, that taxes "if placed upon land will constitute an element of the cost of that which the land produces," has been sharply criticised. The correct explanation of the effect of such taxation seems to be that above given. It is worth remarking, also, that the test proposed for duties is the one by which all taxes should be tried. What effect does the tax have on prices? As under a perfect system, taxation would have no effect on prices, so that tax is the best which affects prices the least.

those depressed, to make the money equal to the exchanges to be effected with it, are agricultural products, coal, and petroleum, into which raw materials do not enter. Grosvenor, iu his late work on protection, has collected the statistics showing that, in every period of high duties, the goods which the farmer consumes have ruled high, while his crops have ruled low.* Unable to account for the latter fact, he simply remarks that "high tariffs in some way deprive the farmer of a fair price for his products." The explanation is plain. A high tariff widely diffused causes a redistribution of prices to make the money equal to the circulation, enhancing the prices of what the farmer buys, and depressing the prices of what he sells.

But our present currency has precisely the same effect, and in a far higher degree. It iuflates paper prices and lowers gold prices; while the farmer buys only for paper, and sells really at gold values. Paper money, by increasing the cost of production in manufactures, and by its effect on retail prices, is a far greater tax on consumption than any tariff ever devised. But, as articles of export must follow the price of gold, the farmer is helpless against this tax, and, as gold has been made one of the cheapest commodities in the country, the currency has a power in depressing the prices of agricultural products in comparison with which that of the tariff is infinitesimal.

In promoting an unequal distribution of wealth also, paper money is a more powerful agent than the present or any other tariff. When men are taxed according to their wants, instead of according to their abilities; when taxes are proportioned to consump-

---

* "Does Protection Protect?" p. 264.

tion instead of to wealth, the poor man finds his wants as pressing as those of his richer neighbor; and, unlike the latter, can make no savings upon which to found a competency.   Not only is paper money a greater tax on consumption than the tariff, but it has also a peculiar effect of its own in rendering the distribution of wealth unequal.   It increases the cost of production, causes prices to fluctuate, and renders credit less accessible.   Greater capital is thus made necessary in business operations, and the natural advantages of the larger capitalist over the smaller are doubled.   Paper money makes it more easy to swell great fortunes, and less easy to found small ones.   It benefits only the rich.   It is the poor man's curse.

CHAPTER XIII.

THE questions to which an inconvertible currency
gives rise are peculiarly questions of morality. When,
by force of law, the standard which measures every
pecuniary obligation is made to fluctuate continually,
one of the parties to every such obligation is licensed
to rob the other. Disastrous as is the effect of such a
currency on the material prosperity of a country, the
manner in which it thus violates good morals is a still
stronger objection to it. But, as this immorality can
only be made apparent by a slight process of reasoning, it is often overlooked, or the conclusions arrived
at in respect to it are diametrically opposite. Yet the
moral questions growing out of an inconvertible currency are of simple solution, and any differences of
opinion about them arise more from self-interest than
from the intrinsic difficulties of the subject.

The primary use of money is to be a standard of
values, as invariable as the uncertainty of all things
earthly will permit. Hence the thing which is the
most stable in value of any known commodity is selected for the office. To this thing, for the sake of
convenience, a name is given. The name, however,
does not affect its value. A certain number of grains

of gold are called a dollar. If a less number receive the name, the value of the gold is the same, though the thing called a dollar is changed. But, in measuring value, it is the thing, and not the name, which is used as the standard. When a plough is sold for a given number of dollars, it is the intention of the parties to exchange it for a known commodity, as much as if it were bartered for a given quantity of wheat. It is in substituting the name dollar for the thing dollar that morality is violated. A smaller measure takes the place of the real measure, and the party to whom money is paid receives less value than is his due.

It is from the same source that the differences of opinion, as to the moral obligations of contracts made with reference to such a standard, arise. One party to a discussion means by the word dollar the thing. Another party means the name, or a thing of less value, to which the name has been temporarily given. The same person also, at one time means by dollar the name merely; but, when his interest in the question is changed, insists that a dollar is one particular thing, to wit : a certain amount of gold, and that the name can mean nothing else.

In a country where paper dollars, convertible on demand into real dollars, have always been used as money, it is easy to substitute the name for the thing as the standard of values, without shocking the public sense of justice. The quality of convertibility may then by law be taken from the paper money, without the immorality of the measure being perceived. The habit of looking upon the paper dollar as a mere symbol becomes so inveterate that it is not understood that, when it is in fact made a symbol, it is also made an instrument of robbery. If an Act of Congress were passed authorizing every man who owed a thousand dollars to be acquitted of his debt by paying five hundred dollars, a universal outcry would arise against legalized robbery. But when, in 1862, by substituting the name dollar for the thing dollar, a free license was given to debtors throughout the United States to rob their creditors, the objectors met only with derision. Creditors, it was answered, received all the dollars their contracts called for, and, though robbed of half their property, were said not to be wronged; for " a dollar is whatever the law makes a dollar." The terrorism of public opinion was used to suppress the suggestions of morality, and the supposed necessities of the occasion silenced justice.

Several circumstances attending the issue of greenbacks not only added to the immorality of the measure, but tended also to diminish the public appreciation of it.

If Congress had expressly restricted the effect of the legal-tender act to contracts made after its passage, the violation of justice would have been less, and the difference between gold and paper would have been brought home to all. But, by specifically excepting past debts from the operation of the law, the object of passing it would have been in part defeated. Greenbacks were issued in order to borrow money by a forced loan. They obtained immediate and general currency, because by their use debtors transferred less value to their creditors in paying their debts, and were none the less acquitted in full.

But, demoralizing as was the action of Congress in

passing the legal-tender act, that of the courts in interpreting it was still more so. Law was never more completely divorced from justice than in the judicial decisions which have grown out of this act. The courts of every State where greenbacks circulate have not only sustained the legality of such money, but in so doing have needlessly violated the principles of morality.

The judges who have upheld the legal-tender act have not endeavored to restrict its effect, as if enforcing with reluctance an odious law, but, on the contrary, have seemed eager to extend it to cases which might well have been considered beyond its scope. Thus no distinction has been made between debts contracted prior to, and those contracted subsequent to, the passage of the act. Yet it does not, in express terms, refer to past debts, and a way was left open to the Courts to diminish the immorality of the law without annulling it. For the questions, whether Congress has power to make paper a legal tender, and whether it has power to make it a legal tender in payment of debts already incurred, are wholly independent of one another. If Congress has the first power, it certainly has no right, by a retroactive enactment, to deprive men of their property without due process of law, and no law ought to be construed so as to have that effect, when it does not, in express terms, include the case.* Yet it has been held by

---

* Since the above was written, the Supreme Court, in Hepburn vs. Griswold, has held that the legal-tender act by its terms was intended to apply to debts contracted before its passage.

That decision, made before the Court had forfeited respect, deserves consideration. The reasons given are not convincing. The

the highest Court of the leading State of the Union, not in the first excitement of the war, when the plea of necessity ruled, but after peace had given reason an opportunity to resume its sway, that a contract made in 1857 to pay $1,400 " in gold and silver coin,

rule of construction is well settled, that no law will be construed to have a retroactive effect, so as to injure vested rights or to deprive men of their property, unless the retroactive intent is expressly specified in the law. But if it is assumed that the legal-tender act, when construed retroactively, deprives men of their property, it must be assumed, also, that the Congress which passed it knew that such would be its effect, and had in mind, at the time of passing it, the rule of construction above mentioned. The legal inference is, that having, with this knowledge, omitted to make the act specifically retroactive, the intent was, that such a construction should not be given to it. It may be said that Congress, being ignorant of these rules of law, in fact intended the reverse. Very true. But ignorance of the law excuses no man. It excuses neither the legislators who make our laws, nor the judges who construe them.

The other reason assigned is equally lame. It is inferred that, because interest and duties only are excepted from the legal-tender clause, therefore no other debts can be included within the exceptions. Very true again. But whether preëxisting debts are included within the exceptions, and whether the law was intended to apply to preëxisting debts at all, are distinct questions. To settle the first negatively, does not settle the other affirmatively. When things intrinsically different are included in the same classification, a quality belonging to part of the class ought not to be predicated of the whole. To classify debts according to their subject-matter, as, for instance, duties on imports, interest on the public debt, and principal of the public debt, and to infer that, because the first two are excepted from the legal-tender clause, and the last one is not, therefore, duties and interest are payable in coin, and the principal in legal tender, would be strictly logical. But, to classify debts according to the time when made, and to determine that the members of this class are without or within the legal-tender clause, lawful money of the United States," was fully satisfied by a tender of treasury-notes, the market value of which, at the time of the tender, as compared with gold, was as one to two and twenty-five hundredths.* Similar decisions have been made in fifteen other States, and finally in the Supreme Court of the United States; and this is now the settled law of the land.

No one will deny that it is a plain principle of justice that a law changing the standard of weights or measures ought not to be applied to obligations already incurred. When the statutes of the State of New York were revised, so as to affect the standard of weights and measures, the operation of the law was expressly restricted to future transactions.† It was provided that "all contracts thereafter to be executed" should be construed to be made according to the new standard. Now, the effect of changing the measure of value is the same as the effect of changing any other measure. One who agrees to sell a bushel of wheat for a dollar is equally robbed under color of law if, before the agreement is fulfilled, the quantity of wheat which legally constitutes a bushel is increased, or the quantity of gold which legally constitutes a dollar is diminished. It would be as easy to give the name bushel to one hundred pounds of wheat, instead of sixty, as to give the name

according as they are included or not in the exceptions of the other class, is bad in logic, whatever it may be in law.

If, therefore, it be admitted that money is always a commodity, it follows, from the accepted canons of construction, that the legal-tender clause was not intended to embrace debts dated before its passage.

* Rodes *vs.* Bronson, 34 New York Rep., 649.

† Revised Statutes, 3d edition, p. 777.

dollar to fifteen grains of gold, instead of twenty-five and eight-tenths grains, and it would be as immoral to apply the new standard to obligations already incurred in the one case as in the other.

When individuals attempt to defraud the community by using false weights and measures, the offence is punished as a crime. But when the government, by establishing a false standard of value, makes fraud a part of every pecuniary obligation, the judges throughout the land hasten to extend the operation of the law. Yet, in the one case, it is only a few retailers who cheat their customers, while, in the other, every debtor is enabled to rob his creditors. In the kind of immorality the transactions are identical. But in degree the petty frauds of the shops cannot be compared with robbery that covers a continent.

But the most immoral decisions to which the legal-tender act has led are those invalidating specific agreements to pay in coin. When the parties to a contract agree, with full knowledge of the difference in value between treasury-notes and coin, and in consideration of that difference, that the debt shall be paid in coin only, a decision which enables the debtor to violate his covenant by paying in paper, wrongs the creditor as much as the act of the thief who filches his pocket-book. No substitution of a name for a thing can cover its immorality; for the parties have distinctly specified what they understand by the word dollar. Nor have these decisions the poor excuse of necessity. When two things of unequal value are made by law a legal tender, the only way to give full effect to both laws is to permit individuals to specify under which law their agreements are made.

The premise from which all these expositions of the legal-tender act are deduced is too plainly false for argument. A dollar is not only a name, but it is also a thing, and the invariability of the thing to which the name is given is the most essential quality of money. Yet it is gravely asserted that value is purely an ideal thing; that it is a quality of money which the law does not recognize, and that the parties to every contract take the risk of any change in the value of the thing called money, before the contract is completed. It is decided that, if a creditor receives the number of dollars agreed upon, although the value of his claim has been reduced " by the agency of paper money, or by simply debasing the gold and silver coin of the country," the contract, nevertheless, has been literally complied with. That such a proceeding is robbery seems never to have dawned upon the judicial mind. Yet it is only in treating of the standard of value that a name is mistaken for a thing. If the name bushel were given to thirty pounds of wheat instead of sixty, any attempt to apply the new standard to agreements already entered into would be speedily suppressed. There is no magic in a name which can work the miracle of turning thirty bushels of wheat into sixty. Yet the opinion prevails in our courts that the name dollar can work a similar miracle with gold.

The same opinion seems to have invaded the pulpits of the country. Whatever may be the theoretical morality of theologians, no case is known where any have hesitated to avail themselves of the legal-tender act to pay, in depreciated paper, debts contracted before its passage. On the contrary, when greenbacks

13

were producing the greatest exhilaration, appeals resounded through the land from pastors to parishioners, entreating them to pay the mortgages on their churches while money was plenty. What greater inconsistency than for one, professing to believe in "a higher law" relieving him from obedience to human laws, which conflict with morality, to preface with such an appeal a sermon from the text, "a false balance is abomination to the Lord; but a just weight is his delight!"

When Congress, the courts, and the pulpits, were so demoralized by paper money, it would have been strange if the people had not been similarly affected. Such was the case. The money provided by the legal-tender act was generally accepted as a means of paying past debts.

In transactions between individuals, this was perhaps unavoidable. But there was no necessity for paying in greenbacks public debts contracted in gold; for taxes could have been increased, in nominal amount, to correspond with the depreciation of the money in which they were paid, without thereby increasing their real amount. Nevertheless, every State where greenbacks were forced into circulation, with one exception, repudiated a portion of its funded debt by paying its creditors in depreciated paper. To Massachusetts alone belongs the distinguished honor of simple honesty. The amount saved by these acts of repudiation was hardly worth the stain they left. The time for the payment of the principal of all the State debts could have been easily extended, and it was only foreign creditors who asked for payment of their interest in gold. Yet when an honorable effort was made to save the good name of the State of New York, by paying the interest on its debt according to contract, the offer was rejected with scorn. Not to support greenbacks was then to be an object of suspicion. To sustain robbery became a test of "loyalty." But a more disgraceful act of repudiation transpired as late as 1868, after necessity could no longer be used as a shield for crime. When the foreign holders of stock of the State of Pennsylvania, which had been negotiated in coin many years before, protested through their agent against "the injustice of the action of that State in forcing its creditors to accept payment in a depreciated currency," the State Treasurer replied : "Your complaints about the injustice of our not paying you in gold may seem just to you, but to us they seem ridiculous."

If this man had spoken for himself alone, his act might have been passed over as a mere sporadic case of moral obliquity. But he claimed to speak for others, and subsequent events have rendered it probable that he had measured correctly the opinions of those whom he represented. It is certainly a fact that the moral sense of the country has been so debauched by paper money that a transaction which ought to have forever disgraced every one approving of it, hardly excited remark.

But immorality of a still more inexcusable kind has resulted in this country from tampering with the standard of value. It is beginning to be generally understood at the present time that to lower the standard is to transfer property from one person to another without the consent of the loser, and without any merit of the gainer. Greenbacks are beginning to be recognized in their true character as instruments of robbery. Yet the advance in morality is small. Those who are loudest in asserting that greenbacks are instruments of robbery are endeavoring to remedy the wrong by making them the instruments of a far greater robbery than any yet committed. It is seriously proposed by the first men of the nation to add a percentage to every debt in the country by enhancing the standard of value; and the best reason that can be given to justify the wrong is, that, because creditors have been robbed, it is now the turn of debtors to meet the same fate. Those who style themselves bullionists now fail to practice the fundamental idea of their creed, and refuse to accept the fact that gold has never ceased to be the standard by which the value of the false standard has been measured. One who really believes that a dollar is only a name can be excused for wishing to tamper with the value of the thing which bears the name. But one who believes that value only can measure value, ought to know that to increase the value of the dollar, so as to affect debts already incurred, is to rob every one who has debts to pay. Yet the bullionists of the country, instead of opposing, have favored this wrong. The policy of resuming specie payments, by elevating the currency to the standard of coin, has met with many opponents. Merchants have feared the bankruptcy it would cause; politicians have trembled at the loss of votes that would follow. But the more fundamental objection to that policy, the fact that it is a crime, has been avoided by all, and by none more than by bullionists.

No argument is necessary to prove that to elevate

the standard by which values are measured, with no exception of past obligations, is as immoral as it is to lower it— As one who has agreed to sell a bushel of wheat for a dollar is robbed if, before the completion of the contract, by operation of law the quantity of wheat in a bushel is increased, or the amount of gold in a dollar is diminished; so one who has agreed to buy a bushel of wheat for a dollar is in like manner robbed if, before the agreement is fulfilled, the quantity of wheat in a bushel is diminished, or the amount of gold in a dollar is increased. As a creditor who holds a note for one thousand dollars would be robbed of five hundred dollars, if compelled by law to receive one half the amount of the debt in full satisfaction of it, so the debtor would be equally robbed of five hundred dollars if compelled by law to pay fifteen hundred dollars on his note. The rule works both ways. Debtors may be wronged as well as creditors by changing the standard of value.

Whether the wrong is committed by directly changing the weight of gold in the coined dollar, or by changing the amount of gold its paper representative will realize, is immaterial. If it were decreed by law that the word bushel in all the wheat certificates current on the Chicago Board of Trade should mean one hundred pounds instead of sixty, not only would the warehousemen be robbed, but also every seller of an option for future delivery. Yet to change the meaning of the word dollar in a coin certificate is in effect the same as to change the meaning of the word bushel in a wheat certificate. When the paper used as money is inconvertible, the effect is still the same. The note then becomes a stamped counter, and is worth what it

will bring in real money. To change the latter amount
is like changing the number of grains of gold in a
coined dollar, or the number of pounds in a bushel.
The plan of resuming specie payments by turning
greenback debts into gold at their face is more immoral than to change the measure of wheat from bushels into centals without excepting past contracts; for
the latter would affect only those who had agreed to
buy or sell wheat, while the former would affect the
parties to every contract to pay money.

But, while the immorality of debasing and that of
appreciating the standard of value are the same in
kind, in degree the latter is the worse. It could
hardly fail to bring commerce to a stand-still, and
bankrupt every one in debt. Some writers argue that
merchants, having full notice of the change, could ar-
range their liabilities accordingly; as if giving a man
notice that you intend to rob him lessens the crime.
It is also claimed that the process being gradual, the
suffering would be less; as if a series of petty larcenies
from many would be less wrong than a grand larceny
from a few. But neither notice to all the world, nor
any protraction of the operation, can remove its wick-
edness. One of the foundations of our social organization is credit. It pervades commerce. Our banks
are founded on it, from the bills they issue to the deposits they receive and the notes they discount.
Credit enters into all mercantile operations, however
much it may at times be curtailed. Nearly all our
States, cities, counties, and towns, have funded debts
contracted during the war. Our public works are
built on credit. The bonds of railroads and other
corporations are counted by millions. But wherever

there is credit there must be a contract of indebtedness and two parties to it. To elevate the standard of value in which debts are paid, is to transfer the property of one of these parties to the other by a trick of legislation. If all the obligations to pay money existing at any one time in this country (not including the public debt of the United States) are estimated as low as three thousand millions of dollars, then to suddenly elevate the value of the greenback dollar from eighty cents to one hundred cents, is to fraudulently transfer six hundred millions of dollars from debtor to creditor; and, though there are many persons who are both debtors and creditors, the wrong of such transfer would be slightly alleviated, but not removed by that fact. If the operation should be prolonged through a series of years, the transfer would take place none the less, though the loss would be distributed among a greater number of debtors, but, as the amount of the exchanges effected with the advancing standard would be larger, the aggregate amount of the robbery would probably be greater. Not only would the losers be robbed under color of law, but the property of the poor would be transferred to the rich. The heaviest loss would fall upon the active and enterprising. The young men struggling to start in the world would be crushed, while those whose fortunes are already made would be further enriched without effort.

But, in order to resume specie payments, something more would be necessary than to elevate treasury notes to the standard of coin. There must be a decline in the prices of every thing bought and sold. The purchasing power of the greenback currency

must be made equal to that of a purely metallic currency, and as the loss of purchasing power, which
greenbacks have undergone, as measured by general
prices, is considerably greater than the apparent loss
represented by the premium on gold, the loss to the
debtor class by increasing the purchasing power of
the present currency to the level of a metallic currency, would be more accurately represented by considering greenbacks worth seventy to eighty cents on
the dollar, instead of ninety. That is to say, the
amount of property which debtors would be obliged
to sell in order to realize a given sum of money would
be increased by a percentage considerably greater
than that represented by the premium on gold.

Now, there would be no way by which debtors
could protect themselves against this loss. Those
whose obligations are already incurred would be compelled to pay from twenty to thirty per cent. more
value than they received when the debts were contracted. Those whose indebtedness will be incurred
while the process of appreciation is going on, will not
have the same means of defence which capitalists
could use while the inflation was in progress. A specific contract law would enable creditors to avoid any
loss from a depreciation of the currency, but it would
not protect debtors against loss from its appreciation.
Capitalists holding treasury notes, soon to become
equal to gold by operation of law, would not sacrifice the premium by converting them into gold immediately. On the contrary, they would turn gold into
greenbacks, and loan the latter, in order to obtain a
transfer to themselves, under color of law, of the
property of their debtors. Measured by its effects,

the policy of elevating a depreciated currency to the standard of gold is more immoral than the opposite policy of depreciating it.

Nor can the immorality of such a policy be palliated by "the tyrant's plea." Necessity is made to answer for the original issue of greenbacks. But important as is a speedy resumption of specie payments to the prosperity of the country, there is no necessity of reaching that end by increasing the value of the present depreciated currency to an equality with gold. The easiest way to resume specie payments is to abandon the policy of appreciation, and to withdraw greenbacks, by funding them without enhancing their market value in gold. Even in that way it would be difficult to prevent creditors from having the advantage. Greenbacks were made an instrument of robbing creditors on the plea of necessity. That plea cannot be used when it is proposed to make them an instrument for robbing debtors. For, in this case, the path of honesty is the easiest to follow. That any other has ever been suggested, results from the illusions of paper money.

If the value of the coin had been directly debased, it would never have been seriously proposed to restore it to the ancient standard, so as to add a percentage to every pecuniary obligation. A law commanding every one, who had agreed to pay one thousand grains of gold for a certain quantity of property, to pay instead twelve hundred grains, could not be enforced in this age. Giving the same name to the different amounts of gold would deceive nobody. Hence it has followed that, where despotic princes have debased their coin, in order to rob their creditors, the original standard has not been restored. A pound sterling, as its name implies, contained in the reign of Edward I. one pound troy of standard silver. To-day it contains a little less than one-third of the original amount. The coin of England at the present time, as compared with that of Edward I., is as 20 to $66\frac{13}{100}$. The French livre, likewise, has undergone successive debasements, until the corresponding coin now contains but one-seventy-eighth part of its original pound of silver.

These fraudulent changes of the standard of value have usually been in one direction. Creditors only have been robbed by them. It was reserved for the despotism of a free government to rob first creditors, and then debtors. By means of the transparent illusion of paper money, the attempt is now making to perpetrate the most gigantic swindle that ever found honest advocates. But the plan of increasing the amount of gold which constitutes a dollar, and that of raising the greenback dollar to the par of specie, are so plainly identical that the scheme is not likely to succeed. It is easier, and more honest, to continue to follow the precedent of debased coin; to let the paper dollar remain at the point of debasement it has reached, and resume specie payments by settling past debts according to the value of the money in which they were contracted.

But, while the honesty of such a policy is admitted in general, it is claimed that there is one class of debtors whose obligations, though contracted in depreciated paper, can be turned into gold, dollar for dollar, without any violation of morality, namely, the tax-payers. Yet the right of one generation to hand down to its successors a mortgaged government, is at best a matter of doubt. The modern funding system, with its accompaniment of indirect taxation, is as surely calculated as the land tenures of the feudal system, but in a less degree, to produce inequality of conditions and an unjust distribution of wealth. It is one of the agencies by which fraud has been substituted for force in modern times, as a means for enabling the few to bestride the many.

To encumber any country, then, with an enormous debt, is a proceeding which ought to undergo the severest scrutiny, and every step of which ought to be beyond suspicion. The consideration which the United States received for the present debt, at a gold valuation, has been variously estimated. It is probable, however, that the purchasing power of the money in which the debt was contracted, had fallen, on an average, owing to the improvident issues of paper, to sixty cents on the dollar. To pay the debt in gold, then, will be to defraud the tax-payers of the country of one thousand millions of dollars. Of the immorality of such a transaction there can be no doubt. The only question would be to decide from what time the immorality should be dated. If there is a valid agreement to pay the debt in gold, the agreement must be carried out according to its terms. For one generation has a legal right, under our laws, to bind its successors. In that case, the wrong would date from the time of incurring the debt. The wrong-doers would be those who were so weak or ignorant as to contract a debt in depreciated paper, and agree to pay it in gold. If, on the other hand, there is no legal obligation to pay the debt in gold, the immorality has not yet been committed, and may be prevented. In that case, those who advocate immorality are those who would rob posterity, by adding, without any new consideration, a thousand millions of dollars to the burdens of the tax-payers. If, therefore, a promise to pay gold did not enter into the contract at its inception, to make such a promise, without any new consideration, would be to taint the whole debt with fraud.

No examination of the immorality of an inconvertible currency would be complete, without mention of its more general effects in demoralizing society.

When, by fluctuations of the value of the standard by which values are measured, the prices of all commodities vary incessantly, the element of gambling enters into all business transactions, and the commercial morality of the nation is undermined. The desire to acquire riches suddenly, and without labor, then becomes contagious. Honest toil, with its slow returns, gives place to speculation, amid the excitement of which the stern requirements of morality are forgotten. Men naturally honest, who, treading the firm foundation of specie, would never have gone astray, deluded by paper money, are enticed into hazardous ventures, and find themselves defaulters before they are conscious of wrong. The bank defalcations, so common as no longer to excite surprise, the countless peculations and forgeries, which have taken place during the era of greenbacks, show the corruption they produce. Specie payments are desirable, if for no other reason, to revive honesty in those filling places of trust.

This haste to be rich is at the bottom of the political corruption of the times. When speculation pervades all business, it stalks boldly into the public

offices, and our legislators and tax-gatherers, instead
of laboring for the good of the people, make their positions mere stand-points for jobbery and money-getting; while the public morals having fallen to the
Spartan level, we blame our officers, not for stealing,
but for being caught. From the same source proceed
in part the evils of the " ring " formations of the day.
In a country of Democratic equality, where, though
individuality is preserved, individuals have ceased to
be great, a tendency arises for those having some
common interest to unite for promoting some common
end, and, while the individuals remain at their former
level, the union becomes great. This tendency is
seen in the formation of corporations for every purpose, and in their tendency to consolidate after being
formed. It appears also in the combinations of workmen to put up wages, of merchants to put up goods,
of capitalists to put up stocks, and of politicians to se-
cretly plunder the people, while openly abusing one
another for falsity to public interests a thousand miles
away. Much of the strength of these combinations,
except of those of the workmen, is derived from paper
money, and, though they would exist without it, they
push to the utmost all its evil effects. Politicians take
advantage of the preoccupation of business men in
money-getting to transfer the government to the scum
of a great city, and the frauds which are bred in one
class are duplicated in the other. While the leaders
of Wall Street make over-issues of stocks, the representatives of the Five Points forge vouchers. It is on the
stock exchange that the worst scandals have transpired. In the whirl of money-getting, nothing succeeds like success. The means employed are immate-

rial. In the general corruption that prevails, courts and legislatures uphold the one who wins. He is the best "operator" who can steal a railway, and buy a judge. Nor are the Erie frauds without a parallel. Those who issued new stock so as to depreciate the value of that outstanding, merely followed the example of the United States, which by issuing legal-tender notes depreciated all outstanding debts. Necessity compelled the directors of the Erie Railway to keep their offices by printing certificates to vote on, and thus robbing the other stockholders. An alleged necessity compelled the United States to make a forced loan by printing legal-tender notes, and robbing every creditor in the land. But unfortunately the parallel does not end here. The "Erie Ring," it is alleged, tampered with our judges to sustain a fraud. But how has the legal-tender fraud been upheld? When the Supreme Court, following the teachings of political economy and of common sense, had decided that as a contract to pay dollars, made while coin was the only tender, was an agreement to deliver bullion of a certain weight and fineness, therefore a law compelling a creditor to accept depreciated paper in its place was void, two lawyers, who in the course of their business had announced a different opinion, were forthwith added to the judges on the bench, and these, instead of declining, as decency suggested, to review the question under such circumstances, proceeded to revive in our midst the realism of the twelfth century, and announced once more the crude absurdity that a dollar is only a name, that value is an ideal thing. Yet so drunk is the nation with money-getting, that neither the immorality of this decision, nor the shameless manner of obtaining it, has shocked the public sense of right.

There is but one way to revive in the public mind the distinctions between right and wrong in pecuniary transactions, and that is, by returning to a measure of values that does not fluctuate. If in the process financial distress arises, and bankruptcy is widespread, such trials are needed to clear the moral atmosphere. Thus will men be taught to live by labor, instead of by their wits; to try and get rich by slow accumulations, and not by a single stroke. Corruption, we may be sure, will diminish with speculation. Honest dollars will bring honest men.

CHAPTER XIV.

THE reasons for the belief that a currency not convertible into coin on demand is a curse to the country in which it circulates having been given, it remains to examine the means by which such a currency may be replaced by the one Nature has provided. Of the seven great nations afflicted at the present time with irredeemable paper, all save one are prevented, by the necessities which involved them in the difficulty, from attempting to escape it. Fortunately, the resources of the United States are so unlimited that a resumption of specie payments in this country can be prevented only by a lack of will, and not of ability. But, while it is generally admitted that the evils of our present system ought to be removed, the chief difficulty in the way of effecting the change seems to be a disagreement as to. the proper method of bringing it about.

Of the several measures proposed for effecting a resumption of specie payments, that known as contraction is most worthy of consideration. As the suspension of specie payments was caused by excessive issues of paper, the conclusion is natural that resumption can be accomplished by the reverse process of diminishing the amount of those issues. The effect of this measure in bringing production to a stand-still, and the immorality of enhancing the standard by which all values are measured, have already been stated. Whether the scheme is practicable remains to be considered.

The possibility of replacing our inconvertible government currency with a bank currency based on coin, by arbitrarily withdrawing treasury notes from circulation, will depend upon the amount of them it would become necessary to cancel before that result could be reached. It is customary in some quarters to deride all attempts to compute the amount of paper money which it is possible to keep convertible into coin on demand, and to assert that such computations are unreliable and useless. A contrary opinion was expressed by John Adams many years ago, in language worth repeating:

"The amount of ordinary commerce, external and internal, of a country," he says, "may be computed at a fixed sum. A certain sum of money is necessary to circulate among the society in order to carry on their business. This precise sum is discoverable by calculation, and reducible to certainty. You may emit paper or any other currency for this purpose, until you reach this rule, and it will not depreciate. After you exceed this rule, it will depreciate, and no power or act of legislation hitherto invented can prevent it." *

* John Adams's Works, vol. vii., p. 195, cited by Bowen, p. 381

If the functions of money and the laws that regulate its circulation have been heretofore stated with correctness, the data upon which this calculation must be based can be readily ascertained. Under the law of the circulation of the precious metals, the amount of specie which circulates in each country bears a fixed relation to the amount of specie which circulates in every other country with which it has commercial relations. No one country can permanently retain more than its share of the circulating medium of the world. The amount of paper money also convertible into coin on demand which can circulate in any country will just equal, or be but a trifle in excess of, the specie which would circulate in that country if paper money were not used. It is possible, therefore, to ascertain approximately the amount of paper convertible into coin on demand, which can be kept afloat in the United States. That amount will be found by taking the sum of that which circulated before the suspension of specie payments, and adding to it an allowance for the growth and development of the country since that time. It was shown in Chapter IV. that the convertible bank-notes, which were ordinarily in circulation during the generation preceding the war, were always fully equal to the natural specie circulation of the country, and frequently in excess of it. The United States always had as much and frequently more paper money afloat than it was possible to keep convertible into coin on demand. The following table shows the amount of paper money in circulation at the beginning of each year from 1834 to 1868, omitting the fractions of millions :

Year.	Value.	Year.	Value.
1834	$95,000,000	1852 estimated	$150,000,000
1835	104,000,000	1853	146,000,000
1836	140,000,000	1854	205,000,000
1837	149,000,000	1855	187,000,000
1838	116,000,000	1856	196,000,000
1839	135,000,000	1857	215,000,000
1840	107,000,000	1858	135,000,000
1841	107,000,000	1859	193,000,000
1842	84,000,000	1860	207,000,000
1843	59,000,000	1861	202,000,000
1844	75,000,000	1862	218,000,000
1845	90,000,000	1863	529,000,000
1846	105,000,000	1864	636,000,000
1847	106,000,000	1865	948,000,000
1848	129,000,000	1866	919,000,000
1849	115,000,000	1867	852,000,000
1850	131,000,000	1868	767,000,000
1851	155,000,000		

Compound interest notes, and the three per cent. certificates used as part of the bank reserves, are included during the war years. The amount of paper in circulation has been nearly stationary since 1868, and no statistics are necessary for the subsequent period.

The average bank circulation during the twenty-six years prior to 1860 was less than $139,000,000. The amount of exchanges to be effected, and the money necessary to effect them, are undoubtedly greater now than before the suspension of cash payments, so that there is need of a greater amount of money than ever before. But the increase is very much less than is commonly supposed. The above table does not show any enormous increase in periods of ten years. If to the circulation of 1861 fifty millions be added for the growth of the country in the intervening time, the sum would probably be above the amount of convertible paper which would readily circulate at the present day. If an expansion of bank-notes to two hundred and seventeen millions in 1857 ended in a panic and a general suspension of specie payments, it is probable that two hundred and fifty millions of convertible paper is all the country could use in 1872. But, if advantage is taken of the occasion to suppress small bills and establish a bank-note circulation strictly convertible on demand, it is reasonable to set a lower limit, and to believe that the average bank-note circulation that the country could readily use is about two hundred millions of dollars. To avoid question, however, the former may be assumed to be the true sum. In all these amounts the money composing the bank reserves is included; for that portion of it used as a reserve to meet deposits, though apparently idle, has, in fact, the greatest rapidity of circulation or effective power of any money in use. Bank deposits, on the other hand, are excluded; for, although they are used as a medium of exchange, they are not used as a standard of value. They are currency, but not money; an effect and not the cause, varying like prices with the amount of money in circulation. In any consideration of the means of resuming specie payments, the national bank-notes also must be included with the treasury notes as part of the circulating medium. Not only is the government liable for their ultimate redemption, but in their effect, in enhancing prices and disturbing the international exchanges, they differ in no manner from the inconvertible paper into which they are convertible. The legal-tender notes, however, which are actually reserved for the redemption of bank-bills, but not those reserved to meet deposits, may be deducted, to avoid all question. In that case, however, the coin and bullion used by the banks as a part of their reserves must be added.   The total amount of the circulating medium now in use may be stated, then, in round numbers, at seven hundred millions of dollars.   The problem for the contractionists to solve is, how to reduce this seven hundred millions of inconvertible government paper to two hundred and fifty millions of bank paper convertible into specie on demand.   The practical difficulties in the way of every measure yet proposed for accomplishing this result are insurmountable.

1. The first difficulty to be encountered, in carrying into effect such a policy, would come from the diminution of the amount of the precious metals in the country, which has already taken place.   The amount of coin in the United States, exclusive of the Pacific States, before the war, was from two hundred to two hundred and fifty millions.   The former sum is probably the nearer the truth.   The additional amount necessary, at the present time, to effect the increased exchanges consequent on our growth would be about twenty-five millions more.   The reasons for the belief that a very considerable portion of the precious metals has been driven out of the country by the use of a false standard, have been given.   But it is clear that two hundred and fifty millions of paper money cannot be kept convertible into coin on demand, so long as the coin necessary for the purpose is not in the country.   Yet the policy of contraction, so far from attracting back our due share of the precious metals, will drive off another part of that which remains. The premium on gold would be constantly depressed by the general belief that treasury-notes would soon

be raised to par, even if the government ceased to apply artificial means to increase the depression, while, owing to the fact that the surplus currency in circulation must be absorbed, the prices of commodities in general would continue to be inflated. The premium on gold would continue to range lower than general prices. Gold would be the cheapest article of export, and would so remain, until contraction, by bankrupting those in debt, had reduced general prices to panic rates. A preliminary, therefore, to a resumption of specie payments by contracting the currency, ought to be to send the premium on gold, if possible, above the average of general prices, in order to make it the most costly article of export, and a desirable article of import. But to increase the premium on gold is wholly contrary to the theory on which contraction is founded, and would be fatal to the continued prosecution of that policy, by rendering its injustice too plain to be longer concealed by sophistry. A high premium would also keep up the prices of those articles whose prices follow that of gold, and, as more money is necessary to effect exchanges at high than at low prices, the steady diminution of the volume of the currency would be more keenly felt in excessive stringency in the money market. It would follow, also, that, when a sufficient diminution of the currency had taken place to justify an attempt at resumption, a sudden decline of the premium on gold would be necessary, which would hardly fail to precipitate a panic that would cause gold to be hoarded and defeat the attempt.

2. But there is still another practical difficulty in the way of the policy of contraction, equally hard to

escape.   The whole money in circulation in this country before the war, including both coin and paper, was never much, if any, over four hundred millions of dollars.   Allowing for an increase of fifty millions of paper and twenty-five millions of specie, the whole amount necessary at the present time would be from four hundred and seventy-five to five hundred millions. If, then, a contraction of our redundant currency should be enforced, when the present amount of seven hundred millions of paper had been reduced to four hundred and seventy-five or five hundred millions, it would just equal the natural and necessary circulation of the country, and there would be little or no premium on gold.   But it would none the less be impossible to resume specie payments.   For, the instant greenbacks became redeemable on demand, two hundred and seventy-five millions of coin would be added to the circulation, which would then amount to seven hundred and seventy-five millions, being seventy-five millions more than before resumption was attempted. It would be necessary, therefore, to continue the process of contraction until a considerably less amount than five hundred millions was left in circulation. But as the latter sum is the natural and necessary circulation of the country on a specie basis, when the inconvertible paper money was reduced below it, there would not be enough left to effect exchanges, except at a very low range of prices.

Prices would then necessarily fall even below the specie standard.   This would, finally, have the effect of attracting specie into the country from abroad. But any thing more than a momentary resumption of specie payments would even then be impossible.   For if the paper in circulation were reduced to four hundred and fifty millions, the addition of the necessary amount of specie, two hundred and seventy-five millions, would still make the total circulation more than seven hundred millions, and specie payments could not be maintained.

If the amouut of paper money, which can be kept convertible, is two hundred and fifty millions, the present seven hundred millions must be contracted to that sum before resumption can become permanent. But when the .inconvertible paper falls below five hundred millions, the natural circulation of paper and specie combined, there would not be money enough left in circulation to effect the exchanges of the country with ease. To continue the contraction till only two hundred and fifty millions remained in circulation would be plainly impossible. A reduction of the currency below its natural amount took place in England at the close of the Napoleonic wars, and, by causing a decline of prices, it rendered possible the resumption of cash payments. The same phenomenon occurred in this country after the revulsion of 1837, and again after that of 1857, and was the cause, in part, of the stagnation which followed those years. But in the present case the amount of the inconvertible paper is so much more excessive, that a repetition of the process is not possible.

It may be said, however, that the object could be accomplished, without thus reducing the amount of currency in circulation, by hoarding specie in the Sub-Treasury while the contraction was in progress, and after the treasury notes had been considerably reduced in amount, and sufficient specie had been col-

lected, the remainder of the notes could be redeemed
in coin on demand. The notes, continuing in circulation until thus redeemed, would then be destroyed ;
the coin exchanged for them would be restored to circulation, and specie payments would be established at
once.   The amount of specie, however, which this
scheme would cause to be hoarded in the Sub-Treasury,
would be fatal to it. It would be necessary for the
government to possess enough specie to redeem and
cancel all its treasury notes, and as the amount of
national bank-notes is three hundred millions, the
banks also would be compelled to redeem and cancel at least fifty millions of their notes, and stand
ready to redeem the rest on demand. There is no
source from which such great accumulations of specie
could be derived: and if it were possible to make
them the whole supply of gold in the country would
be tied up, and the premium would rise to unheard-of
figures. This is simply a scheme to compel the Treasury to "corner gold." The effect on the policy of
contraction of enhancing the premium on gold has already been sufficiently considered.

3. Whenever a contraction of the legal-tender
notes is enforced, a triple contraction of the instru-
ments·of exchange will take place. Greenbacks, bank-
notes, and bank deposits, will be contracted together ;
besides which, all the instruments of credit used as
currency will be diminished. Bank loans and discounts would then nearly cease. All the resources of
the banks would be required to protect their own notes
and demand liabilities; and even if it were in their
power, they would be slow to make loans to merchants
and business men, the majority of whom would be

14

candidates for bankruptcy. Government bonds would afford an investment for all their loanable funds, with high interest and no risks. If an ordinary bank contraction of a few millions results in a panic and general ruin, it is difficult to estimate the ruin which a government contraction of hundreds of millions, protracted through a series of years, would produce. The contraction which took place in 1866–'68 is not a safe criterion by which to judge of the future. After the close of the war, the withdrawal of the government from the markets as a purchaser, the change of employments, and the universal belief in a speedy return to specie, rendered a general decline of prices inevitable. By this decline a portion of money was thrown out of employment. The necessary exchanges could be effected without it. The contraction of the legal-tender notes was made at this time, and merely absorbed this surplus currency, for which there was no further use. The stagnation which that process caused resulted, not from any want of currency, but from the tendency to hoard treasury notes so as to secure the rise in their value. The contraction never was carried far enough to affect the circulation of the banks. The full limit of three hundred millions of national bank-notes allowed by law was filled when the contraction of greenbacks ceased. The banks had increased their issues during the process, instead of curtailing them. The full effect of the measure on business cannot be known until the contraction of treasury notes has been carried far enough to compel the banks to contract their notes, and consequently their loans. Whenever that point is reached, the whole machinery of exchanges will come to a stand-still. The injustice of enhancing the standard of value so as to affect past debts will become painfully manifest, and, in the reaction that would follow, creditors would be more likely to suffer than debtors.

Since the repeal of the law authorizing the Secretary of the Treasury to contract the legal-tender notes, the policy of contraction has been apparently abandoned; but among its advocates are still numbered nearly all the leading men of the nation, who claim to be versed in political economy and finance, and a return to it may be forced, whenever the danger of losing elections seems sufficiently distant, unless, in the mean time, the illusions of paper money can be dispelled.

Several schemes for bringing about specie payments without contraction have been proposed. But it is unnecessary to refute the errors contained in them. If specie payments cannot be reached by means of contraction, they certainly cannot be reached without it.

The authors of all these quack remedies for restoring the metallic medium, without regard to the amount of paper based on it, overlook the law of the circulation of the precious metals—as stupid a blunder as that of an astronomer who should commence the calculation of an eclipse by denying the law of gravitation. The precious metals circulate from country to country, as if all trade were barter, and as if they had never left the form of bullion. Their use as money only makes the desire for them universal, and renders their movements through the channels of commerce more rapid than those of any other commodity. No one country can retain more than its due share of the metallic medium. Whenever such an excess exists, prices are enhanced, imports are increased, and the specie is sent abroad to pay for them. Whenever inconvertible paper is made convertible into specie on demand, or one portion of it (treasury notes) is made thus convertible, and another portion (bank-notes) is made convertible into the former, the effect on the international exchanges is the same as if the whole paper, less the reserve to meet bank-notes, were, in fact, transmuted into gold. If our seven hundred millions of paper were at once turned into gold, and the gold could be made to circulate as rapidly as paper, general prices would remain as high as they now are, and would be higher in our markets than in any other. Commodities would be attracted hither as fast as we could consume them, and the specie would all be shipped back to pay for them. Gold flows to the country where it will buy the most, and from the country where it will buy the least.

There is another plan for reaching specie payments without trouble, as attractive as it is delusive. As the United States are increasing rapidly in population and wealth, it is popularly believed that by waiting long enough the country will "grow to" the currency now in circulation. Such would undoubtedly be the case. But the important question for consideration is, how long before specie payments would be reached by waiting until the growth of the country rendered necessary a circulating medium of seven hundred millions of dollars in paper. It is maintained by some, that, since inconvertible paper has come into circulation, the method of doing business has changed, owing to an alleged curtailment of the credit systen, so that more money is necessary now to effect the exchanges than before the war. But it is not shown, that with a return to specie payments will not come also a return to former methods of doing business, and until this probability is disproved, no reason can be given for supposing that the amount of money required to effect the exchanges will increase faster in the future than in the past. On the contrary, as steam is rendering communication more easy from year to year, as population is tending to become more and more concentrated, and the use of the economizing expedients of credit is daily rendering less money necessary to effect the exchanges of commerce, it is reasonable to believe that the amount of paper money which the country will need will not increase as rapidly in succeeding generations as in that covered by the table given at the beginning of this chapter. Assuredly, if the currency is regulated by suppressing small bills and enlarging the specie reserves, the amount of paper which can be kept convertible on demand will increase very much less rapidly than population and wealth. If the rate of increase is the same as that which appears from the table, say about fifty millions every ten years, it would take one hundred years from 1860 to raise the necessary paper circulation to seven hundred millions. If the increase is geometrical, doubling every twenty years, it would require nearly forty years from 1860 for the country to grow up to that amount. By gradually contracting the currency, the end might be accomplished sooner. Thus, by supposing the two improbable things, that contraction would be submitted to, and that the need of paper money increases geometrically with population, the earliest day which could be set for resuming specie payments by exchanging the present inconvertible government currency for a convertible bank-note currency would be twenty years distant. The disease requires a quicker remedy.

The scheme for escaping, by further inflation, the injustice of enhancing the standard of value, is not worthy of serious discussion. Though it is just to pay debts with money of the same value as that in which they were contracted, it is not just to still further depreciate money already depreciated. To pay a debt contracted in paper worth seventy cents on the dollar with paper worth fifty cents, is not to pay the debt with the currency in which it was contracted. Such a proceeding, however, would be strictly in accordance with " the theory of greenbacks," the decisions of the courts of fifteen States, ending with the Supreme Court of the United States, and the precedents established by all the States but Massachusetts in paying their funded debts. The citizens of the State of New York, for instance, could not reasonably object to a measure which would be in strict conformity to the decisions of their highest tribunal and their own practice.

The pretext on which the demand for a further issue of treasury notes is based, is wholly untenable. It is asserted that more currency is necessary to transact the business of the country. The error consists in mistaking an increase of paper money for an increase of capital. What is really needed is more loanable capital. This, however, is a product, not of the printing-press, but of labor. A farmer who raises a thousand bushels of wheat, for which he receives a thousand dollars, adds two hundred dollars to the loanable capital of the country, if he saves that sum out of the proceeds, to loan to his neighbor. But the government, which increases its issues of inconvertible paper, adds nothing to the capital of the country. It simply causes prices to rise. An increase of the instruments of exchange is not of itself an increase of capital. It is an effect, and not a cause. As capital accumulates, the amount of it which takes the form of money is increased, and all the other instruments of exchange are necessarily increased in proper proportion; for the reason that the amounts of the exchanges to be effected, and of the instruments necessary to effect them, are greater than before. But no particular sum of money, nevertheless, is necessary to effect the exchanges of any country. The amount required is purely a question of prices, the rapidity of circulation being considered constant. One hundred millions of dollars can be made the medium of effecting as many exchanges as one thousand millions, but at a lower range of prices. The matter of chief importance is, that prices in each country should bear a proper relation to prices in every other country, in order that commerce may flow in its natural channels. When gold is the basis of the currency, prices are regulated by the laws of trade, and of the circulation of the precious metals. When the order of Nature is not interrupted by foolish legislation, the amount of money in a country is self-adjusting. It adapts itself in accordance with natural laws to the capital of the country and the amount of exchanges to be effected. What is needed in the United States is not more inconvertible paper, but to return to the only money current in the markets of the world.

The only honest, and the only practicable method

of returning to specie payments has already been alluded to. The principle on which it is based is so simple and just that it is surprising that reasonable men should ever have advocated any other. If a debtor owes one thousand dollars, payable in treasury notes worth eighty cents on the dollar, his creditor is equally well off, whether he receives eight hundred dollars in gold, or one thousand dollars in paper. The way to specie payments, then, is to settle all obligations incurred under the legal-tender act, according to the value of the money in which they were contracted, and to restore to contracts, made before the passage of that act, their original standard; to abandon the attempt to elevate greenbacks to the level of gold, and to withdraw them from circulation without increasing their value. That resumption, whenever it takes place, will be based on this principle, is not doubtful. There is room, however, for a wide difference of opinion in respect to the practical measures to be adopted in carrying it into effect. The measures used, and the time of their application, will depend largely on the political and commercial events of the immediate future. To the probable course of the latter only can reference here be made.

There is a possibility of the recurrence within a few years of one of those periodical upheavals in commerce which seem inevitable to nations in a progressive state of wealth. The cause at the bottom of commercial revulsions, as shown in a former chapter, is usually an accumulation of capital in the loan market, and a decline of rates of interest. This leads to visionary investments in speculative enterprises in the course of which vast amounts of capital are either destroyed, or, being changed from the circulating to the fixed form, are no longer loanable. Another cause, which in the United States, at least, has always appeared on the surface of such occurrences, is a defect in the machinery for effecting exchanges, which has stimulated an increase of bank loans, and an expansion of bank-notes on a market already ripe for them. In the historical crises of 1837 and 1857, both of these causes were combined. At the present time they are both again at work. The production of wealth and accumulation of capital in this country have, it is true, been diminished by the losses of the war, and the needless burdens imposed by a barbarous system of finance. But by these same causes the distribution of capital has been changed. It has been concentrated at the financial centres, and brought under the control of speculative operators to an extent never before witnessed. At the same time, in England and Germany, there seems to be an unusual accumulation of capital, and a consequent lack of paying investments at home. Bubble enterprises of various kinds are, of course, ready for the market, in addition to which large transfers of funds to this country are taking place. If a crisis in the London market should result, it would meet with a responsive echo in New York, marked by a rise of the gold premium. These transfers of foreign capital also are likely to stimulate our loan markets, while the defects in the machinery for effecting exchanges are ready prepared to aggravate a speculative fever, and to make more fatal the resulting collapse. Our banks are freed from the restraint which paying specie imposes, and the legal restraints it has been attempted to substitute are of doubtful efficacy. At the same time the decline of the premium on gold carrying with it the prices of large classes of commodities has set free currency which must be absorbed in use, and that use may be as a reserve for bank expansion. If these causes lead to excessive investments in mining shares, railway enterprises, or real estate at inflated prices, the usual collapse will follow. Then the evil effects of inconvertible paper will be fully felt. The destruction of loanable capital and loss of confidence would cause excessive stringency in the loan market, which would probably be immensely aggravated by a rise of the gold premium, carrying with it the prices of many commodities. But the worst effect of the inconvertible paper would be the impediments it would place in the way of recovery from such a disaster.

In 1857–'58, the decline of gold prices made this a cheap country in which to buy. Production was vastly stimulated thereby, and in the years 1859 and 1860 the results of labor in producing wealth were more satisfactory than in any other years of our history. But if such a crisis occurs during the era of greenbacks, the increased cost of production, and the uncertainty of the future which they create, would seriously impair the efforts of capital to retrieve the disaster by engaging in legitimate production.

Then would come a proper time for adopting measures to enforce specie payments on the principle of paying debts according to the value of the money in which they were contracted. The prostration already existing could not be greatly aggravated by such legislation, and its enforcement would leave the way open for an active union of capital and labor to restore prosperity to the country.

But while the tendencies exist which may culminate in a commercial revulsion, such contingencies as short crops, a European war, or repressive legislation, may counteract their effect. The likelihood of such an event, however, is one of the elements to be considered in examining the problem of the restoration of specie payments, and the possibility of its occurrence ought to teach that the road thereto has many turnings.

But in the mean time the supposed near approach of paper to an equality with gold has led to discussion of the merits of another form of paper money that deserves notice.

It is maintained by some writers that the cheapest and best money is paper not redeemable in coin on demand, but just equal to it, as tested by the absence of any premium on gold. All the plans now in vogue for restoring specie payments contemplate, not an actual return to convertible bank-notes, but merely the establishment of a currency of this kind. To elevate treasury notes to the level of specie, temporarily at least, might not be very difficult. If the natural circulation of this country be placed at five hundred millions of dollars, of bank-notes and specie combined, then to contract our present circulation by two hundred millions might be expected to bring down the premium on gold to par. But owing to the curtailment of credit in commerce, the diminution of the use of options on the stock-exchange, and the absorption of currency in retail prices, more currency is now used than would be possible in a natural state of things. It is probable, therefore, that a contraction of one hundred millions would be sufficient to make treasury notes convertible by exchange at the Sub-

Treasury, leaving bank-notes convertible into them. In such case no coin but a little silver would be added to the circulation, and it might be kept thus nominally convertible by exchange for a considerable period. Such a proceeding, however, would not constitute a return to specie payments, and such a currency would be no improvement over that now in use. Being issued by government, it would be subject to government interference. But to drag the most delicate and sensitive part of the machinery of commerce into the arena of politics, and to make the whole business of the country dependent on the changes of political parties, has already become unendurable. The government, moreover, would have no means for judging of the amount of currency needed by the commerce of the country. Bankers have such a test in the amount of notes they can circulate without being called upon to redeem them. But to exchange treasury notes for gold at the Sub-Treasury would not furnish the government a similar test. The premium on gold, or the absence of any, would not be in this case, any more than in the cases already considered, a sure criterion of the value of money in exchange. Small bills would of necessity form a part of a currency of the kind supposed, and its purchasing power, as measured by general prices, would inevitably be considerably depreciated, while gold remained at par. In that case foreign trade would be affected, and manufactures and commerce would suffer. The adjustment of the international exchanges is a matter of such exceeding nicety, that it will bear no interference of government. Nature has provided in the precious metals a self-adjusting regulator of commerce, which governments never fail to derange when they meddle with it. To elevate our present currency to par, therefore, would not improve it. On the contrary, when a currency is not really convertible and self-regulating, it is desirable that gold should be at a premium as high as can be borne, without producing stringency in the loan market, in order to counteract, if possible, the increased cost of production which such a currency creates. But to keep a currency of this kind at the par of gold, for any period, is practically impossible. Combinations of capitalists would probably be formed to get possession of all the government gold, and make a profit on it by selling it out again at a premium; while the first European war, or civil commotion, or financial revulsion and decline of bonds, would send gold to a premium without any increase of the quantity of paper; and it is the experience of mankind, without a single exception, that no government issuing paper money can long resist the temptation to over-issues.

Paper money, not convertible on demand, has the defect of being inflexible. Its amount does not vary with the number of exchanges to be effected. The marketing of the crops causes a greater need of money at some seasons of the year than at others. The course of trade varies from year to year, and the demand for the instruments of exchange varies accordingly. When coin is used the amount of money in circulation adjusts itself naturally to the amount of exchanges to be effected. The precious metals flow from one country to another as they are needed. Specie, also, being the universal representative of values, is hoarded, and thus withdrawn from circulation, and

is restored to activity again when called forth by an
unusual demand. Paper money, on the other hand, has
only a local value. Its quantity cannot be diminished
by shipments to other countries, nor does the practice
of hoarding it ever become general. The amount of
it to be circulated remains the same at all times, independent of the exchanges to be effected with it. It
accumulates, therefore, at the centres of trade at some
seasons of the year, to be used in stock-jobbing, and
at other seasons a scarcity of it arises. This scarcity
also is frequently increased arbitrarily by those inter-
ested in a decline of prices.

This defect of an inconvertible currency it is proposed to remedy by making treasury notes convertible
into bonds, and bonds reconvertible into treasury
notes, at the pleasure of the holders. The error of the
advocates of this plan lies in supposing that the exchange-value of money, as marked by prices, and the
rates of interest paid for the use of capital, are directly dependent. Prices, however, are vastly more
powerful than rates of interest. Thus if the price of
any commodity falls a few cents in a short space of
time, the decline may be at the rate of fifty per cent.
per annum, or a rise to the same extent may be equal
to one hundred per cent. per annum. The holders of
commodities consequently can afford to pay exorbitant rates of interest in order to prevent prices from
declining, or to cause them to rise. Precisely this
phenomenon has frequently been witnessed on the
stock-exchange, where commissions of one-sixteenth,
one-half, and even as high as three-quarters of one
per cent. per diem are sometimes paid for "turning
stocks." If, therefore, bonds were convertible into

treasury notes at the pleasure of the holders up to a certain limit, those speculating for a rise of prices would be likely to pay rates of interest high enough to induce the holders of bonds to convert them into money; and the result probably would be that the limit would be always filled. The amount of capital that naturally seeks investment in government securities at low rates of interest is comparatively small, and is daily invested in that manner by the purchase of bonds. To make bonds reconvertible into money would not increase the amount of such capital. Nor would it give the currency such flexibility as specie gives. Prices are the controlling cause of the flexibility of a specie currency, and not rates of interest. The measure proposed must be regarded as an abandonment of the policy of ever appreciating treasury notes to the par of gold, and from that point of view is highly desirable. If the rate of interest yielded by the bonds were placed low enough, the measure could finally be made use of in reaching specie payments.

CHAPTER XV.

IN any scheme for withdrawing the treasury notes
of the United States, and resuming specie payments,
one of the first considerations ought to be, whether
the plan proposed is in strict accordance with the
legal obligations entered into by the government in
contracting the indebtedness. The reason for such
honesty, however, is not that a breach of faith would
be ruinous to the public credit. The argument from
expediency is entitled to but little weight. One of
the happiest events that could befall the nation would
be such a limitation of its credit that not another dollar could ever be added to its obligations. The most
active element in that financial feudal system, by which
in these latter days a few are elevated over the many,
is the facility which credit gives for swelling the public debt. Among the reforms of the future, a place
may well be left for a constitutional limitation, which
would restrict each generation to spending its own
money only. A breach of the public faith, therefore,
is to be avoided; not by reason of any damage it
would inflict on the public credit, but from those high-

er considerations of morality which enable men to do good for its own sake, and to shun evil from a love of right. That such a course is wrong in itself, is a sufficient objection to it, without weighing its expediency.

In considering whether treasury notes should be elevated to the par of specie, it is to be borne in mind that there are two distinct classes of persons to be affected by the measure, whose rights are different, and whose cases ought to be considered separately. Such a proceeding would affect both the obligations of individuals to one another in paying debts contracted under the legal-tender act, and the obligations of the government toward its own creditors, the owners of its notes. The latter class, measured by the pecuniary value of the securities it holds, is of comparatively little importance. Whether treasury notes, deprived of their quality of money, and made government securities simply, shall be raised from ninety cents on the dollar to par, is a question of forty millions of dollars, more or less. But whether treasury notes, being the standard of value in all pecuniary obligations, shall be elevated to the level of specie, is a question involving hundreds of millions of dollars, the solvency of the whole trading class, and the happiness of the nation. Whence the opinion is derived, that the government has legally bound itself to perpetrate the enormity of thus elevating the standard of value, is difficult to perceive. No promise or contract was made to resume specie payments in that manner or in any other. Indeed, such a promise would be wholly inconsistent with "the theory of greenbacks." The Congress which made treasury notes a legal tender, believed that they were as valuable as specie, and that there was no necessity of any promise ever to make them convertible into specie. The same men in the next Congress attempted to do away with the premium on gold by an act of legislation. The courts, regarding value as wholly an ideal thing, have been unable to perceive any difference in value between specie and treasury notes, and the law has recognized no such difference. The dollar, therefore, which is intended in every contract made under the legal-tender act, is the paper dollar, or dollar of account, and the government has never promised nor agreed to change these dollars into real dollars. Nor has it ever limited any time within which to make its own notes equivalent to specie. Greenbacks might continue inconvertible into coin to the end of time without any violation of contract. That it was believed by the Congress which authorized their issue, and by the public generally, that specie payments would ultimately be resumed by rendering them equal to specie, does not alter the case. The existence of that expectation is one of the reasons that no pledge was required of the government to return to specie payments in that particular manner, and within a limited time; but this expectation, nevertheless, having never been put in the form of a legal obligation, ought to be disregarded now that the logic of events has proved its realization to be impracticable as well as immoral and unjust. Whether constitutional limitations, therefore, would not restrict the United States from depriving individuals of their property by thus enhancing the standard of value, is a question that need not be examined at length. It is sufficient to remark, that the guarantee, that no man shall be deprived of his property without due process of law, is violated as directly by enhancing as by depreciating the measure of values, and that when such violations are permitted government fails in its most essential attribute, that of affording security to its citizens. The question of practical importance is to determine what would be the legal obligations of debtors and creditors toward one another in case of the repeal of the law making treasury notes a legal tender, and their withdrawal from circulation.

A law, which provided that every debtor owing nine hundred dollars should pay his creditor one thousand dollars, would be in direct conflict with the constitutional guarantee above mentioned. Yet this is precisely what would take place if, by repealing the legal-tender act, every greenback dollar were changed into a gold dollar, and the latter course would be as illegal as the former. The fact that the name dollar has been given to the unequal values, does not change the case. That which it is forbidden to do directly, cannot be done indirectly. Congress, therefore, has no power, under the constitution, to transmute paper into gold, dollar for dollar, by repealing the legal-tender act. In case of its repeal, without any clause saving past contracts, the courts would be bound to make such contracts payable in gold, according to the value of the money in which they were contracted, and to send each case to a jury to determine the value of the money intended by the parties. One way of removing all doubt on the subject would be to provide, in the law containing the repeal, at what percentage in coin greenback contracts should be settled. And whether Congress made such a provision or not, each State could establish such a percentage for its own courts. The only limitation on the power of the States is contained in that provision of the constitution of the United States which forbids them from passing laws impairing the obligation of contracts; but, as the law in question would provide for carrying out contracts according to the intention of the parties in making them, this restriction could not be invoked against it.

There is a precedent of such a law in American history, which has been approved by the court of highest jurisdiction.

"In November, 1781, the Legislature of Virginia passed an act calling paper money out of circulation, and also another act directing the mode for adjusting and settling contracts made in that currency.

"The second section of this latter act, after stating by way of preamble, that 'the good people of the State would labor under many inconveniences for want of some rule, whereby to settle and adjust the payment of debts and contracts entered into or made between the first day of January, 1777, and the first day of January, 1782, unless some rule should be by law established for liquidating and adjusting the same so as to do justice as well to the debtor as the creditor,' enacts that, from and after the passing of the act, 'all debts and contracts entered into or made in the current money of this State, or the United States, excepting at all time contracts entered into for gold and silver coin, tobacco, or any other specific property, within the period aforesaid, now remaining due and unfulfilled, or which may become due at any future day or days for the payment of any sum or sums of money, shall be liquidated, settled, and adjusted agreeably to a scale of depreciation, hereinafter mentioned and contained; that is to say, by reducing the amount of all such debts and contracts to the true value in specie, at the days or times the same were incurred or entered into, and upon payment of said value so found in specie, or other money equivalent thereto, the debtors or contractors shall be forever discharged of and from the said debts or contracts, any law, custom, or usage to the contrary in any wise notwithstanding.'

"The fourth section establishes the scale of depreciation, which shall constitute the rule by which the value of the debts, contracts, and demands, in the act mentioned, shall be ascertained."

Of this law, Chief-Justice Marshall, in delivering the opinion of the Supreme Court, said: "The act is applied directly to the date of the contract, and the motive for making it was, that contracts entered into during the circulation of paper money, ought in justice to be discharged by a sum differing in intrinsic value from the nominal sum mentioned in the contract; and that, when the Legislature removed the delusive standard by which the value of the thing acquired had been measured, they ought to provide that justice should be done to the parties." *

The example of the Virginia of Washington and Jefferson, approved by Chief-Justice Marshall, is one worthy of imitation in any age or country. Justice has not changed since 1781; and the fact that the paper money then used had depreciated lower than

* Faw *vs.* Marsteller, 2 Cranch, p. 10 (1 Curtis, 428).

that now in circulation, does not affect the principle. The rights of all parties ought to be guarded in removing the delusive standard of value, as well when it has depreciated to only eighty or ninety cents on the dollar, as when it has fallen several degrees lower. The degree of the depreciation does not alter the justice of the case, or the obligations of the law-makers. If, therefore, the Government of the United States had the power to elevate its treasury notes forthwith to the level of specie, it ought to provide, before so doing, that the obligations of individuals should not be affected thereby, but should be settled according to the value of the money in which the debts were contracted.

In writing of paper money, the question of the resumption of specie payments might be brought to an end at this point, and the obligations of the United States toward their creditors, and the proper method of funding the public debt, might be left for a separate investigation. The rights of private creditors and of public creditors under the legal-tender act, however, are so intimately connected, that both must be settled together. In fact, the chief difficulty in the way of a just resumption of specie payments is the claim of the public creditors that their rights are different from, and superior to, those of private creditors under that act. In considering the manner and the effects of a resumption of specie payments, therefore, it becomes necessary to examine the merits of this claim, and to consider the legal liabilities which the United States entered into in negotiating the different securities of which the public debt is composed.

The first question which arises is, whether there is

any obligation ever to pay the legal-tender treasury
notes in gold at their face. In order to establish such
an obligation it must be shown that there is a difference between these notes and private debts. If it is
just to settle the latter according to the value of the
money in which they were contracted, it is likewise
just to pay the former at the same percentage, inas-
much as the government received no greater consideration for its indebtedness than any other debtor.
The only thing that could change the rule would be a
difference in the terms of the contract. But no such
difference exists. The law is in these words:

"And such notes herein authorized, shall be receivable in payment of all taxes, internal duties, excises,
debts, and demands of any kind due to the United
States, except duties on imports, and of all claims
and demands against the United States, of every kind
whatsoever, except for interest upon bonds and notes,
which shall be paid in coin, and shall also be lawful
money and a legal tender in payment of all debts,
public and private, within the United States, except
duties on imports, and interest, as aforesaid." Treasury notes are a "claim against the United States,"
and a "public debt." Being included within two of
the provisions of the legal-tender act, they are doubly
payable in what that law has made a dollar. Great
stress, it is true, is laid upon the use of the word
dollar. "The United States will pay the bearer one
dollar." This, it is insisted, means $25\frac{8}{10}$ grains of
gold, nine-tenths fine. Read by itself, such undoubtedly would be its meaning; and it would be an obligation, moreover, to pay that dollar on demand. No
rule of our law is better settled, than that a note, in

which the time of payment is not designated, is payable whenever presented. In the words of Chancellor Kent, "If no time be expressed, the law adjudges that the money is payable immediately." One of the most essential qualities of negotiable paper is, that the money should be payable at a fixed and certain time. If, therefore, the treasury notes are to be construed solely according to the promises contained on them, each note is legally payable in coin, whenever presented to the proper officer of the government, and, if payment is refused, the United States are guilty of a flagrant violation of contract, and of an undisguised act of repudiation. This objection can only be avoided by construing the whole contract together, and considering the reverse of the note as well as its face. Each note contains the assurance that it is a legal tender to pay all debts, public as well as private, and all claims against the United States. This is equivalent to saying that the dollar mentioned in the note is not the coined dollar, the only one recognized up to that time as a legal tender, but the dollar of account, or conventional unit of computation, of which each note is itself made the representative without regard to value, that being only an ideal thing. In this way only, can the refusal to pay treasury notes in coin on demand be upheld.

There is another consideration which leads to the same conclusion. ' If the coined dollar had been the dollar intended by that word contained in the treasury notes, then the only reasonable construction of the legal-tender act would be, that these notes were a legal tender only to the amount of their actual market value, and not of their nominal value. The law does not itself specify to what amount, or at what value, each note should be a legal tender. As government securities, their value was sure to fluctuate as compared with gold, and if they had been promises to pay, or representatives of real dollars, to have made pre-existing debts payable in them at their face would have been an undisguised act of robbery. The robbery was disguised therefore by considering each note to be itself a dollar, and not a representative of one. Such has been the decision of all the courts thus far. A dollar is whatever the law makes a dollar, and the law has made treasury notes to be dollars. This, it is true, is a shallow device for concealing robbery and repudiation. But it has proved none the less effectual.

The word dollar, therefore, used in the treasury notes, has the same signification as in private debts contracted under the legal-tender act. The dollar mentioned is understood to be the dollar of account, or whatever the law makes a dollar. Every man who has made a note under that act has promised to pay dollars. Yet no one has ever supposed that gold dollars were intended. In the case before cited, Chief-Justice Marshall thought "that contracts entered into during the circulation of paper money ought, in justice, to be discharged by a sum differing in intrinsic value from the nominal sum mentioned in the contract." The use of the word dollar in the contract did not affect the justice of the rule in that case; and the rule applies with as much force to the treasury notes of the United States as to any other debt. The promise to pay real dollars was intended to be, and was understood to be, nugatory. The only method

15

of payment provided by law was to receive the notes for taxes, and in payment of loans whenever negotiated. If the notes had simply been stamped "this is a dollar," their legal effect would have been the same, and the fact that greenbacks are mere stamped counters would never have been questioned.

It follows, from the fact that the legal-tender notes are mere counters, that when they are paid in coin, they ought to be paid according to their actual, and not according to their nominal value. The holder of a ten-dollar note would be precisely as well off to receive nine gold dollars for it as to hold it; and the United States have not only a moral but a technical legal right to pay him in that manner. There is a practical objection, however, in the way of such a course. To raise the amount of specie necessary to pay the treasury notes, even at ninety cents on the dollar, would be difficult, as it was part of the original contract under which they were issued, that "such United-States notes should be received the same as coin at their par value in payment for any loans that might be thereafter sold or negotiated by the Secretary of the Treasury." Under this provision the government is precluded from negotiating a loan for coin only, until the treasury notes are all funded, and in case any holder of such notes should tender them in payment of any loan, and should meet with refusal, he could justly claim that the United States were liable for the difference in price, if any, between his notes and the bonds.

It cannot be maintained, however, that the government has ever precluded itself from naming the rate of interest to be yielded by the bonds, into which treasury notes are to become convertible. The act under which the first issue of notes was made contained a provision making them convertible into six per cent. bonds at the option of the holder. This option was repealed by a subsequent act, after sufficient time had been given to the holders of the notes to avail themselves of the privilege, if they so desired. The fact that notes are still in circulation on which the device is printed that they are exchangeable for six per cent. bonds, has given rise to the claim that the government has precluded itself from funding them into any other class of bonds. To this it is answered that, the notes being money, to fund them is for the government to borrow money, and that therefore the time and manner of making them fundable is for the convenience of government, and not of the holders of the notes. No limitation of the time during which the option was to run having been specified, it was clearly the right of the government to fix such a limit, in order to give the holders of the notes sufficient opportunity to avail themselves of their privilege, and afterward to borrow money at its own convenience only, and on better terms, if possible. The United States, then, having retained the right to specify the terms on which all the treasury notes shall be funded, the result can be made as advantageous to the tax-payers, and to those who have contracted debts payable in them, as to pay them at a percentage of their nominal sum. If treasury notes were deprived of the quality of being a legal tender in payment of private debts contracted after a given date, the holders of them, as fast as they ceased to be current as money, would desire to convert them into interest-

bearing securities. The United States could then
fund them at a low rate of interest, and, if the rate
were properly named, justice would be done alike to
the tax-payers, the note-holders, and private debtors.

The next question which arises is to determine in
which sort of money the funded debt of the United
States is legally payable.

In considering the question, it is worth remember-
ing again that, legally, there is no difference between
gold dollars and paper dollars. The courts say the
judges who preside over them must recognize as a dollar whatever the law makes a dollar, and as the law
has made both gold coin and treasury notes to be
dollars, payment of debts in either is equally legal.
The only practical point is to determine to which of
the parties to a contract belongs the option of selecting between the two. If the choice is left to the creditor, he naturally selects the money which is the more
valuable. If to the debtor, he, with equal sagacity,
selects that which is less valuable, value to both of
them being the reverse of an ideal thing. If neither
sort of money is specified in the contract, the option
belongs to the one who has the money to pay. If, on
the other hand, gold is specified, then, under any just
construction of the laws, the option belongs to the one
who is entitled to receive the money. The legal-tender act, by its terms, expressly applies to all claims
against the United States, and to all debts, public and
private, within the United States, except duties on imports and interest on the public debt. The same rule,
in reference to selecting the money in which the debt
is to be paid, applies, therefore, to the public debt as
to the debts of individuals. As the man, who, having the

option of paying his debts in the currency in which they were contracted, worth seventy cents on the dollar, should, nevertheless, insist upon paying them in a currency worth par, would be considered demented, so those who would compel the United States to pay their debts in the more valuable currency, if the choice has never been legally relinquished, ought to be placed in the same category. The pecuniary affairs of the nation ought to be administered in accordance with the same principles of justice as those of an individual, and the rights of the tax-payers ought to be as jealously guarded by the law-makers as those of an individual are guarded by himself. There is this difference, however, between the government and individuals, that no question can arise as to the legality of a specific contract to pay coin, when made by the former. The law authorizing the agreement renders it beyond attack. In order to determine, therefore, with which party the option of selecting the currency in which the public debt is to be paid, has been left, all that is necessary is, to discover whether any specific contract to pay coin has been entered into by the government. Such a contract must be sought in the law authorizing the issue of bonds, and not in the bonds themselves; not only because the government can only make a contract in pursuance of law, but because no mention of the money in which the bonds are to be paid is contained in any of them. They are all alike payable in dollars, but, whether in gold or paper dollars, the bonds themselves do not specify.

Various attempts have been made to spell out a specific contract to pay coin from the law authorizing the issue of the bonds known as five-twenties; and, notwithstanding the noisy vituperation of the advocates of that view of the question, the argument to sustain it has never been stated with full force. Though the law authorizing the first issue of these bonds does not specifically provide for the payment of the principal of them in coin, it contains provisions from which such an intention can be inferred with some show of reason.

1. As treasury notes are not a legal tender for the payment of the interest on the bonds, the interest is left payable in coin, and is computed at six per cent. in coin, as if the principal were also a certain sum of the same money.

2. Treasury notes are made receivable " the same as coin at their par value in payment for any loans sold or negotiated by the Secretary of the Treasury." It might be claimed that, as the notes were specifically made equal to coin when used in payment of the loan, it was intended that the debt incurred should be payable as a coin debt.

3. Duties on imported goods are made payable in coin, and the coin is set apart as a special fund for the payment in coin of the interest on the bonds (treasury notes not being a legal tender for that purpose), and for " the purchase or payment of one per centum of the entire debt of the United States " within each year.

From all these provisions taken together, the inference may be drawn that it was the intention of the law that the principal of the bonds issued under it should be payable in coin only. That such was the expectation of the law-makers can hardly be doubted. It was the general opinion that specie payments would be resumed after the close of the war by elevating treasury notes to the standard of gold, and that all debts, public and private alike, payable in the distant future, would thus become payable in coin only. If specie payments are resumed in that manner, the expectation will be realized. But the question of practical importance is to determine whether, in the event of resumption by repealing the legal-tender act, and settling past debts according to the value of the money in which they were contracted, the bonds of the United States would be legally payable in coin at par, or in coin at a percentage of their nominal sum, in the same manner as private debts. That there would in such case be no difference between the principal of the five-twenty bonds issued under the act of February 25, 1862, and private debts, is a conclusion which cannot be escaped.

The provisions above mentioned cannot be fairly construed to amount to a specific contract to pay coin.

From the fact that the interest is computed in coin on a certain sum, it by no means follows that the sum is intended to be composed of gold dollars, instead of paper dollars. The law recognizes no difference between the two. According to " the theory of greenbacks," under which the bonds were issued, there is no such difference ; and it cannot be doubted that the Congress which passed the law saw no incongruity in making the interest payable in coin, and leaving the principal payable in lawful money.

From the fact that treasury notes are made receivable the same as coin in payment of loans, no inference can fairly be drawn as to the kind of money in which it was intended the bonds should be payable. This quality was evidently given to the notes to increase their value without any reference to its effect on the bonds. The interest on these was specifically made payable in coin in order to sustain their value, and notes were made convertible into them the same as coin, in order to partake of this advantage. Nothing, therefore, can justly be inferred from this fact as to the sort of money in which the bonds were to be paid.

Peculiar stress has been laid on the fact that a sinking fund for the payment of the debt is set apart in coin. To this it is a sufficient answer, that the measure is a mere fiscal arrangement of the government for its own convenience, and does not constitute a contract with the holders of its bonds. But, moreover, the fact that the coin may be devoted to the purchase as well as to the payment of the debt, is entitled to all the weight that has been given to it on the other side. The provision for payment, even if it meant payment in coin, wonld be nugatory so long as the bonds were below par. But there is nothing in the fact that the duties are made payable in coin, and the coin set apart to pay the debt, which would prevent the government from converting the coin into "lawful money," and paying the debt with the latter. Whether such a course would be legal is to be determined by the other provisions of the law, as to the money in which the bonds are made payable. To pursue such a course with the bonds specifically made payable in coin would be a violation of contract; but to pay in that manner bonds which are not specifically made payable in the more valuable currency, would simply be to do what every wise man would do in the management of his own affairs. These provisions of the law of 1862, neither singly nor together, are sufficient to withdraw the bonds issued under it from the general provision of the same law, that treasury notes should be a legal tender in payment of all claims against the United States, and of all debts, public and private, except duties on imports and interest on the public debt. They do not cause the principal of the debt to be included among the exceptions. The interest and custom duties are specifically excepted. But, if certain debts are specifically excepted from the legal-tender clause, the implication is irresistible that it was not intended to except any others. As the interest is by name excepted, therefore the principal is expressly included. In the same manner, the specification in some loan acts, that the bonds are to be paid in coin, shows that those bonds were intended to be paid in a different manner from the bonds issued under an act where coin payment is not mentioned. It should be remembered, also, that a bond is both "a public debt" and "a demand against the United States." It is therefore twice as much within the legal-tender clause as a private debt. The undeniable fact is, that the law-makers entertained the expectation that the public debt, being payable in the then distant future, would, in the natural order of events, become payable in coin, or its equivalent, by the elevation of treasury notes to par. This expectation, however, was never reduced to the form of a contract, and no intention was ever in any manner shown to apply a different rule to the principal of these bonds from that applied to private debts. In short, there is no

specific contract to pay coin, and, in case of a return
to specie payments by settling past debts according
to the value of the money in which they were contracted, a court of justice would be compelled to
apply the same rule to the bonds issued under the law
of February 27, 1862, as to the debts of individuals.

No question as to the kind of money in which the
bonds issued under the law of March 3, 1863, known
as ten-forties, are payable, can arise. The principal
of the bonds issued under that law is expressly made
payable in coin. The same provision is contained in
the law of March 3, 1864, authorizing the issue of
two hundred millions of bonds. Nearly four millions
($3,882,500) of five-twenty bonds were issued under
this law, and any discrimination in favor of the holders of these bonds would be to them a mere matter of
good luck. Yet that is no reason for fulfilling the
contract otherwise than according to its terms. The
law of June 30, 1864, repealed the two preceding
laws before the full amount of bonds authorized by
them had been filled, and provided for the issue of
four hundred millions of other bonds, without specifying that the principal of them was to be payable in any
thing but lawful money. The law of March 3, 1865,
under which six hundred millions of five-twenty
bonds, or seven-thirty notes convertible into them,
have been issued, contained the following provision:
" And the principal, or interest, or both, may be made
payable in coin, or in other lawful money." This
sentence, it will be remarked, is in the disjunctive
throughout, and contains a direct authority to the
Secretary of the Treasury to make a specific contract,
binding on the United States, to pay the principal of

the bonds issued under this law in coin. Yet no such contract has been made by that officer. Nothing is said in the bonds or notes as to the money in which they are to be paid. By what process of reasoning the conclusion is reached, that, in the seven-thirty notes, issued under this authority, the word dollar means other treasury notes, and, in the five-twenty bonds, gold coin, is not clear. The only way in which that meaning could have been given, was by specifying in the bonds that they were to be paid in coin. No such provision having been made, they are expressly payable, like any other debt incurred under the legal-tender·act, in lawful money at the option of the debtor.

The first and second series of the sixes of 1881 were negotiated before the passage of the legal-tender act, and that portion of the debt, having been incurred in specie, ought to be paid in the same money. The third series was issued under the act of March 3, 1864, and the principal is payable, therefore, in coin.

From this examination it appears that the principal of the ten-forty bonds, and of the few millions of five-twenty bonds issued under the law of March 3, 1864, is specifically payable in coin, and that the sixes of 1881 ought to be paid in the same manner. These bonds compose but a small part of the public debt. The great bulk of it, therefore, is payable, like private debts, in whichever class of legal-tender money the debtor prefers; and the option to pay the five-twenties at the expiration of the shorter term, at the pleasure of the United States, includes the option to pay them in the less valuable currency.

But it is urged that—by reason of certain advertisements of the loan agents of the Treasury Department, that the principal of the bonds would be paid in coin, and of certain letters of successive Secretaries of the Treasury to the same effect—the government is cut off from exercising this option. To this it is a sufficient answer, that the Secretary of the Treasury has no power to bind the government, except that which he derives from the laws under which he is acting. Nor could one Congress ratify any promises of that officer, so as to bind a future Congress, except by a law duly enacted. Each Congress must seek the contracts binding on the government in the statutes of the United States "published by authority," and the official acts done in accordance with them, and not in newspaper advertisements and fugitive letters. But these letters were not written until long after the bonds authorized by the law of 1862 had been negotiated. They cannot affect those bonds, therefore, either as a part of the contract, or as a contemporaneous interpretation of it. And, the Secretary of the Treasury having failed to exercise his authority to insert in the bonds issued under the law of 1865 a specific contract to pay coin, the omission, as to those bonds, cannot be supplied by private letters.

There is this further consideration, also, that none of these letters of the Secretaries of the Treasury contain a contract, or any thing that can be construed into one, to pay the principal of the bonds in coin. That of Secretary Chase, dated May 18, 1864, which is the one principally relied on, merely states that "it has been the constant usage of the department to redeem the funded or permanent debt in coin," and adds, "these bonds, therefore, according to the usage of the government, are payable in coin." The letter of Secretary McCulloch, dated Nov. 15, 1866, is to the same effect, and merely states that it is the "established policy of the government" to pay all bonds in coin. Not only do these letters fail to constitute a contract to pay coin, but they are notice to all the creditors of the government that the payment of the bonds in coin would depend wholly on the continuance of a usage or policy of the Treasury Department, which had never received the sanction of law, and which would be liable to be reversed by a new Secretary of the Treasury, or any future Congress. The payment in coin of the loan of 1842 did not establish any precedent for the payment in gold of bonds negotiated after the passage of the legal-tender act. On the contrary, it established the precedent of paying the bonds according to the value of the money in which the debt was contracted.

But it is claimed that there is an honorary obligation to pay the war debt in gold. To this it is answered, that trustees have no right to give away the money of their beneficiaries. Congress acts in a fiduciary capacity for the tax-payers of the country, and for generations yet unborn. Congress has no right to pay the debt except according to contract. Any other course would be binding neither legally nor morally, and would taint the whole debt with fraud. A gift not actually executed by payment could be revoked whenever the beneficiaries of the trust obtained the power to revoke it by electing a Congress pledged to the measure.

The question of the payment of the public debt has been examined thus minutely because it is the chief obstacle in the way of that more important measure, a return to specie payments. But, when the conclusion is reached that public and private debts must be settled in the same manner, the way is clear to provide for the settlement of both on the principle of equal and exact justice to all men. As the debts of individuals contracted under the legal-tender act would, on the repeal of that act, become legally payable according to the value of the money in which they were contracted, so the debt of the United States would, in that event, become legally payable in the same manner.

The only practical result from this conclusion with regard to the public debt would be, that a way would be opened for readily re-funding it at a lower and uniform rate of interest. Instead of selling gold bonds at a discount, to pay paper bonds at par, the process could be reversed.

This construction, also, could be made practically effective in re-funding the five-twenty bonds at a lower rate of interest, long before the question of settling private contracts could be reached. Thus, if the monthly payments of the public debt, instead of being made by purchases at par in coin, were made by redemptions of bonds selected by lot, and paid in greenbacks, a motive would be furnished to all the bond-holders to fund their bonds in a new security, payable specifically in coin. The reduction of the interest would be the consideration to the United States for paying the principal in coin, and this agreement would be the consideration to the bond-holders for submitting to the reduction of interest.

All these conclusions, it is supposed, have been

changed by the so-called public credit act, passed since the foregoing was written. That law is in these words: "Be it enacted, etc., that, in order to remove any doubt as to the purpose of the government to discharge all just obligations to the public creditors, and to settle conflicting questions and interpretations of the laws by virtue of which such obligations have been contracted, it is hereby provided and declared that the faith of the United States is solemnly pledged to the payment in coin, or its equivalent, of all the obligations of the United States, not bearing interest, known as United-States notes, and all of the interest-bearing obligations of the United States, except in cases where the law authorizing the issue of any such obligation has expressly provided that the same may be paid in lawful money or other currency than gold and silver. But none of said interest-bearing obligations not already due shall be redeemed or paid before maturity unless at such time United-States notes shall be convertible into coin at the option of the holder, or unless at such time bonds of the United States bearing a lower rate of interest than the bonds to be redeemed can be sold at par in coin. And the United States also solemnly pledges its faith to make provision, at the earliest practicable period, for the redemption of the United-States notes in coin."

That this law does not change the legal conclusions herein arrived at, appears from several considertions.

1. It is an attempt of Congress to exercise judicial functions, and while Congress may perhaps have the power to construe its own contracts, though it has no power to construe private contracts, yet the con-

struction which one Congress enacts is not binding on its successors, and, if plainly wrong, ought to be repealed.

2. As the law neither mentions nor purports to contain any consideration, it does not constitute a contract, and may be repealed by any future Congress without injury to private rights.

3. If legal-tender notes were not payable in coin by force of the law under which they were issued, then, to make them so payable now, is to add to their value, and to compel debtors who have made contracts under the legal-tender act to part with additional value in paying their debts. It was held by the Supreme Court, while yet honest, that, to compel creditors to receive depreciated paper in payment of debts contracted in coin was to deprive them of their property without due process of law, and was therefore a violation of the constitution. But evidently, to compel debtors to pay coin or its equivalent, when they only contracted to pay depreciated paper, is to deprive them in like manner of their property without due process of law. It is the same boot, only transferred to the other leg.

4. This law disregards the contract made with the holders of treasury notes, and contained in the legal-tender act, that such notes "should be received the same as coin, at their par value, in payment for any loans that might be thereafter sold or negotiated by the Secretary of the Treasury," a contract which is still to be found printed on some of those notes. The public credit act implies that bonds may be sold at par for coin while treasury notes are selling at less than par, in which case the latter could not be received in payment

for such loan. A negotiation of this kind has actually been consummated in the case of the five per cent. bonds, and the contract of the United States with the holders of their treasury notes, to receive such notes the same as coin in payment for any loans sold or negotiated after their issue, has been openly repudiated. Congress, in order to give to the bond-holders more than their contract calls for, has taken from the note-holders part of the consideration which their contract distinctly specifies. If our government can thus flagrantly violate its contract with one class of its creditors in order to benefit another class of them, the question naturally arises, What is its contract worth ?

Congress, in passing this law, has utterly disregarded the "theory of greenbacks," in accordance with which the legal-tender act was framed, in order to defraud the tax-payers for the benefit of the bond-holders. It is a singular coincidence that a coördinate department of the government has revived that theory in full force, in order to defraud creditors whose debts were contracted before the passage of the act, for the benefit, principally, of a few great railway corporations.

The public credit act affords an admirable illustration of the fact, a disregard of which by legislators is a prolific source of evil, that every law has more than one effect. It was intended to settle the manner of payment of the principal of the five-twenty bonds. That question, however, even granting that those bonds are within the terms of the act, which in fact they are not, it has left precisely where it was before the law was passed. The practice of paying those bonds in coin had already been established, though improperly, by the Treasury Department, and would have been continued without the law, until Congress directed the exercise of the option to pay them in lawful money, and any future Congress would still have precisely the same power to so direct, as if the public credit act had never passed.

But though the law failed of the effect intended, it has had other effects not intended. It has delayed the refunding of the debt. When a six per cent. bond, payable in gold, can be bought at the same price as a four per cent. bond, there is no inducement to money-lenders to subscribe for the latter, and, as the option to redeem the six per cent. bonds may be made effective at any time, they do not rise above par so as to bring up the lower class of bonds to that price.

This law also has had the effect of compelling the government, during the depreciation of treasury notes, to negotiate loans for coin only, thus causing a deplorable breach of the contract with the holders of such notes.

It has had the further practical and disastrous effect of depressing the premium on gold by causing our bonds to rise to par in the foreign markets, thus robbing our producers of a part of the price of their products, more than neutralizing the protective effects of our tariffs, and wholly paralyzing our foreign commerce.

The public credit act was extorted by fear of the monstrous proposition to pay the debt in greenbacks, and to obtain the greenbacks by printing them, a proposition only less monstrous than the decision of the Supreme Court, by the terms of which such a proceeding would be both legal and moral.

The proper answer to have made to the claims of the bond-holders for protection against so dangerous a catastrophe would have been, that Congress must decline to usurp judicial functions by interpreting contracts, that it could not obtain the gold to pay the bonds as the option matured, having precluded itself by its contract with the note-holders from negotiating a loan for coin only, but that it would afford the desired protection in the only legal manner left, by exchanging the old bonds for new ones at a lower rate of interest, and making both principal and interest specifically payable in coin. The new bonds in such case would probably have sold at a higher price than the old ones, and the exchange would have been made voluntarily, just as the seven-thirty notes were converted into five-twenty bonds. The party in power could then have imputed to itself the credit of having relieved the burdens of the tax-payers by re-funding the debt, and could have thrown on the opposition all the odium of the "greenback heresy." The public credit act is not only illegal and unjust, but, what in politics is considered worse, it is a blunder.

The legal-tender act has produced some strange inconsistencies.

Thus, the Governor of New York, in his last message, says, "the unpaid principal of the war bounty debt was, on the 30th September last, $16,887,206. This portion of our debt was contracted, and is to be paid in our present legal-tender currency. The residue of the State debt, which amounts to $12,595,495, was contracted before the war in gold, and the honor of the State and good faith demand that it shall be paid, both principal and interest, in gold coin." The only exception taken to this is, that the proposition to pay the ante-war debt in gold does not accord with the decision of the Supreme Court, and ought not to be entertained. When the holders of the Pennsylvania State debt, contracted before the war, made a similar claim, their demand for justice was not only rejected, but with the rejection was coupled an insult.

If we turn now to the Federal Government, we find that the claim that its war debt contracted under the same legal-tender act, in a currency worth on an average sixty per cent., should be paid in gold, has not only been allowed, but its opponents have been covered with vituperation. It may be dishonorable to inquire into the consideration of our war debt, but when the court of highest jurisdiction decides that value is only an ideal thing, that a dollar is whatever the law makes a dollar, and that for individuals to pay in depreciated paper debts contracted in gold is both legal and moral, there are those who will insist that the same justice be meted out to all, not the justice of a packed court, but justice derived from the rule that all debts, public and private alike, ought to be paid according to the value of the money in which they were contracted.

CHAPTER XVI.

THE pattern after which most of the schemes for effecting a resumption of specie payments in the United States are modelled is the legislation of England at the beginning of the present century. A brief examination of the experience of that country with inconvertible paper money is necessary, therefore, in order to show what points of resemblance and dissimilarity exist between that experience and our own, and in order to derive a fruitful lesson from one of the most instructive cases history affords. The contest now proceeding in this country, with respect to paying in gold debts contracted in depreciated paper, is paralleled by that which took place in England subsequent to the year 1819. The difference between the two cases, however, is very great, and the inapplicability of that precedent to the affairs of the United States can be readily shown.

1. The most obvious distinction is the time at which the objection to the injustice of that policy, in the two countries, was first made. In England it was claimed that it was grossly unjust to compel the payment in a currency of full value of debts " contracted between 1797 and 1819, when

the Bank of England was exempted from giving
cash for its notes," and the depreciation of the currency during that period was represented to have
averaged from thirty to fifty per cent. This protest,
it will be observed, was not entered until after the
contraction had taken place, and the resumption of
specie payments had become certain, and was persisted in, after that event, with the practical conclusion that the nation ought either to reduce the value
of the sterling money, or "return to the depreciated
currency, or strike off from mortgages or other private
debts of old standing a percentage corresponding to
the estimated amount of the depreciation." To such
a claim the ready answer was made that it came too
late. No government could pry into the business
affairs of individuals long since completed, to ascertain who had suffered wrong by the use of a false
standard of value, and to compel the gainer to refund
a portion of his profits. To have returned to the depreciated currency, or to have reduced the standard
of the coin, would have inflicted a greater injustice,
without redressing the wrongs aimed at; for the relations of debtors and creditors had wholly changed
in the mean time, and to have injured the creditors
of that day would not have benefited the debtors of
ten years before; while the national debt had passed
in large part into the hands of innocent holders, who
had paid for it in a currency of full value. It had become impracticable, therefore, to redress the wrongs
complained of.

In the United States, on the other hand, the objection has been made in season. Though an immense
amount of injustice has already been inflicted by tam-

pering with the standard of value, the crime of transmuting paper into gold, dollar for dollar, can yet be avoided. But in so doing it will become necessary to take things as they are. To restore to creditors the value of which they have been robbed by the legal-tender act is now impossible. To elevate greenbacks to par would not accomplish it; for the same persons who were creditors, while the depreciation was in progress, are not the creditors of to-day. The most that can be done, is to restore to all existing debts, contracted before the passage of that act, their rightful standard. The same answer can be made to the demand for raising the value of the current paper money to a metallic standard, that was made in England to the demand for the restoration of the depreciated currency, or a reduction of the value of sterling money. To do so would interfere with existing rights; as it is now impossible to ascertain the particular persons who were either benefited or injured by the depreciation of the money, " to attempt to retrace our steps would be, not redressing a wrong, but superadding a second act of widespread injustice to the one already committed."* The only way to avoid a second act of injustice in this country is to accept accomplished facts, and restore cash payments by settling all outstanding debts according to the value of the money in which they were incurred, as near as practicable.

2. But the circumstance which is of chief importance in rendering the English precedent totally inapplicable to the financial situation of the United States at the present time, is the difference in the kinds of in-

---

* Mill, " Principles," etc., Book III., chap. xiii., sec. 6.

convertible paper money used in the respective countries.   The two currencies belong to separate species;
the most important distinction between them is, that
in our case the notes used as money are made by law
a legal tender, and were issued by government as a
forced loan; while in England the notes were issued
by the banks, and were not a legal tender between
man and man, that quality having been given to the
notes of the Bank of England at a much later day
(1834).   The bank, it is true, was authorized to suspend specie payments, having been forbidden by an
Order in Council from making payments in cash,
which restriction was subsequently confirmed by Act
of Parliament.   It does not appear, however, that the
country banks suspended altogether.   Nominally, gold
might have been demanded for their notes at any time,
but in practice they redeemed them only by exchanging them for those of the Bank of England; while all
debts of individuals were throughout the suspension
legally payable in coin of the realm.   When payments
were suspended in 1797, public meetings were held
throughout the country, at which pledges were made
and a general agreement entered into to use bank-notes
as the equivalent of coin, and they continued to be
so used to the end by common consent.   The law was
laid down by the courts in 1801 * that the debtor was
entitled to demand coin; but no attempt was made to
enforce this liability until 1811, when Lord King, impelled, apparently, by a desire to make "a political'
point," issued a circular to his tenants, requiring them
to pay rents on all old leases in coin or its equivalent.
This proceeding was met by Lord Stanhope's act, so

* Grigsby vs. Oaks, 2 B. and P., p. 526.

called, making it a misdemeanor to purchase or sell coin for more than its nominal value in Bank of England notes, or to receive or pay notes for less than their nominal value, and removing also the remedy by distress in case a tender of notes had been made. This law did not make bank-notes a legal tender, and, as was pointed out in Parliament, could have been easily evaded. But, unlike our Stevens gold bill, which seems to have been modelled after it in some points, it answered the purpose for which it was intended. No further attempt was made to enforce payment of debts in coin, and Bank of England notes continued practically, though not legally, a legal tender.

But from this fact an important result followed. The Bank of England gained no power of forcing its notes into circulation beyond the actual demands of the community; a power which it would have obtained if the notes had been made both a legal tender and not redeemable. That institution continued to conduct its operations after the suspension in the same manner as before. It issued its notes only in the usual course of business. It discounted all mercantile bills that conformed to its rules, and the amount of its own notes in circulation depended on the public demand for them. It was restricted, also, from advancing to the government any sum exceeding £600,000, so that no forcible issues of inconvertible paper were made. The amount of Bank of England notes in circulation increased gradually, and, twenty years after the suspension, the amount of notes of five pounds and upward had doubled. It seems sufficiently well established, however, that the excessive issues of inconvert-

16

ible paper were owing, in the main, to the country banks. The number of these institutions more than doubled in the first ten years of the suspension, and, as was natural in doing business without the restraint of paying specie, they abused their credit and made improvident advances to their customers. The belief that the suspension of specie-payments was but temporary, and liable to terminate at any day, was sedulously kept alive throughout its whole duration. The public faith in the Bank of England was so great that a want of confidence in the currency never found expression in a premium on coin. There was no speculation in gold as a commodity, not simply because it was forbidden by law, but because 'Bank of England notes were, in fact, "held in public estimation to be equivalent to the legal coin of the realm." It was only during the last six years of the war that gold rose to any considerable premium as marked by the price of bullion, and this price seems to have been determined principally by the state of the foreign exchanges. The demand for it to send abroad to support the armies operating in foreign countries, to pay subsidies, and to settle trade balances, seem to have been the chief causes which affected it. The highest price reached was forty-two per cent. in 1812 and 1813; and the price of gold was as far from marking the depreciation of the currency during the suspension of specie payments in England, as the gold-room price has been in the United States. Prices, however, in that country, rose considerably. The greatest depreciation of the currency as marked by general prices has been variously estimated at from twenty-five to seventy-five per cent. Though it has been hotly contended that this rise was not owing to excessive issues of inconvertible paper, there is no reasonable doubt that it must be attributed to that cause. The fact so much relied on that the price of gold varied, neither with the prices of commodities in general, nor with the amount of paper in circulation, has no bearing on the question. Gold was affected by causes peculiar to itself, and, confidence in the inconvertible paper remaining unimpaired, its price in paper depended mainly on the demand for it to ship abroad. The fact that it rose to a premium proves that the currency was depreciated, though it fails to prove the degree of the depreciation at any particular time. But whatever measure of depreciation is used, it is certain that the inconvertible currency of the United States has depreciated far lower than did the bank currency of England, and this difference alone renders the remedies applied in the one case wholly inapplicable in the other.

3. The manner in which specie payments were brought about in that country affords another point of contrast. The resumption resulted, not, as is commonly supposed, from Peel's bill fixing a day certain, after which the bank was compelled to pay cash for its notes, but from the voluntary action of the country banks and mercantile classes in contracting their liabilities, and thus preparing themselves to resume long before the day appointed by law. This action followed naturally from the belief in the immediate resumption of specie payments, and from the previous legislation of Parliament. The order in council, prohibiting the bank from paying cash, was posted February 27, 1797. Mr. Pitt declared this restriction to be merely a pre-

cautionary measure, which would be removed in a few weeks. Parliament, forthwith, legalized the measure by the Restriction Act, and limited its duration to the 24th of June of the next year. In June the restriction was continued till one month after the commencement of the next session, and the law was finally amended so that the restriction on cash payments should continue "for six months after the conclusion of a general peace, and no longer." When, therefore, in 1815, peace was finally declared, the expectation that the law would be enforced, and specie payments be immediately resumed, was universal. Every one, accordingly, began to prepare for that event. There was a total destruction of confidence, and credit was contracted in all its forms; but the greatest contraction was by the banks other than the Bank of England; and, though the total contraction of paper money from 1814 to 1822 was £43,467,978 ($215,000,000), the amount of the notes of that institution of five pounds and upward in circulation remained nearly stationary. The extent of the contraction can be appreciated best by considering its effects. General prices declined extensively. Distress and bankruptcy were universal. The year after the close of the war was the most disastrous period known in England since the Norman conquest. "There was a universality of wretchedness and misery which had never been equalled, except, perhaps, by the breaking up of the Mississippi scheme in France."* To have caused such a degree of bankruptcy, the contraction, not only of paper money, but of the whole fabric of credit based upon it, must have

* 2 Carey, "Social Science," 378, quoting Francis Horner. See "Alison's History of Europe," vol. iv., chap. 2.

been very great. Gold declined in price with other things, and at the end of 1816 had fallen from fifteen per cent. to almost nothing. The severity of the revulsion caused a temporary cessation of the attempt at resumption, but, as confidence was gradually restored, the attempt was renewed. Peel's bill was passed, graduating in a decreasing scale the amount of its notes which the bank should give for a fixed amount of bullion, so that at the end of three years, viz., May 1, 1823, it should commence the redemption of its notes in coin. The act was to take effect from February 1, 1820, but, within a few months of its passage, gold fell to par wholly independent of its action, and specie payments were virtually resumed. The bank directors, however, applied to Parliament for the passage of a new act, wholly removing the restriction on cash payments. This was done, and specie payments were legally resumed on May 1, 1821. In producing the resumption, Peel's bill had no effect, except in stimulating the banks and commercial classes to make the necessary efforts. The previous contraction had prepared the country for it, and as confidence was restored, and business extended, there was need of more money to effect the exchanges, than at the height of the panic, so that specie payments were finally resumed after a slight expansion of the currency over the figures of 1816, instead of a further contraction.

If now we turn to the United States, we find a very different series of events. There was a general expectation that, when the war closed, specie payments would be resumed in some manner, though the government had made no pledge on the subject. Yet the

only effect of the expectation was a great depression
of the premium on gold.　There was no considerable
contraction of credit.　On the contrary, the banks
steadily expanded their liabilities, while the withdrawal of treasury notes was proceeding, and, when the authority for that measure was terminated, they had increased both their deposit-liabilities and their circulating notes.　If, therefore, the example of England is to
be followed in this country, contraction must be commenced over again.　It must be enforced by the government until it reaches the banks and the people, and
causes a contraction of credit in every form.　We
must also endure a financial revulsion similar to that
which took place in England in 1815–'16, but greater
by as much as the amount of paper money in circulation is greater.　At the end of the revulsion, an act of
Congress, modelled after Peel's bill, graduating the
figures at which the Treasury should be compelled to
redeem its notes, and fixing a day certain for the resumption of specie payments, would be in order.　But
to imitate that precedent, leaving out the contraction
and the misery of a great financial revulsion, is to leave
out the essential part; while to go to work to produce such a revulsion, when the excitement of actual
war is over, and the plea of necessity can no longer be
invoked, would be a crime without a parallel.　No
technical legal plea for such a course can be made.
The government of the United States has never promised nor agreed to elevate its treasury notes to the par
of specie, so as to affect private contracts made with
reference to them as the standard of value and measure of indebtedness.　Even if it had promised to pay
gold dollars for them, that obligation would not pre-

vent the exception of private debts from the enhancement. In other words, there is no contract to prevent the government from first fixing the percentage at which debts contracted in paper are to be paid in gold, and afterward disposing of its treasury notes on whatever terms are found at once legal and practicable. In England, on the other hand, the legal fiction that gold was the only standard of value, having been persisted in throughout the suspension, and the government having solemnly promised to elevate the paper money to the par of gold within six months after the conclusion of peace, not to have done so would have been a flagrant violation of contract. In fact, the promise was not fulfilled according to its terms; for resumption was delayed for nearly six years, instead of six months. And, if the paper had been depreciated as low as ours, there is no probability that the promise to resume in that particular manner would ever have been made good.

The only provision of our laws which can be compared with the English pledge to resume within six months after peace, is the prohibition against issuing more than four hundred millions of dollars of plain legal-tender notes. This is equivalent to a pledge to all creditors, including the bond-holders, not to debase treasury notes by further issues, and to violate it at this day would be inexcusable.

From this comparison it is evident that the English suspension of specie payments and our own belong to distinct classes. The former was a bank suspension unaccompanied by forced issues of inconvertible paper, and deriving its authority from common consent rather than from the sanction of law—differing from other

bank suspensions, however, in the time through which
it was protracted, and the greater degree of depreciation the notes reached; while our currency belongs
to the class of legal-tender paper money forced into
circulation by government. Our treasury notes differ,
as money, from the French assignats and the Continental currency only in the smaller quantity of the
issues, and the lesser degree of depreciation they have
reached. There is but one method of restoring a
currency of this class to the metallic standard. It
must be converted into gold at less than its face.
There is not an instance in history where legal-tender
paper money, materially depreciated, has been made
equal to coin, dollar for dollar. The Continental currency of the revolution and the French assignats
sank so low as to be extinguished. Austria, during
the wars with Napoleon, issued paper money which
depreciated to such a degree that in 1811 it was called
in, and replaced by other notes at the rate of twenty
cents on the dollar. After the peace of 1815 these
notes, and the subsequent issues, were taken up at
forty cents on the dollar, being at the rate of eight
cents on the dollar of the original issues. Russia has
gone through with the same process. The government notes issued as money, having become depreciated, cash payments were resumed in 1839, by making
them convertible into the notes of the Commercial
Bank of St. Petersburg at the rate of four for one.
There is no material difference between the paper
money now circulating in the United States and
that which has been scaled down in these countries to
the level of gold, except in the degree of the depreciation.

There are many persons to whom such a course seems disgraceful. These should remember that equal and exact justice is always honorable, and that whatever disgrace may accompany such an escape from the evils of depreciated paper, must be referred to its original issue. Those who have disgraced us are the authors of the financial policy which has rendered such a proceeding inevitable. Many persons will also probably insist that such a proceeding is partial repudiation. But these forget that the repudiation has already taken place. To permit paper money to depreciate is an act of repudiation. To withdraw it at its value in gold is only to remove the veil, and make the reality visible to the dullest comprehension. Gold being the standard of values, to accept it as such is not repudiation in the absence of any contract to the contrary.

But there is a method of withdrawing the present currency, suggested in a previous chapter, which avoids even this objection. If the legal-tender act were repealed as to future contracts only, leaving all entered into before a day named payable in treasury notes, the price of the latter could be regulated by the rate of interest yielded by the bond into which they would become convertible. Thus, if the interest of United States consols were fixed at four per cent., the lowest rate named in the present funding bill, they would sell, probably, at something above eighty in gold. Greenbacks would be worth, within a fraction, the same price as consols, and all debts contracted in them would be settled in a currency of the same value as that in which they were contracted, as near as is practicable. There would be no repudiation, even in form, in such a measure. The actual number of dollars specified in the contract would be paid. But the value of those dollars would be established according to the demands of justice. At the same time, the vested right of every holder of legal-tender notes (if the legal-tender act is legal) to use them in payment of debts contracted, while they remained a legal tender, would be regarded.

But there is another argument against selecting England as our model in resuming specie payments, which, though not strictly logical, is entitled to weight. The financial policy of that country at the beginning of the century was thoroughly Tory. The Reform Bill had not then been passed. The few governed for their own good first, and for the good of the many afterward. It is after the precedents of this period of English history that the financial legislation of the United States, since 1862, has been modelled. We have had a tariff as high as the most persistent corn-law Tory ever advocated, and, though it has failed of its intended effect, it serves to show the school of political economy to which our legislators have belonged.

Our internal revenue taxes have been diffused over as many articles as possible, in accordance with the English practice of that generation, founded on the mistaken belief that revenue increases with the number of taxes imposed. There is a satirical description, by Sidney Smith, of taxation in his day, containing the following well-known passage.

"Taxes upon every article which enters into the mouth, or covers the back, or is placed under the foot —taxes upon every thing which it is pleasant to see, hear, feel, smell, or taste—taxes upon warmth, light, and locomotion—taxes on every thing on earth, and the waters under the earth—on every thing that comes from abroad, or is grown at home—taxes on the raw material—taxes on every fresh value that is added to it by the industry of man—taxes on the sauce which pampers man's appetite, and the drug that restores him to health—on the ermine which decorates the judge, and the rope which hangs the criminal—on the poor man's salt, and the rich man's spice—on the brass nails of the coffin, and the ribbons of the bride—at bed or board, couchant or levant, we must pay." *

This is one of the selections contained in every school-reader, and is the only political economy taught in our common schools. Our legislators, deriving their learning from those much-vaunted institutions, seem to have taken this satire in grim earnest. By modelling their tax laws after it, they have made it prophecy.

An attempt, also, has been made in this country to convince us of the truth of the Tory doctrine, that a national debt is a national blessing, and, though the lesson has been derided in theory, it has been fearfully practised.

Paper money, likewise, with its fatal facility for "fertilizing the rich man's field with the sweat of the poor man's brow," has been forced upon us, while a monopoly of issuing bank-notes has been conferred on the banks actually established. All that remains to complete the parallel with the Tory England of half a century ago, is to transmute paper fortunes into gold, dollar for dollar, and to tax the people to accomplish it.

If universal suffrage is only a bait to allure the

* *Edinburgh Review*, 1820; "America."

people into the trap set for them, the scheme may succeed. If, on the contrary, it is a means for enforcing the rule that the end of government is the greatest good of the greatest number, paper will be converted into gold only at its actual value in gold.

But there is one point of English practice which we may well follow. That nation has never been guilty of the folly of attempting to make the preservation of specie payments depend on the price of its government securities. English consols have never sold at or above par, except temporarily. Nor have the securities of any European nation sold uniformly at that rate. To make the resumption of specie payments in this country depend on the price of our bonds, as is generally proposed, is a measure without a precedent, and which cannot succeed. A necessary preliminary would be a universal conviction that the debt ought to be paid at par in gold, and a general abandonment of all schemes to pay it according to the value of the money in which it was contracted. Justice, however, refuses to change, and the desire to enforce it, so far from being abandoned, is likely to gain ground. To make our bonds sell at par would require, also, a continuance of the present exorbitant rate of interest. Even if these prerequisites existed, specie payments would, after all, depend on the fluctuations of the stock-market. To make them depend on the way the wind blows would be as sensible. A necessary step toward resumption is to effect a total divorce between the exchange-value of money and the market value of government securities—between the circulating medium and the national credit. This can be done only by using as money that which is the standard of all values.

But there are serious objections to making United States bonds sell at par, even if it were possible to keep them there. It is, or ought to be, the policy of the nation to put its debt in process of extinction. If the bonds sell below par, instead of paying them at their face the Treasury will buy them at their market price, and the lower the price the less money will it take to pay the debt. To enhance the price of government securities, therefore, is to increase the burdens of the tax-payers. "To elevate the national credit" is part of the scheme for defrauding the people.

The reduction of the interest on the debt of the United States to the English standard, even if bonds fall below par, is preëminently desirable. No method of effecting that reduction can be devised that would not leave our debt a harder bargain for the tax-payers than the portion of the English debt contracted during the French wars. That nation sold its stock so as to receive for it about 58 for 100, and paid three per cent. interest. We realized for our bonds about the same average, and have paid six per cent. interest. English war-financiering was just twice as good as American. Their stock, however, is redeemable in coin. The greater portion of ours is payable at the option of the debtor, in paper. Certainly the legal right which Congress has thus retained of compelling a reduction of the interest, in consideration of adding to the principal the difference between depreciated paper and gold, is a right the exercise of which has already been too long delayed.

CHAPTER XVII.

THE conclusion has been reached in preceding chapters, that, in resuming specie payments, liabilities incurred during the circulation of depreciated paper ought to be adjusted according to the value or purchasing power of the money in which they were contracted, and that, as past debts cannot be thus settled in accordance with justice, so long as the legal-tender act remains in force, the first step toward specie payments must be to get rid of that enactment. The most obvious way of removing a bad law is to repeal it, having due regard to rights which have vested under it. But in this case it is necessary to provide for the immediate future as well as the past, and to furnish the country with a currency to take the place of that withdrawn, in such a manner that commerce may move on without derangement. The road to resumption is not to elevate treasury notes while possessing the quality of current money to the par of specie, but to deprive them of this quality, making them government securities only, and substituting for them as money a mixed currency of specie and bank bills. A necessary preliminary to establishing such a currency is to restore to the country its due share of the precious metals, now driven off to foreign lands. Specie must be collected, not simply in the vaults of the sub-treasury, but in the coffers of the banks and the pockets of the people. Private hoards now thoroughly depleted must be refilled. It is a fatal defect of every scheme for resuming specie payments by elevating treasury notes to the par of gold, that it not only does not provide any way for meeting this deficiency, but that it tends inevitably to increase it. There is no motive to the banks or the people to accumulate coin, if the whole supply is to be held in the sub-treasury, and the government is to assume the task of resumption. It is one of the worst effects of the intrusion of government beyond its proper sphere in furnishing the circulating medium, that the people learn to rely on the government alone to cure the defects of the currency, and individual efforts cease. Before specie payments can be fully reached, this order must be reversed, and the burden of the task must be thrown on the banks and the people, where it properly belongs. The general measure necessary for accomplishing this is to cause the scale of average or general prices in this country, as measured by the standard of gold, to fall below the scale of such prices in the countries with which our commercial relations are intimate. Under the law of the circulation of the precious metals, gold has flowed out of this country, because a dollar in gold has less value in exchange in the United States than in any other part of the world. Gold will not flow into this country until a dollar in gold will buy more in the United States than in other countries. A partial means of producing this result is to so reform our system of taxation, and concentrate indirect taxation on a few articles, that the cost of production may be lessened. But the most important prerequisite is to cause treasury notes to be quoted at a discount, instead of gold at a premium, so that the foreign producer shall no longer have two profits in selling his products in our markets, one on the sale, and one on the purchase of the gold to remit home. Whenever such a consummation is reached, and gold is fully restored to its proper place as the sole measure of values, the scale of general prices will inevitably fall below the level prevalent before the war, unless during the process of resuming specie payments the flow of the precious metals can be turned toward the United States, and our due share of the circulating medium of the world can be gradually distributed through the land. That this can be accomplished without a continued depression of prices from the gold rates now prevalent, measured by converting treasury notes into gold at the current premium, is not probable. If the gold is not actually in the country, prices must decline, when it again becomes the standard; and this decline is necessary in order to attract it hither. The debtor class would suffer consequently, if specie payments were restored at once by converting treasury notes into gold at the value marked by a premium no higher than ten per cent. If prices declined from the present rates in gold, debtors whose obligations are already incurred would be compelled to sell more property in order to realize the money to pay their debts in gold, at ninety-one cents on the greenback dollar, than if the present depreciated currency continued in circulation. If the average advance in prices over those prevalent in 1860 is thirty per cent., not only would the decline equal this percentage, but prices might fall even lower, before our share of the precious metals could be attracted back to us, and in that case present debtors would be worse off than if greenback debts were settled at seventy-seven cents on the dollar. Even if the process were prolonged through a term of years a certain amount of distress would be endured. The nation is drunk with paper money, and it cannot recover from the debauch without suffering. A financial depression, and an era of low prices are needed, however, in order to restore commerce to health. It is only through such an experience, that the haste to be rich without work can be cured, and the lesson taught, that wealth is the fruit of labor. It is the only way to cause extravagance to be replaced by economy, and habits of integrity to become prevalent through the land.

When low prices are the result of a want of confidence, and are accompanied with the hoarding of capital, they mark a period of disaster. But considered of themselves they are not an evil. When low prices prevail, speculation languishes. Men are then compelled to live by labor, instead of by their wits. Capital seeks productive instead of speculative enterprises. Manufactures and commerce flourish; for a period of low prices is a period of cheap production. The purchasing power of money is increased, and all men prefer to buy in the markets where their money will buy the most. Low prices are a benefit also to those who work for wages; for it is then, usually, that wages have the greatest purchasing power. That an era of low prices will prevail in the United States, whenever gold is fully restored to its proper office as the sole standard of values, is probable.

It would be a rash conclusion, however, to believe that a simple repeal of the law making treasury notes a legal tender, would restore specie payments. Nor would that result follow, even if a provision were included for the adjustment of all past debts in gold at a percentage of their nominal sum. The country would then be left in a position similar to that existing during an ordinary bank suspension, and the condition of affairs would resemble that which prevailed in England during the long suspension. Treasury notes are current as money, not only because they are a legal tender, but because they are of small denominations, and payable to bearer. To remove the former quality would still leave them current as money. For there is not sufficient specie in the country to take their place, and the people would possess no other currency; while the banks would be wholly unable to redeem their liabilities at ninety cents on the dollar, or at any other percentage; their bills, consequently, remaining convertible into treasury notes only, would, like them, continue in circulation as money. Though it is necessary now to provide for past debts, in accordance with the same principle enforced when the continental currency of the revolution was withdrawn, and which was applied in most of the Southern States, after the close of the Rebellion, in settling liabilities expressed in Confederate money, the resemblance extends no further. Paper money in those cases dropped out of circulation at once, because it had become worthless; and prices fell excessively low, until a supply of the more valuable currency had been attracted in. An extremity of suffering, and bankruptcy, consequently, was endured in those instances which in our own case can be avoided. The problem with us is to withdraw the depreciated currency, without permitting it to appreciate, and still using it as a circulating medium, while the withdrawal is in progress, so that the commerce of a great nation may move on in its usual course. In order to accomplish this, it will be necessary that two currencies of unequal value should circulate side by side. The rule that the poorer currency tends to supersede the better, must be reversed. But so powerful is this rule, that the difficulties in the way of overcoming it are enormous. So inveterate becomes the habit of using a paper currency which has circulated unquestioned for years, that to replace it with the metallic medium is an operation requiring the most skilful as well as energetic legislation. A generation of men is growing up to whom coin is a tradition. To teach them its superiority, and to induce them to restore it, is not the work of a day.

A simple repeal of the legal-tender act, therefore, unaccompanied by other measures, would not in all probability have any great effect. Treasury notes would still remain current as money by common consent and imperative need. The difficulty and the immorality of causing their value to appreciate would still continue as great as ever. As universal bankruptcy was caused in England by a voluntary contraction of a paper currency which had never been a legal tender, so bankruptcy ten times as great would be caused in the United States by a forced contraction of a currency which had ceased to be a legal tender. It would be necessary, therefore, in withdrawing treasury notes, to provide for contracts entered into after the repeal of the legal-tender act, as well as those incurred before. The latter could readily be provided for, either by a scale of depreciation, or by excepting them from the effect of the repeal. The former could be provided for in no other manner than by preventing treasury notes from rising in value, while their withdrawal was progressing. To do this would be easy. Treasury notes with us are money. In the markets of the world they are simply government securities. As government securities their value could be made to depend on the rate of interest yielded by the bonds into which they were fundable. If past contracts incurred under the legal-tender act were settled at a percentage of their value, treasnry notes themselves would be included in such settlement. If the repeal were restricted to future contracts only, the treasury notes would legally remain as now, payable in other treasury notes only. In either case the easiest, and the most equitable way of disposing of them, would be to make them receivable for taxes, and convertible at the option of the holders into interest-bearing securities. If strict justice is to be done between debtor and creditor, a rate of interest ought to be selected that would cause treasury notes to sell for a percentage of their face, corresponding to the loss of purchasing power the currency has experienced. If prices have advanced on an average thirty per cent., then treasury notes have a little less than seventy-seven per cent. of the purchasing power of our former metallic currency, and in resuming specie payments the price of greenbacks as government securities ought to be made to coincide with their value as money. As a decline of gold prices is necessary, before the metallic medium can be fully reinstated, a part of the decline ought to be caused by a rise of the premium on gold; or, if treasury notes are quoted at a discount, by a fall of their quotations. The rate of interest then selected for the bond into which to fund them, ought to be one that would cause them to sell in the immediate future at from seventy-five to eighty cents on the dollar.

But, as treasury notes under this arrangement would continue for a time at least to be current as money, the holders of them would probably find greater profit in using them as money, than in converting them into bonds bearing a low rate of interest, and would only convert them as fast as they fell out of use as money. Their withdrawal, then, would progress but slowly, and the government would come into possession of them principally by receiving them for taxes. It would probably be found necessary to cancel a portion of those thus received, in order to force coin or convertible paper once more into circulation. Treasury notes would continue to be used temporarily in payment of the current expenses of government, but what greater objection there can be in paying them out when quoted at a discount, than when gold is quoted at a premium, is not easy to perceive. Nor if they continued current as money, would it be easy to cause them to be quoted at a discount. To effect this would require sufficient time for the business of the country to adjust itself to the change. It would require also the establishment of a general conviction that they would never be elevated to the par of gold. When the policy of appreciation had been distinctly and finally abandoned, and the opposite measure of funding treasury notes at so low a rate of interest as to make their price in gold conform to their purchasing power as money had been fully established, the business community would begin once more to use gold as the standard of values, and treasury notes would begin to be quoted at a discount.

In the cities having a foreign commerce, where values are to a great extent measured in gold at all times, the change could be effected rapidly. In the city of New York, for instance, where a large amount of business is already transacted on a gold basis, to extend the use of specie would be easier than in other parts of the country. Merchants would adopt the practice of keeping two bank accounts, one in current funds, and the other in coin or its equivalent, and, as the withdrawal of inconvertible paper progressed, it would be comparatively easy for the banks and mercantile community to make the accounts kept in specie predominate, and finally to cause treasury notes to be classed with uncurrent funds, like country bank-bills under the former system. They would then be bought and sold by brokers like other government securities, and would cease to be money, except to some extent in retail dealings.

In this way could death be brought into the Gold Room, and paralysis over the Stock Exchange. An end would thus be put to some of the disgraceful accompaniments of stock-jobbing, which are deranging the business of the country, retarding its development, and debauching the morals of the nation. . If, in the process, there should occur such a withdrawal of loanable capital from Wall Street that the concentration of securities among a few owners would be more difficult, and the power of a few stock-jobbing autocrats forever broken, the whole country would be benefited.

Whenever specie is thus restored to circulation at the money centres, the rest of the country will be ready to follow the example. The ease, however, with which it can be substituted for paper will vary in different portions of the Union. The experience through which the South has passed has not been such as to enrapture the people of that region with paper money. Through the suffering that resulted from the destruction of one currency they have learned the defects that belong to the whole class. The South has now no paper medium of its own. Being cut off from the benefits of the National banking act, by the limitation of bank-notes therein prescribed, it can only obtain a paper currency from the North, and, in so doing, must suffer all the evils of paper money without any of its benefits. It must part with as much value to obtain one hundred dollars of greenbacks or bank-notes, as to obtain ninety dollars in gold. And the latter sum, though nominally smaller, has, in the markets of the world, fifteen to twenty per cent. more purchasing power than the former. Cotton, the staple product of that region, commands gold at the will of its holders; and, as the rate of premium on gold has long been, and is likely to continue, considerably below the diminution of purchasing power which greenbacks have experienced, as marked by general prices, the South must suffer a considerable percentage of loss in converting the gold received for its cotton into the paper medium. It will display wisdom, therefore, in declining to become a field for the circulation of Northern bank-bills, and in regarding greenbacks as the most odious badge of subjugation.

Texas has persistently refused to accept, as money, either the treasury notes of the Confederacy, or those of the United States; and the exceptional prosperity that State is now enjoying, ought to be an example to the rest of the ease with which specie may be retained as the circulating medium without the aid of any law more powerful than public opinion, and of the benefits which must accrue from such a course. Whenever, therefore, the policy of withdrawing treasury notes without increasing their value is distinctly established, the South will be ready to follow the example of Texas. Cotton will bring the needed gold, and a convertible bank-note currency can be readily created.

In other parts of the country, particularly at the West, the process will be slower and more difficult. Greenbacks will be clung to with tenacity, and it is probable that they will continue to be used as money, at least in retail dealings, until finally withdrawn and cancelled.

The real difficulty in resuming specie payments is with the banks of issue scattered through the country, who are fattening on the substance of the people. Many of the country banks were never possessed of any specie, and all of them are now nearly depleted of it. They must be furnished with a motive, and a necessity for accumulating specie reserves. A repeal of the legal-tender act would leave bank-bills to be paid in the same manner as other private debts. If such a repeal should take place at the present time, the banks necessarily would continue to redeem their

bills in treasury notes only. But if these are never to
be elevated to the par of specie, and the government
is not going to resume in that manner, the banks
must learn to take care of themselves, and cease to
lean on a superior power. If a future day were fixed,
and the redemption, in coin, of all bank-bills issued
or reissued after that day, should be enforced with
sufficient penalties, the banks would be furnished with
a period of probation during which to accumulate
specie; and the danger of losing their circulation
would supply them with a motive for commencing its
accumulation. If the date fixed were distant, and the
restriction of the amount of bank-bills were removed,
specie banks would be established in many parts of
the country. The old banks, also, would begin to
issue convertible notes, and the transition from an
irredeemable to a redeemable currency would be
facilitated. It is probable, however, that this cannot
be accomplished without a general curtailing of bank
loans, and considerable suffering on the part of the
speculative community. Borrowers, however, would
suffer infinitely less from these measures than from
any others that have yet been proposed. That such a
policy would be considered by the bank managers as a
great hardship is also extremely probable. They have
for years had all the benefits of furnishing a circulating medium, without any of its responsibilities. They
have grown rich by aid of that monstrosity in finance,
bank-bills convertible only into inconvertible paper.
They have leaned on the government so long, and have
become so thoroughly impressed with the idea that
the government is to bear the burden of resuming
specie payments, and that they will have nothing to
17

do but to follow in its wake, that they will probably consider themselves wronged when their rightful responsibilities are once more imposed upon them, and that burden is placed where it properly belongs. If the banks are to escape becoming odious to the people, not only must their present monopoly of issuing circulating notes be brought to an end, but they must also prove themselves of use in the difficult task on which the country is entering.

The measures, which, following one another at successive intervals, would be likely to produce specie payments with the least hardship and the most justice, may be briefly summed up as follows:

1. Repeal the public credit act, and refund the debt, as suggested in Chapter XV.

2. Repeal the legal-tender act, leaving all liabilities incurred between February 25th, 1862, and the time of the repeal, except specific contracts to pay coin, payable in treasury notes, and make these receivable for taxes, and convertible at the option of the holders into bonds bearing a low rate of interest. The treasury notes received for taxes could then be cancelled as fast as a surplus accumulated, and as the business of the country could endure. It would be necessary also to provide for greenback contracts having many years to run, and not specifically payable in coin, such as railway bonds and leases in perpetuity, by a scale of depreciation.

3. Leave all bank-bills, except those specifically payable in coin, redeemable in treasury notes, until a day named, and compel the banks to redeem in coin all bills issued or reissued after that day.

The result of many of these measures is altogether

conjectural. It is impossible to know the practical operation of a law until it has been tried. A seemingly trivial detail may change its whole effect. As such laws could only be put in force one after another, new necessities would probably be developed with each of them. The general principle, however, that the value of treasury notes ought not to appreciate, so long as they remain current as money, cannot be doubtful.

During the process of resuming specie paymeuts, a favorable opportunity will be offered for changing our monetary standard, so as to make it conform to any unit of international coinage that in the mean time is agreed upon. Whatever measures may be adopted for settling greenback debts, according to the value of the money in which they were contracted, an allowance can readily be made in such settlement for any change in the value of the coined dollar. The main thing to be considered would be whether it is worth while to make the change.

The benefits to be derived from an international coinage are largely overestimated. It would save travellers much annoyance and some expense; while if accounts could be kept in coins of equal value, the labors of book-keepers, and accountants would be slightly diminished. But in foreign commerce the precious metals are used only as bullion. Whether in the shape of coin or bars, they are measured on the scales, like wheat, or coffee, or sugar, or any other commodities whose values are compared by weight. In settling international balances this is the most convenient method, and no system of international coinage will ever make coin other than bullion in such transactions, or substitute the one in place of the other. A similar overestimate has appeared in applying the decimal system. In keeping accounts and making numerical computations, to proceed by decimals is the most convenient plan. But the natural and convenient subdivision of the dollar is into halves, quarters, eighths, and sixteenths. The want of coins to express these fractions is felt in retail trade, and is particularly prominent in California at the present time. This use of a decimal subdivision of the dollar comes from a logical adherence to theory in contempt of facts, that betrays the French origin of the decimal system. In undertaking an international coinage, there would arise a similar danger of overdoing it, and its success would be a step further toward obscuring the fact that money is always a commodity, a clear realization of which by the public would do more than any thing else to prevent all legislative tinkering with the currency.

In discussing the future financial policy of the United States the question of first importance is, What shall the currency be made after specie payments are fully restored? Shall we return to the defective system that existed before the war, with its small bills, its scanty reserves, its insecurity, and its expansions and contractions; or shall we set bounds to the encroachments of credit, and establish a currency founded on specie in fact as well as in name?

The changes which the last decade has wrought are most plainly visible in the financial wants and capabilities of the country. Not only has wealth accumulated, but its concentration has increased the amount of circulating wealth, or capital directly computed in money; and, in many parts of the country, all necessity for economizing capital by the extension of credit in the form of bank-bills has passed away. At the same time, by incurring an enormous public debt, a large portion of which is held abroad, we have given " hostages to fortune." The shipment of our bonds home for sale will perhaps have less effect in draining our gold than is commonly supposed. In that event the prices of bonds in New York will decline—that is, interest will rise—until the export demand is brought to an end. These transfers of our government securities, however, will cause the circulation of the precious metals to and from this country, to depend more upon rates of interest, and less upon prices of commodities than formerly. They will render our floating reserves of specie liable to be checked against suddenly. The movements of the great bulk of our stock of the precious metals will remain, as heretofore, determinable by the prices of commodities. But a diminution of the floating reserves of specie held at the commercial centres will necessarily disturb the whole commerce of the country, and the constant liability to incur such a loss will render imperative an extension of the element of specie in our currency. Not only must the reserves held by the banks and moneylenders be increased, but the hoards in the hands of the people must be enlarged, in order to furnish a source whence the floating reserves may be replenished. The circumstances of the country, therefore, have materially changed since 1860, and it has become necessary, as well as possible, to curtail the element of credit in our currency. As in manufactures we have reached a point where by reason of our desire to compete in the foreign markets free trade has become needful, so in financial matters we have reached a point where the stability which specie gives can no longer be declined.

This changed condition of the country will of itself bring a stronger infusion of coin into the currency, and greater moderation in the use of credit as an instrument of exchange will be forced, without any active interference of government.

The manner in which a mixed currency can be regulated, and the extent to which government ought to interfere with it, were pointed out in Chapter VII. Whether our future currency ought to be regulated by means of the national banking system, remains for consideration. If the views expressed in that chapter are correct, but one opinion can be given : the national banks ought never to be permitted to survive the restoration of specie payments. The defects in the details of the bank act cannot be here specified. Only the general principles with which it conflicts will be mentioned.

The most obvious objection to the system is the one formerly made against the Bank of the United States. It introduces into federal politics a money power likely to oppose, by improper means, all legislation hostile to its supposed interests. This danger is not fanciful. It is doubtful whether any law could be got through the present Congress for refunding the debt, or for restoring specie payments, if distasteful to the national banks. It would not be necessary for them to contribute a fund " to influence legislation," as they are already amply represented on the floor of Congress in the persons of their officers and stockholders. The most dangerous outgrowth of federal centralization is this tendency to make laws, not for the good of the people, but for the advantage of proprietary interests. Political parties divide on one question, or one group of questions, as, for instance, those growing out of slavery, and with reference to these questions the people are represented. But there it ends. On questions of tariff, currency, the debt, and public domain, special interests only are recognized in Congress. The laws on those subjects are made, not by Congressmen as representatives of the people, but as representatives of the manufacturers, banks, bond-holders, and railways. To go through the Senate and select the Senators who were elected to represent railway corporations first, and their States afterward, then to pass to the House, and designate the members who were elected to represent banks and tariff rings in preference to their constituents, would afford results not flattering to parliamentary government.

Many instances of the power of proprietary influences over legislation can be given.

The principal obstacle to-day in the way of specie payments is one powerful railway corporation, whose leases in perpetuity would be likely to bankrupt it in case of an increase of the value of money. Its freights and fares would then be at lower rates, and likewise its expenses, leaving its net profits greater, as measured by the purchasing power of the money received, but computed in a smaller number of dollars than before, while its leases would still call for the actual number of dollars specified in them. Resumption brought about by elevating the value of greenbacks, would probably ruin a company with such liabilities, and it is doubtful if resumption by settling greenback debts with reference to values can save it from bankruptcy.

Another example of the power of the capitalist class in shaping legislation is witnessed, when the annual tariff-tinkering takes place. The producers, whose wares are subject to foreign competition, then form themselves into rings to aid one another in obtaining protective duties, and their most impudent pretensions are listened to with deference by Congressional Committees, while it is tacitly understood that the consumers have no rights that Congressmen are bound to respect. If an occasional tub is thrown to the whale, it is in the shape of removing the duties on tea, or coffee, or sugar, which the consumers hardly feel, in order to retain more securely duties on raw materials like iron, that are felt by the whole people in the prices of almost every thing they buy.

An aristocracy is defined to be a government by a privileged order. To meet modern forms this definition must be changed. An aristocracy in this age is a government administered by a privileged class to protect or increase its own proprietary interests. If names are disregarded, and essentials only are considered, the government of the United States, as now administered, comes within this definition more clearly than that of Great Britain. Our privileged order is not composed of individuals whose greatness is recognized, and to whom a title is given, but of aggregations of individuals who form a ring, or a corporation, and receive in the latter case a corporate name; and, though the units are constantly shifting, the aggregation perpetuates itself. Our privileged order transmits its powers, not to its heirs, but to its successors. Another difference is, that with us this class, in return for the powers granted to it, renders a public service by assisting in the production of wealth. But it cannot be shown that the interests of our manufacturers and banks, as advocated by themselves, do not conflict with those of the mass of the people. They make use of their power over legislation to gain an advantage Nature has never given, in appropriating to themselves an undue share of the products of labor. The laws enacted through their influence, for imposing taxes proportioned to consumption, including protective tariffs, and for transmuting paper contracts into gold, dollar for dollar, including the public debt, are contrary to justice, and inconsistent with the well-being of the masses of the people. The same scheme of taxation and currency, established in a country where all the available land had been occupied, and population had begun to press upon the means of subsistence, would produce a degree of pauperism and degradation not exceeded by that existing in any part of Europe.

The national banking system as one element in this plan for establishing a proprietary instead of a popular government, ought to be broken up, and the banks remitted to the States, where they can be managed, without meddling in politics.

The remaining objections to the bank act come from the fact that it involves an intrusion of government beyond its proper sphere. This appears at several points.

The bank-notes are virtually a government liabil-

ity, with bonds put up as collateral. It is no part of
the duty of the United States to supply the people
with a currency. But if the government is going into
the banking business, it ought to become primarily
liable on the notes, and make all the profit from issuing them, rather than stand in the position of an accommodation indorser for the banks.

The requirement of security to guarantee the ultimate redemption of the notes is wrong in principle, as
heretofore shown. It is not the ultimate, but the immediate value of the notes, that should be secured.
If, however, government indorses them, or takes the
best collateral in the market to secure them, their ultimate value becomes so sure that further restraints are
necessary to prevent excessive issues, even when the
notes are redeemable in specie on demand. This necessity is met by the provision requiring the banks to
keep on hand, for the redemption of their demand liabilities, a certain percentage of lawful money, or of
specie after the return to a metallic basis. But so
strong would be the tendency to make over-issues of
notes whose ultimate redemption was securely guaranteed, that the percentage of specie would never conform to the requirements of the law, unless closely
watched by the government. The officers, therefore,
called bank examiners, would be necessary, and we
would thus have in the United States a mixed currency whose convertibility into specie on demand
would be regulated, not by the watchfulness of the
people in the management of their own pecuniary
affairs, but by the watchfulness of the bank examiners.
No more flagrant intrusion of government beyond its
proper sphere could be devised. It is probable that

such legislation would produce a long train of evils not now visible,.besides failing of the effect intended. In periods of excited speculation, if not at other times, the examiners would ·be: likely .to collude with the banks, and wink at evasions of the law. Of collusion and corruption in a bank examiner, a notable instance has already occurred. To compel the banks both to give security for their notes, and to keep on hand a fixed percentage of specie, would be found too onerous for them ; as they could make on the capital invested in bonds a higher rate of interest than they would yield. If a percentage of reserve were required, that alone would be sufficient, without requiring also collateral for the notes, while both provisions are wrong in principle.

Another objection of. the same class is, that the bank act furnishes a uniform currency. The only uniform currency needed after specie payments are reached is that issued from the mint. The more uniform in its qualities convertible paper is made, the more apt is it to become uniformly redundant. The notes then obtain a wider circulation, and are slower in coming home for redemption. The banks accordingly are thus enabled to keep a greater amount of them afloat. This objection is met by the plan of central redemption, which involves another violation of correct principles. The chief gain to the public from banks is the increase of capital they bring to be loaned to those engaged in active enterprises. The use of bank-bills can be justified only from the addition they make to this loanable capital. Banking capital, therefore, ought to be localized, and not centralized. Each· community ought to have all the profit to be derived from its own banks. If, however, the country banks are compelled to redeem their bills at the commercial centres, a portion of their funds will be kept there in any event, and a tendency would exist to send thither at times further amounts to be loaned on call. There would be danger, also, that the coin would be counted in the reserves twice, once by the city, and once by the country banks, thus rendering the currency more susceptible to the effects of a foreign drain of specie. The notes also would in this way obtain a wider circulation in times of prosperity, and in a commercial revulsion could be presented for redemption with double facility, thus intensifying the panic throughout the land. Uniformity is the last quality that in a country as diversified as the United States a bank currency requires. Different communities have different needs. The mining, the agricultural, the manufacturing, the commercial States have different opinions on the currency question, and can keep different amounts of convertible paper afloat. If the whole subject were remitted to the States, where it belongs, the kind of currency needed by each would develop itself by a slow growth, in accordance with a natural process of evolution; while specie would remain the one uniform currency for all. The machinery of the bank act with its security for notes, its arbitrary reserves, its central redemption, and its bank examiners, will probably be found too onerous for the banks, after specie payments are resumed, particularly if they are selected as subjects for both Federal and State taxation. It is probable that many of them will then voluntarily return to State jurisdiction even at the sacrifice of their circulation.

If the policy prevails of terminating the national banking system with a return to specie payments, an opportunity will be afforded in the process of resumption for summarily disposing of it. The banks could be permitted to issue all the notes redeemable in specie on demand they could keep afloat, without lodging any bonds with the Treasury Department to secure their redemption, and, as fast as the notes redeemable in legal-tenders were withdrawn, the bonds collateral to them could be sent back to their owners. The banks could continue their names and corporate existences under State laws, and no disturbance of business would ensue. They could then be subjected by Congress to the liability of involuntary bankruptcy on application of any creditor whose claim had not been paid in specie on demand, and if the Federal government appropriated to itself, by means of a stamp duty, part of the profit of issuing circulating notes, the currency would be sufficiently regulated without its further interference.

If the conclusions reached in these pages are correct, the hope is not unreasonable that out of this present chaos of paper money may be evolved the most favorable opportunity in American history for establishing a currency secure and self-regulating. When the nation is fully disgusted with the wrongs now inflicted upon it the time for reform will be at hand, and the means of reform will then be found ready. The precedents, in accordance with which the much-needed regulations of our future mixed currency can be enforced, have already been established. The statesmen on whom will devolve the duty of organizing a sound system of finance, will find all the mate-

18

rials prepared for them. When specie payments are finally restored, the rest will become comparatively easy. It will then be possible to maintain a better-regulated mixed currency in the United States than we have ever yet had, or than any other nation now possesses. The way will then open, as capital accumulates, for the gradual diminution of the element of credit in the currency, and for the use of a circulating medium composed so largely of specie that it will never fail in stability.

The United States can only reach the full material development of which they are capable by the expansion of their commerce. The capabilities of our country for production are so enormous that the markets of the world must be opened to us, or production will halt. But our commerce cannot expand until our producers are enabled to use the same instrument of exchange as the rest of the world. Placed athwart the commerce of the globe, nothing can prevent us from monopolizing the largest share of its profits but national ignorance. The Romans made of the Mediterranean a Roman lake by conquering the countries bordering on it. Americans, winning only victories of peace, can make of the Pacific an American lake by covering it with their commerce. We cannot, however, enter upon the career Nature has marked out for us until we have learned that our country is no exception to the laws of political economy.

THE END.